MARIA AND THE ADMIRAL

MARIA AND THE ADMIRAL

Rachel Billington

First published 2012
by Orion Books
This Large Print edition published 2013
by AudioGO Ltd
by arrangement with
The Orion Publishing Group Ltd

Hardcover   ISBN: 978 1 4713 2334 8
Softcover   ISBN: 978 1 4713 2335 5

British Library Cataloguing in Publication Data available

Printed and bound in Great Britain by
MPG Books Group Limited

To Kevin

CHAPTER ONE

I had thought of starting this story in my last years when my most constant companion was that dear little creature, the leech. Eleven years held captive in bed, or at least bedroom, is enough to try the patience of a saint and I was never that. Nor was I old at that time although, in the 1830s, to reach fifty years of age was old enough. I was famous, however, as a writer. So, looking backwards from age to youth, where should a writer start her story? At a high point of drama, perhaps.

Let me start, then, in a sailing ship attempting to make its way round Cape Horn, the most southerly and terrifying of all land masses. We are in the midst of a dark, boisterous sea, over us a dense, grey, cold sky. The albatross, stormy petrel and pintado are our companions. Below deck an even more dismal scene is being enacted, for both the captain of the ship and his trusty first lieutenant are dangerously, possibly mortally, sick.

I was that captain's wife and the year was 1822. I had nursed my husband since we'd left Rio de Janeiro a month earlier when he was already ill, and had had scarcely a night's sleep since then.

The barometer dropped lower and the weather worsened. After a terribly violent gale from the south-west, with snow and hail squalls, the sails were whitened and ice cased the rigging so that the men could not grip and fell to the deck, breaking heads or limbs.

Then there was a short respite. I may be forgiven, I hope, for quoting from my own journal:

1

I was glad today when the dead-lights were removed, to see the bright, blue, but still boisterous sea, spreading with ample waves curled with snowy tops, in the sunshine; it is many days since we have seen the sun and the white birds flying and chattering, or wrestling on the water, while the ship, like them, sometimes bravely mounts the very top of the wave and sometimes quietly subsides with it . . . A few minutes after noon, an iceberg was reported on the lee bow . . .

Soon after that the icy gales were back. The dead-lights were back, turning the cabins into fetid little caves of darkness. Nothing stayed where you put it. Bottles, boxes and plates, if you were fool enough to get them out, danced a mocking jig before hurtling to the floor. I was too experienced a sailor to fear the weather—I trusted the crew to save us from a watery grave. But, for my patients, another kind of death, torrid and pain-racked, beckoned. I did not describe the filthy odours, the disgusting fluids and putrid flesh. Or, worse still, the appeal of desperate eyes.

My journal was published in 1824 by John Murray, that estimable businessman and man of letters, who presented the world with so many travellers' tales. As a woman I stood out, which made me proud but not popular. Members of the female sex were not expected to be independent. It was always my trouble, although hardly my fault.

After my death I was saddened, although not totally surprised, by an entry in my friend Lord Holland's journal referring to myself: 'Her works I have not read, but I believe they are unfeminine and abusive.' You, who live in another age, cannot be expected to appreciate how easily notoriety can be acquired by any woman of spirit who breaks through the conventions of her time.

It may be clear by now that I am writing this document from beyond the grave. The grave is in Kensal Green Cemetery, London. This was a new and fashionable final destination when I was placed there in 1842. It was a pleasant, countrified place, which I had chosen for myself. Two years later my second husband, Sir Augustus Callcott, joined me. I have to confess, however, that I was surprised at the plainness of the stone slab laid above us— less surprised that it so quickly became derelict, vegetation obscuring the names of those buried therein. There were no children to tend it.

What goes round, comes round, and in 2008 my grave—our grave—became the centre of attention, the moss removed, a plaque applied. There was a little ceremony, the stone slab draped in a Chilean flag—I had not felt so warmed in years. Yet it was strange to be honoured in a country not your own. 'A Friend of the nation of Chile,' as the inscription on the plaque reads. Even though the traffic hurtled along Harrow Road, made noisier because a wall around the cemetery had crumbled into ruin, it was a dignified and even moving event, with the distinguished Chilean ambassador reading an encomium. Afterwards my admirers (if I may with modest accuracy call them that) were served drinks and what are now called 'nibbles', as if we were goats, in the Dissenters' Chapel. I was never a Dissenter, of course, but modern life seems to take little care of religious propriety.

Cape Horn, you may know, which we left a page

3

or so ago in turbulence and mortal fear, is, or was in 1822, the difficult and dangerous route to Chile. I am designated for ever a friend to Chile but only because of a noble person who was a friend to me. He, who is the main subject for this book, now lies in far greater state than I in Westminster Abbey.

Yet that ceremony of recognition for my own place in the history of a far-off country (with a descendant of John Murray present as well as other British dignitaries) gave me the idea of writing a true account of my life. Not my whole life, but the part that meant most to me. I did begin a memoir when I was still alive. We are back again to that old, but not very old, lady, sick, bored, lying in bed and dictating the story of her life to her good friend the Hon. Caroline Fox, Lord Holland's sister. I always had grand connections wherever I found myself, which says more about the power of the intellectual—if merely a woman—than my breeding, although that was not insignificant. In Edinburgh, when scarcely more than a girl, I was known by my peers as 'philosophy in muslin'. I was proud of the term then, but now I am not so sure for I see they were making fun at my expense.

But I am jumping around in the most addle-pated way, more with the disordered mind of an old person than that of the roving spirit I have become. The sublime poet and freedom fighter Lord Byron (a John Murray author, like myself) was wrong about that.

So we'll go no more a-roving
So late into the night
Though the heart be still as loving
And the moon be still as bright.

4

He was a treasured acquaintance but we fell out over a small criticism I ventured. Small criticisms, I sometimes think, are taken hardest. Of course it did not lessen my lifelong admiration for his work.

My dictated memoir is a lively work, or so I thought when I reread it recently. It tells the story of Maria Dundas ('Maria' pronounced to rhyme with 'pariah'), growing up in Papcastle near Cockermouth in Cumberland. My early childhood was happy enough; I was entertained by tales of smugglers, storms and shipwrecks when we were living by the sea, changing to ghosts and witches when we moved inland. We were a naval family so I seldom saw my father, Captain Dundas, until, when I was eight, he swept me away from everything I knew and took me to London. I never saw my beloved mother again—she was an American, who was known as the 'Virginian Nightingale' for the place of her birth and the sweetness of her voice.

Instead I was to be the poor relation in my uncle's house in Richmond and in a school run by the two Miss Brights, daughters of the Reverend Bolingbroke Bright. It has the ring of fiction about it, as recent commentators have noted, the all-but-orphaned child, plain but clever, making her way in a harsh world. I am likened to Jane Eyre, although I consider her a pallid, spiritless type of heroine.

I describe myself as plain but it was more that I had been allowed to run wild and spurned girlish artifice. In later years, when my character was more fixed, several portraits were painted of me which show that my features were strong but not without symmetry and grace. The most masterly is owned by the National Portrait Gallery in London, although if you wish to view it, you will have to persuade the curator to release it from the vaults in South Wimbledon. It was painted in Rome by Sir Thomas Lawrence in 1819. I was there with my first husband, Captain Graham. Sir Thomas, as swift as any to capture a likeness, was bet by our friend, the painter Charles Eastlake, that he could not complete the picture in two hours—and he did, although not the draperies. Even two hours' doing nothing seemed a dreadful consumer of time to me. You can see the impatient energy in my face. At any rate, it was painted in Eastlake's studio and he obtained the picture, exchanged for a couple of his elegant Roman landscapes.

My memoir carries my life forward only to 1807. For those who care to read it, my cousin by my second marriage, Rosemary Brunel Gotch, printed the full text in her biography of me published in 1937 and, to this date, the only true biography. Soon that will be a hundred years ago. How time flies when one is dead! Recently something has been published about me called *A Literary Biography*, which I have to admit appeals to my vanity. It is written by Regina Akel, a clever Chilean lady who has tried, after some research and some invention, to measure the self in my writing with the living self. I leave it to others to judge her success. It is, of course, written from a modern feminist viewpoint.

I hardly like to remember the reasons I gave up dictating my memoir: the bleedings, the fevers, the weakness, shakings, headaches, all the bodily infirmities that lay low even the strongest. You, from the modern age of antibiotics, cannot comprehend such physical sufferings.

But death for me was a well-understood enemy.

I had been fighting it tooth and nail since I was diagnosed with consumption more than thirty years earlier. My whole life was an evasion of death. In a little commonplace book I kept when I was twenty-one (held for posterity in the Bodleian Library, Oxford), I record a frightful period of illness near death. When it eventually passed, I wrote a note for myself on 10th August, 1806: 'May thy returning health be well employed that I may live for ever!' I make no comment on what I'm doing now!

Death was with me always. So, we are led back by a harsh connection of thought to Cape Horn, to the wild awfulness of Nature at its most despotic and the dying hours, for so they proved to be, of a good and honourable man. My first husband, Captain Thomas Graham, was never a firebrand. I understood that at once from our meeting aboard His Majesty's ship *Cornelia*, a 32-gun frigate. He was travelling out to India where he would be assigned a vessel. I was twenty-four years old, and accompanying my father to Bombay where he was appointed commissioner of the Navy. Like any vulgar girl, I knew I must find a husband. Not that I ever admitted to such an ambition in my lifetime. We all have a story at our core that we may disown or admit. It is often about love. Graham had never been my story, nor was Callcott later, although I loved them both as a wife.

I was born for many lives but only one man, and it is our story together that will eventually form the heart of this book.

But first let us flash back to the Captain Graham I met on the way to the subcontinent in 1809. The voyage had unpleasant moments—the

7

first lieutenant of the ship was a pompous fool and I made the mistake of publicly mimicking his ridiculous ways. All the same, the journey gave me a husband. It makes me smile now to think my attentions first settled on another man, Mr Charles Taylor, more obviously educated and attractive than Graham. How kind of the Fates to draw us apart! (I suspect now he wanted a less opinionated wife.) Captain Graham and I dealt so well together that, until his death, we never had a quarrel, although over twelve years we travelled round the world often under the harshest of conditions, with the added disadvantage of my unreliable health.

It was during the years of my marriage that I was first published, by Longman and then by John Murray. *The Journal of a Residence in India* came out in 1812 and, I can proudly assert, it is one of the earliest records by a woman of life in that fascinating country.

But this is not the story I want to tell. My true story started as we braved Cape Horn and my dear husband, from whom I'd never had a cross word, died in my arms. Is it cruel and as you, in the twenty-first century, would say, 'inappropriate' to record my husband's death as the beginning of my story? I had nursed him as devotedly as any wife and recorded for posterity my feelings as finally all efforts were in vain:

20th April, 1822
Today we made the coast off Chile. From the 3rd of April, it became a register of acute suffering; and, on my part, of alternate hopes and fears through days and nights of darkness and storms, which aggravated the wretchedness of those

8

wretched hours. On the night of the 9th of April, I regularly undressed and went to bed for the first time since we left Rio de Janeiro. All was then over, and I slept long and rested; but I awoke to the consciousness of being alone and a widow, with half the globe between me and my kindred.

Many things very painful occurred. But I had comfort, too. I found sympathy and brotherly help from some, and I was not insensible to the affectionate behaviour of my boys as the midshipmen were called.

Mr Loudon and Mr Kift, the surgeon and assistant surgeon, never left the bedside, and when my strength failed, my cousin Mr Glennie, and Mr Blatchley, two passed midshipmen, did all that friends could do.

But what could any human kindness do for me? My comfort must come from Him who in His own time will 'wipe off all tears from faces'.

I referred, somewhat theatrically, to my own death. Now I suspect I wrote it, some time after the miserable event, with the intention of wringing the hearts of my readers. But this must be too cynical: I was a widow in the turbulent seas of the South Atlantic, alone in the way the hierarchy of the ship dictates, my only true friend my young cousin Glennie.

We had rounded the Horn at almost the moment Graham's soul passed—as if the ice had gripped his lungs and, vice-like, stopped his breath—but we still had hundreds of miles to beat our way up the coast with the south-westerlies ever against us. Despotic Nature had done her worst, taken one more innocent victim, but we must continue with

9

the struggle.

Even I, experienced in tragedy and separation, as all sailors' wives must be, might have been forgiven for allowing misery to overwhelm me. But I had the first lieutenant to nurse and then my dear Glennie fell ill. I was also conscious of my duty in escorting my husband's body to its final resting place. Many believe that burial at sea was the tradition during the era I describe, and that was often so, particularly after or even during a battle. But in peacetime a captain deserved better. So Graham remained in the stateroom, laid out in his dress uniform with jaw bound and sword at his side, while I made my bed in Glennie's cabin, on the floor beside him.

The ship moved ever forward, northwards slowly, slowly sailing up the coast of Chile. We had left the icebergs behind and instead saw dark swathes of green forest and red soil. Then I beheld one of the greatest natural wonders of the world: the Andes. How could a heart, even as battered as mine, not be exalted by the sight of this seemingly unlimited range of mountains that followed the coastline, sometimes hardly separated by more than a strip of land, sometimes modestly retreating in a forest of peaks surging eastwards as well as north? At dawn their snowy tips were bathed with rosy pink, in the day they were sun-gilded, as rich as any Inca gold. At dusk they were veiled in a blue haze, which merged into purple or mauve.

The ship sailed on, a bravely moving island in the great expanse of the Pacific Ocean. I stood on the deck, as scrubbed and ordered as when its captain still lived, and contemplated my position. I looked towards the majestic mountain range, in natural beauty and magnitude far beyond human comprehension, and it seemed that the narrow strip of land that ran between sea and mountains was diminished almost to nothing. Yet this was a place of human habitation, the ship's destination, a country, even now fighting the final battles for independence from the Spanish oppressors.

With my husband lying cold below, I let the warm breeze blow on my face and swivelled my head from mountain range to ocean and back to land again. Above my head, the vast pyramids of sail, stretched taut to catch the slender wind, caused the ropes and masts to creak and moan. The sun sparked off the well-polished brass, and the buttons of a red-coated marine appearing from below.

Around me the seamen went efficiently about their business. Two officers talked not far from me. None looked my way.

'I am alone,' I told myself, once, and then again and again. 'Now that the captain, my husband, is dead, I am nobody. This ship on which I have lived for so many months owes me nothing. When we arrive at the harbour of Valparaíso, I must remove myself, lock, stock and barrel, and live where charity dictates.'

In this way I tried to convince myself of the miserable reality. Yet always in my sight were the magnificent Andes and the unlimited horizon of the Pacific. They told me a different story, a story of new beginnings, of freedom, beauty, inspiration.

My eyes began to hurt with the intensity of my staring. The brightness shimmered across my skin, entered my brain. This was the exhilaration of facing the unknown that explorers will devote their whole lives to experience. At what was the lowest

11

point of my fortunes, I felt a corresponding surge of pure excitement.

I was alone, yes, but that in itself was a challenge and my whole life up to this point had taught me that I had the strength to overcome the odds. I should have turned to my God and, perhaps, in a way, I did, recognising in the great natural beauty with which I was surrounded His all-powerful hand.

Tears filled my eyes, and if the lieutenants had looked in my direction, they would have concluded, with perfect good sense, that they were the tears of a new widow with 'half the globe between me and my kindred'. Now, nearly two hundred years after that moment, I shall admit that the tears of sadness and nervous dread were mixed with the tears of one who looks into the sun and feels her heart flame up in exhilaration.

CHAPTER TWO

The good *Doris* sailed slowly into Valparaíso's harbour. A gentle wind blew from behind us; the sun, too, was behind, sinking in rich golden rays that cast long shadows on the ships already moored. There were many, sails reefed, swaying gently on their moorings. The most action came from a multitude of boats darting among their grander cousins. On shore small figures, occasionally illuminated by the sun, moved without haste, a dignified frieze, although they were probably about usual port business at the end of the day. There were buildings, although not as many as there were ships and few of consequence. I picked out a church tower and the outlines of a fort. Above them rose steep cliffs, green-clad in the rifts that divided them into two dozen or more sections and turned a deep crimson in the more rocky parts. Some buildings clung to the lower slopes, and I guessed by shadowy parts that there were also smoother plains.

We were to spend a last night aboard ship but already I could see boats heading our way and suspected there would be those on board who would try, out of the kindliest of motives, to direct my fate one way or the other. But I had known these moments before and was armed against persuasion. As we entered Valparaíso, sun sinking, rosy mountains ahead, I had already decided to remain there. How long I could not predict, but I was certain that my future was in this emerging country rather than in turning tail and fleeing back to England.

Around me all the preparations went on for a ship at anchor. Even if we would not go ashore that evening, news was on its way to us. That evening there were a dozen round the captain's table, despite the absence of the poor captain and myself. I spent the evening in Glennie's cabin, stitching my black fustian and merino, adding a ruffle of silk where I deemed it necessary. Judging by the buildings I had seen, there would be little ceremony at Valparaíso but I knew that my almost notorious lack of interest in feminine finery sometimes made me negligent and I did not want to give offence.

The hours of darkness deepened and the voices of the men at table rose, although at intervals hushed respectfully on account of the dead—little goes unheard on a frigate. I shook out my black skirts and packed away the others in my trunk.

My journals I put in another, with my paintings and, most important of all, my books. Wherever I have lived or travelled, books have always been my closest friends. Some of these I had used to teach the midshipmen their Latin and French. It was not without dropping a tear that I wrapped up and put away my Froissart and my Cicero, my Chaucer and my Bible. Where and when would I be unpacking them again? Yet despite the tear, despite all my regrets that the life of an estimable man had been cut short, my heart was still pierced by the dart of excitement.

It was in this moody time of reflection, the cabin dark, save one dripping candle, that Mr Dance, the first lieutenant, whom I had nursed on the journey, brought to me a certain Captain Ridgely of the United States Ship *Constellation*. There were ships of many nationalities in the harbour. Napoleon had died on St Helena a year earlier and there were no wars between European countries, or between Great Britain and America; ships travelled freely to represent their country's business interests. It was in just such a concern that Graham and I had left Portsmouth for Valparaíso as part of the South Atlantic and Pacific Fleet.

Like many of his compatriots, Captain Ridgely was a kind, straightforward man, although his dark red face, as homely as a sugar beet, told me that he'd not declined the wine we'd brought aboard in Rio. His voice was loud with that not unattractive drawl. 'The commodore,' he told me, speaking slowly as if to a halfwit—sober mourning can be confused with a low mental understanding—'has offered to delay the sailing of the *Constellation* so that letters from His Majesty's Ship *Doris* may round the Horn in safety.' Putting his large hands together as if in reverential prayer, he added, 'If you, madam, wish to return home, we will delay our sailing still further.'

Both men bowed to me and I, indeed, felt duly grateful. But how to explain convincingly to them that I had no wish to return to England? I hesitated, then was struck by the realisation that the same feminine frailty that might lead me to seek the comforts of home might also be a reason to avoid such a long and hazardous voyage so soon after I had just endured one, and under such painful and arduous circumstances.

'Your commodore is generous, Captain Ridgely,' I said quietly, although I gazed at him directly in order that he could see I was not prevaricating. 'But I fear I must decline the offer for I have neither health nor spirits for such a voyage yet.'

Both men blinked doubtfully. I had seen the same suspicious expression on Dance's face when he watched me listening to a seaman's tale of love and constancy. Once, I had held in my hand a shining ringlet and Samways, a seaman, apparently rough-hewn as a rock, had sighed to me, 'One day you *must* see her—she will look at you. She does not often look, but when she does it pierces to the very soul!' Later I had informed Dance, of whom I was fond, that he must not raise his eyebrows at me as I listened to such simple confidences: an educated man should not forget that all humans love the same.

I could see he was wondering what I was up to now as I made my excuses to Captain Ridgely on the grounds of ill-health. He knew my independent spirit too well. Yet finally he decided to believe that

15

I had given in to feminine weakness; it flattered both officers' sense of manliness.

I lowered my eyes modestly and they assured me that they would do everything in their power to arrange for my stay in Valparaíso to be comfortable and restorative. We parted amicably.

But hardly had I nipped the small remains of the candle and substituted another than Dance was back. I had heard the piping and shouting that signifies someone of importance had entered the ship a few minutes earlier.

'Don Jose Ignacio Zenteno, the governor of Valparaíso, requests your presence. He is in the stateroom.' The lieutenant had become much more formal and stood more nearly to his gangly height.

Yet when I got to Don Jose (having adjusted my turban and put a black shawl around my shoulders), I saw an unimpressive man, whose swarthiness, long moustaches and gaudy jacket and necktie suggested he was not entirely European. We met in the stateroom, from which Captain Graham's body had been removed since my last visit. There were bottles of brandy and glasses on the table and the air was thick with alcohol fumes and smoke from cigars and pipes. I tried not to show my discomfort because the governor was bound to be important to my future in Valparaíso.

We sat at a table, Don Jose opposite me with two officials, even shorter than him and clearly unused to the restrictions of formal clothing, each trying vainly to ease his neck collar or waistband, standing behind him. The lieutenant and I sat opposite, with two fine red-coated marines behind us.

We proceeded to all the formalities of respectful wishes to His Great Majesty King George III on the

16

one side and a somewhat more muted admiration of General O'Higgins, the 'supreme director' of independent Chile, on ours. At that time Chilean and Spanish politics were not something in which the British government wished to take sides.

Personally, I had always been for independence as I would support the overthrow of oppressors anywhere in the world, including our own country. But I was aboard a British ship and had no wish to cause difficulties. This exchange was carried out in the most curious mixture of languages. Both male parties felt that they knew the other's tongue and neither was prepared to give ground. I, as it happens, encouraged in my studies by my periodic illness, knew four languages before I was twenty and many more (including Greek and Persian, which I heartily recommend) by the time I reached Chile. Since Graham's death, I had been studying Spanish, which was like an opening book to me—but of course I kept silent.

At length Don Jose turned to me, his square face lengthening as far as it was able.

'Señora, Madama, Doña, Milady'—his English became more and more impenetrable. His message, however, was almost brutally clear. Put into the King's English, he said, 'Tomorrow morning, with all due ceremony and respect, the honoured Captain Graham will be carried from the ship and buried in a spot I have appointed within the fortress, out of your sight. This will be carried out with such service as your church demands'—this was kind as he was, naturally, a papist—'and I can promise the attendance of soldiers.'

Using my most gracious Spanish (and enjoying Dance's schoolboy smile at the governor's astonishment), I thanked him for his generosity and thoughtfulness. Those of you unused to the ways of the Navy in the early nineteenth century may be surprised by the speed with which my husband was despatched since we had been in the harbour only a few hours. But we had sent a cutter ahead with the news and we were flying our colours half-mast high.

Understanding all this, I confess nevertheless to a momentary sense of weakness. The *Doris*, which had been my home for a year, would sail away the moment supplies were received and a new captain appointed. My 'boys' would go with her, Blatchley, Tunis and Witty, my lieutenants, Dance, Chandler and others. This could be a matter of days or, at most, a few weeks.

Slowly, I made my way to my bed beside Glennie. He was sleeping more peaceably than he had for many nights. I admired his girlish complexion and stroked back the damp curls from his face. He woke and muttered that I should not watch over him. But where else was I to go? Darkness and the fusty close odour of a small cabin combined to depress my spirits. I left the cabin, having determined to say my last farewells to my husband. Instead I found myself heading to the steps that led up to the deck. It was dark and I had brought no candle. I knew the men were not asleep because from the stern of the ship I could hear singing and raised voices. They had not been allowed onshore yet, but clearly some independent soul had procured beer or wine beyond their usual allowance. I even thought I could recognise Samways striking out in his good strong baritone, 'The Girl I Left Behind Me'.

As my head reached the deck, followed soon after by my body, I realised a group of men were

18

dancing, their bare feet with soles as horny as shoe leather beating on the wooden floor. Again I was swept by nostalgia for this world I was about to leave behind. We might not have battled against an enemy but together we had struggled with natural elements as dangerous as any human. One of the men out there would not be dancing now without my attentions after he has fallen from the trysail mast, breaking his arm and collar bone. But it is amazing what good nursing can do. Our dear surgeon, Mr Loudon, would have given him up for dead.

Wrapping my shawl closer—although it was hardly necessary, the night was so still and mild—I went further on deck. There I saw Mr Chandler by the wheel with Mr Dance at his elbow, and nearby two midshipmen, Blatchley and the little fellow called Witty. When they saw me, they drew respectfully away but I had already heard what they were talking about and noted their upturned faces. 'Orion,' one had said, and 'Mars', another.

So I, too, looked heavenward and gasped at the wondrous scintillations I saw there. The Milky Way cascaded across the darkness while many others I knew by name seemed to form a coronet or sparkle in its wake. Immediately, my spirits revived and I called out, 'Who can show me the Southern Cross?'

Eagerly, they crowded round, suspecting that I, who had been teacher to many of them, knew the answer to my own question.

'There!' cried Mr Witty, who had so laboured over his Latin.

'Over here!' cried Mr Tunis, as quick with his mathematics as any captain of the Blue.

For us Europeans, the excitement of beholding

19

the Southern Cross is that, by definition, it can be seen only in the southern hemisphere. So we exclaimed over its bright points and felt that the sum of our life had been increased by such a sight. For myself, it affected me even more deeply and, once again, my heart pounded with the joys of a new world opening.

The two officers had not joined us in admiring the starry firmament but continued with their quiet conversation. They were speaking of Chilean politics, I realised, for suddenly Dance raised his voice: 'Whatever rules our government may pass about British officers employed in the service of other countries, I defy you to call Captain Cochrane anything but a hero. A hero first to his own country and then to Chile.'

'You mean *Admiral* Cochrane,' replied Chandler, mockingly. He was a mean sort of fellow, who was to be maimed by a falling bowsprit on his thirtieth birthday. 'He had to cross the globe to become an admiral.'

'A hero, nevertheless,' repeated Dance, firmly.

At that moment, he happened to turn in my direction, and I could not resist saying, 'Bravo! A more courageous admiral never commanded a ship.' Like most of the English population, I knew Captain Cochrane's record in the wars against Napoleon Bonaparte, who had recognised his adversary's genius by christening him Le Loup de Mer, the Sea Wolf.

The officers turned away again unhearing, the midshipmen went to watch the seamen, hoping, no doubt, for a swig of illicit alcohol, and once more I was alone in the night.

At that time I knew very little about Lord

20

Cochrane's naval victories over the Spanish. As to his present whereabouts, beyond that he was still away from Valparaíso, or his future intentions, I knew nothing. I was aware, however, that he had fled England after being wrongly accused of Stock Exchange fraud and spending a year in prison. As soon as he was released and invited to create a Chilean Navy, our jealously vituperative government had passed a law called the Foreign Enlistment Act to try to stop him serving in another country. But they had been too late, and for the last two years he had been engaged in pushing the Spanish out of Peru and Chile.

I should record here that Lord Cochrane had entered both Captain Graham's and my own life on many occasions previously. Graham was a very young midshipman in His Majesty's Ship *Thetis* when Lord Cochrane was an older one. The captain was Sir Alexander Cochrane, Lord Cochrane's uncle. All three of us came from distinguished naval families who had originated in Scotland. In London, although I could not call us friends, we bowed if we met in a drawing room or social event. He was a noticeable man and I flatter myself that I was a noticeable woman. Although we spoke briefly, we spoke with understanding.

Our paths had taken very different courses, certainly. I had become an author. Lord Cochrane had moved from the highest rank to a convict who was sentenced to be put out in the stocks and pelted with rotten eggs by the common man. (As it happened, he was so loved by the common man that, in order to avoid a public uprising, the stocks were summarily abolished, never to be revived.)

We were merely acquaintances, therefore, but

21

with a shared background and liberal outlook that, if events had been different, might have made us more. Soon to be cast adrift in a strange world, I was looking for a star to guide my course. That evening, Le Loup de Mer, the victorious admiral of the Chilean fleet, took hold of my imagination and became that star.

CHAPTER THREE

The emotional extremes of such a night rendered sleep impossible and I made no pretence of undressing but took myself off to the stateroom. There, I read passages from Tacitus that Graham and I had studied together on our first voyage to India when, indeed, we had plighted our troth. Then we had looked to having children together, but now the books we had studied, and perhaps the books I had written, were all that could be a memorial of our union.

Before dawn, I was on deck again. At first there was a thick mist that Dance, in his usual obliging way, informed me was very common on this coast and called a *neblina*. I could scarcely see the ships nearest to us and the air was cool and dank. Sounds, however, were magnified so I could hear the commands from a ship that was to leave harbour and even individual calls from the shore. Already, there was much activity and I thought I detected marching feet, which might be the guard mustering for Captain Graham's last procession.

The mist remained thick and clinging but it was only when I sensed my presence on deck was

22

becoming an embarrassment that I went below and followed my nose to fresh-brewed coffee. The embarrassment was because a group of seamen, under the command of Mr Loosey—a correct young man who was trying to grow a moustache—was preparing the captain's barge to take his corpse across the bay.

In fact, I was far more upset by what I found below. The servants of the new captain, a Captain Vernon of His Majesty's Ship *Blossom*, (whom I thoroughly detested without ever having met him), had arrived with their master's belongings to make ready the cabin for him. Although my boxes were packed and ready to go, it was a shock to see another man's things take over the place where Graham and I had been happy enough for a year. The chance of a ship's command is always uppermost in every naval officer's mind. For example, the novelist Jane Austen's distinguished admiral brother gained himself a ship by noting through a telescope a ship entering Gosport harbour flying its flag at half-mast. He was offering himself to the Admiralty in a moment.

Soon after Captain Vernon's servants, another boat came out of the mist. This time it was the American Captain Stewart's wife offering me a cabin aboard the *Franklin*, which her husband commanded. I declined, yet was beginning to feel more and more out of place. The Navy of various countries wished to dispose of a captain in a proper manner without any woman queering the pitch. So when a third boat arrived with an offer from a Mrs Campbell, the Spanish wife of an English businessman, to receive me into her house until I could find lodgings, I accepted almost readily. Mrs

23

Campbell herself did not come, but an employee of her husband who, I guessed correctly, hailed from the small Scottish town of Douglas where I had spent my early childhood.

Thus it was from the window of a stone-built house on the waterfront that I watched my husband's bodily departure from this vale of tears. I was accorded the liberty of being alone. The *neblina* had melted away and brilliant sunlight sparkled off the waves. A north-westerly wind had sprung up so the captain's barge and the boats accompanying it threw up white spume around the prows. As the barge, rowed by a dozen strong seamen, left the *Doris*, the ship fired a cannonade of guns, echoed by other ships at harbour and answered a minute or two later by guns in the fort where the captain was destined. The sound rolled round the bay, then reverberated against the newly revealed cordilleras and echoed back. It was a magnificent display, worthy of a greater man than Captain Graham.

I did not have such a good view when the barge came ashore but I could hear bands strike up, not just British in origin but Spanish and American too. The sound was the better for being anything but funereal. I pictured the scene as the draped coffin was carried up the steep path to the fort. There, I imagined no more, although I could hardly fail to hear yet another rolling cannonade from the fort. Instead I read from my Bible Psalm 107, verse 30, which is read every Sunday on board ship by God-fearing captains. I had heard it so often that I hardly needed to consult the Holy Book:

They that go down to the sea in ships, that do business in great waters; These see the works of

24

the Lord, and His wonders in the deep.

A burial place is a chancy matter. I've already talked of my own grave—derelict for nearly two centuries before it was rejuvenated. Captain Graham's fate was more mysterious. He was buried safely enough, one must presume, and the place of the fort exists even to this day, but of his grave there is no sign.

A few dogged persons, interested in my history or simply the history of the British in South America, have turned detective and tried to track Graham down. Evidence pointed to a cemetery within Valparaíso, one half of which is reserved for foreigners, Cementerio de Dissidentes (strange that such a place should figure twice in my life— or, rather, death). Surrounded by a high white wall, the Chilean cemetery spreads high up on a *cerro*, the name given to the steep hills that run down towards the harbour; the numbers of *dissidentes* graves confirms how many foreign non-papists have populated Valparaíso over the years.

In my life after death, I have watched men and women trudging round in a dedicated sort of way as they examine the multitude of names on the gravestones. They arrive in the middle of the day after a severe climb upwards. Soon they spot a largish white memorial to the men in the employment of the Royal Navy. They stare, take off their hats, wipe their faces and, with the pounding hearts of bloodhounds, read off the names. I could tell them they are wasting their time. This graveyard was only founded in 1836, and although the bodies of some who died earlier were transferred here, Graham was not among them. He

25

lies still, I am sure, in the grave prepared for him at the Fort San Jose on a bright April morning in 1822.

I myself never had any wish to visit his grave. I lived in an unsentimental age when death, unless heroic, was too common to be commemorated. Maybe Graham's plot once had a stone to mark it but I could not even be certain of that. At any rate Valparaíso's history of dramatic earthquakes and floods, which is so central to my own story, altered the landscape of the city so that a solitary grave would easily disappear without trace. The surprising thing is that the old fort remains, still on a promontory overlooking the bay, although the sea has removed itself many metres further out.

Ironically, it is now called, with no basis in fact, 'Cochrane's House'. It is no accident that the great man's spirit lives on through fiction at least as much as through history. While he was still alive, Captain Marryat who had served under him as a midshipman on HMS *Imperieuse*, used his dramatic experiences in *Frank Mildmay, or the Naval Officer.* Marryat at first hid his authorship and I remember well when, in 1829, the word was out that he had written it. Later, C. S. Forrester based his Hornblower series on Cochrane and, in modern times, Patrick O'Brian created another Cochrane with the dauntless Captain Jack Aubrey. Thomas Cochrane was too much of a giant among men to fit into history, just as he was too much for the establishment of his day.

But we have left me, a new widow, in the house of strangers, hearing, but no longer seeing, evidence of her husband's burial. Soon enough the ordinary sounds of a busy port overcame the ceremonies of death. Some I could identify: trains of mules bringing provisions for the ship, their sharp hoofs clacking where there were cobblestones on the front, although there was little enough of that sign of civilisation. My brief walk from the shore to the house had confirmed my view that Valparaíso was far less developed than you would expect of a busy port. I soon learnt that the Spanish had considered Chile the least profitable and most far-flung country of their empire and had shown little interest in developing it. For many years, they had allowed no foreign ships into Valparaíso. The Americans were the first to come, whalers from the south.

Yet a city did gradually grow. My journal records my first impressions:

It is a long straggling place, built at the foot of
steep rocks which overhang the sea, and advance
so close to it in some places as barely to leave
room for a narrow street, and open in others,
so as to admit of two middling squares, one of
which is the market-place, and has on one side
the governor's house which is backed by a little
fort crowning a low hill. [*I did not, you may note,
make reference that this was the burial place of my
late husband.*] The other square is dignified by the
Iglesia Matriz, which, as there is no bishop here,
stands in place of a cathedral.

I have not yet mentioned my skill as a painter. One of the first paintings I executed was of the Iglesia Matriz, as it existed in 1822 before the earthquake struck. It shows a low, whitewashed building with red tiles and a simple cross. Beside it there is a slightly taller, free-standing bell-tower, with a rather more elaborate cross. It is surrounded by low buildings, not unlike a row of English cottages. In the foreground three peasant women, one wearing the typical wide-brimmed hat, lay out baskets filled with flowers.

Too much is made today of those who can wield a brush as well as a pen. In the days before photography any traveller who wished to help his reader imagine the site he had visited turned out pictures. My paintings, which were engraved for my published journals, are now collected in the British Museum, where anyone, on producing identification, may shuffle through the boxes and doubtless admire those that are more colourful and dramatic.

To return to my journal:

> From these squares several ravines or quebradas
> branch off; these are filled with houses, and
> contain, I should imagine, the bulk of the
> population which I am told amounts to 15,000
> souls; further on there is the arsenal where
> there are a few slips for building boats, and
> conveniences for repairing vessels, but all
> appearing poor; and still further is the outer fort,
> which terminates the port on that side. To the
> east of the governor's house, the town extends
> half a quarter of a mile or a little more, and then
> joins its suburbs the Almendral, situated on a
> flat, sandy but fertile plain which the receding
> hills leave between them and the sea.

I had scarcely finished recording this when I fell ill. The long voyage, the nursing of the sick, the lack of sleep, the loss of a dear companion would have affected a stronger body than mine. Now I spent the hours lying in my narrow bed, watching the sun sweep through the unglazed window and move slowly across the whitewashed walls. I was too sad and ill to receive visitors. Only the Campbells made their way to my bedside. I have nothing in common with those who trade for money but Mr Campbell's Scottishness was in his favour and he could, at least, bring news of the world outside. Mrs Campbell, on the other hand, was totally without education.

Her conversation when she came to me went like this; 'Mrs Graham'—pronounced more like a fish name than that of a human—'you are well?'

What question is that to a woman prone on her sick bed?

'You are too kind,' I would respond. 'And tell me how is little Rosita today?' Although Mrs Campbell could not provide me with conversation, she did have two charming children who chattered away at my bedside in a delightful mixture of Spanish and English. The boy, unluckily for him and his mother, was called Archibald after his father. In Mr Campbell's presence, his wife tried, with much tongue-twisting and eye-rolling, to pronounce the name, but the moment the busy father left the house, Archibald became Marco, with good cheer all round.

I make fun of her but at the time I was more tolerant. Her mother was certainly Indian, taken as wife or mistress of a Spaniard just as Mr Campbell had taken her. She was extremely pretty, with a smooth golden complexion, large black eyes and long curly hair, which in the home was plaited down her back in the Chilean fashion. It was, of course,

29

a marriage of convenience and both sides counted themselves lucky, her mixed race discounted by her beauty, his age (he was at least twenty years the older) and grizzled looks—he had lost an eye—by his relative wealth and position.

Nor did I patronise either of them for that. Marriage was not then a matter of romance, whether in the remote part of the world where I found myself or in England's Home Counties. Any fan of Miss Austen's work will be only too aware that money and position greatly influenced any sensible girl's approach to love. In passing, I might note that I read all her works as they came out and found her innocent and lively manner well suited to my sick beds at various times; sadly, I had none of her novels to hand in Valparaíso. My only caveat was that she made so little of her knowledge of the Navy. Two long-lived brothers—I have already mentioned one—who eventually became admirals (although after her death) gave her ample experience of the profession's fascinations.

It is true that in *Persuasion* Miss Austen paints a recognisable portrait of two very worthy naval men. Admiral Croft is a rear admiral of the White and had made a fortune while based in the East Indies. Captain Frederick Wentworth, the object of the insipid Anne Elliott's affection, has been made a commander after action in St Domingo and thus becomes a suitable husband in the eyes of her snobbish family. Anne had the sympathetic habit of doing something we Navy wives all practised: studying the Navy Lists in the *Naval Chronicle* to see how our men progress.

The trouble is that Miss Austen was never aboard a ship in motion, from what I can tell. The sea had not entered her blood as it had mine. Even as I lay, head aching and body aflame, in my little room in Valparaíso, I was consoled by the sounds of the harbour: the heavy wooden wheels of the ox carts, the yellings in a multitude of languages, the rolling barrels, the shrieking gulls, the slapping waves against the harbour walls. When the wind blew through my window I smelt salt water and fish and imagined myself at sea.

I liked life aboard ship. I liked living with men, particularly the young and healthy. Writers now emphasise the discomforts of a sailing ship and it is certain that there was little space aboard a frigate where three hundred men must co-exist with as much as eight miles of rigging, three main masts, ten or more sails, up to a dozen boats of various sizes and, in the case of Doris, thirty-six large iron cannons. Moreover, at the beginning of a long voyage there would be enough animals to stock a farmyard, not to forget the rats that, although useful in times of starvation, were generally most unwelcome guests.

But unless supplies ran out, and assuming the men could be kept from drinking more than the regulation amount, there was exercise, food, company, somewhere to lay their heads and plenty of air. I've seen men pressed on board with caved-in chests, grey skin, flat feet and pimples like the heads of volcanoes who, after a few months on a well-run ship, would make Michelangelo reach for his chisel.

A captain makes the ship in his image. A disciplined, moral and courageous man, not too quick with the cat but ready to use it when necessary, will have cheerful, obedient men aboard.

31

A brutal captain will soon turn the men into brutes, and a cowardly captain will have his men, officers too, shrinking from the face of battle. Most of all, the captain must be a leader.

As my health recovered, I was seldom left alone in my little room on the front. Messages of goodwill arrived from naval officers and others of all nationalities, including the governor. Offerings of cakes or fruit were brought, sometimes by servants, sometimes in person. Owing to adverse winds, the *Doris* did not sail until May so my 'boys', Mr Blatchley, Mr Witty and Mr Tunis, came daily with the news that entertained their young minds. It was, of course, all about the war fought against the Spanish and therefore about the great Admiral Cochrane. My cousin Glennie, more or less recovered in health, would sit with me for an hour or two.

We were in high expectations of ultimate victory over Spain. 'Oh, to be on board, guns run out, chasing their ships!' Glennie could fight a whole battle in my little room but he turned out to be right, although we only knew it a week or two later. After two and a half years at the head of the Chilean fleet, Cochrane chased the last two Spanish ships into patriot ports where they surrendered.

He then sailed on into Callao, Lima's port, where General San Martín, commander in chief of the patriot forces, had set himself up as protector. Later commentators on my writings about this gentleman have almost universally declared me unfair, suggesting that I was led astray by my preference for the British hero, and it was true that the two men disliked each other on sight, despite fighting on the same side. Luckily, General

O'Higgins, supreme director of Chile, managed to get on with both of them.

As I listened to the stories of unwinnable victories, the spirit of adventure, which had led me to stay in this faraway place, revived.

'Now, Mr Campbell,' I said, when that grizzled gentleman visited one evening, with Rosita and Archibald tugging at his coat-tails, 'I cannot presume on your hospitality further. You must find for me a modest house where I may reside quietly.'

'Reside *quietly*, madam!' The honest fellow laughed heartily. 'Why, you have a wider acquaintanceship in Valparaíso than I have after living here fifteen years.'

'People have been kind,' I admitted, with a ladylike blush.

'Governors, commodores, captains, handsome young officers with their buttons shining and hair watered have all come to pay their respects to the desolate widow.'

This was presuming too much. 'The naval fraternity look after their own,' I replied, pursing my lips.

But this man (hardly a gentleman) had lived too long away from the civilities of sophisticated behaviour to be restrained by my expression. 'Leaving aside the young naval gentlemen,' he continued, 'any one of your ad—' he was about to say 'admirers' but changed it suddenly— 'acquaintance would provide you with far more spacious and elegant quarters than you have here.'

'Ah, Mr Campbell, you mistake me,' I retaliated, in tones of asperity. He was a man used to dealing with traders. 'I arrived here, true, as the widow of a captain of His Britannic Majesty's Navy but I am, in my own self,' I could not help emphasising the words, 'a writer, a published and therefore *professional* writer. I wish to live not in an endless round of gaiety and gossip but in a way that affords me the time to study and to note the customs of the country in which I find myself. When I used the word "modest" to describe the dwelling I desire, that is an accurate description.'

I saw by his face that my words had astonished him but also that my plain speaking had gained its effect. He now believed me and bowed in an accepting way. I decided to press home my point.

'I have heard of a part of Valparaíso called the Almendral, which is quiet and countrified with fruit trees and an excellent view of the harbour. This is the sort of place that would suit me admirably.' I had also heard that anyone living there risked being robbed or murdered so I was not surprised when the good Mr Campbell expressed himself horrified at the idea.

'A lady on her own may as safely live among the savage Indians in Chile's south,' was how he put it.

I remained firm. 'My dear sir, you indeed have the advantage over me of knowing the country but perhaps I have done more to study human nature. I will feel very safe, because I believe no one robs or steals without temptation or provocation. As I have nothing to tempt thieves, so I am determined not to provoke murderers.' I might have added that I had lived among bandits in Italy and published a book about it.

The conversation finished there, however, and a few days later I had the satisfaction of hearing a solid cottage had been found for me in the Almendral. Mrs Campbell, shocked, told me that my neighbours would be Chilenos, small farmers, almost peasants. I patted her hand consolingly.

* * *

I set off for my new home on a clear autumn day— the beginning of May, according to the calendar, but the weather told a different story for this land in the southern hemisphere. The dry season was still with us and more to be enjoyed by the rains that would follow in a few weeks. Of the dank *neblina* there was no sign. A side-saddle had been procured for me and a tolerably fine horse called Charles, which had the habit of shying at anything bright or unusual in our path. This uncomfortable behaviour was encouraged as my small party of horses, and mules to carry my boxes, was increased by many of the company of the *Doris*, officers, my boys and my old friend Samways, leading some seamen decked out in their shore-going finery of broad-striped trousers, red waistcoats, shiny tarpaulin hats, wide straws or spotted handkerchiefs over their heads and all with long, swinging pigtails. They gave me huzzahs every few moments, which soon attracted the loafers on the front, the boys with colourful ponchos, the men in their tall hats and wooden clogs. Even the peasant women, come into town with figs, lemons and pomegranates, picked up their baskets and followed.

My procession, for such it became, wound down the main street (the only street of any note) where small shops sold the silks of China, France and Italy, the printed cottons of Britain, rosaries, amulets, glass beads and combs from Germany. The British shops, I noticed, were more numerous

35

than any other, stocking hardware and cloth as well as the framed saints, tinsel snuff boxes and gaudy furniture that the astute Birmingham artisans had concluded were more suited to coarse transatlantic tastes.

Reading this sentence, I fear a modern reader might accuse me of racism. I was ready enough to recognise the true arts of Chile, the hand-woven and hand-dyed cloth, the perfectly cast pottery bowls, even if the decoration was simple. But I could not admire the cheap and gaudy goods with which Europe cajoled and sometimes spoiled the dignity of this emerging nation.

I rode my sprightly horse with my head high and attendants close, and was pleased when the governor, Don Jose Zenteno, sent a message of goodwill and others who'd paid me kindness did the same. I did not want them to think that, by withdrawing to the Almendral, I was turning my back on their town.

'So, cousin,' said Glennie, who had stayed at my side from start to finish of my public and, I must admit, slightly absurd progress, 'now you have your wish, what will you make of it?'

His youthful high spirits had led him to ask such a question where he would not usually have presumed. I answered him gravely, 'If you tell me of the success of the Chilean fleet with Admiral Cochrane at its head, then I will know how to answer you.'

He could not quite make this out and went off at once to oversee the entrance of my wooden bedstead into the house. I smiled to myself and, sliding off my horse without the help of anyone (a luxury in those times when a gentlewoman was considered incapable of any action without a servant), I took stock of my surroundings. It was more charming than I had expected. Around me flourished not only the almond trees for which the area was named, but also olives, pear, apple, quince, orange and lemon, with some fruit still remaining on them.

Looking down between them, I could see the beautiful sweep of the bay and the ships of all nationalities safely anchored there. I was glad that I had not lost my view of the sea. Behind the house the red ravines rose majestically, sometimes streaked with the white of marble stone. Nothing grew in them, and the ground was scarred by the courses of winter rains, but all around was scattered vegetation, some cultivated.

The cottage was solidly built, its thick walls whitewashed and broken by only one window, unglazed but with an ironwork grille over it. I went inside.

'It's so dark,' complained Glennie, looking aghast at the heavily beamed and truly dark main room.

'No more than the midshipman's berth,' I replied, smiling, 'where you so long to go.' But he was right, and in the small bedroom where there was no window or door, it was black as pitch. I should need a good supply of candles if my programme of reading was to be continued as the nights set in. To the positive were the respectable pieces of furniture I had been loaned and the view through the open door, although that, too, had its drawbacks: a path, beaten solid by the hoofs of mules as they took firewood and other necessaries into town, passed nearby.

When my escort departed, with many promises to return the following morning, I was alone but for a couple of servants and glad of it. My published journals speak of my sorrows and sadness, but this, I should confess, was more to meet the expectations of my readers than to describe the reality.

At about three p.m., a Chileno, wearing the traditional poncho, tall hat and heavy spurs on his boots, appeared with fresh milk and an offer of any assistance I might need. I welcomed him more warmly than if he had been the governor himself, bearing hot beef and a flagon of wine. I tried out my Spanish and what Señor Juan Miguel understood from me I do not know— probably my position as a woman without a family presented an insurmountable barrier even without linguistic problems—but I understood from him that a Chileno lady of ninety years was my nearest neighbour: she invited me to visit and meet her family the following morning. It seemed that already my determination to live among the local people was bearing fruit.

CHAPTER FOUR

The lady was indeed aged, yet still upright and dignified, with a thick silver plait down her back. I found her settled on the veranda that encircles all Chilean houses, protection against sun or rain. To the sides and over the roof grew myrtle, laurel and jasmine. She sat somewhat queenly, a rosary round her neck, on a carved wooden chair while around her played a bevy of black-eyed, rosy-cheeked grandchildren or probably great-grandchildren.

The moment I appeared, with my servant, Felipe, dragging unwillingly behind me, the matriarch instituted a whirlwind of activity. As a manservant produced a chair for me, the children ran into the garden, returning with mimosa, roses, carnations, jasmine, sweet peas and scabious, which they piled into my lap until it overflowed.

They were shooed away by a procession of stately mothers and some younger girls. Most had adorned their black hair with a flower so that it was as if the attendants of the Goddess Flora had arrived. I used my Spanish to praise everything I saw, while one of the younger women struck up in something I took to be a native language before, just in time, I made out its remote cousinage to English!

'Thee Keengie Horge way thank. Way hank por favor Admiral Cochrane.'

Of course, the last two words made all things clear but I was amazed, nevertheless, that such simple people knew of the saviour who had come into their midst. I could not help smiling, however, at the linking of his name with that of King George, whose government had tried to stop him leaving England.

Now a table was carried out, covered with a somewhat grubby cloth. While in Valparaíso, I had been warned against *matee*, the local drink. 'Every person uses the same straw,' Mrs Campbell had advised me, in shocked tones, although doubtless herself brought up with the practice. At least I knew what to expect when a rather fine silver pot appeared with a silver tube, holes pierced in it at the end.

The *señora* gestured for me to go first and I

39

gestured to her. Eventually I agreed and sucked up the *matee*, which turned out to be an unthreatening mix of a herb-like dried sienna, sugar and lemon. Nor did I suffer at any time from sharing a straw with these healthy, beautiful people. Afterwards, I called Felipe for a bag I had brought and unpacked my sketching equipment.

Artists all over the world, and from time immemorial, have had to contend with an enthusiastic crowd of spectators such as that which gathered, pointing to everything in view and exclaiming with delight at any recognisable mark on my paper. Yet the joy in that moment was very great, with linnets and blackbirds singing around me and swallows making their arrow-like darts across a rivulet that ran through the bottom of the garden. My sketch was not a great success, yet I walked back to my house in the afternoon sunshine with a sense that I was not just waiting for my new life to begin but was already, if only in a minor way, engaging with this new country.

I was still several steps from my home when I was overtaken by Glennie riding a small but elegant horse and accompanied by Lieutenant Loosey, whose moustache at least seemed to be flourishing under Chilean skies.

'You are late, sirs!' I called out, remembering that they'd promised to be with me first thing in the morning.

Loosey reined in his horse—Chilean bits are cruel so that, checked abruptly, the poor horse nearly stood on his hind legs. Glennie performed the same sudden stop, although with less of a flourish. He was still not quite strong.

'We have a reason, madam!' Glennie, who was

liable to excitement, raised his hat and waved so that his hair, too, stood on its end and waved. 'You will see in under the half-hour. We are the forerunners.'

So, they dashed ahead while I, with Felipe, followed sedately, although I would rather have been with them, being as keen to be mounted as you, in another age, might race along in your Renault Clio.

At the house, the two men stood impatiently, as the young will, swishing at grasses with their crops, then making aim at a bumble bee that had no difficulty in avoiding them but made the horses jump.

I went inside to find refreshments and almost at once heard the sound of more hoofs approaching. I looked out and saw a train of three mules with, atop the first, a small, doll-like woman, whose extreme discomfort I could tell even at a distance.

'Who is that?' I called out, immediately suspicious.

'She's your p-present,' Loosey replied, with a carefree smile, belied by the stutter. The smile died away as he saw my expression.

'Explain yourself, sir. Who is this uncomfortable lady?'

Glennie, now properly anxious, although with a self-righteous air, came closer. 'She is Mrs Henrietta Headingly,' he murmured, 'a naval widow who has come as your companion.'

'My companion!' Female companionship is not beyond my skills. In later years the Hon. Caroline Fox became my greatest confidante and support. Over a decade I addressed hundreds of letters to her as she did to me. You may read them now

41

in the British Library. But that was when sickness confined me to my room. In my prime, I always preferred men, and in Chile I was very much in my prime. The sad little bundle, now approaching at a slightly faster pace, was not for me.

'I do not wish for a lady companion.'

Glennie chewed his lip and Mr Loosey gazed at the sky as if he hoped to be whisked away by a tornado.

'She is not exactly *our* present.' Glennie frowned so hard his nose concertinaed. 'We are her escort. She has been sent to you by Captain Dean, Commodore Stewart, the governor, and all those who have your best interests at heart.' He blushed as he pronounced these words and I realised, with a sense of doom, that he had learnt this message by rote and that the all-male establishment of Valparaíso was speaking through him. I was to have a lady companion and here she was.

'Good afternoon, madam,' I said, as the bundle crumpled to the ground. Her face was just as I had expected; pink, egg-shaped and painted in the middle with small unremarkable features. She was too puffed to reply so I turned to Glennie again. 'Are those her boxes?'

'Yes,' admitted Glennie. He had known me too closely to deny my displeasure, and I saw a look pass between him and his friend, then a smile.

Loosey's smile threatened to turn into a boyish guffaw. He stepped closer to me and whispered, 'She says she's usually known as Hettie Heavenly. You see, Henrietta Headingly, Hettie Heavenly.' At this he roared, and so did Glennie.

This was rude. Doubtless the woman was a fool but if we must cohabit she could not be insulted.

'Give Mrs Headingly your arm to the chair,' I said reprovingly, to Loosey, and to Glennie, 'Help the men in with the boxes.'

In this way Miss H., as I called her in my journals, came into my life. Everything about her was dull because she had never had a thought that wasn't conventional, quite like the pug-faced parrots that squawked about the garden, although admittedly prettier. She would have seen herself as the heroine of a Dickens novel—if the famous author had lived in her time.

There was only one striking thing I discovered that first evening as she drank too deeply of the strong Chilean wine: despite being married to a captain (albeit he'd never made post) and despite having two sons at sea (Edgar, fifteen years and Clarence, thirteen years), she *detested* the Navy.

'I was so very young when we married,' she told me and crooked her little finger at her glass as if we were taking tea at Court rather than picnicking in a Chilean cottage. 'Mr Headingly snatched me from the bosom of my family.'

'The bosom?' I echoed facetiously. Perhaps luckily for our forced companionship, mockery, like so much else, was not in her repertoire of understanding.

'We were met a week,' she continued, her blue eyes round, 'and married in the morning. He sailed away and when he came back there was Edgar. Then he sailed away again, and when he came back, there was Clarence but, oh dear, what a surprise! *He* was missing a leg.'

'A leg!' I exclaimed to cover a snort of laughter. What portion of anatomy would next burst from my lips, I wondered. Her manner of delivery, whether about arriving child or departing leg, had not varied, although maybe her eyes had opened even wider. 'Did you never think of accompanying your husband on board ship?'

'No, indeed not, madam. In my experience women who go on board ship invade a man's world. Besides, the sea winds so coarsen their complexion that one can hardly tell if they are female or male.'

Thus she dismissed more than a decade in which I had accompanied Captain Graham around the world, ever-widening my delight in the new and unexplored. Before I could sound 'complexion' as my next body part, this naval scourge elaborated on her theme.

'The Navy has a reputation for gentility but in my view it is a home for the ne'er-do-well and the scoundrel. Even Admiral Nelson behaved in a way no gentleman would countenance.'

By now her cheeks were painted, like those of a doll, with the bright pink spots of a consumptive although, as I was to learn, she was the heartiest of women.

'May I ask how you arrived in Valparaíso if you think ships are not for ladies?'

At this she drew a handkerchief from her sleeve. 'In the two years I have been here,' this was news to me, 'how often have I remembered that fateful morning when Captain Headingly took me on board?'

'And did he die at sea?'

She nodded gravely.

'Heroically, perhaps?'

The handkerchief was pressed to her eyes. 'He fell overboard.'

Perhaps I'm wrong to describe her as dull

because, looking back at the scene and the curious blankness with which she described a remarkable event—I have never heard of a captain falling overboard, for good, as it were—she might have been some kind of genius.

'His missing leg made him somewhat unbalanced. The wind was strong, his grip on the rigging weak.'

'He could not be rescued?'

'We were flying along at seven knots. The waves were high. It was dusk.' She removed the handkerchief. 'So, you see, we're both in the same boat.'

'Scarcely a boat,' I quipped.

She sighed heavily. 'Both stranded on foreign shores. Both needing a new husband to start our lives again.'

Even allowing for the effects of Chilean wine, this was outrageous. I found I had sprung to my feet but, as a sharp retort formed, I saw her little face staring up at me with some faint intimation of uneasiness, and relented. She was not worth my anger.

'Come,' I said. 'We must prepare for bed.'

At least I had the pleasure of watching her discomfort as I refused her the share of mine and pointed her to a bench in the main room. I left her one guttering and rather disgusting Chilean candle and took myself two brought from England with the intention of re-forming my mind in the cool delights of Milton. I was pleased to discover in his description of Paradise, a passage that so reminded me of the countryside in which I now resided:

45

> *The roof*
> *Of thickest covert, was in woven shade;*
> *Laurel and myrtle and what higher grew*
> *Of firm and fragrant leaf: on either side*
> *Each odorous bushy shrub*
> *Fenced up the verdant wall.*

I had noticed as Miss H. unpacked her boxes that, apart from the expected Bible, she did not possess one book.

*   *   *

The next morning I made a plan for several longer expeditions, both into the countryside and back to town. The weather, unfortunately, did not co-operate, setting into either rain or the dreaded *neblina*. After two days of this, in which I read Lord Byron out loud, and Miss H. darned her stockings, I announced, 'Today we will call on La Chavelita,' which I had discovered was the name of my stately matriarchal neighbour.

As before, our welcome was warm, not reciprocated by Miss H. 'Oh, my boots!' she screeched, in the greatest agony—far greater than when she had revealed her husband could fill only one boot at a time. 'This red mud is as bad as clay.'

'It *is* clay,' said I, setting myself happily beside our hostess on the veranda. The distant view was screened by the rain, but the flowers and shrubs in the garden glowed even more brightly in their shrouded light. Beside me I had many an eager face whose owner laughed and chatted as I grew more confident with my Spanish.

Soon we were invited to stay for lunch, which I

accepted eagerly.

'Oh, Mrs Graham!' How Miss H.'s blue eyes rolled in appeal as, according to local custom, we stuck our fingers into a lamb stew dripping with gravy and other less definable specialities. Inexorable, I waved away the offer of a plate and spoon, which, our hosts had heard, was the European way.

'When in Rome, do as the Romans do,' I admonished Miss H., who would, I soon saw, rather have starved. Her trial continued with the arrival of the inevitable *matee* and its shared drinking straw. The Englishman abroad has been the subject of many studies, in some of which I have featured. Nottingham Trent University—'Not Oxbridge', I hear the intellectual snobs of you cry, and I might have thought the same, but it's extraordinary how lying underground for a century or two sharpens your sense of perspective. If scholarship takes the form of a research project under the auspices of a 'Centre for Travel Writing Studies', then I would be a fool to complain.

The point I intended to make was that women travellers come in two sorts, just as they do at home: those who wish to conform and those who wish to explore. It hardly needs saying that Miss H. fell into the former category and I into the latter. It looks odder abroad because the conformist is trying desperately to reproduce the old world rather than adapt to the new. Miss H., with her Sidmouth sensibilities, was certain to be unhappy. However, on that wet day in the Almendral, she took a little revenge on me, even if she did it unconsciously.

'My dear Mrs Graham,' she exclaimed, coming alive again after food and drink had been removed, '*now* I see where we are!'

'I rejoice for you.' It was true that the mist had lifted, displaying the width and depth of the garden.

'It was one of Lady Cochrane's favourite places for a picnic,' she continued complacently. 'She would ride out here with her children, her chosen friends and admirers, a retinue of servants. Once I was among the company and I have never seen such merriment. Riding, dancing, singing, Lady Cochrane excelled at everything.'

She then launched into tales of Lady Cochrane's adventures while in Chile, her bravery, her beauty, her conquests of man and beast.

'Was Admiral Cochrane with her much?' I enquired, with assumed languor, only hoping that we could have less of the *wife* and more of the *man*.

'He was at sea very often. On one occasion, indeed, she was on board during an attack at Callao and lit a cannon with her own hands when a seaman failed in his duty. The whole crew, on becoming victorious, sang the National Anthem in her honour.'

'I believe,' said I, 'that after lighting the cannon, she fainted away with the shock of the explosion.' I had heard this story while in Valparaíso. Tittle-tattle is the staple of a small society. It was impossible, however, to staunch the breathless flow of admiration.

'One day she paraded in front of the Chilean troops and quite astounded them with her horsemanship as she controlled a fiery steed, "*Que hermosa! Que graciosa! Es un angel!*" they cried.' Here Miss H. caught the attention of our hosts who, despite her execrable accent, recognised their own language. When she went on to cry louder, in a thoroughly overexcited way, the name 'Cochrane',

48

they bowed and smiled and clapped their hands. I could not blame them, but how awful it was to hear the name of such a hero on the lips of such a pathetic human specimen.

Encouraged by her reception, Miss H. told further tales of Lady C.'s bravery: her crossing the Andes in October, sleeping on a bullock's hide at Puenta del Inca and avoiding being pushed over a precipice by a Spanish soldier.

Unimaginative, conventional ladies lose all sense of proportion once their attention is caught by someone unusual in their experience. The truth is that Kitty Cochrane, as all London knew when she ran off with His Lordship to Gretna Green, was an extremely pretty sixteen-year-old bastard with a Spanish dancer for a mother; she had caught the eye of a man who, like so many brilliant seamen, had no idea about women. When I knew him better, I felt even more certain that he had mistaken his animal passion for love, and pity for her situation had aroused his chivalry. That she was uneducated to the point of being a simpleton, he had overlooked and continued to overlook, since they were apart so much, for many years. He had found a subject for his romantic nature. Towards the end of his life he wrote a letter to his son, Captain Eustace Cochrane, warning him of the mundane problems at the heart of a bad marriage, which clearly referred to his own:

I hope your brother and yourself, if such an event shall be contemplated, will secure enough, not for your living alone, but for the consequences of married life: for, believe me, that after the honeymoon is past there is the

49

education of children to provide for, their
advancement too in life—But above all, there
is the necessity that the Hon. Mrs Horace shall
not get out of humour, and make your life one
continued scene of bickering and reproach,
because the Hon. Mrs Somebody Else keeps
a carriage; can give better or more numerous
parties—or dress better! My dear boy, guard
against this species of ever-preying misery above
all else! For, like the perpetual drop of water, it
will wear the heart, or harden it to stone.

Eustace Cochrane never married. His hot-headed father had fallen for a fool, who thought fashion and position (which she had never had before he took her up) the most important thing in the world. She had no way of understanding the true qualities of the man she had married, which went far beyond pleasing society—indeed, he had proved his contempt for society by the very act of marrying her. It was an irony that she was too foolish and he too romantic to admit.

She liked parties because she was pretty—nothing wrong in that you may say, but Cochrane loathed parties. Her greatest moments were when the world, or that small part of it around her, cried, '*Que guapa! Que hermosa! Que preciosa!*' All her exploits were performed in the public eye. Like her mother, the unknown Spanish dancer, she needed a stage to be happy because without an audience she was nothing.

This was the woman whom one of the great geniuses of the nineteenth century had chosen to marry, one picked out by the great Lord Byron, who wrote, 'There is no man I envy so much as Lord

Cochrane.' This was the woman who was bringing a flush to Miss H.'s silly round cheeks and a sparkle to her aimless eye.

At the time, I knew only some of the information recorded above, so it was absurd to be depressed by Miss H.'s adulation of the wife of a man I still scarcely knew, whatever my imaginings for the future. But the rain was coming down in leaden sheets, buffeting the flowers and quite obliterating the silvery sheen of the sea far below. It seemed to flatten my spirits. I found myself unable to prevent Miss H. embarking on yet another story—this time about Kitty's wounding by a stiletto as she defended her husband's papers against a marauder.

I felt insignificant, a poor widow, not even a mother like my ghastly companion. Kitty (or Kate, as Cochrane's most recent biographer has insisted was her proper name—for my part, kittenish she was, so Kitty she'll be) had used her youth and beauty to ensnare a man as far above her as the sun above the earth. On that grey afternoon I echoed Byron's lines:

> *I stood*
> *Among them but not of them; in a shroud*
> *Of thoughts which were not their thoughts.*

Yet these few words of poetry served to remind me of the power of my pen, which is stronger and lives longer than any posing act.

'We should leave,' I said, rising as I spoke. In my mind's eye I saw my writing-desk with white paper, ink and quills waiting for me. There was my place, a commentator on life wherever I found it most interesting.

CHAPTER FIVE

My determination to provide material for my
journal, the Chilean fleet's continued absence
and Miss H.'s continued presence encouraged
me to visit the festival of Nuestra Señora del Pilar
la Avogada de los Marineros, which celebrated
St Peter's feast day. Fishermen toured his statue
around the harbour, accompanied by boats, bands
and salutes from rockets and guns.

We rode down to join the celebrations at the
Church of Le Merced, whose spire I could see
from my house. It was a fine bright day and, as we
rode, I made notes on those also on our road, no
Europeans in this slightly removed place, apart
from an English butcher who had built quite a
palace above my home. Most were decked out
in ribbons and flowers, some riding the elegant
little Chilean horses, others on mules. Once we
overtook a whole train of mules and carts come
from Santiago, where they'd been carrying goods
including, they told me, two pianofortes. The
Chileans were very fond of music of all kinds. The
journey had taken the muleteers less than three
days, which I considered good going for ninety
miles, some of it over the foothills of the Andes.

Miss H., of course, could not approve of me
talking to 'the natives'. She looked even more
askance when we found that we were meeting La
Chavelita in a kind of public house, across the road
from Le Merced, and that other rooms soon filled
with revellers, entertained by copious amounts of
drink (although I saw not a person drunk), lively

music and gambling.

The religious part of the ceremony also displeased my companion and I myself found the papist habit of carrying their painted Virgin about the town—on gracious visits to San Joseph, Santa Dolores and Santa Gertrudes—too absurd to raise religious thoughts, but when she was returned to her own altar and we struck up with 'Ave Maria Stella', I was duly moved. How often I had heard those lines on a balmy evening in Italy:

> *Star of the dark and stormy sea,*
> *Where wrecking tempests round us rave,*
> *Thy gentle virgin form we see*
> *Bright rising o'er the hoary wave.*

Poetry has always had the power to move my thoughts to another sphere. I am not alone in this. When Lord Byron's *Childe Harold* was first published it sold five thousand copies within a week. Perhaps I lived in a more poetic age.

As we rode home on that dark night, our servants laughing and chatting, the smell of damp rosemary, sage and jasmine rising, the moon, in gauzy mist shining above our heads, I chanted to myself such verses as I could remember and felt my head filled with a thousand wondrous sensations.

There were other expeditions after this one, grander affairs to Valparaíso where I and Miss H., sparkling as best she could, ate with the governor, Don Jose Zenteno, and whichever naval captain invited us.

As May approached June, news—more often gossip—came from the battlefront in the north: Lord Cochrane was in Peru, meeting with San

53

Martín; Lord Cochrane had not gone ashore; Lord Cochrane was coming to Valparaíso; San Martín was to oust O'Higgins; San Martín was to meet with Bolivar in north Peru (as Bolivia was then called); Lord Cochrane was attempting to get payment out of San Martín for his crews who had so honourably discharged their duty; Lord Cochrane lay in Calloa Bay with his guns shotted but might be expected soon. There was talk of little else.

One of my kinder new friends was the American consul, Mr Hogan. I dined more than once at his home, with his wife and daughters and whoever else was visiting Valparaíso. His house was simple, in a row of solid buildings that boasted an overall pediment.

Mr Hogan was a very whiskery sort of man who owned a whaling fleet and believed that only good things come from the sea. In his house I met many naval men of all nationalities. The Spanish might still hold on to Chile in the far south but in Valparaíso there was an excited air of opening opportunities. One afternoon, a certain Captain Guise came to dine. He was lately of the Chilean Navy. He was exceedingly polite to me, and appeared to be a good-natured gentleman-like man. Miss H. certainly thought so. Imagine my surprise when his conversation about the engagements with the Spanish centred not on the heroic fight for independence but on the opportunity for accumulating wealth in these rich provinces. He was, in short, an adventurer! Nor did he feel the shame that might have induced him to dis-Guise his ignoble aims.

At my small protestation of disbelief, he pushed aside his wine and looked hard at me. 'Madam, you who have been born and bred to the British naval service'—I had briefly told him my history—'know only too well that the cruel life at sea would be intolerable without the prospect of sudden riches above the small sums paid out, often irregularly. From the great Admiral Nelson to the loblolly boy, seamen have always counted on their share of the prizes, and that's the way things are run. Nelson himself famously commented after his capture of Toulon in 1793, "All we get is honour and salt beef." ' He paused and leant back in his chair, securing his thumbs in his waistcoat. 'Why only last year Lord Cochrane captured the ship in which San Martín stored his treasure and stole from it a yacht-load of silver and seven sacks of gold.'

'*Stole*, sir?' I put down the glass I was holding.

Guise's face had darkened terribly as he brought forward Lord Cochrane's name and, too late, I remembered that he had hoped to command the Chilean fleet himself. Although he had fought nobly under Cochrane, he had eventually fallen out with him and gone to work on San Martín's staff.

'Lord Cochrane's motives were honourable,' intervened my good friend the American consul, soothingly.

I know that my own face is not inexpressive if I am aroused to anger, particularly on behalf of someone I admire. 'He paid over the majority of the money to his sailors, which was far overdue, leaving some for the Army. He kept none for himself.'

'A man who fancies himself Robin Hood,' muttered the bitter captain, his face darkening still further, 'is hardly fit to command a navy.'

'My dear sir,' began I, trying hard to moderate

my tone, 'you yourself have described the naval system in such a way as to suggest such behaviour is expected and necessary.'

'You do not steal from your own side, in this case your own commander.'

There was that word again, 'steal'. I've always had a high colour but I could feel it rising dangerously. Around the table Mrs Hogan and her daughters were looking at their fingers while only Miss H. seemed to be enjoying the disagreement. She was hoping, I suspect, that I might be put down. Restraining my feelings and mindful of my duty as a guest, I resorted to generalities: 'It is wonderful that such a young country as Chile should have had the foresight to confide its future into such able, firm and honourable'—I bowed to the consul—'hands as belong to Lord Cochrane. I fondly trust that the benefit of this sage measure will be permanently felt.'

It was obvious that Captain Guise did not find my words as general as all that, but before he could speak again, the Hogan family rose in concert and shepherded us all from the room on to a terrace that overlooked the bay. They made sure I stood at one end and the jealous captain at the other. A cool wind blew from the north-west, fanning hot cheeks and distempered minds.

After a short while I indicated to the consul that it was time I left. He made no effort to delay me and I would have been off as soon as the horses and escort could be assembled. But at that moment Miss H. measured her length on the floor, going from the perpendicular to the horizontal in one.

'My dear Mrs Headingly!' exclaimed the kind Mrs Hogan, anxiously. 'Emily, dear,' her eldest daughter, 'hasten and bring my smelling-salts.'

Even the irascible Captain Guise joined in this emergency and with 'all hands to the deck' Miss H. was soon off the deck and sitting on a comfortable cane chair.

I looked at her and she looked at me. 'I fear you are not ready for a journey,' said I, with syrupy sympathy.

'Dear Mrs Graham . . .' she began in a delightfully wavering voice before seeming to swoon once more.

'She may stay here,' pronounced Mr Hogan. 'You may both stay.'

Miss H.'s eyelids flickered and something near a smile twitched her rosy lips.

So it was that with Bella, my maidservant, newly acquired that day, Felipe, and my Chileno escort I set off back to the Almendral.

As I spurred my horse up the rutted track—the rainy days had caused a stream to burst its banks and dig holes where it would—I revelled in my newly gained freedom. No one, I dared to hope, would foist another 'companion' on me. I have too much independence of mind to wish to join those females who are permanently excluded into second place; I had relied on education to raise me from their dreary ranks—I used to be told that it was a pity I was not a boy for then my talents might be of use.

Now I looked forward to hours of quiet study and absorbing exploration. I could not have forecast that the very next day my waiting would be over and my new life would begin.

CHAPTER SIX

2nd June, 1822

A rainy morning, and feeling cold, yet the thermometer not below 50 of Fahrenheit. While I was at breakfast, one of my little neighbours came running in, screaming out, 'Señora, he is come!'

'Who is come, child?'

'Our admiral, our great and good admiral, and if you come to the veranda, you will see the flags in the Almendral.'

Accordingly, I looked out and did see the Chilean flag hoisted at every door: and two ships more in the roads than there were yesterday. The *O'Higgins* and *Valdivia* had arrived during the night, and all the inhabitants of the port and suburbs had made haste to display their flags and their joy on Lord Cochrane's safe return.

The drizzle cleared, the mist evaporated and a brilliant sun sparkled on the crests of the little harbour waves, as if the very sea laughed and celebrated.

'Bring me my shawl,' I directed Bella whose pretty dark eyes were still fixed on the scene in front of us.

Like the agile goats and unnamed goat-relatives that live on the mountains, I gathered my skirts and scurried higher up the *cerro*. There, I could look down and see sharper the scene at the harbour. As I watched the boats, the launches and gigs buzzing round the two great ships, like bees around a honey pot, I concluded, with sentiments of relief, satisfaction and anticipation, that at last my natural friend had arrived.

On that bright morning, I admitted to no more than that. As a widow of middle years, I must leave girlish fantasy to the heroine of a romance (although not Maria Edgeworth's young ladies, who have more sense—just think of dear good Belinda). Yet my heart beat faster and my cheeks flushed even as I told myself we were merely acquaintances with a shared background and outlook. That was already a lot. Most likely, if we set aside the naval fraternity, I was the only person capable of understanding and sympathising with every aspect of his life.

He might have been unaware of his need for me, but I felt keenly the need of a powerful friend like him. In my lifetime women who made their own way in the world were highly suspect. By staying on in Chile, a widow and alone, I had marked myself out as a danger. 'A danger to what?' you of the twenty-first century ask. I answer: 'A danger to society.' Even in that faraway place, I was a threat to the settled British, who became ever more absurdly parochial the further they travelled from home. (After my death, I viewed the apogee of such behaviour among the ladies of the British Raj in India.)

The few weeks I'd moved in Valparaíso society had given me ample time to decide whom I wished to be my friends. In that summer of 1822 I strenuously noted the point in my journal.

It is curious, at this distance from home, to see specimens of such people as one meets nowhere else but among the Brangtons, in Madame d'Arblay's *Cecilia*, or the Mrs Eltons of Miss Austen's admirable novels. Yet these are, after all, the people most likely to be here. The country is new; the government unacknowledged by our own; the merchants are chiefly such as sell by commission, for houses established in larger and older states; and, as all Englishmen, from the highest to the lowest, love to have their home with them, the clerks, who fall naturally into these sort of employments, either bring or find suitable wives: therefore society, as far as relates to the English, is of a very low tone.

Reading this now, I am slightly shocked by its patronising air, accurate though I was in my description. But that is a dull modernising. I did continue to point out that these same uneducated people owned kind hearts. But who is to barter a kind heart for a small mind? When society tutted that I had 'set my cap' at Lord Cochrane, I cocked a snook at them—I never wore anything but a turban.

I had to wait four impatient days to meet the Admiral. Our first engagement took place after a papist celebration of *corpus domini* at the Iglesia Matriz. I attended with dear Mrs Campbell, whose brother Don Mariano de Escalada (a finer-looking man than I would have expected) was preaching. Since my friend had put off her French or English dress and adopted Spanish costume, I went so far as to borrow a mantilla to drape over my head and shoulders.

'Anyone would take you for a *señorita española*!' cried Mrs Campbell, clapping her hands.

I was pleased enough with my supposed

60

appearance to walk unselfconsciously through the streets. We were preceded through the crowds by a couple of boys carrying missals and carpets for us to kneel on. At the entrance to the church I all but bumped into Miss H. since the thick black lace of the mantilla somewhat obscured my view.

Having first attempted to avoid me, she then exclaimed, to do her justice, with some appropriateness and even wit, 'Still doing as Rome does, I see, dear Mrs Graham.'

'Or Madrid, in this case,' I responded, and we laughed falsely together.

Inside, the dim air was thick with incense and candle fumes plus the even stronger aromas of too many people crammed into a large space but not large enough. Through the musky gloom glittered the effigy of the Virgin Mary, dressed in hooped white satin with silver fringes, and a diadem of stars, the whole reflected by looking-glasses set around her. On either side stood Saints Peter and Paul, robed as priests of the Church.

Worshipping at graven images is bad enough but my tolerance was further tried when the congregation was called upon to kiss a reliquary, origin unspecified. The ceremony was held in the presence of my patron, the governor, who did not arrive till eleven o'clock by which time several young ladies had decorously fainted and the guttering candles had turned the air black.

Nevertheless, I forgave Zenteno's tardiness since the whispers around the church indicated that he had been in conversation with the Admiral. The service, particularly the sermon, was carried out in a very proper spirit, with reference to the moral freedom conferred by Christian teaching, which is,

61

of course, but a short step to political freedom.

We emerged, blinking like owls, into a surprisingly sunny afternoon and found ourselves further entertained by the display of about a hundred and fifty boats and canoes, adorned with national colours, firing rockets in the bay before setting off to sing hymns and chant at every church or little cove. From a distance the effect was of a myriad dragonflies skipping over a pond and, for a moment, however unlikely, put me in mind of home.

But I was very tired and, like tourists round the world and over the centuries, felt the need to put up my swelling feet. Thus abandoning Mrs Campbell, I repaired with my maid to a house belonging to my newest acquaintance, Mr Hoseason. Did I know Lord Cochrane was taking dinner there? I believe Hoseason had told me he acted as agent for the Admiral. Did I retain my mantilla because I thought it becoming? My journal gives no clue: I preferred to attend to the political.

'Mrs Graham, madam. Your servant.' Mr Hoseason was a pompous sort of man, a bachelor, tall and thin, overly impressed by rank. But he kept a well-run kitchen, his meat more finely butchered than was usual, his chairs and table more commodious. For these reasons, which he, doubtless, understood, his dinner times were always well attended.

I stood for a moment at the entrance to the drawing room. Disguised by my lacy drapes, I felt able to contemplate the scene undetected. Lord Cochrane stood in the centre of a group of naval officers. He was head and shoulders taller than any other, a man whose massive talents were matched by his frame. Having been much at sea recently, his face was sun-darkened, setting off, even at the distance I stood, the brilliance of his blue eyes and his fair to auburn hair.

Like many heroes of his generation, he was much painted over the years, although his total came nowhere near Wellington's, which ran into hundreds—sometimes in later years the duke would sit for half a dozen artists at one time. All the same, there are Cochrane portraits, Cochrane statues, even Cochrane plates. But when I picture him, I think of a stained-glass window in the *Museo Naval* in Valparaíso, just a few hundred feet or so from the house where I met him on that evening. In the window, he is more than life-sized, wearing full-dress uniform with a sword at his side and his favourite extra-long, two and a half foot telescope in his hands. Judging by his hair colour and his girth he is pictured in his mid-forties, as he was during his time in Chile.

Incidentally, this charming *Museo Naval*, whitewashed and built round an elegant courtyard, features the Sir Thomas Lawrence painting of myself with the attached epithet, 'Maria Graham. A personal friend of Admiral Cochrane'. So be it. I do not object. On that evening in Valparaíso, that was precisely what I hoped to be.

As I stared at him from under my mantilla and thought of how shamefully he had been treated by his country, lines of Shakespeare came into my head. England,

Like a base Ethiope, threw a pearl away
Richer than all his kind.

I must have murmured the lines aloud because Mr Hoseason bent to me. 'I beg your pardon, madam, you are waiting for an introduction.'

'I was recalling Shakespeare,' I replied, somewhat tartly. 'I am acquainted with His Lordship over many years. I was considering how England's loss has been Chile's gain.'

'Indeed so.' Taking my arm he led me, as it were, on to the stage.

Before leaving this little curtain-raiser, however, I wish to abuse one of the editors of my journal who pointed out that I had misquoted Shakespeare. She was right. I admit it freely. But what she had not understood was that the heads of the educated of my generation were filled with quotations, to be used as expressions of the moment and not to be judged against some yardstick of exactness. Whether the base man was an Ethiope, an Indian or a Judaean is of interest only to bores and pedants!

I moved slowly across the room, which was not big enough. I was conscious of my upright carriage and supposed that my face glowed with anticipation. The officers around me parted. We stood face to face—or as far as we could since, although I am not short, he was a good six inches above me.

'Señora.' He bowed.

'My lord.' I bowed too and moved my mantilla a little aside from my face. The effect was gratifying in the extreme and I realised he hadn't recognised me before.

'Mrs Graham. I had heard that you were in Val—' He hesitated, almost stuttering with pleasure. Or so I thought until he resumed. 'I beg to offer you my deepest sympathy. Captain Graham was a first-rate seaman, a . . .' He hesitated again, searching, I had to assume, for more words of approbation, although 'first rate' was already beyond what my poor Graham could have expected.

Immediately I acknowledged to myself it was right and proper that he should salute the passing of a fellow officer so graciously. It was only my stupid woman's heart that had beaten too fast and imagined another cause for his emotion. Yet I knew well enough how deep is the love between naval men. Hatred, such as arose between Cochrane and Earl St Vincent, of the English Admiralty, is even deeper.

'You are kind, my lord. Captain Graham would have been gratified.'

'I understand you have taken a house?'

So he had talked about me—or heard talk about me, which came to the same thing.

'It is in the Almendral, a very peaceful area.'

'And full of bandits, if I am to believe common gossip.'

'Never believe common gossip,' I replied, and we looked a little solemnly at each other, acknowledging, perhaps, that gossip gave us both reputations yet neither of us cared a jot for it. 'My neighbours are good, hard-working Chilenos,' I added. 'They have become my friends. No bandit would be allowed across my threshold.'

'They are a fine people. I am proud to have been made a Chilean citizen. I have a house myself, in the south, and another estate nearer here. I plan to import English agricultural methods.'

While we talked thus, I noticed an air of surprise among the officers, who had retreated a little but

65

not out of earshot. Lord Cochrane was always loved by officers and men alike but he was not thought quite ordinary. As a man of action on the foredeck, he was impetuous, cunning, daring, bold, but in the drawing room he was often withdrawn and sometimes silent. But here we were, exchanging pleasantries as if we were old friends meeting at Holland House.

We talked for some time about Chileno farming, which was extremely antiquated, and Lord Cochrane became heated over the place of the modern plough. Like his father, the old and eccentric Earl of Dundonald, he was always interested in inventions. I then thought it necessary to enquire after his wife. 'Perhaps Lady Cochrane will enjoy planning your new house with you.'

A sad, muffled look came over his face. 'Lady Cochrane finds the heat difficult. The children too . . .' Once more his voice trailed away. It is an unfortunate fact that the strongest of men can be bemused and befuddled by a particular kind of pretty, silly woman.

'The climate is not easy,' I agreed, without pointing out that the Chilean winter, which we were now entering, was much the same as winter in fashionable Bognor.

By now the room had become considerably more crowded and I was aware that the deferential circle around us had become three or four deep: they would not much longer be denied the company of their hero.

Bowing to the inevitable, I stepped a little aside, 'I should be honoured if you could escape your duties long enough to pay the Almendral a visit.'

'Yes. Yes.' For the first time he raised his blue

eyes to the gathering. 'I shall do that. My duties, as you say, take me tomorrow to Santiago where the director, General O'Higgins, resides, but rely on it, I shall find my way to your peaceful area.'

For a moment, I thought he bent forward as if to kiss my hand in the Spanish fashion. But that was fancy. He was already politely, if wearily, listening to a stocky individual with a ridiculously ill-tied cravat. Hands twitching to make it straight, I removed myself to a side room where there was a bench for me to sit and rest my feet, and peace to collect my thoughts.

We had not talked of the things that most concerned everybody in Chile. Politics had been far from Lord Cochrane's mind as he spoke to me and I thought it gave him pleasure that it was so. He was, I have already implied, a man more for actions than words. Yet, as Admiral of the Fleet he was at the centre of the stage. In particular, I longed to hear his views concerning the Protector of Peru, Señor San Martín. Apparently Chile's ally, he was now generally believed to be a man of self-serving and despotic nature. Moreover, he was rumoured to be planning to publish a direct attack on the Admiral's good faith.

I looked round the room in which I found myself. There was one window, which showed a square of sky with a line of sea at the bottom. The floor was wooden, with chairs and benches set around the walls, some covered with rugs as is the Chilean custom. Through the open door, I perceived a scene of noisy animation, punctuated by the braying laugh that characterises the English at pleasure.

I was in danger of feeling the self-pity of the voyeur, although I had chosen the role for myself,

67

when three officers burst upon me. They were from His Lordship's squadron: Captain Crosbie, an exuberant flame-haired Irishman, Lieutenant Moreland, English, though hardly less lively, and Captain Wilkinson, a thick-set sensible man. Since the *Doris* had sailed, I was sadly short of any naval friends and therefore had been glad to make their acquaintance earlier in the day.

Crosbie hailed me unceremoniously: 'We have been discussing General San Martín. What line do you take, Mrs Graham? With all your book-learning, do you defend the man as a wily leader and patriot or think him the devil incarnate?'

Before I could present any case, although I knew little enough, Wilkinson interrupted, 'Surely no rational man can describe the present government of Peru as anything but tyrannical, stained by cruelties more like the frenetic acts of the Tsar Paul than the inflictions of even the greatest military tyrants.'

'Cruelties, sir?' began I, but got no further before Crosbie returned to the fray, flinging his hat on a chair as he spoke, as if to give himself more freedom to denunciate.

'I have a letter from Mr Dance of your old ship, the *Doris*.' Here, he paused to extricate the letter from his inner pocket. 'It says that an elderly respectable woman in Lima, having imprudently spoken too freely of San Martín, was condemned to be exposed for three hours in the streets in a robe of penance; and that, as her voice had offended, she was gagged, and the gag used was a human bone. She was taken home, fainting with a natural loathing, and died!'

Such were the shouts of disgust for a man who

could order these actions that I would have needed the eloquence of Portia to argue the despot's case, were I inclined to do so, which I was not. San Martín's shabby treatment of Lord Cochrane was too well known. Now my new friends vied for further instances of the inhumanity of Peru's so-called 'Protector'.

'You have seen the *Milagro*, in port now?' continued Moreland. 'It is full of Spanish prisoners, to whom San Martín had promised security and protection. However, after paying half their property for letters of naturalisation and permission to leave Lima with the rest, they were seized and stripped on the road to Callao, huddled on board the prison ship and soon will be sent to join the other captives, probably for life, since they are only to be liberated when Old Spain acknowledges the independence of her colonies.'

'Can any man be so base?' I interjected, almost as passionately as the young men.

'Worse is to come,' continued the brave lieutenant, 'for these poor people have arrived without the common necessities of life, and might indeed perish even before they reach their everlasting gaol. But one man has taken pity and, out of his own purse, has seen their most pressing wants are supplied.'

'And the name of that man?' I prompted. In truth I knew the answer because this noble story was doing the rounds in Valparaíso but could not resist hearing it spoken.

'Admiral Lord Cochrane!' They made so much noise that several faces, including Mr Hoseason's, appeared curiously at the door.

These young enthusiasts, you must recall, were

not long back from a war. They had fought and killed and seen their brothers killed. Their lives had been at the mercy of the skill and imagination of their commander. Their spirits were still tuned to a high degree. Nor had the war yet been fully won because not only southern Chile but much of Peru, always essential to Chile's security, was still in the hands of Spanish royalists. They might be called to fight again.

I myself had grown up when our war with France seemed unending. I came from a naval family, so the news of battles at sea was not background. I had read the *Naval Chronicle* before I picked up *Castle Rackrent*. I understood, therefore, the European rules of war, the honour a captured enemy officer must be accorded, the importance of a strict morality being upheld by the man in charge. Virtue in wartime is a first necessity.

So I spoke soberly to these honourable young men: 'Would that His Lordship could inspire these people with some of the humanities of war as practised in Europe.'

But they looked away from me and, following their gaze as I finished my sentence, I saw that the Admiral himself stood at the door, his eyes upon me.

Unable to master a blush, I moved aside, for he was entering with Mr Hoseason and others behind them. At the same time, servants carrying trestles and platters arrived from another door behind me. It was clear that we were to eat in this room. Suddenly overcome by faintness, I sought a chair. As soon as I had composed myself a little, screened as I was by the press of backs, I decided I would leave. The day had been long; already the light from the square window showed a richer glow. If I wished to get home I must start the journey now.

I would flatter myself if I thought I would be much missed. I had made my mark but that was all. Nevertheless I harassed my poor Bella on her uncomfortable saddle and my two dull Chileno boys so that my Charles and their mules should bring us back the sooner and I could sit alone with my writing-desk and put down the experiences of the day. I would not put down everything, I need hardly say, but the act of writing would give me a chance to dwell on the happiest moments.

Above all, I remembered the look in His Lordship's eye as he stood at the door and heard me extolling the virtues of a man who understood the morality of war. He had seen, I imagined, even as my horse stumbled his way up the steep path through the increasing darkness, an intelligent, graceful woman, who spoke her mind freely among men and, although not without pretensions to looks, spurned the usual female arts, the simpering and deferring, the ribbons and the buttoned ankle, as being but insipid fare to a man of strong character . . .

I had just reached this point in my thoughts, proving to my satisfaction that I was destined to be His Lordship's companion, when my foolish horse, frightened by the hoot of an owl, darted sideways. He went one way and I, pride coming before a fall, went the other. My head hit a stone and the last thing I saw was the Southern Cross spinning above the horizon.

CHAPTER SEVEN

A delicate constitution such as mine must always suffer repercussions after a fall. A bleed followed and I was forced to spend several days in bed.

The weather was chill and gloomy so I was delighted when the same three officers I had met with Lord Cochrane decided to build me a stove in my little sitting room, complete with funnel. Hitherto, I had used an open brazier, which filled the air with charcoal fumes.

'We should be burning coal,' stated Lieutenant Moreland, as he blackened his hands in my interest.

I lay watching them work from the couch on which the undesirable Miss H. had slept (the gossips said she was chasing Captain Crosbie, whom I believed well able to run before the wind). 'And why do we not use coal?' I asked, ever glad to inform myself and thus my journal and the wider public.

Moreland pushed his lanky hair from his face, which was streaked as black as a Negro's. 'There was abundant coal in Concepción, not more than a few hundred miles to the south, but the Spanish did not allow trading along the Chilean coast so it was cheaper to bring it thousands of miles from England.'

'Cheaper, but not cheap?'

'Not at all cheap.'

'So we use charcoal. Well, the woodcutters, whose trails are all in the hills above, may profit from it.'

'Indeed.'

At which the young men returned to their noisy work and I returned to my peaceful book. My contentment in enforced leisure might have been less if I had been unaware that, since our meeting, Lord Cochrane had ridden to Santiago where he remained. Again gossip flew about his sayings and doings. His detractors spoke of his greed in trying to extract his wages from a country starved of funds first by the Spanish and then by war. His admirers—myself, his captains and lieutenants among a multitude of others—pointed out that he was only trying to extract, like an unwilling tooth, money due to him after nearly three years in which he'd risked life and limb.

Lord Cochrane's experiences in the Royal Navy had taught him that you fight twice for your prize money: once on the deck of a ship with your sword in your hand and once with the Admiralty, who deals it out. Many considered the second the more formidable enemy. General O'Higgins, however great a leader of this newborn country, was not convinced by His Lordship's arguments.

Never for a moment did I doubt the Admiral's honourable motives. I mused and the lines of my beloved Milton passed in front of my eyes:

Love virtue, she alone is free,
She can teach ye how to climb
Higher than the sphery chime;
or, if virtue feeble were,
Heaven itself would stoop to her.

It was nearly an entire month before His Lordship returned. My health renewed, I was on a path above my home studying a plant called *culen*, which I knew was medicinal and much prized as a charm against witchcraft, when I heard a salute from the bay below. Leaving Bella behind, I hurried to my favourite vantage-point from which I had often admired the shadows over the sea as the clouds rolled swiftly along, sometimes concealing and sometimes displaying the cliffs of Valparaíso. Today my interest in the view was more particular. The salute had been fired from an English frigate, His Majesty's Ship *Aurora*, the smoke from which, after creeping in fleecy whiteness along the water, gradually diluted into volumes of grey cloud, and mixed with the vapours that lay on the bosom of the hills.

It could only signify one event: Lord Cochrane was returned from Santiago and going aboard the frigate. As the smoke cleared I was indeed able to see his gig, gilded and bright with flags, alongside the *Aurora*.

I watched till my eyes protested against being screwed up another moment, then slowly descended to my house. The day before, I had visited Lac Laqunilla in a company from Valparaíso. Now I sat on my veranda and tried to describe the outing for my journal but my thoughts were elsewhere.

At four o'clock, when the light was already fading, I gave up and sat staring at the tops of small fruit trees, a few crudely tiled rooftops and the casings for vines. I had passed scarcely more than ten minutes in this unproductive state, when I heard noises, at first I thought from the Almendral's one inhabited street, but the sounds drew nearer. Horses! Mules, bearing goods to Valparaíso or travelling empty back again, often passed my door, oxen too, pulling wooden carts, but horses very seldom—unless their riders were coming to visit me.

'Bella! Prepare the tea things. *Matee*, too.' I had begun to like the stuff. 'And bring out the silver teaspoons and the best tablecloth.'

'Señora! Señora!' wailed Bella, who seldom managed to carry out my wishes at the first command.

I dashed to my dark little bedroom, felt around for my prettiest violet turban. When at home I had graduated a little from unflattering black. I teased out the curls around my face and took out from lavender my Indian paisley shawl. Black, but pretty. Then, still ignoring Bella's complaints, I quite grandly renewed my place on my very ungrand veranda.

How was I so sure it was His Lordship come to visit? I cannot answer that—except in terms that would severely undermine my credibility as an intellectual—although since the definition of an intellectual is one who deals in abstractions, perhaps there is some link. Let us say the horses approached more rapidly than usual and their feet sounded heavier on the ground as if bearing the weight of someone mightier than most.

They came into view, Cochrane at the head, riding a horse marked with brown and white blotches like a circus animal. Behind were Captain Crosbie and a man I knew to be a Dr Craig, from the flagship *O'Higgins*. These last two must have come out for the exercise since they cantered on past the house, doffing their hats to me as they passed.

'Mrs Graham!' cried Captain Crosbie.

'Your servant!' cried Dr Craig. And they were

gone. Meanwhile two *peons* had come to take hold of Cochrane's horse.

'Your mount has more the look of a cow than a horse,' said I, quite losing my composure as he bent over my hand.

'A horse is faster but not so useful in the face of hunger or thirst,' he answered, as if it was a serious matter.

Little did I know how apposite were his words. As we settled ourselves on the veranda—he with some difficulty since both the space and the chair were small—and began to utter the civilities usual on such occasions, Bella appeared, bowed almost double at the presence of such an august visitor.

'Señora. Señora,' she began again, tears trembling in her dark eyes.

Such was her panic that I imagined a calamity and, excusing myself from His Lordship, took her to one side. 'What is it, girl?' I asked her, kindly enough, in my very much improved Spanish, at which she broke into such a flood of tears that I could hardly hear her message. It seemed, however, to include the word *leche* repeated in a rising tone of despair.

I glanced at my guest but he seemed happy enough, eyes indeed half closed—any sensible man of action, when finding himself in a safe harbour, takes the chance of rest.

'*Leche*, Bella. For the tea?' Finally, the matter was explained, and not so very tragic: there was no milk.

Smiling rather, I returned to His Lordship and explained the situation. 'I fear I brought it on myself by pronouncing such an insult on your horse.'

Immediately he rose to his feet, transformed into a towering figure of energy. 'A cow!' he bellowed, looking out at the landscape, now shrouded in softly falling rain. 'My kingdom for a cow.'

In a minute he had ascertained from Bella where the nearest cow grazed, commanded Felipe to attend with a rope and a bucket and off he went up the hill. Perhaps I should have sat decorously waiting but I have never liked to be left out of any jaunt. Yet what an unlikely procession we were: out in front the long-legged Admiral, hatless, his thick tail of hair down his back, his uniform epaulettes and buttons gleaming even in the dim weather; next the stocky Felipe, laden with the heavy rope, trying to keep up; then Bella skipping along with the bucket as if she were a milkmaid (which, quite possibly, she was before she came into my service); and finally myself, panting and skipping, slipping and jumping in my best buttoned boots.

Eventually a small patch of grass under a fine Chilean palm tree revealed a small bony cow, who looked at her unusual visitation with commendable equanimity.

'Does the cow have an owner?' I gasped out to Felipe, not wishing to offend my kind neighbours.

Felipe seemed offended by my question as if it impugned the worth of the cow. 'It is a cow from a very good home,' he answered, or something to that effect. It hardly seemed worth pursuing the subject since Lord Cochrane had already taken the bucket and, seeing the cow needed no lassoing, had turned the coil of rope into a useful seat beside the animal's udders.

'You don't mean to milk her yourself ?' I exclaimed.

77

He bowed before seating himself. 'Nothing would give me greater pleasure, madam, than to furnish you with the requisite for an elegant tea table.' At that, and under the horrified gaze of the servants, he began to squirt the milk with a deft professional touch.

Damp but triumphant, we soon returned to my cottage where we resumed a more conventional afternoon's entertainment. His Lordship's prowess as a milkman reminded me of his interest in farming. I had hardly uttered the words 'agricultural improvements' before the silence that had been threatening to fall was broken by a torrent of words.

'You, who live outside the city, if we can call Valparaíso such, will have perceived the antediluvian nature of the implements used to till and plant this country, blessed as it is with all the riches that generous Nature can bestow, based on a productive soil, and a climate that offers sun and rain in equal proportions.'

'I have not yet seen a spade made of anything but wood,' said I, entering enthusiastically into his theme. 'And a day or two ago I saw a peasant digging with the blade-bone of a sheep tied to a stick.'

'I have heard it said that the ancient people of Chile ploughed their land with the horns of goat and oxen,' contributed the Admiral.

'Now that is impossible,' I contradicted, because, even with him whom I most revere, the truth must be told, 'since oxen only entered this country with the coming of the Spanish.'

' "Ancient must give way to past," ' smiled His Lordship, 'although I will not give up my goats.

78

I shouldn't be surprised if goats have been here since God separated this continent from the waters around it.'

'We may agree on goats.' I inclined my turbaned head.

'A toast to goats.' Solemnly we raised our cups of now cold tea to an animal with few attractive personal traits but that surpasses all four-legged mammals in its ability to survive.

'I understand you have already brought modernity to your Quintero estate.' In this way, I set him off again.

'Ah, Mrs Graham, there is a long way to go before modern Europe can come to Chile, the country that has truly become my adopted home.'

'And how is your estate at Concepción?'

'You, madam, who are reputed to know more about this country in three months than I do after three years—although most of that time was spent in its service on board ship—will know that the south is hardly secured from the ferocious Indians known as Araucanians, let alone the Spaniards.'

'Yet it would be a great thing to have a peaceful estate in such a place.'

'Yes. Yes. There is so much to do in a new country, a newly independent country, whose previous experience has been one of oppression. I believe the Chileans to be a race of great ability. The Chilenos on my ships fought and died with great courage.'

My interest was immediately heightened. How can animals and agriculture compete with the merest whiff of politics? I longed to ask not only about San Martín but also about Don Bernardo O'Higgins, the director of Chile, whom I knew

79

admired his Admiral, even without acceding to all his requests. Unfortunately the thudding of hoofs announced the return of Captain Crosbie and Dr Craig.

Exhilarated by his ride, Crosbie flung himself out of the saddle and precipitated himself on to the veranda where, standing between us, he looked from one to the other and bellowed (in the way men do after violent exercise), 'Sir, madam, may I assume that in our absence you have sorted out South American affairs of state? Or perhaps pursued even deeper matters and discovered how to create the Philosophers' Stone!'

Seeing that he was making fun following my reputation as a blue-stocking, I was tempted to rejoin with a quotation from the Milton I had just been reading:

How charming is divine philosophy
Not harsh and crabbed as dull fools suppose . . .

But I did not want to cramp Crosbie's style, or to appear as a prating elderly widow in the eyes of one of the Admiral's most trusted officers.

Instead I tossed my head and cried archly, 'How mistaken you are, Captain Crosbie. *Lapis philosophorum* has been far from our thoughts. Our conversation has encompassed the world of cows and goats before moving on to spades.'

Dr Craig, coming more slowly, arrived in time to hear my comment. He had a seamed and sallow face, like an old man's, although he could not have been more than thirty. He bowed before saying seriously, 'If only more clever women would turn their brains to such practical uses, I have no doubt the world would increase the sum of its knowledge by more than double. I am looking forward to welcoming the first female doctor, not midwife, of which there have always been many, but trained medical doctor into our ranks.'

This was very flattering to me and I took to Craig at once. 'So you do not believe the advice that Lady Mary Wortley Montagu gave to her granddaughter, to conceal whatever learning she attained with as much solicitude as she would hide crookedness and lameness?'

'Certainly not. I have seen enough surgeon's assistants on board ship, the so-called loblolly boys, who are on occasion female, to recognise that sex is no barrier to learning.'

'Hey-ho!' intervened Crosbie, still in high spirits. 'A learned lady may be useful when it comes to catching the blood after a limb is chopped but what sort of wife will she make? Quite a harridan, I should suppose, not far from Shakespeare's celebrated shrew.'

I allowed the doctor to take up the cudgels for the fairer sex and looked with some concern at His Lordship. During our intercourse, he had slumped lower and lower in his chair and now I saw his eyes were closed. Now and again, a gentle snore broke the surface and I guessed that, as with all large men, these might soon rise to volcanic proportions. Yet I hesitated to wake him. It was obvious that he was worn out and that, sitting on my little veranda, he felt completely relaxed. I was complimented, and noticed, as if it was an omen, that a brave ray of sun had pierced the clouds and lighted on his noble frame.

Whether the sun or the gargantuan snore that

indeed broke from him, or the noisy appearance of a cart pulled by four oxen, disturbed him, he came round abruptly and stood to his feet as if a drum roll had beaten him to deck.

'We must be on our way, Mrs Graham.'

I also stood. The doctor and Captain Crosbie, who had never sat for there was scarcely room for all of us, bowed politely.

But their departure was easier said than done because even three determined English gentlemen (one Irish, but I count him as honorary) cannot pass on horseback when a Chilean cart with four sturdy Chilean oxen are in their path. Moreover, the recent rain had encouraged mud and the mud had encouraged holes. In a second the cart was as securely stuck as a cork in a bottle.

Once again a transformation came over my eminent guest. Under his command branches were cut and laid under the wheels, the oxen harnessed more productively, the driver substituted by Captain Crosbie who, crying, 'This is far more entertaining than the drawing rooms of Valparaíso,' lashed the oxen so unmercifully that I had to plead on their behalf.

With the cart departed, amid many international protestations of goodwill, mainly consisting of 'Bravo', from Crosbie, the men returned to the veranda where I had stood watching.

'Quick, Bella, bring in a few bottles of wine. From the case by the door.'

You see, I understand when a glass or two of white wine is just what is needed. I had taken off the *Doris* a case of the best South African wine, called Constanza, which Captain Graham had bought on our voyage to the Cape.

As sailors like their grog, so officers like their wine. I have seen four or five bottles go in a sitting when only one person is drinking. Bella was kept busy going backwards and forwards to the case while Dr Craig, with his deft surgeon's fingers, had the corks out in a trice. I, too, drank, but modestly, lest my ready tongue decided to make a fool of itself.

Captain Crosbie took the floor with stories of their last sailing. Deferring always to Admiral Cochrane, who seemed content to say little, he described their recent voyage when they had chased two Spanish ships as far north as Acapulco. On their voyage back to Peru their water had entirely gone. 'I was reduced to catching rain in the brim of my hat, fortunately a hat with a wide brim. The men got the sheets out and tried to make a useful reservoir. Ain't I right, your lordship?'

'Our ships were exceedingly poorly provided for,' confirmed Cochrane, with a gloomy air.

'Which has caused us a huge deal of trouble,' continued Crosbie, blithely. 'If the opium-eating San Martín had . . .'

Lord Cochrane frowned heavily, then turned to me. 'An afternoon without politics is a pleasure indeed.'

Crosbie took the hint and the conversation turned scientific as Dr Craig argued the case for rainwater over spring water, interrupted after a few minutes by His Lordship whose face had resumed its usual benign expression, turning once more to me.

'I believe, madam, I have not told you the reason of my visit.'

I performed a gracious bow and waited

expectantly, somewhat surprised. Had he needed a reason?

'I wish to invite you on an historic voyage aboard my steamship, the *Rising Star*. It is the first of its kind to cross the Atlantic. On the seventh of July I intend to take it to my estate on Quintero Bay. I would be honoured if you would be one of my guests.'

This was a fair invitation indeed, one that the ladies of Valparaíso would kill for. 'Have you invited many aboard?'

'The governor, Don Jose Zenteno, and his wife, some Chilean friends . . .' His voice trailed away; the guest list was of least importance.

'I am honoured to accept. I have seen the ship in the harbour with its great chimneys.' I dared a criticism. 'It is not *graceful.*'

'Ah, but you should visit the engine room. There is a thing of beauty!' He came so close in his enthusiasm that I could smell the sweet liquor on his breath, with an undertone of some kind of root, carrot or turnip. His lips were red and smoothly elastic. 'That is what I wish you to view. A person with your appreciation of mechanical innovation will be in awe of such man-made wonders. I may stand for hours, watching, amazed, as cogs fit into cogs, levers into other levers, pistons slide in and out, like . . .' He paused, lost for a simile, and Captain Crosbie gave an absurd guffaw, which I ignored.

This description may make His Lordship sound ridiculous but this would be a false impression for, with the inventor's light making his eyes shine, he was more impressive than ever.

Soon after this, the whole party really did leave

and I, with my blood heated, not only by the wine, tried vainly to settle with my journal.

I noted the visit thus: 'His Lordship rode down to my house in the evening for tea.' Enough, I felt, for my readers. Elsewhere I commented that he was disinclined to talk about politics, although his officers were not. My imagination dwelt on the *Rising Star*, this machine brought from the northern to the southern hemisphere, proving that the old world was ever capable of renewing itself. Chile was so backward that a printing press had only recently been set up. I replayed our conversation in my mind and tried to find a place for myself in his life.

As darkness settled in new waves of misty rain upon the countryside, I imagined myself as his amanuensis—never his wife—standing at his left hand (let the silly Kitty have the status and public attention of the right hand) and understanding, as no one else could, his dreams. My powers of communication were so much greater than his—like many sailors, words seldom served his purposes as well as commands or example—that he needed me to make sure that the dreams were turned into reality.

To make this point clear, I would ask my readers to refer to His Lordship's earlier career as a Whig Member of Parliament when, although loved by the voters, he became unpopular in the House not just because of the content of the speeches, thought revolutionary by most standards, but because of their inordinate length and convoluted construction. Brilliance, even genius, is not always conveniently packaged, although I note that in the twenty-first century a talent for the second is often confused with the first.

Let us say only that Lord Cochrane, a naval commander of the first order, needed someone at his side when on *terra firma* and the person most fitted to be that someone was me. Or so I thought on that murky and far distant night.

Perhaps more honourable than what may, in some sense, seem self-serving ambition was my growing admiration for the emerging country in which I found myself, cast up on its shores, almost as if shipwrecked. I shared with Lord Cochrane his belief in its future. I felt like Daniel Defoe, the author of *Robinson Crusoe*, whose hero was a castaway on Juan Fernández, an island off Chile's coast. While collecting narratives of English adventurers in Chile, the writer described this land as a terrestrial paradise and the inhabitants as beings worthy to possess it.

Undoubtedly I was on my way to earning the soubriquet engraved on the plaque so recently applied to my gravestone: 'A Friend of the nation of Chile'.

CHAPTER EIGHT

7th July
Yesterday morning I rode early to the port, on Lord Cochrane's invitation, to join a party which was to sail with him in the steam vessel, the *Rising Star*, to his estate of Quintero, which lies due north from this place about twenty miles, though the road by land, being round the bay of Concón, is thirty.

86

So I opened my description of an extraordinary day and night. Our company consisted of Don Jose Zenteno, his daughter, Señora Doña Dolores, the Honourable Captain Frederick Spencer of His Majesty's Ship *Alacrity*, who eventually became a rear-admiral and succeeded his brother as 4th Earl Spencer, Captain Crosbie, Captain Wilkinson, some officers of the Patriot Squadron, with whom I was not acquainted, besides some other gentlemen. These 'other gentlemen' were, in the main, Chilenos and included the curate of Placilla, a village near the mouth of the little river Ligua, which runs into the Bay of Quintero.

To my great pleasure, the Admiral escorted me on board himself at ten a.m. He did not take me to where the other guests were congregating, but immediately led me down many dark ladders and narrow, low-ceilinged corridors (luckily, the hoop of my skirt was not great and, as a naval captain's wife, I had learnt agility), to the very bowels of the ship where the great machinery thrust. It consisted of two steam engines, each of forty-five horse-power. His Lordship pointed out to me, with justifiable pride, how the wheels were well covered so as not to show from without. He explained to me all the workings of the various parts of the engine and I paid a deal of attention. Any seaman or seaman's wife will tell you that a form of transport that entirely depends on the vagaries of the wind is unreliable indeed. Coleridge in his 'Lays of the Ancient Mariner' so brilliantly described the calm, 'a painted ship upon a painted ocean', while the dread of beating up against a strong north-westerly breaks the sleep of even the most stalwart captain. As an aside, I cannot resist noting that Lord

Melville, the first lord of the Admiralty (the body that had so vilified Lord Cochrane), declared in 1826:

Their Lordships feel it their bounden duty to discourage to the utmost of their ability the employment of steam as they consider that the introduction of steam is calculated to strike a fatal blow to the naval supremacy of the Empire.

How narrow-minded! How bigoted!

'Oh, my lord!' I exulted, as we scorched our faces against the vast furnaces—I had to shout above the engines, although they were scarcely warming up. 'What a magnificent example of the triumphs of man over the obstacles Nature seems to have placed between him and the accomplishment of his imagination!'

Our faces equally red, we gloried in the machinery and might have stayed till we expired in our own sweat, if a crowd of officers hadn't joined us so that the foreman of the engineers begged us to leave or his men could not prepare the ship for departure.

With some reluctance, Lord Cochrane led us on deck where we were greeted with huzzahs and a kind of unceremonial ceremony, for this was a day for pleasure. The sky was surprisingly clear and bright, the crimson cliffs glowed, the water sparkled a brilliant blue, and all around the ships and boats, either moored or moving, decorated the beautiful harbour.

Impulsively, I turned to His Lordship, who had not left my side and was still not quite surrounded by others. 'With what rapture would the breast of

Almagro have been filled, if some magician could have shown him, in the enchanted glass of futurity, the port of Valparaíso filled with vessels from Europe, and from Asia, and from states not yet in existence, and our stately vessel gliding smooth and swiftly through them without a sail, against the wind and waves.' I'm not sure if he heard the end of this little speech, although I knew he would have echoed its spirit, because he was drawn away by the insistent Zenteno, who wished to point out to him plans for a bar against the inward-blowing winds.

I was happy enough to be on my own for a moment, looking up to the two magnificent chimneys from which smoke belched, feeling the throb of the engines under my feet, as we drew away quicker and quicker from the flotilla of small boats that had accompanied us thus far. The waves were not strong but increased as we passed out of the harbour, ornamenting a glossy viridian with delicate white crests. I turned my head backwards for a moment and saw His Lordship at the rail, his blue coat reflecting the sky, his thick red-gold hair as bright as the sun, strength and determination in every line of his body.

At that moment Captain Wilkinson approached me. Returning to my previous theme, I spoke freely: 'Do you not agree that we carry on board a hero whose name, even in Peru and Chile, will surpass not only Almagro's but those of his more famous companions, the Pizarros?' With hindsight you may say that I was somewhat carried away in this estimation. You may not even have heard of Almagro, the man who conquered Peru and Chile in collaboration and competition with Pizarro.

Captain Wilkinson, however, knew exactly what

I meant. He drew up his lanky height and pointed his nose skywards as if to dare disagreement from the gods, 'Courageous as a tiger, honourable as a lion, wise as panther.' He would have appreciated the great statue of the Admiral that now stands on Avenida Brasil in Valparaíso. Around it are well-carved reliefs of his various naval victories, ending with his extraordinary capture of Valdivia. A century after his death, Chile's great poet, Pablo Neruda, hailed him with a many-versed hymn of praise, opening:

Lord of the sea, we call you, singing, to battle
We are as water and sand oppressed,
We are a people mute and besieged
Lord of the sea, we call you, singing, to battle
Spanish chains deny us the seas.
Our hopes wither in the Spanish night.
Lord of the sea, grief and rage await you in the
*   harbour,*
Southern seas are calling you, Lord of the sea . . .

'Mrs Graham, may I give you my arm?' My thoughts were interrupted by Captain Spencer, a handsome and well-made man with the graceful manners of the aristocracy. 'We are invited to partake of champagne and Chilean delicacies on the lower deck.'

'You have my arm,' I responded, suiting actions to words, 'although I am somewhat unconvinced of the concept of Chilean delicacies.'

'I find the food fresh and of good quality,'

'You are right,' I agreed, and we looked at each other with mutual goodwill.

The scene below was festive, the babble of

Spanish and English competing with the closer reverberations of the engines and confined by the low ceiling. The officers were kept busy opening bottles of champagne so the continual explosions, not unlike rifle fire, punctuated the chorus of happy voices and male laughter.

I was shown a seat at the side of the room next to Señora Doña Dolores. Apart from myself, she was the only woman present, a little younger than I and substantially built, with lustrous black hair and unusually pale blue eyes that proclaimed Don Jose, or more likely his wife, could claim Spanish origins. After a few civilities about the honour we shared in being aboard on such an auspicious day, we settled to a conversation (carried out in Spanish) about fireplaces, the superiority of the English grate over the *brasero*. Although the señora was polite, I could see that she kept her lips pursed whenever she was not actually conversing (although that sounds grandiose for her comments on the merits of coal over charcoal) and that her blue eyes slid away as if they must not meet mine.

It was, I suppose, as if she found herself sitting next to one of Wilkinson's leopards, an animal of a different species from her own, alien to the country and, by common agreement, dangerous. I find codes of behaviour are always more rigid where the Roman Church holds sway. I was a foreigner, a Protestant and a widow, who refused to hide under a black veil or, like Miss H., to make clear that my life was dedicated to finding a husband: it was rumoured she had already become engaged to an American Captain B. More shocking still, I went about freely and independently, with only a maid and a *peon* to accompany me.

91

I did not make anything of this difficulty in my journal because I did not wish to seem a poor victim of tittle-tattle. I was proud in life, as I am no longer in death. Señora Dolores' behaviour hurt because I knew it meant she had been listening to Englishwomen's tales.

Yet I had only to lift my head to the Englishmen in the room to feel all my confidence return. Here was the future of Britain, with these fresh-faced captains and lieutenants, grouped even now around the Admiral, the greatest of them all. As I thought this, he himself came over to me, bowed coolly to the *señora* and, taking my hand, led me to the table where the 'delicacies', actually the usual *porotos* (beans) and *charqui* (leathery strips of beef) were laid out.

There we were accosted by the curate of Placilla, who held a glass brimming with champagne, which, judging by his speech, was not the first or even the second. 'My Lord High Admiral,' he began, or something grandiloquent to that effect—he was speaking in Spanish, 'for this divine white beer, I will grant absolution absolutely unconditionally for a thousand years.'

'And can you guarantee the Holy Spirit will descend with every gulp?' demanded Captain Crosbie.

'The spirit in the bottle will rise up and meet the spirit of his maker,' vowed the priest, reeling somewhat, not only because of the drink but because now that we were in open seas, the smooth progress of the ship was broken by undulations.

Their riotousness attracted the stubby, self-important figure of the governor, who drew Lord Cochrane aside.

'The Chilenos have never tasted champagne before,' whispered Spencer, in my ear. 'They are drinking it like weak beer.'

It was cruel to laugh, but we did, my anti-papist feelings at that time making me unsympathetic to a priest in his cups. I may add that my subsequent history and my passage through the jaws of death has made me more tolerant of the beliefs of others—even if, in some cases, they seem nearer superstitions.

At any rate, the deed was done. The men were drunk, and when we returned to the deck, they could scarcely keep their feet. This was made worse by the gradual increase of a boisterous sea, stirred up by a stiff wind blowing from the north-west, which also brought a few puffs of grey cloud on the horizon, intimations of a natural war being fought somewhere else, but perhaps approaching.

The Admiral having descended to his beloved engines, I stood at the taffrail with the governor, both of us entirely steady on our feet, I through long experience and Don Jose because of his short legs and low centre of gravity. It has always been my habit to seek out the company of the powerful. Comments from such men inform my journal with a credibility that was, in the early nineteenth century, hard won by someone of my sex.

So, Don Jose Zenteno, a disloyal braggart, as it turned out, became the object of my attentions. He held forth about the future of Chile as we passed by the various inlets and small harbours, which I longed to know more about.

'Chile is at last free of the oppressor. We are a great people who have been slaves too long. Valparaíso is already the centre of trade on the

93

east Pacific. As the first democracy of the South Americas we will act with renewed vigour and reap the rewards for ourselves.'

His confident platitudes were hard to separate from the wind, the slapping waves and the dark beat of the engines, so I intervened with a question: 'Would it not be wonderful, Your Honour, if these little harbours could be increased in size and capability and become the outlets for agricultural produce, for sheep's wool, cow hide, corn and vegetables, so that they need no longer travel the torturous roads of sea path or the hills of the Andes? Would that not open the whole country to new trade?'

'I see that the Señora Graham has thought deeply about our country,' growled Don Jose, with a fierce frown.

Undeterred, I carried on, the wind in my sails— or perhaps I should say, the steam in my chimneys. 'We can imagine a time when the *Rising Star* is not the only steam vessel in these waters. Nothing can be better adapted for packets on these coasts.' I have to admit that this idea leant much on my earlier conversations with Lord Cochrane. I continued, despite the governor's fidgeting and looking over my shoulder: 'The regular ships that now force other craft out as far as Juan Fernández, in order to make a reasonable passage from Lima to Valparaíso, are never so strong as to hinder the workings of a steamship. Besides, the facility of communication between these as well as the intermediate ports would not only promote their commercial interest but be a means of security against the attempts of any enemy these countries have to fear from abroad.'

94

This speech was long, far too long for Don Jose, who became less and less inclined to listen.

I stopped speaking and the governor began a meaningless response to disguise the fact that, as governor of Valparaíso, he had no wish to share his profits with other ports. We were both diverted by a noise above the chug of the engines and, glancing behind me, I saw that half a dozen or so Chilenos, overcome by the 'white beer' and the motion of the ship, were bent over the side emptying the contents of their stomachs.

It was not a sight for ladies, although one I had seen often enough during my time at sea. As I turned away Captains Spencer and Crosbie arrived on either side and directed my attention to Quintero Bay, now quite easily visible.

'We should make harbour in an hour or even less,' Crosbie told me.

'With the wind against us too,' added Spencer. 'I shudder to think of the rope-pulling necessary to hold our course in a sailing vessel.'

'I think I am quite converted to steam,' agreed Crosbie. 'It is so easy to—'

He stopped mid-sentence for at that precise moment the engines cut out and immediately we found ourselves wallowing, like any old tub, at the mercy of wind and waves.

All was consternation. The Admiral reappeared and informed us that a small bolt in the machinery had given way, principally from imperfect fitting. This, after all, was a trial run. 'Since we are nearly abreast of Quintero,' he announced, looking about with his sharp admiral's eye, 'I suggest that we carry on, trusting to the tide to take us into port.'

We were all, or the sea-going section of those

assembled, perfectly aware that the captain of the ship does not ask opinions but makes decisions, so this so-called suggestion was voted by acclamation.

Our spirits were high, and the beautiful bay, with Lord Cochrane's unfinished house, seemed close enough to take a boat to or even swim. But it was not. So near and yet so far. Helpless, we stood at the rail and willed the ship forwards.

The evening closed in, and it was a dull, raw, foggy night. Those not accustomed to the sea, even if they had not partaken of the 'white beer', grew faint and weary. A very fresh contrary wind had sprung up so eventually they decided to go below and find what rest they could on narrow bunks or hammocks.

Preferring to remain on deck, I stood beside Captain Spencer. We could see His Lordship beat the rail in frustration. Now and again he put his famous eyepiece up—as if he could see anything between boisterous black waves and even blacker clouds.

> *'And in the scowl of heaven each face*
> *Grew dark as they were speaking.'*

I spoke quietly enough but Captain Spencer heard it. He turned to me, 'Let us rejoice that no one's life is at risk, there is no enemy fire, no dangerous exposure at the carronades, no rocky shores that sink their teeth into the heart of your vessel. The situation we find ourselves in is a troublesome difficulty but no disaster.'

'The Admiral has had the reputation since the Napoleonic Wars as a man tenacious under adversity,' I said. 'I feel sure he will convey us to

Quintero harbour.'

'With the engine dead and the ti
uncooperative, he has but one option,' sa
Spencer.

'Rig the sails!' The order was repeated roun
the ship in the usual bellowing way, even if the me
were no more than a few feet apart.

The crew rose to the challenge: rope and sails
were produced like magic and put to the yards. It
seemed as if the old world would vanquish the
new, but either a malicious spirit was keeping pace
with the ship or the new world struck like a snake
in its death throes, but for the moment the foresail
rose, to a quickly hushed huzzah, the two chimneys
lashed out and tore right through it.

Once more we were buffeted ignobly by a
howling and contrary wind. The Admiral came to
me, his hair streaming out from beneath his hat.
'It is time for you to go below.' His calmness was
impressive but it is never wise to witness a man's
humiliation so I obeyed at once.

Unfortunately I had been assigned a bed with
Señora Doña Dolores who filled the whole small
cabin with herself and her snoring. It is no credit
to myself that if she had been a gentleman I would
have taken the squeezing and the noise in my
stride but, as it was, I crept away again and found
a sheltered corner tucked snug against the mizzen
mast.

Despite the bad-tempered wind and the cross
rolls of the ship, I must have slept because I woke
as a grey dawn silhouetted a large man staring
down at me.

'At least you had a pleasant night.' I recognised
the voice of His Lordship.

s, indeed.' I rubbed my eyes and tried to
ten my cap.

e furniture has been tossed all over the place,
hey complain in their cabins.'

e seamen do not complain, I make certain.'

stared away from me. 'The seas are running
than ever so that, despite the sail properly
e are still no nearer our destination.'

gaining more wakeful faculties—His
ship had at first appeared to me almost as if
a dream—I stood up and smoothed down my
rt as best I could. The ship was not happy in her
urse. That was immediately clear. She alternated
sliding sideways with a bounding forwards,
nterrupted by sudden leaps, which could be
backwards, forwards or sideways.

'And no sign of abatement,' said I, scanning the
horizon like a true old salt.

'None.' He frowned mightily. Our conversation
was unusual because it seemed as if he wanted me
to give him permission to turn round and return to
Valparaíso. 'I had been counting on showing you
my estate.'

I did not want to turn round. He did not want
to turn round. 'For sure a hearty breakfast with a
tot of brandy in the tea will raise the spirits of your
guests wonderfully.'

His brow cleared; his hand gripped mine and for
a man no longer young, who had forgone a night's
sleep, it was an exceedingly strong grasp.

' "Then imitate the action of the tiger," ' I cried.
' "Stiffen the sinews, summon up the blood." '

The breakfast did all I had imagined. Even the
curate, clinging to the table, made a fair repast of
beef and pastries. 'By the Almighty who cares for

the smallest beetle,' the foolish man declared, 'I believe this is the finest, sturdiest ship I have ever ridden in.'

Unfortunately the weather was not so easily seduced and our progress was remarkable by its absence. At length, alack, we turned for home and, as a horse on the return journey sets its head high and pricks its ears, the ship leapt forward in a smooth, steady course. By one thirty p.m. we were in sight of Valparaíso, having passed the vineyards of Viña del Mar.

When we landed on the quay from the boats, Mr Campbell was also there, overseeing the unloading of a ship. Noticing, doubtless, our chastened looks—every loafing sailor could see we had come back by sail and some did not forbear to sneer or laugh, shouting witticisms, such as 'Not the rising but the *Sinking Star*', he hailed us in his good baritone.

'We can welcome you back with good news at least. The United States has recognised the independence of the South Americas.' His beard waggled with exhilaration.

The braying and stamping of the mule train waiting to be loaded for its journey to the capital overwhelmed some of his words, but we thought we understood enough to cheer and, shortly afterwards, Mr Hogan also came with the same information. A fastidious man, he held on to his hat, which threatened to fly off in the still blustery wind, while picking his way among the boxes and mule droppings. Eventually finding a dry and quiet space, he spoke to His Lordship and those of us in earshot.

'The Congress of the United States has

acknowledged the independence of the Spanish American colonies of Mexico, Colombia, Buenos Aires, Peru and Chile.'

'Oh, joyful intelligence!' I exclaimed, forgetting my place.

'The United States of America,' continued Mr Hogan, with understandable pride, 'itself so lately emancipated from the thraldom of the mother country, is the natural asserter of the independence of their American brethren.'

This could have been taken by an Englishman other than the Admiral as casting aspersion on his country, particularly since Great Britain showed no sign of recognising the existence of an independent Chile. But His Lordship had, of course, thrown in his lot with Chile.

'It has turned out to be a day of celebration,' he said remarkably cheerfully, 'if not for new methods of transportation by sea, certainly for a new country.'

Mr Hogan then invited the Admiral, myself and several officers to take dinner that evening. The only question was where I could spend the intervening hours, somewhere I could rest and tidy myself. Lord Cochrane, Mr Hogan and my officer friends had already bowed their au revoirs when Mr Campbell, who had been unashamedly listening in, suggested Mrs Campbell and the children would be most pleased were I to visit.

So along I went, stepping briskly over the stony quay while avoiding both the governor and his daughter, who had stopped to talk to friends and, by their expressive gestures and raised eyes, were describing the terrors and failures of their voyage with as much pleasure as previously there had been

100

pain.

In ten minutes I had reached the Campbells' house. Archibald and Rosita met me with all their pretty chatter. They led me, as if I hadn't been gone for six weeks, to my old room, which was even smaller than before, owing to a dozen towers of packing cases.

'Mr Campbell has some very delicate china inside,' his loving wife told me, although I could see very well that 'DYNAMITE', and 'GUNPOWDER' was written on the side. Clearly the astute man of business did not consider that the present peace would hold for ever.

After all, this was a country used to a way of life ordered by force rather than democracy. I was contemplating these dire forebodings, staring into the bowl of water provided for me to make my ablutions, when my vision became affected in the strangest way, almost as if I had tears in my eyes. Then I realised the water was behaving unnaturally, swirling agitatedly before forming into little peaks like whipped white of eggs. Next the floor began to quiver.

'Earthquake! Earthquake!' The little children ran into my room. Like all Chilenos, even young ones, they were both unafraid and respectful of the regular movements beneath their feet. But it was my first experience.

'Ah, yes, an earthquake,' I agreed, bravely clapping my hands as if at a brief entertainment, for already it was over.

With the help of Bella, who had looked for me on the quay before being directed to the Campbells', I continued my preparations for the evening—clean gloves, clean shoes, a clean cap. I had nothing more.

Quietly, I rose and went to drink *matee* with Mrs Campbell before setting off for Mr Hogan's house. As I left, she picked out a small, sweet-smelling jonquil from the many in her hair and tucked it neatly into my cap. She smiled at the effect. 'Even a widow may wear a flower.'

CHAPTER NINE

Dinner was quiet at the Hogans until after we'd eaten when the Admiral made his appearance. At once the somewhat dull company was galvanised. Half an hour later His Lordship's secretary, Mr Bennett, a clever but eccentric man, dressed as if he were the Doge of Venice, arrived from Santiago.

Mr B. had brought with him a Spanish soldier, Colonel Don Fausto de la Hoya. Clearly a gentleman of good lineage, he was now haggard in the extreme, with the grey skin of a man who had been starved of food and light. The moment he saw the Admiral, he began to utter a stream of gratitude, both in Spanish and well-pronounced English, proving he was educated as well as suffering. With some difficulty, he was restrained from throwing himself at his generous conqueror's knee.

We were all agog and Mr Bennett, rather histrionically and in an odd Lincolnshire accent, explained the history to some of us.

'The colonel was captured at Valdivia and His Lordship, in the manner of European rules of engagement, obtained from the government a promise of generous treatment. Instead, he was treated with the same cruelty and injustice as all the other prisoners of war of every rank. He was thrust into a dark dungeon, and there detained without fire, without light, without books.'

We all expressed horror at this savage behaviour, and I added, 'As if the cruel treatment of individual prisoners could have forced Old Spain to acknowledge the independence of Chile!'

Mr Bennett agreed before continuing, 'Don Fausto has now been liberated on parole by Lord Cochrane's intervention.'

At that time His Lordship himself came over and introduced his prisoner to us, as if he were an honoured guest rather than a prisoner of war. Such was the convention among naval officers fighting in European wars. One English captain of my acquaintance had spent nearly as much time dining on *pâté de foie gras* and good red Burgundy in a French ship-of-the-line as he had commanding his own ship.

The evening continued pleasantly. Two of Mrs Hogan's daughters had pretty voices and their mother played on the piano with a fine air and an excellent finger. Even the presence of the swooning Miss H., with all her dimples and wiles, did not diminish my enjoyment. (We managed the whole evening with no more than a polite bow across the crowded room.) Soon the young, who included Chilenos as well as Americans and English, were clamouring to dance; a guitar was found and a fiddle, and soon quite a little orchestra was set up.

While this was in progress, His Lordship and I took chairs side by side with Mr Hogan, Mr Bennett, Captain Spencer, Don Fausto and several others. To be seated beside the gentlemen at a gathering was always an honour and I felt it keenly. At the same time, I would have been glad to be back on that windy deck when there seemed to be only the Admiral and myself in the world.

The talk, unsurprisingly, centred on the opportunities presented by American recognition of Chilean independence.

'Are you comfortable now, Your Lordship,' asked one American businessman, who perhaps did not realise the sensitive nature of this question, 'that the Chilean Navy will be paid the money owing them?'

'I am not comfortable, sir,' came the stern answer, 'and will never be so until every seaman has the proper sum in his pocket.'

I could see that the American had another question, which might be even less acceptable to His Lordship. Before he could open his mouth, Mr Hogan used his consular skills to lead him off with great determination to admire a view of the harbour through a further window. It was unfortunate that rumours in this place continued to accuse the Admiral of procuring large sums of money and secretly sending them back to England where, of course, Lady Cochrane and his children lived.

(Posterity continues to accuse him of obsessing over money. The facts of the matter are that Lord Cochrane was owed many thousands of pounds by the Chilean government and never received more than a fraction of it. Only after he had been in England for very many years did he finally manage to extract a paltry six thousand pounds.)

The number of dancers increased in number and

enthusiasm. I was sipping a glass of wine quietly when Captain Crosbie, face as scarlet as a poppy and hair flying loose from its ribbon, descended upon me. 'Not dancing, Mrs G.? If you can waltz as well as you ride, you'll shame us all. Pray stand up with me when the music sets off again.'

I smiled at the young puppy's intentions— although he was a puppy who had fought and killed as many men as a Mussulman has wives. 'You forget I am widowed, Captain.'

'You are right. I did forget.' He gave me a sly look. 'It must be the flower in your cap.'

I had not thought him so observant. 'Go and dance with Mrs Henrietta Headingly.'

'You may be widowed, but she is engaged,' he answered, before whirling away.

Lord Cochrane did not talk to me in any personal way until the evening was drawing to a close. We stood together by the door to the room.

'You are returning to your home tonight?'

I acknowledged this. 'My man servant and maid are waiting outside with horses and *peons* with torches, although I can see through the window it is a fine, moonlit night.'

If he thought it strange I should travel thus alone, he did not show it (as it happened, Captain Crosbie accompanied me, amusing himself by hallooing at imaginary bandits). Speaking with the diffidence I'd already noticed when he addressed me, the Admiral added, 'I shall call on you tomorrow, then. I have something to bring you. Two somethings.'

Unlike many ladies, I did not try archly to guess what they might be, but responded simply, 'I shall look for you, sir.'

So we parted.

That night after I had got my good captain away, with more than a tot or two of my good Constantia wine, I lay on my couch, unable to sleep or, perhaps it would be truer to say, unwilling to sleep. My thoughts moved too quickly between the past, with its doubts and difficulties, and the present, which offered tantalising flashes of happiness. Like a young girl, my heart was in turmoil, and like many a young girl, I turned to Byron. Only recently John Murray had sent me a case of books, including Byron's three plays recently published by him, *Sardanapalus*, *The Two Foscari* and *Cain*.

Tragedies and *Mysteries*, as they are called, they yet suited my mood: Lord Byron cannot write without stirring our feelings. I was particularly gripped by the depiction of Lucifer in *Cain*. Since the sublime Milton, no writer had depicted evil with greater power and imagination, yet I knew from Murray that Byron had been much vilified for it, as if he himself was the seductive enemy. I had heard that Byron, like Cochrane, was an outcast from England, travelling in Italy, and I, too, identified myself as a kind of outcast. I read through the night, heard the first cockcrow and rain drizzling on the tiles, then dozed off just before Bella brought in my chocolate.

CHAPTER TEN

My first waking thought was that it was not schoolgirl romance that linked Lord Cochrane and myself but an instinctive understanding of

106

and respect for each other's qualities. Between a man and a woman in the year of Our Lord 1822, this was all the more remarkable, despite Mary Wollstonecraft's publication of *Vindication of the Rights of Woman* thirty years earlier. Instinctively, Lord Cochrane looked past a woman's clothes and saw someone he wanted to know better. Not everyone of the female sex would be pleased with this but I, 'philosophy in muslin', felt chosen.

An hour later, he was with me. At his side was the handsome Captain Spencer, Captain Crosbie, Dr Craig, Mr Bennett, who in daylight I saw had a cast in his right eye, the prisoner, Colonel Don Fausto de la Hoya, a shy young man and an extremely large dog.

They were too many to fit into house and veranda, but since it was raining, we had no choice. His Lordship took the chair he had had before and the rest drew themselves around as best they could, the mighty dog lying uncomfortably under his master's long legs. Thinking to entertain those who had not tried *matee* before, I went to order a pot, and when I returned I found that only His Lordship, the young man, who spoke English with a Spanish accent, and the giant dog remained. As before, the others had gone for a ride.

As I sat down, the dog crept out and stared at me with amber eyes. Long soft ears fell at either side of his face, like a judge's wig. I don't know what he thought of me but we certainly took each other in.

'He's a pointer,' said Lord Cochrane. 'A gun dog that is known here as Perdiguero de Burgos. His name is Don.'

'I hope he is a Chilean not a Spanish *don*,' I responded, a little facetiously, for while I admired

107

his colouring, patterns of liver against a cream background, good enough design for a dandy jacket, I was recalling Byron's lines about his beloved dog, Lyon: 'Lyon, thou art an honest fellow, Lyon. Thou art more faithful than men, Lyon; I trust thee more.'

'Don is the first of my presents,' said Lord Cochrane, and I thought I perceived a deepening of the red in his already weather-darkened complexion. 'I shall be going to my estate in Concepción in a week or so where I have too many dogs to need another. He will serve you well and make sure you are safe.'

I was so overcome by his thoughtfulness that I could hardly stutter my thanks. Unfortunately, the joyful confirmation of his care for me was lessened by the news of his leaving Valparaíso. 'Will you be away long?' I asked, when I had found my voice.

'A month. Two months. I'm not certain. I have four months' leave from the Navy.' He looked at me gravely. 'I have another present for you. Vicente,' he addressed the young man, who stood uncertainly. He was small, with lustrous black eyes and a delicate, almost girlish mouth. Although his skin was sallow, he reminded me of dear Glennie, now at sea with the *Doris*.

'Vicente was brought up in Quito, although born in Cundinamarca, and has been on board my ship for more than a year, mainly because he has nowhere else to go. In that time he has shown a considerable talent for drawing and I thought that . . .' here he hesitated, remembering, perhaps, that he was not a captain aboard ship able to order things as he wanted '. . . with your knowledge of the arts you might be able to help him develop

108

his skills.' The Admiral's blue eyes looked at me appealingly. 'It is a present that can be refused and certainly returned.'

This was embarrassing for poor Vicente, whose English was quite good enough to understand his Lordship's final remark.

'A dog has no choice but a man may have some control of his future,' I said, looking at the boy. 'Does Vicente wish to be my student?'

'Ah, yes, Señora, a thousand times yes. I have heard so much of your painting and I know so little.'

This was flattering. I didn't remember talking about my art to his Lordship so he must have heard of it from elsewhere. As he took on the smug expression of someone who always knew he was right, I smiled at his *protégé*. With no midshipmen around, I was missing my maternal role. 'You will discover I am a hard taskmaster.'

He bowed with some elegance. 'It will be my pleasure.'

This decided, he strolled off with Don to explore his surroundings. I was alone with Lord Cochrane. This may not sound so dramatic, but in 1822 the habit of privacy was not established and very few occasions permitted the luxury.

We sat quietly as the rain stopped and a soft mist gradually drew back to reveal the sun, brightening the garden. His Lordship, despite his genius, did not suffer from an excess of self-knowledge and I suspect he hardly recognised our situation beyond a sense of comfort. When he did speak, I was surprised by his subject.

'I have been hearing the news from Greece. It is a noble country that is suffering much bloodshed.

109

But there is no price high enough for freedom from tyranny.'

'I understand that some two thousand Greeks and the same of Turks have been massacred since the struggle for independence began.' I could see these shameful figures did nothing to halt his train of thought, although he was reputed in the Navy to take care that no life was lost unnecessarily. Indeed, one of his criticisms of the Navy was that the greatness of a victory was judged in part by the number of lives lost—on your own side as well as the enemy's.

'Would you ever consider offering the patriotic Greeks your services?' I asked for, after all, a strong Greek Navy could save Greece from the Turks just as much as the Chileans from Spain.

'There have been approaches.' He paused. 'There have been approaches from various countries seeking freedom from their oppressors.' My heart pounded. Here was further proof of his confidence in me. Yet I could hardly bear the thought that he might be snatched from my presence.

He sighed, then straightened his bearing. 'I am admiral of the Chilean Fleet. I am a Chilean citizen.'

We were interrupted by the return of the bounding Don, who seemed set on knocking me off my chair. There was, however, no sign of Vicente.

Lord Cochrane bent down and absentmindedly stroked the dog, his strong hands caressing him with surprising tenderness. The dog, as dogs do, seemed to smile, pulling his muzzle back and raising his head. The sight aroused me in a feminine way, and I even felt jealous. I wanted to feel those fingers stroking my face. Without thinking further, I stretched my hand down to the dog so that, inevitably, I met and touched His Lordship's.

I looked up at him, with an expression not of canine devotion, I trust, but of affection and admiration. It was, also, I suppose, an invitation.

The blue eyes met mine. His hand, the one not holding mine over Don's head, came up behind my neck and pressed my face towards his. We kissed.

I often think of that first kiss. Much is made of sexual intercourse as if this is the truest way to intimacy of body and mind. Yet the kiss, an expression of desire for union, so close to the source of all emotion and action, the brain, must be in many ways at least as important as a coupling carried out as far from the head as, in a map of the world, Valparaíso is from London. Our kiss joined us with our whole beings. Whatever might follow could scarcely take us further.

But now rather languorously, Vicente was approaching us. The languor, of course, might have arisen from doubt whether to advance or retreat. In the end he followed Lord Nelson's advice always to attack from the front, and carried on towards us. Don leapt off the veranda to greet him.

While His Lordship smiled composedly, I began to babble: 'Did you know that Lord Byron has a veritable menagerie with him in Italy, or so Mr Murray tells me? Ten horses, eight enormous dogs, three monkeys, five cats, an eagle, a crow, a falcon, five peacocks, two guinea hens and an Egyptian crane, many of which live with him in his villa.'

I suspect that the young man understood half of my words but all of the emotion behind them. I did not want Vicente to replace Miss H., a watchdog

111

for the conventions, but as an acolyte who would consider any behaviour I chose as *sans reproche*.

He came and sat with us while His Lordship asked, 'You join the ladies who admire Lord Byron as a great gallant, I surmise?'

'As a great poet,' says I. 'His gallantry is for others to know. Even a genius may have moral weaknesses.'

'That is without argument.'

'And possibly,' I decided to exaggerate and lighten the tone, which would suit our circumstances better than a Bible lesson, 'the greater the genius, the greater the weakness. But I do not admire Lord Byron only for his poetry. I admire him for his defence of liberty. In that, surely, we can find accord.'

'In truth, I have not read his poetry, nor any man's poetry beyond the classics: Ovid, Lucullus, Horace. But I was in London during the scandals of which he was at the centre when there was little sign that he cared about liberty. I believe he spoke only once or twice in the House, and spoke so hotly that he left those noble gentlemen more enraged than convinced. As you know, I was elected a Member of Parliament for Westminster and have some experience of these things. If you wish to defend liberty, you must stand up and state your case, not gallivant abroad with peacocks, monkeys and whores.'

He had become passionate. It was obvious that his year in prison, when he was loved more by the common people, his voters, than by his equals, apart from a few reformers such as Cobbett (who himself spent time in prison), smouldered in his heart. I suspected I would not persuade him of the merits of Lord Byron and quite wished I had never mentioned his name. Perhaps absurdly, I even wondered if he felt jealous of a man I admired so deeply. Or perhaps it made me too like the teams of other goggling ladies. (When Byron left England for ever from Dover a few inquisitive society ladies dressed as chambermaids took a final peep.) An even more lowering thought was that the handsome m'lord might be a hero of Lady Cochrane's—even if she got no further with books than their covers.

'A glass of wine, gentlemen?' I stood up briskly. The name of Lord Byron would never pass my lips in my true hero's presence again. Yet, then again, I remembered Byron's admiration for Cochrane. As I went to find Bella, I thought that a poet may admire a man of action but a man of action is unlikely to admire a poet.

CHAPTER ELEVEN

The morning in which I gained a dog, a student (to my relief, Vicente did not stay with me but arrived each day at ten a.m.) and the close attention (I do not claim more) of an admiral set a pattern for the days that followed.

His Lordship generally arrived at two o'clock, after my lesson, often in company, who soon rode off, followed by the sound of guns as they banged away merrily at wild fowls. Once they even hit a *huemul*, the small Chilean deer. The grey Spanish colonel turned out to be an outstanding shot and returned triumphant more than once with a scrawny clutch of woodcock relatives, from which poor Felipe must singe off the feathers.

Left to ourselves, Lord Cochrane and I, side by side on the veranda, 'covered the waterfront', a phrase appropriate enough in the circumstances. He told me, for example, the story of his famous capture of Valdivia from the Spanish garrison in the summer of 1820.

'Valdivia had always been considered impregnable,' he explained, spreading his large hands to make a map. 'General Freire thought I was a madman even to attempt it. The harbour is formed by the river of Calle-Calle, which, widening opposite to the town to an estuary of four leagues broad, narrows again at its mouth to half a league. Four considerable forts defended the narrow entrance, and at the Morro Gonzalez, or Englishman's Bay, there were upwards of one hundred guns, the fires of which cross each other from every point.' His eyes narrowed and grew bright as he recalled one of his greatest victories. Sailors have always liked to tell of battle. Most women do not want to hear such tales. But I was agog: this was history in the making, the events he described having taken place a mere two years earlier. The consequences were still unfolding. In my sketch of the history of Chile, which introduced my published journal, much of my information came directly from His Lordship's mouth.

'So how did you breach these formidable defences?' I asked.

'Under a Spanish flag.' He smiled. 'I sailed into the harbour and learnt the state of the fort and its garrison. In fact, I was so close in that I had a health inspector aboard who never suspected a thing.'

114

He smote the arm of his chair with childlike glee. The male animal is never happier than when in action—if heroic, all the better! Some of you may question the morality of this victory, whose success rested on a well-executed piece of trickery. But those were the rules of the times: captains carried aboard the flags of every nation and chose one as the most practical disguise, sometimes only revealing their true allegiance just before an engagement. That was the only rule: you must fight under your nation's flag.

'And what next?' I pressed, for he had been diverted a moment by Don, who had appeared with a large rabbit dangling from his jaws.

'Good fellow.' He released the rabbit, which flopped down dead. 'Now find us a fine cock pheasant.' The dog leapt away as if he had perfect understanding or, more likely, shared his master's joy in the chase.

'So, then,' His Lordship turned back to me, 'I procured two hundred and fifty men from a somewhat reluctant General Freire, who was further north in Concepción, and with three ships, the *O'Higgins*, *Intrepid* and *Montezuma*, sailed back towards Valdivia, pausing ten leagues southwards and, putting soldiers and myself in a smaller vessel, made for Englishman's Bay. Once there and unseen, they marched two abreast towards the strong stockade of the first fort, which had six guns trained towards the beach.'

'And where were you?'

He laughed, I think, at my expression of wonder. 'I was in a little gig being rowed along the beach from where I might direct operations more easily.'

'Exposed to those six guns?' I looked admiring.

'Indeed. But the hero of the hour was a young Chileno midshipman who, perceiving one of the pales of the blockade to be rotten, prised it away and, removing his large hat—a not inconsiderable sacrifice—went through. Others followed, the gap was widened and, in short, the fort was taken. There followed the greater forts of Corral, Amargos and Chorocomayo. Colonel Fausto de la Hoya was captured here and what remained of his regiment.'

'So when your ships sailed in, there was little resistance?' I knew the answer but wanted him to complete the history.

'The Spanish flew precipitately, abandoning town, remaining forts, standards, barrack stores, military chests. In short, the whole was in my hands.'

'A triumph! And the losses?' Again, I already knew the answer.

'The enemy's loss in wounded and killed was great, seven hundred lost. I take no pleasure from it. On the patriot side, on *our* side, six were killed and eight wounded.'

'And with this noble victory, the Spanish supply routes were cut.'

He bowed at the compliment, knowing it to be true, and for a while we sat comfortably silent together. For once it was not raining and I rested my eyes on the scene Vicente and I had been sketching that morning. I wondered if Lord Cochrane would like a report on his *prot*égé's abilities. I would have told him that his natural talent gravely lacked the example of European painters. It was a comment on the artistic life here that the only sculptors were those who carved the

116

head, hands and feet of those saints who were to be dressed and put up in church.

But as I thought of speaking, I noticed that His Lordship's face no longer wore the peaceful expression of a man recalling past success but a more anxious, troubled look. I could guess where his thoughts were taking him. I had lately learnt that the strutting Don Jose Zenteno, who was both governor of Valparaíso and Navy minister, had welcomed the victory of Valdivia but secretly criticised Cochrane for attempting such a risky venture without authority. Ever since, he had undermined Cochrane's position with the director, General O'Higgins. Since San Martín and the Admiral were already at loggerheads, this made his position at the very least unstable.

Wishing to dispel His Lordship's frowns, I quoted, in order to show my understanding, from a Spanish poet:

'Envy is Honour's wife, the wise man said,
Ne'er to be parted till the man was dead.'

He stared at me, surprised, perhaps, that I could read his mind. 'You have a poem for every eventuality.' He smiled.

I smiled too. 'I am trying to avoid Lord Byron in your presence.'

'Pray do not inconvenience your poetic sensibility.'

Thus a lighter tone was established and I gave my artistic report on Vicente. His Lordship listened with interest, although his knowledge was not great. Yet, as with many men of genius, he was always interested in gathering information.

117

Later, we had many talks about his ill-usage by various members of the Chilean directorate, but not then. That afternoon we talked a little more, then strolled arm in arm towards the stream that edged my property. It ran briskly after so much rain, so pure and clear that, bending down, we were able to perceive, as if in a magnifying glass, every pebble, frondy leaf and near-transparent fish.

I conquered the temptation to quote Milton and my virtue was rewarded with a second kiss. Ah, can anything be more glorious to a woman than the desirous warmth of a beloved man? Oh, the touch of hot skin and panting breath!

The guns that had been firing all afternoon, coming rather closer, alerted us to our returning escort. So we stood apart.

The men were in high humour. They had bagged more partridge than was quite respectable and literally had stuck a feather in their caps. We had only our flushed cheeks and quickened breath to proclaim our festive air. Even Dr Craig, a sensible, sober man with whom I usually discussed medicinal herbs, asked me jokingly, 'Have you and the Admiral set the world to rights, Mrs Graham?'

His Lordship answered for me: 'We have set ourselves to rights, which is all any mere mortal can claim to do.'

'But you have done so much more,' I protested.

'We'd need a priest and a lawyer to settle the point,' suggested the doctor.

'The curate of Placilla, perhaps,' added Crosbie, referring to the 'white-beer' priest on board the *Rising Star*. 'He would settle any argument for a glass of liquor.'

We walked slowly up to the house, disputing

absurdities all the way. I was on Lord Cochrane's arm and the others around us, even Colonel Fausto, pleased to be in each other's company.

'Shall it be *matee* or wine?' I asked, when we reached the veranda. Felipe waited attentively with some other servants. My question was treated as a mere witticism and soon those who could find seats were seated and the rest standing, but all with a glass in hand.

Below the veranda, a horde of dogs lolled on the ground, disappointed, doubtless, that the partridge had been spirited far from their jaws. Don took his place under the Admiral's legs.

We continued to talk without much sense about entertainments. 'If you bring me a nice Broadwood piano I will play for you,' I told them. 'Or we can summon my neighbour to pluck her guitar.' This was voted the better option, although no music at all could be counted the greatest pleasure.

Dr Craig recalled the evening before when Captain Crosbie had stood up more than once with Miss H.

'If that lady flies her flag at you, it's best to take to the boats,' put in Captain Wilkinson, making us laugh with his imitation of her pursed little smile.

'I understood she was engaged to an American captain,' said I.

'And who made you understand it? The captain or the lady?' asked Crosbie, with a knowing smile.

'You gentlemen are cruel!' I riposted, as if to defend Miss H.'s honour, but they all knew too well my experiences with my past companion.

During this somewhat vulgar discourse, His Lordship was quiet but it was the quiet of contentment. Young men in a far place are liable to loosen their moral purse-strings. Yet these men were not profligate. Like most seamen they would pay to have their male urges satisfied but, in general, their instincts were good and true. Miss H. drew ridicule because of her cant and hypocrisy— everyone knew she'd take a tumble with any gentleman who allowed a whiff of the marriage vow—but nevertheless they held most of my sex in high regard. They thought us lesser beings, certainly, in accordance with the views of the times, but that itself led to chivalry and romance.

I, as an independent widow, was set apart from this. Although my friends from the *Doris* were still at sea, these new friends had inherited their goodwill towards me. I do not believe I flatter myself when I say I was one of them.

*   *   *

Evening was casting blue shadows across the grass when Lord Cochrane rose to his feet. He stood for a while, staring into the distance, perhaps trying to see his ships in the port below. A seaman's eye is said to be better than an eagle's for spotting a mast, friend or foe. He turned to me and sighed heavily. 'You have no immediate plan to return to England?'

'As you see, I am at home here. I am writing for my journal. I have friends.' I smiled.

But his mood had become heavy. 'Do you ever consider that this country, trapped between mountains and sea, may never overcome such isolation?'

'The mountains and sea are Chile's glories.'

'The desert to the north, the ice floes to the

south, are they glories too?'

I knew about the glooms of men who were not naturally introspective. San Martín's devious hostility had lowered His Lordship's spirit about the future of the country to which he had tied his prospects. General O'Higgins had not done enough to countermand this view. Four months' leave was not to him a joyous prospect, unless he could use the time for some great work.

'A newly independent country must always face especial difficulties. You yourself have overcome the greatest obstacle in the Spanish oppressor.'

Our companions had walked away to where the *peons* held the horses and we moved slowly towards them.

'My mother died when I was ten.' He spoke as if this was a continuation of our conversation. I waited. 'My grandmother brought up myself and my brothers. I am indebted to her for having avoided every kind of vice that surrounded me on entering the Navy. She told me that success is sure for a man who is open, true and honourable. I have endeavoured to follow her precepts, but she did not tell me that for every man who tries to do good there is one engaged in the pursuit of wickedness, who will do everything in his power to see the forces of evil triumph. In San Martín I have met that man.' He paused, glanced at me, as if hoping for contradictory words. But what could I say? Cheerful words are meaningless to a man who is cast down.

The pause turned into a longer silence. We had stopped walking and a soft drizzle joined the falling night. Ahead of us the horses fidgeted, one whinnied, and from further down the hill a donkey uttered its desolate croak. His Lordship seemed lost in soulful thoughts. His large head sank on to his chest. Perhaps he imagined an English home, his wife, his young children, who resided in Tunbridge Wells. But I think not. It was the black dog that had got him, which sinks its teeth only into the best of us.

I patted Don, a dog of a very different nature, and pronounced with, I hope, a mixture of sympathy, understanding and encouragement, 'May I count on a visit from Your Lordship tomorrow?'

He turned his eyes on me at first with a lack of focus and then with a sudden blitheness that flung out all his past conversation. 'You may!' he answered, in a powerful voice, and with that he was off to his large cow-coloured mount and the cavalcade streamed away down the hill.

CHAPTER TWELVE

Don and I returned to the house quietly. I sat in the darkness, illuminated poorly by two guttering candles, and tried to write from the objective stance of an historian the present state of Chile. But my lord's mood had infected me: the candles guttered, the ink splattered, and finally I aroused myself only by recording the bitter diatribe against General San Martín, which did my reputation more harm than the general's. Two centuries later, I can see the good in him: twice he rejected ultimate power, first in Chile before my story begins when O'Higgins took over, then in Peru, as I shall record later in this book. He had his principles. I made him the sinner to Cochrane's saint; the greater his sins, the greater my hero's good. The story of every hero needs a villain.

That night seemed particularly long, my only comfort the large, warm body of Don, who at first acted out canine dreams with twitching and whimpering, then setted into a heavy, still somewhat noisy slumber.

'Come, Don,' said I, as at last rosy-fingered dawn made a delicate appearance at the uncovered window. 'Let us take a stroll.'

Felipe, still wrapped in his poncho, followed us, the dog trembling, not with cold, although the air was exceedingly cool, but with the excitement of the fresh smells all around him, and the lady entranced by the loveliness of nature. The morning soon became as fine 'as that on which Paradise was created' and as I wandered around collecting wild flowers I thought how love expands the heart for appreciation of the wonders of this earth. In the sandy lane nearby I found a variety of the yellow-horned poppy, the pink-flowered mallow, vervain, trefoil, fennel, pimpernel and a tiny scarlet mallow. I gathered them until my bouquet was so big that I had to hand some to poor Felipe. All were imbued with my heightened emotions.

We had gone some way from the house and I was beginning to feel the pangs of hunger when I noticed that Don's behaviour had changed markedly: his tail drooped, his back dropped and he slunk along the ground. Behind me, Felipe muttered something I did not understand. In a hedgerow nearby, a bevy of starlings rose suddenly, swirled in the air, leaving agitated patterns on my eyes, then returned whence they'd come.

Suddenly the ground beneath my feet began to sway, accompanied almost immediately by a noise like the explosive escape of vapour from a closed place. Near me, Felipe tore the hat from his head and, falling to his knees, cried, *'Misericordia!'* This was the biggest earthquake I had experienced yet and lasted for more than a minute, followed by another, smaller, shock.

I, who had never felt any upset on the stormiest ocean, felt all the usual effects of sea-sickness and might have fallen to my knees with Felipe, were the *'misericordia'* not part of the performance. The sensation was disagreeable in a way unlike other convulsions of nature. In all others it seems possible to do, or at least attempt, something to avert danger. We steer the ship in a storm for a port; our conductors promise to lead the lightning harmlessly from our heads, but the earthquake seems to rock the very foundations of our globe, and escape or shelter seems impossible.

It passed. The world righted itself and everything but our increased heartbeat seemed as before. Slowly, we gathered the scattered flowers that Felipe had flung away in his fear, and Don's tail rose, if not to its full perpendicular, to an angle of cautious optimism. We started back.

As we walked downwards, I dimly perceived that these earthquakes, must be understood not just as an important part of life in Chile but also as being woven into my friendship with Chile's hero. Lord Cochrane had talked of the Andes, the Pacific Ocean, the northern desert and the southern ice floes, but to this must be added the force that lay beneath the ground. In my, literally, shaken state, I tried to put together my happiness as I had wandered, full of love, among the flowers and the suspicion that, beneath all this prettiness, a growling enemy lay in wait.

'Señora! Señora!' Bella came running to greet me. I could tell her all was well.

The day took its usual pattern. Vicente arrived some time after ten o'clock with his charming indolent air. 'An earthquake is nothing to me,' he assured me. 'Earthquakes are for women and the uneducated.'

He was young and away from home—if he had a home—so I patted his arm and admired his bravery.

We sat together and I drew Felipe, a subject Vicente thought unfit for a serious artist until I pointed out that all men were the same under their clothes and perhaps, like the classicist, we should sketch Felipe naked—at which point he became far more terrified than he would have been at the largest earthquake and unequivocally changed his attitude: 'What dignity! What bravura! See the way he wears his poncho as a knight wears his cloak. Note the angle at which he holds his stick, the length and thickness of his moustache.'

So Felipe, all unknowing, missed a fate that I'm sure would have seemed to him worse than torture and death while I gained a respectable portrait of a Chileno in his costume, which, like my other artistic efforts, may be found at the British Museum. I am less certain what Vicente gained.

At half past one when we were just finishing a light repast of cold meat, bread and fruit, His Lordship appeared. He seemed restless and did not settle into his accustomed place. He pulled Don's ear, picked up a piece of meat in his fingers, as if to

125

eat it, then threw it to the dog. His only companion was the wry Dr Craig, who raised his eyes at me but I turned away. I would do nothing behind His Lordship's back. Every few minutes he stared down to the harbour so it was not difficult to see where his thoughts lay. A man with enemies can never have a quiet spirit.

'May I propose an expedition, sir?'

'You may.' He hardly looked at me.

I persevered: 'I have discovered that all the coarse pottery is made at a place called Rinconada, which means "nook". We may walk there in less than an hour.'

If I had hoped for a 'Lead on, Macduff' spirit, I was disappointed, but he nodded dejectedly and, after I had collected my shawl, we were off, Felipe leading the way, with Lord Cochrane's servants, the doctor, myself, Vicente and His Lordship following.

It is extraordinary how quickly a man of genius may revive when given something for his mind to work on. Rinconada turned out to be an unprepossessing place but all the more interesting for that. We found it beyond a crumbling wall, which had once been the far boundary of the port. Looking for a manufactory, all we saw was a row of poor cottages, made only of twisted branches with grass for roofs, in front of which sat women, so bundled up in skirts and shawls that they seemed hardly human.

His Lordship, striding by in his blue coat, shining buttons and white trousers, looked like a colossus from another race—as I suppose we all did to some extent. 'No machinery! No division of labour! Not even a potter's wheel!' His astonishment brought him out of his hag-ridden state but I feared he

126

might think the less of his guide for leading him to such a drear place.

'I am assured,' I began defensively, 'that the *ollas*—jars for cooking and carrying water—the earthen lamps and braziers were all made here.'

'Aha!' The Admiral bent from his great height and saw that in front of the cottages rows of pots, had obviously been put there for sale.

The workings of this peasant industry now aroused his curiosity and he instructed Felipe—Colonel Fausto and Vicente had walked away as if to avoid being tainted by too close a contact with humble workers—to find a woman to tell us the method of production. His Lordship's Spanish sounded curiously English to my ears, but he was used to commanding subordinates to his will and a respectable woman was soon produced from a respectable-looking cottage—which is to say there was visible inside a bed made of thongs and posts rather than a pile of skins.

'I shall be guinea pig and try my hand.' I sat myself on a sheepskin under a penthouse of green boughs and began to imitate a little girl who was working a saucer. To my surprise, Lord Cochrane then took a lump for himself.

So we sat, side by side, and I am not ashamed to admit he was far the better potter and completed, with no effort at all, a fine two-handled jar. But seamen are all good with their fingers, having as midshipmen a full training in the art of sewing as well as with a cat's cradle of ropes. That the Admiral was not too high and mighty to try his hand in the company of Chileno *peons* displayed his rare nature: one minute a commander, the next a humble student.

Not that humble, however.

'Felipe, ask them where is the oven!' This in a peremptory bellow.

By now, after two hours or so, we each had a little group of our own work but, in my view, they were not yet ready for firing.

'They must be polished first,' I protested, as I had seen the shiny finish to the pots, essential if they were to be watertight.

He conceded with fair grace and our woman instructress, understanding my Spanish, produced from a leather pocket at her front a smooth shell. This she rubbed over the clay, using a little water, at first gently, then with greater force as the clay hardened, until a perfect polish was produced. We followed her example with vigour until my fingers and hands quite ached.

At last all was ready and Lord Cochrane looked around with happy anticipation. The satisfaction of setting a well-made pot in an oven is equal only to baking it out, still well made. He was due for disappointment. The baking in this poor region was in holes scraped off the side of the hill, the fire made of small thorn branches, which grow sufficiently ardent. But there was not sufficient then collected and the evening was drawn in.

'A job left undone is a job ill done,' remarked His Lordship, frowning. I feared for a return of his bad-humour.

'They will fire your pots as soon as they can,' said Vicente, who had eventually made his own Gothic creation before carrying on a desultory conversation with an elderly spectator. He turned to me. 'Would you say I could make a Venus de Milo out of this clay?'

'The clay is good,' I answered, 'so the only question is your talent.'

At which His Lordship broke into hearty laughter, and I saw that the afternoon had not been wasted.

We returned to my home and the air was sweet with the smell of mimosa and the slight stringency of eucalyptus. The Admiral could not stay longer because he had a dinner with one of O'Higgins's men from Santiago, but he left reluctantly. Although we had not been alone together, even for a minute, I felt that our friendship and his keenness for my company continued to grow.

I was, however, disturbed by the hasty arrival, just as my guests were saying their farewells, of Mr Bennett. Scarcely giving me greeting, he drew his master to one side. Determined not to eavesdrop or, worse still, to look as if I was eavesdropping, I nevertheless understood by his gestures that he was informing the Admiral, with all due deference, that he was already late for what was to be a very important meeting.

Wistfully, and not disowning some feelings of guilt, I watched the Admiral ride off without a backward glance.

CHAPTER THIRTEEN

The progress of love is not for outsiders, unless written with a poet's pen. Recently I looked again at my cousin Rosemary Gotch's biography of me. It is a fair work and I am generally grateful. However, in her description of Captain Graham's proposal to me on board HMS *Cornelia*, she quotes from my unpublished diary (now lost), which she rightly describes as the 'crude stilted diary of a girl of 23'. Two examples: 'I feel his cold trembling lips as they touched mine . . .' and 'He whispered to me the delight he anticipated in being the father of my children . . .' How embarrassing! Even with the excuse of my living in a more romantic age—or, let us say rather, in the age of the Romantics—these words have so little meaning as to be gibberish.

I needed a husband so I found my dear Graham and, as I have written earlier, we sorted very well together. But there was no passion on my side, as these and other even more embarrassing lines seem to suggest. The only truth might be found in the 'cold lips' that trembled as much with the poor captain's temerity at taking me on as with desire. But I did everything within my nature to make him happy and would have borne his children with enthusiasm, had God seen fit.

*   *   *

During the afternoon following our visit to Rinconada, His Lordship came with his usual companions. Dr Craig announced that he was going to look for the *culen* plant, about which I had told him so much. Colonel Fausto had stayed in town, suffering from the toothache, but Crosbie and Wilkinson were there until they left to go hunting. (Poor Felipe was quite at a loss as to how to deal with the resultant game, until I suggested distributing it to the neighbourhood, as was done on occasion in Scotland. This filled poor people's stomachs and increased my popularity.)

'My lord, may I have the honour of making a bust of your excellency's head?' Vicente had brought from Rinconada a lump of clay and pulled a chair in line with his patron.

'Not at all. You may not. Certainly not.'

'You must revert to Venus de Milo,' I called after the rejected would-be sculptor, as he decided to exchange clay for a gun. Don followed him happily, after a perfunctory lick at His Lordship's boot.

'You study this country as if you were employed to do so.' His Lordship addressed me seriously.

We sat by side, the afternoon was peaceful, a gentle sun brightening the view, and I took his comment peacefully. If he had been another, I might have protested that I *was* employed, by John Murray Publishers, to study the country. In the Admiral's case I merely felt complimented that he had noted my serious interest in the country, which, as far as I knew, he was still planning to make his own.

'I am much looking forward to studying your estate at Quintero,' I said, a little daringly. 'So far I have had little chance to travel far into the countryside.'

'The failure of the *Rising Star* is to blame. You may think I am downcast about that. I am not. I am so certain that the future of shipping lies with steam that I have already arranged for the parts of two more ships to come to Valparaíso.'

This was the true genius of Cochrane, the man of vision, who disturbed and provoked but would never give ground when he thought he was in the right. As he spoke eloquently, expanding his understanding of the aquatic world, he took hold

131

of my arm as he would a fellow naval officer's, and then my hand, which I assumed a tribute to my female sex.

'England, which thinks itself so forward in modern inventions, is in fact filled with pompous laggards. My dream is to show that this brave new continent can be in the forefront of new thinking!'

My hand was squeezed till the bones rubbed together, but I was quite carried away by these brave words. I still applaud them. Unfortunately history relates that the machinery for the two potential steamships was left in the warehouse that first received it, the timber used for building by which Don Jose Zenteno, that false friend, made large sums. 'It is the bright day that brings forth the adder; And that craves wary walking.'

The squeezed hand was gradually released; the flow of words ceased. I gazed at him with my large dark eyes (always my best feature) and saw the flame of desire lit in his bright blue ones. We rose and slowly went together into the house and from thence to my bedroom, windowless and as black as the pitch that the Earl of Dundonald was trying to sell to the Admiralty.

This is not a novelettish book—not Richardson's *Clarissa* or even Maria Edgeworth's *Helen*—so I will not try to titillate with what did or did not go on in that little square room on the other side of the world. Earlier, I recorded my distaste for the overblown and untruthful description of Graham's and my pledge on board HMS *Cornelia*, with such absurdities as 'That night our souls were solemnly united.' I shall merely state that for an hour or two His Lordship and I thought only of each other, and when we left as quietly as we'd entered, our mutual respect was as high as ever. 'Adulterer,' I hear someone cry. Ah, yes. Without admitting the sin, I refute the claim. His Lordship's loyalty never left his family. Nor had he left their side but they his. I wished to please him. That was all.

Vicente was already back when we came out on to the veranda. He sat on the wooden steps, rather sulkily swishing at his leg with a stick. I thought how old we must seem to him.

'It's a dull day,' he said in Spanish.

His Lordship, settling himself on his chair, said nothing but looked sympathetically. He was always kind to the young.

'Tea, *matee*, wine, brandy?' I spoke gaily for so I felt. From up the hill, the sound of horses and men, with loud voices, drew closer.

'Not a breath of wind,' said the Admiral.

'A day for the steamship.'

'True. True.' But I was glad when he did not take up the subject again, lapsing into comfortable silence. Vicente continued to beat his stick.

The horses arrived behind the house, and Felipe and Bella came out to serve us.

Captain Crosbie appeared out of the twilight; we all stared because he seemed to be transformed into some kind of bush or tree. Behind him Captain Wilkinson and another figure were also transformed.

'Birnam Wood come to Dunsinane,' said Lord Cochrane, standing to get a better look.

'We come as friends, not enemies,' called Captain Wilkinson. He was so tall with his bough of oak that a bird could have roosted there.

'In fact, we come as walking hides,' boomed Captain Crosbie.

133

'An experiment, I see!' The Admiral roused himself further. As he went off the veranda to join them, a whole crowd of green parrots wheeled above his head.

'Not on my bough!' cried Wilkinson, as if he heard my thoughts. He flung branches and leaves to the ground.

'Was your ruse successful?' asked His Lordship, seriously.

'There's a question.' Crosbie waved his branch about as if in a high wind. 'It certainly had an effect on the horses.'

'They bolted,' expanded Wilkinson. 'And poor old Smith-Watson took a tumble.'

Poor old Smith-Watson, whom I had not met before, looked duly shamefaced, and I peered at him more closely for they had now neared the veranda. I saw there was no such person as Smith-Watson: this was my aristocratic friend the Hon. Captain Frederick Spencer.

'Dear sir, please discard your family tree and accept my humble hospitality.' My attempt at word-play fell on deaf ears.

'And the birds?' pursued His Lordship. 'Were they taken in?'

'You must tell by the size of our bag.' The two men walked off to where they had left the game, for all the world as if they were on the grouse moors of Scotland.

*   *   *

I was happy that afternoon, and on the afternoons that followed. I knew the end would come but I hoped that His Lordship's intention to leave for his

134

estate at Concepción might be pushed away.

Hunting continued, until I suspected that all birds had been wiped out for many leagues around. Killing comes easy to young men, whether of human or animal. But my heart was wrung when I heard a rustle in the bushes and discovered a wounded bird, broken wing trailing, bead eyes pleading. Don was the quickest form of execution with a snap of his gun-dog jaws. I did not live at a time of sentiment.

Fishing took the place of shooting. Here His Lordship was more involved and I, too, making flies, which became increasingly elaborate as his inventive mind was pitted against the wily Chilean fish. One of these flies was of my own design for which I plucked a red-gold hair from His Lordship's head, a dark hair from mine, and snipped a hook from his jacket. I kept that and had it till the day I died.

More time was spent standing over a stream, trying to chart the way of the finny race, than actually wielding a rod. As it was still the rainy season, the skies were often grey and low, the earth brilliant red and the shrubs and grass green as the parrots that flitted above.

The men, I noticed, took no care of the rain, allowing themselves and their clothes to become as sodden as if they'd been swimming. I felt sorry for their servants but the sight charmed me.

'Did you fish during your growing up?' I ventured to ask His Lordship one afternoon when, unusually, he'd come on his own. I knew his boyhood home had been Culross Abbey House, built above the Firth of Forth.

He stood back from the river, hardly more than a

stream flowing swiftly downwards, and stared at me with little understanding. Despite his forty-seven years and his bulky height, his ruddy cheeks, dripping-wet shock of hair and look of surprise reminded me of a nine- or ten-year-old boy, the very age he had been, indeed, when his beloved mother died.

'Don't all boys fish?' He walked towards me, rod in one hand. 'Now I'll tell you, Mrs Graham, that which I loved most of all: taking a boat out all by myself on the Firth of Forth. I used to bring along one of my younger brothers but then they were forbidden to come as it was too dangerous. I'd set out before first light, looking at the sky as dawn rose to check for squalls. There's nothing so free in the world as a man on a stretch of water with nobody but himself and his maker. I thought that then and I think that now.' He came closer so that I could see the brightness of his eyes on either side of his proud beak of a nose. 'Whenever I felt ill done by—no Eton or Harrow for me but a succession of incompetent tutors—I remembered those hours on the water. And oh, if the rising sun found strength enough to push apart the lines of blue and silver clouds left over from night, then what more could a human hope for?'

His hand gripped my shoulder, the warmth and damp filled with manly strength. I felt a shiver of delight that I could scarcely repress. 'You told me you do not read poetry but you have a poet's soul.'

He laughed. 'A seaman who spends too much time staring at sky and water. Come, we are wet enough for one afternoon. Let us go inside.'

This was the man I loved. I fell in love with the hero, then found the man, the boy, the poet. On our way back, I quoted Wordsworth at him:

> *'It is a beauteous evening, calm and free,*
> *The holy time is quiet as a Nun*
> *Breathless with adoration; the broad sun*
> *Is sinking down in its tranquility . . .'*

During this time of what, I hope without sacrilege, might be termed 'breathless adoration', I hardly descended to town. If I had, I might have been forewarned of what was to come.

Ten days after Lord Cochrane had first visited me for tea, his secretary, Mr Bennett, came again. As it happened I was on my own, since His Lordship had taken it into his head to lead an expedition to locate the source of the Estero de las Delicias that ran near my house. Feeling the intimations of a headache, I had stayed behind, at first on the veranda and then, as a gusty wind threw spikes of rain at my face, inside. I had thought his approaching horse and servants Lord Cochrane returning.

'Oh, Mr Bennett!' My disappointment must have been obvious. I liked Mr Bennett, who is to play a bigger part as the story carries on. In fact, his real name was William Bennet Stevenson, a published writer, but I gave him a pseudonym in the journals and so he may remain—except when I dub him Don Benito as a tribute to his tales of travels in Peru and Chile.

He had come to tell a less entertaining tale that afternoon.

'Madam.'

I saw at once by his face, which had none of the clownish gaiety I had come to associate with him,

137

that he had bad news. 'The government is at war with each other? San Martín has seized power? The Admiral's fleet is needed at once?' I was facetious, but happiness has that effect.

'No. No. Not at all.' He was sweating profusely, despite the cool temperature.

'Not at all,' I repeated. 'But His Lordship is wanted?'

'To the contrary.' He produced a handkerchief and rubbed it between his hands. I noticed that even his eye without the squint was not meeting mine.

'Bella! Tea!' I ordered. 'Please, sit,' I said to Mr Bennett.

'Are you alone?' He sat down and, as I nodded, relaxed a little. 'You are a woman of great intelligence.'

I nodded coolly. I had begun to suspect what he had come to say and was trying hard to contain my fury. After all, my schoolgirl nickname had been 'Tiger', following an incident when I'd sunk my teeth into another girl's flesh.

'May I speak openly as to a friend?' His little mouth, which I had once thought amusing, pursed.

I looked down so he shouldn't see the fire in my eyes.

'There is talk.'

'Enough!' I held up my hand. 'You have said enough. I understand Mr Hogan is at home this evening. I shall attend. I have not seen the family for some time.'

'The Admiral cannot come so often. Every day . . .'

I stood up, made my skirts rustle as if they, too, were angry. 'This evening I shall be in Valparaíso.'

138

'His Lordship is expected at his estates in the south immediately. He has told me he will go.'

How strange it was that this intelligent man, of whom I later became so fond, should have brought to an end this first joyful interlude. He should have warned me to let several days elapse before I showed my face at the Hogans'. Perhaps he was afraid of my talons.

CHAPTER FOURTEEN

Black is a dramatic colour, I tried to reassure myself as I prepared for the evening. With my dark eyes, dark hair and high colouring, I would not look faded as most widows of my age. In order to wear a lighter, fuller skirt and lace around my neck, rather than my more sensible riding habit, I had ordered a carriage—although carriages in Chile were more like carts. I hung an amethyst in each ear and looked in my mirror to see the candle give them a crimson heart. It was unlike me to care so much about my appearance.

Unfortunately, I arrived at the Hogans' in a thunderstorm and the bottom half of my skirt was soaked in the time it took to jump from cart to house. The journey had shaken my body mercilessly, reminding me how much I prefer a horse. Bella tried to straighten a black plume in my headdress, doubtless bedraggled, but I pushed her aside. My heart beat far too fast.

'"*If it were done when 'tis done then 'twere well It were done quickly,*"' I told myself, or maybe spoke aloud because the servants at the door looked at

139

me oddly.

'Mrs Graham. My dear!' Mrs Hogan, a true friend, was at my side at once. 'Such an age since we saw you!' She blushed, which did not suit her sallow American complexion.

But I was glad of her kindness as she led me into the room. Supper had already been served and there was music and dancing in a further room. 'We have Argentinian beef,' she said, taking me to a chair.

The thought of Argentinian beef made me turn as pale as my friend was red. 'If there is an ice perhaps.' This was a new delicacy made with ice blocks sailed up from the far south. I knew that the Hogans—with all their countrymen's pride in new fashions—would be glad to provide it.

As she signalled for a servant, I looked around and saw that this outer room was almost empty, apart from some salty old captains of various nationalities with weathered faces and bandy legs. My friends, I guessed, were all within. But it was sensitive of dear Mrs Hogan to give me time to recover from the journey.

'We hear you have taken an art student. Isabella was jealous.'

I took a glass of wine from a silver tray and my sip turned into an unrefined gulp. 'I fear Vicente is nothing like as good a student as your dear Emily would be. I trust the family are well?'

'Indeed. Emily is pining for America, however. I told her at her age she should be pining not for a country but for a man.' This innocuous remark set her blushing all over again.

I stood up. 'I must not keep you any longer from your other guests.'

'But your ice!'

Ignoring this bleat, I swept towards the entrance to the other room, meaning to burst upon them and collect friends about me. But the back of an upholstered lady blocked my progress. She turned to me: Miss H., garlanded with the new glories of her engagement, shiny ringlets, pouting bosom, squeezed-in waist. I was about to give her a polite nod when she averted her silly face, turned up her nose and marched away. I had been cut by Miss H.!

Any of you who have undergone this experience unexpectedly will know how difficult it is to challenge. The removal of the adversary makes protestation impossible, unless preceded by an undignified chase. A man could throw down his glove—a leather slap on the wooden floor would be better than no slap at all (duelling was still an option, remember)—but a woman could only stand and gape, humiliated beyond repair.

Some repair was presented immediately by Captain Crosbie galloping off the dance floor and taking me in his arms. Perhaps I looked ready to faint. Was it my imagination or had the music stopped? In such a situation, I find one often goes deaf as a post. He led me to a chair where Mr Bennett, Captains Wilkinson and Spencer joined me. Spencer was particularly assiduous, rattling on with unusual animation, but I heard nothing. I noticed, however, that no lady approached me, apart from the warm-hearted Hogan family, to whom I shall ever be grateful.

As uncomfortable ladies have over the years, I took out my fan, and flapped it in front of my face, although I was cool rather than hot. I accepted a second drink and, after a while, found my voice

141

again.

My deafness receded as the music struck up. Never had I felt more lonely.

I had a dream, which was not all a dream.
The bright sun was extinguish'd . . . and the icy
* earth*
Swung blind and blackening in the moonless air.

The guests, even my naval friends, seemed only characters strutting and fretting on a stage. I had known the Admiral would not be there and that he was in talks with General O'Higgins before leaving for Concepción and then his estate but, nevertheless, I pined for his commanding presence.

I left as soon as possible. Dr Craig, who had arrived too late to witness the worm turning, commented sagely, as he handed me into my rattle-bone carriage, 'Tittle-tattle has a way of hurting those who deal in it.'

He was a good, kind man—I had seen him dress a wound incurred by one of my huntsmen with great gentleness—but I had no wish to discuss personal matters with him. I looked up at the dark sky from which fine needles of rain fell, ' "For the rain it raineth every day." '

'Mrs Graham can ever produce the apt quotation.' He bowed, and I was nearly jolted off my wooden plank as the mules set off with a homeward nose.

'Señora!' exclaimed Bella, who had been waiting in the carriage, crossing herself twice or thrice. I could have done with a blessing myself, but contented myself with patting her hand.

It had been a day of joy and a day of humiliation.

142

Why should we who are placed in the hurdy-gurdy of this world expect better?

*   *   *

The night passed as nights do and, in the light of a shockingly beautiful dawn—silver-violet on the sea and amber-gold on the hillside—I made new resolves.

Among the acquaintances I'd made in Valparaíso were a Mr and Mrs Miers. They were quite different from the normal society met there, being educated and curious in the ways of the country. Indeed, Mr Miers was both a businessman and an explorer, publishing an account of his travels around the same time as I published mine. Despite our friendship, honesty compels me to admit that his are exceedingly dull, but neither he nor his wife was dull in person, in fact rather the opposite, being distinctly adventurous. I decided to set out, as soon as it could be arranged, to their home, a little way along the northern coastline, beyond the larger estates of Viña del Mar.

Since this is a truthful record, I should add that less than a day's ride from the Mierses' would bring me to Lord Cochrane's estate of Quintero. This was the place that the *Rising Star* had failed to attain and I naturally harboured an intense curiosity to see it, even in its owner's absence.

The waiting was wearisome and lonely since most of my friends had accompanied His Lordship to Concepción. I consoled myself by doing some serious botanising, which I wrote up for my journal and which prepared me for meeting Mr and Mrs Miers, who were more expert than I in local flora

143

and fauna. Twice I rode down to Valparaíso, calling only on the Campbells and Hogans and shopping for my journey. I was cheered out of my sadness by the hustle and bustle of the port, before spending an hour or more watching ships coming and going until I began to shiver under the increasing wind. Then, instead of enjoying my love of waves, salt air, sea-birds, skies, ships and boats, I contemplated what might have been that could never be.

Seeing tears roll down my cheeks, Bella took my arm and led me away. Sometimes a servant can be of more use than a world full of friends.

*　　　*　　　*

At length I was on my way. Felipe and Bella came with me and Don bounded at our side. A Captain Henry Cobbett had volunteered to be my guide as far as Concón. He had been captain of the *Valdivia* under Lord Cochrane, although I had not met him previously. He was a nephew of the political essayist and radical reformer William Cobbett, who had been a friend of His Lordship during his political past.

The nephew, judging by his jutting brow and determined expression, was as obstinate as his uncle. On the other hand he was intelligent and communicative so that I happily consented to him as my escort. I wanted to believe that the Admiral had given him a nudge in my direction.

The ride to Concón was fifteen miles, some of it winding along the edge of precipices, much of the road so bad that it would scarcely seem possible in England. The Chileans are generally admirable horsemen but poor Bella struggled along behind the captain until I almost wished I'd let her stay at home. The happiest among us was Don, who continually disappeared inland at the squawk of a bird or the rustle of a rabbit and once nearly bounded off the edge of a cliff when a kittiwake called to him.

'Have you been this way often?' I asked Cobbett, as we came in sight of Viña del Mar and cantered over a fine stretch of grass.

'I have friends among the Carrera family who own the land around here.'

'And beyond to Concón?'

'That less often but I know the views of sea and cordilleras are picturesque in the extreme.'

He was right. While we waited for Bella to catch up, I loosened my horse's reins and let my eyes feast on the ruby mountains with the volcano of Aconcagua on one side, and the emerald-green ocean on the other. From there we descended to the banks of the great river, also called Aconcagua.

'I believe the Miers house is this side of Concón.' He waved his hand further to the north. 'Quintero is over the hill and beyond an expansive lake.'

'Have you been there?' I asked, somewhat haughtily to disguise my emotions. I needn't have worried: Cobbett was far too self-centred to concern himself with anyone else's feelings.

'Once or twice. The house is being built with a commanding view of the great Quintero Bay. It is far better sheltered from the fierce north-west winds than Valparaíso and would have made a better harbour. But the most rational plan is seldom followed.'

A gloomy fellow indeed. How I wished for a Crosbie! We continued on our way until by chance we came across the Mierses themselves, out collecting rare bulbs and plants. Three *peons* attended them with baskets, already half filled. They were an enthusiastic couple, quite opposite physical types—he like a stringy little monkey, she as round as the bulb she held in her hand.

'Mrs Graham!'

'Mrs Miers! Mr Miers.'

We embraced more cordially than the length of our friendship warranted but there is always something unexpectedly delightful in meeting your own countrymen very far from home. With my 'pleasant's and 'picturesque's, I have possibly not indicated just how wild and uninhabited this region was, always bounded by salt water and rocky outcrops from the cordilleras, as the lower slopes of the Andes were called.

'Madam, I shall take my leave,' said Captain Cobbett.

I waved my escort goodbye with many thanks but few regrets and, having ascertained that the Mierses' home was not far, sent Felipe and Bella ahead with my horse, while I stayed with my horticultural hosts. Happily, we exchanged information.

'Now, dear Mrs Graham,' said Mr Miers, at length taking off his thick leather gloves and brushing earth from his face, 'we must pass by my machinery!'

'Certainly,' I agreed, only a little wearily as we began to walk slowly towards the sound of a powerful river.

'Perhaps you know the history,' suggested Mr Miers. 'I brought the components of an apparatus for rolling copper and stamping metal from

146

Atlantic to Pacific only to discover the country was not in a high enough state of advance to use it.'

A fine mill came into view. It had been a long day and the moon was rising over the water. 'At least we have here both a flour mill and a saw mill, for sawing barrel staves, on which some of my machinery may be used.'

I allowed my mind to drift and I fear my admiration was more for the flocks of water-birds finding their night-time roost than the details of the mill. After many long minutes, Mrs Miers took my hand out of its glove and, finding it cold, interrupted her husband: 'My dear, Mrs Graham is frozen near to death and you keep her here with talk of cogs and wheels.'

So we set off for their house, which was simply built on one floor in the Chilean style, and my health was soon restored with brandy and hot water. My happiness increased when Mr Miers announced that we should ride over to Lord Cochrane's estate after breakfast the following day.

*   *   *

The morning was soft and bright, the horses, including my dear Charles, fresh and lively—indeed, for once I was grateful for the cruel Chilean bit. Looking at my published journal, I find I cannot better the description as we went on our way:

13th August
After fording the rapid river of Aconcagua in three branches, the road of three leagues lies along a wild and desolate tract of sea-beach. On one hand are great sand hills, where no green

147

things find root, and which are high enough to exclude the view of every other object; on the other hand, a tremendous surf, which permits not the approach of boat or canoe, beats unceasingly. Halfway between Concón and Quintero, the great lake of Quintero communicates with the sea. In mild weather it only drains through the sand; at other times it breaks through its bar, and the ford is not always passable. When we passed, it was covered with various kinds of water birds: the flamingo with its rose-coloured bill and wings; the swan of Chile, whose feet are white and his neck and head jet black, a brown bird, with wings like burnished bronze, and a head, bill and feet exactly resembling the Egyptian ibis; and geese, water hens and all the duck tribe, innumerable.

'Soon we will be leaving the beach,' announced Mr Miers, as we paused for water and a biscuit. 'Then you will see an altogether different landscape.'

He was right, for now we ascended a low hill and immediately entered a broad green forest walk, so level that it seemed to be a work of art. On either side there was brushwood between us and the taller trees, whose leaves breathed odours, gave shelter to flocks of wood-pigeons, ground doves and partridges, among whom Don seemed bewildered with joy; every now and again he looked back as if reproachfully because there was no gun of the party.

'The south-west wind here bends the trees into the same figure as it does in Devonshire,' I pointed out, 'except where the hills afford shelter.'

148

All this time I was expectant to see His Lordship's house. I knew it was not finished but imagined the loving care with which he would have chosen the site, the design and the materials. It represented his future in Chile.

(It was as well that neither he nor I could see what lay in store for this promising land where herds of cattle made their daily migration from the wood to the open plain, from the plain to the wood. Two hundred years later, the name 'Gasmar' has taken the place of 'Cochrane' and a vast spread of oil refineries, huge chimneys, gasometers, all on a gigantic scale, cover the coastline and above for several miles. Vile odours complete the atmosphere of hell that industrial progress has created.)

'You see the house now, Mrs Graham. On the point.' Mr Miers held out his arm.

I looked and was disappointed. How often does the imagination outstrip reality! Although the view of the bay was splendid, the surroundings were by no means as pleasant as lower down and further inland. Yet as we walked among the buildings, rooms being detached one from the other and grouped round a main house constructed with natural tree trunks, I found my heart beat absurdly fast.

I recalled that scene in Miss Austen's *Pride and Prejudice* when Elizabeth is caught by Mr Darcy looking over his grand country residence. It is a scene of high emotion. Unfortunately, I knew only too well that Lord Cochrane was many hundreds of miles to the south. Some Chileno workers had taken our horses so we proceeded slowly on foot. At the veranda of the house, supported by pillars of twisted tree trunks, Mrs Miers took my arm. 'Are

149

you as awestruck by our heroic admiral as everyone else? Save San Martín, we may assume.'

'You read my mind.' I turned to face her. She did not know of His Lordship's tea-time visits to my home, or so I chose to assume, and it was a glorious relief to speak freely of him. 'If the master were present now,' I began, 'we would not think of the house. Though not handsome, Lord Cochrane has an expression of countenance that induces you, when you have looked once, to look again and again. It is as variable as the feelings that pass within, but the most general look is of great benevolence. His conversation, when he does break his ordinary silence, is rich and varied; on subjects connected with his profession or his pursuits, he is clear and animated. If ever I met with genius, I should say it was pre-eminent in Lord Cochrane.'

Mr Miers had joined us during my discourse and I saw him and his wife gaze at me with some surprise.

'I see you are indeed an admirer,' said Mrs Miers, smiling.

I smiled, too, for I was not in the least ashamed of my seemingly adulatory description of a great man. Others might take note of his faults or, more truly, weaknesses, for all men have weaknesses (and very often they concern pride and money), but that was not for me.

While we made explorations, Felipe had arranged for a dinner to be laid out in the main room. As we ate our cold meats and drank our red wine, I looked up at the sturdy rafters and sighed for what could not be. My attention was diverted by a cheeky little sparrow that flew in through the open doorway and tried to steal the bread from our very plates.

'He does not appreciate we are English,' said Mr Miers. He pushed his plate to one side so that the bird could dart at it more easily. 'Since the weather is holding, I suggest we visit the gardens after dinner.'

We walked the league to the gardens in high spirits and were rewarded by finding ourselves in a beautiful secluded spot where, in one fenced space, trees such as larch and oak and beech were being raised. (Two hundred years later some of these are noble trees and one oak is labelled, fancifully enough, 'Maria Graham planted this.')

The vegetable garden was equally well organised with vegetables unknown before in Chile, such as carrot, turnip and various kinds of pulse. We delighted the gardeners with our constant questioning and appreciation.

The man in charge, Don Rafael, a hale and hearty man with a hat as tall as a steeple, set off with praise of his master that was hardly less fulsome than mine.

'Is he so advanced in his agricultural projects?' asked Mr Miers, who spoke Spanish well.

In answer he showed us modern farming equipment and I sighed, remembering one of my earliest conversations with Lord Cochrane had been on this very subject.

'Will the Admiral be here soon?' asked Mrs Miers, curiously.

'*Si Dios lo quiere* . . .' replied Don Rafael, crossing himself.

To which I could have added 'Amen'. In a strictly Anglican sense.

151

*   *   *

We were to spend the night at Quintero, in the small dark rooms usual for sleeping. Despite our energetic day of riding and walking, I was still awake enough to discover some designs for small boats fit for coastal trade, which I conceived had been drawn by His Lordship's hand. I pored over these as evidence of his interest in Chile's future and drew Mr Miers's attention to them. Mrs Miers had already retired to bed. We bent together over our one candle like conspirators over a secret map.

'In your opinion Lord Cochrane intends to make Chile his home?' asked Mr Miers, with a somewhat doubting countenance.

'He has said so.'

'What he has said in one set of circumstances may change in another. There is talk of civil war. The country may yet not hold together. San Martín is always inscrutable, and General Freire, although at the moment his hands are full in the south with the Indians and the Spanish, has no admiration for O'Higgins.'

'All the more reason for the Admiral's presence.'

'Do you not think he will not want to clear his good name in England?'

'Not when he is called to defend freedom wherever it may be in the world.'

As we discussed the garbled politics of South America, and the candle guttered and snuffed, neither of us suspected that the very ground we had been traversing all day with such interest would destroy so many hopes and plans for a brave new world.

152

CHAPTER FIFTEEN

There followed for me a time of endurance. In my journals you may read that I travelled a great deal, across the Andes, spent two weeks in Santiago and met many people of various persuasions, including General O'Higgins, the supreme director. I will enlarge on some of this, which I wrote about with gaiety and humour, but it was not my choice. One word from the Admiral, or even the knowledge that he had returned to Valparaíso, and I would have dropped all my courageous journeying and frantic scribbling. But Lord Cochrane remained on his estates in the south.

A small consolation, as I did my organising from my little house on the Almendral, was my growing intimacy with Captain Spencer. His ship had still not sailed and he was often at a loose end. Like me, he was bookish and came regularly to borrow from my library.

'Now, Mr Spencer,' I told him one morning, when my plans to visit Santiago were well advanced, 'you may escort me over the Andes as far as I need to go and barter quotations all the way.'

He frowned regretfully so that his straight aristocratic nose wrinkled sweetly. 'I cannot leave the *Alacrity* for so long but I will set off with you and find you a hearty young companion for the rest of the journey.'

In this way the Honourable Frederick de Roos, a midshipman on HMS *Alacrity*, came into my life. He was another of my 'boys', whom I tried to help and who gave me such joy. Dear Freddie was

153

not only affectionate and intelligent but also the grandson of a duke.

Our departure became a celebration when a dozen or more of my good naval friends, with the addition of Miss Emily Hogan and the Campbells, arrived at my house for breakfast and to escort me, as they insisted, to the first post-house.

'Are you always surrounded thus, *ma mère*?' enquired Freddie, as we set off at last.

'A lady on her own arouses charitable instincts,' said I.

He looked dubious. 'Is that truly the reason?' He thought a bit before adding, 'I can't say I've ever seen you on your own.'

'If you could see me on my own I wouldn't be on my own,' I pointed out, laughing.

Many people cross mountains so I will not burden you with descriptions of the rugged roads or majestic views as we made our way to the first town of Casablanca. Bella rather shocked me by being quite fagged after a mere thirty miles. 'Look at Don,' I told her. 'He's bounding still and, although smaller than you, has run all the way without the luck of a ride.'

'But, Señora, Don is a dog!' wailed Bella, affronted now as well as fagged.

To which any answer I might have given was drowned by Freddie's bellow of laughter.

'I am glad your Spanish is progressing so well,' I told him. 'Now help Felipe with the horses while Bella and I make ourselves comfortable inside.' Seeing his face fall, I added, 'I shall order their best wine for our supper.'

The inn had only one peculiarity: it was kept by an English Negro, who thankfully understood

154

something of the comforts required by the English and presented a very tolerable resting place to a traveller so that I had no need to unpack my travel bed.

The next morning the views of the woody valleys, even at the great height of the Cuesta de Zapata, the smell of mimosa, the deep glens and the snowy pinnacles of the mountains tempted me from my descriptive ban. Yet again when we arrived at our inn, Bella was the most fatigued of our party, and even dear Freddie was swaying on his horse, which proves that youth and health are not the hardiest of travel companions. When I lay down—on our own mattresses suspended above a mud floor—I quoted Shelley to myself:

> *Like a high-born maiden*
> *In a palace tower*
> *Soothing her love-laden Soul in secret hour . . .*

and I pictured a certain heroic countenance.

On the third day we reached the highest point of our journey and began our descent. From the pass of Pudahuel we stared down and Freddie cried out, like the child he was, 'There, *ma mère*, the city! Oh, what a sight!'

'So often in Chile,' said I, 'the want of human habitation throws a melancholy over the face of Nature, but here those spires of dazzling whiteness assures me that Art has conjoined with her sibling Nature.'

This was a bit high-flown and not altogether honest since my mood craved more the solitude of craggy heights than cities and social intercourse, but my habit in life has always been to move onwards.

So when, an hour or two later, Freddie pointed to a train of horses, mules and even a carriage, far below, I answered cheerfully, 'I suspect that this is Don Jose Antonio de Cotapos and his family come to meet us.'

My plan to stay in an inn had been overruled and the dignified Don Jose Antonio, his wife and his large progeny of pretty daughters, were to be my hosts in Santiago. My subsequent tourism in and around Santiago always found me in a group eager to see I was entertained and invariably ending in singing and dancing, which I enjoyed exceedingly: there I could sit and admire without being forced to spout one platitude after another.

Only two days after my arrival on 24th August, I was honoured by an invitation to attend the supreme director, General O'Higgins, at the palace. Whether it was a compliment to my breeding, my fame as a writer or my friendship with Lord Cochrane, I could not say.

I dressed attentively and Bella was decidedly impressed by the result, although her comment might have been better phrased: 'Ah, Señora, at last you look less like a muleteer and more than a lady!'

The de Cotapos family accompanied me, which cast me in the role of peacemaker since their close relations had fought against O'Higgins only a few years earlier. Although the distance to the palace was very short, a carriage was ordered because Santiago had pretensions to grandeur: citizens and visitors alike were expected to behave with all due formality. However, Señora de Cotapos and her daughter Doña Mariquita surprised me with their coarse black shoes and cotton stockings.

'Ah, Señora Graham,' confided the matron, noticing where I was looking, 'We wear these to fulfil a vow we made to Dios if the life was spared of a certain old and sick gentleman.' I could admire their inspiration if regretting their superstition.

His Excellency General O'Higgins's welcome was exceedingly warm: 'Señora, Mrs Graham, it gives me so much pleasure to meet the famous English lady, both author and traveller.'

The room we were received in was furnished in international accord; English cast-iron grates, Scotch carpets, French china and time-pieces; there was little or nothing that looked Spanish, let alone Chilean.

His excellency also spoke perfect English since he had spent several years at an academy in Richmond, Surrey. 'I believe I had the acquaintance of an uncle of yours, Sir David Dundas, a very valiant surgeon.'

I agreed this was more than possible. 'He was surgeon general to George the Third, a great favourite with His Majesty, and lived in rooms in the Old Palace, Richmond.'

'And perhaps you know Dr L. and Mrs P. and Lord R.?,' he asked me, all of whom I did know, which made for a very friendly conversation. He was dressed in his general's uniform and was not distinguished in person, being short and fat, with a coarse, ruddy complexion and a fair colouring that obviously owed more to his Irish extraction than his Spanish. He was in fact the bastard son of a former viceroy of Peru, although looked down on by my hosts, mainly, as far as I could understand, because his inherited estates of sixty-four thousand acres were composed of despised 'frontier' land.

157

As at any gathering in Chile, politics quickly became the subject of conversation. Various views were put forward about the projected constitution, although the military men present, as international as the furnishings, many French, had nothing to offer on the subject and only opened their mouths to quaff their wine.

'You will already know, madam,' said the general, abruptly, to change the subject, 'that education is sadly lacking among many of my countrymen. But you may not know the number of schools newly founded.'

I listened attentively as he listed them, even if I would have preferred more politics.

The general lived with his mother and sister and it was the former, a small, elegant figure, who suggested we should have musical entertainment. Doña Mariquita played French tunes with an elegant air so I was free, once more, to observe. Among all the other charming guests, and sitting rather too close to me, was one fat lady, swathed from top to very large bottom in pale blue satin. She ordered a box to be placed before her into which she spat dextrously.

I whispered to my neighbour on the other side, 'Do you practise such a habit?'

She answered, with indignation, 'You must not judge the new Chile by the habits of the old.'

Before I left the palace, I had a final conversation with General O'Higgins which gave me much to think about. He took my hand and seemed about to kiss me farewell, when he paused. 'As an Englishwoman, you must find Admiral Lord Cochrane's admiration for General Napoleon Bonaparte somewhat curious.'

I was in a quandary. There was a French colonel only a few yards away. Why had the general brought up the subject? It could only have been to prove that his admiral was not always of sound judgement.

'You know of Lord Cochrane's plan for the man who fought to conquer and rule your country?' he prompted.

'General Bonaparte died on St Helena in May 1821. That was a year before I came to Chile and became reacquainted with His Lordship.' I smiled slightly, with what I hoped was sound diplomacy.

'So you were not aware that the admiral of our Chilean Navy planned to rescue Bonaparte from his exile and carry him across the seas, probably in one of his steamships, which, it is true, have had a setback.' Here the general paused for an undiplomatic chuckle. 'You were on the *Sinking Star*, I believe?' Now he had a little audience, most of whom, however, comprehended little more than his jovial expression, since he spoke in English.

'Steamships are the future in sea travel,' I responded, still calm.

'So he tells me. But to return to the French general, Lord Cochrane's plan was to bring him here and set him up as ruler of South America. How do you say to that?'

There was only one answer: 'I cannot imagine anyone more fitted to rule the country of Chile than you, Your Excellency, you, who have experience of Europe and the Americas and whose blood runs with a true belief in *liberté*, *égalité*, *fraternité*. There are those who pronounce such ideas and those who conduct their lives under their precepts.'

He nodded at this and seemed ready to let me

go. But at that moment two young Araucanian women, one a mere girl of perhaps thirteen, came up, pulling his coat and saying something in their own Indian language. He responded kindly, talking back to them.

'Their language is very beautiful,' I dared to interject, at which the general said a few more sentences for my benefit.

We were friends again, but our Napoleonic conversation had taught me that although he was a friend of Lord Cochrane he was not unreservedly so, and I resolved to tell His Lordship. In my passionate soul, I wished that the Admiral had thought of himself as ruler of South America rather than the bourgeois colonial demagogue who had crowned himself emperor.

On our way home in the cumbrous carriage, I commended the general for his kindness to what I understood to be Araucanian orphans.

Señora de Cotapos immediately withdrew behind her fan, which she had felt no need of all evening, and her husband began a long rigmarole about the murderous habits of the Indians. At this point Doña Mariquita gave a quickly stifled giggle so that I realised there was a story behind the story and resolved to seek it out.

The truth came the next morning when Doña Mariquita willingly divulged that the two Indian 'orphans' were the general's mistress and his daughter. The scandal was silent because his mother and sister accepted the situation.

'Ah, he is a fine, brave man,' said Doña Mariquita, 'and a Catholic, although the Church is not fond of him since it is rumoured his new constitution will limit its powers. But a Chilean

160

constitution seems a long way off, with all the silly arguing that goes on.' She laughed merrily.

Having a higher view of constitutions, I made no comment, and handed over the little brooch with a Scottish thistle, which I had promised, and bade her a happy morning with her children.

I often felt an alien amid the Chilean families, which extended to many generations of siblings and cousins living together. There were spinsters and widows, of course, but they were all relatives and had a role to play. Yet my hosts were so generous with their attention that I could not be sad for long. Besides, there was dear Freddie to enthuse about our next interesting expedition, often out of town.

I scribbled down for my journal the picturesque attire of our company as we processed through the countryside, stopping at villa or chapel:

Don Jose Miguel de Cotapos, wore his poncho of plain vicuna wool, his broad hat, his silver-mounted bridle and stirrups, as we rode off to a casita about five miles eastward of Santiago. Most had Chileno saddles, with all manner of carpets and skins upon them. All the ladies had English saddles, the greater number wearing coloured spencers and long white skirts with close bonnets and flowers; two had small opera-hats and feathers and beautiful silk dresses; only my maid and I had sober riding-habits. We looked like some gay cavalcade in a fairy tale, rather than people going to ride soberly on earth; and I was sorry that I could not sketch the figures. Here Mariquita in scarlet and white, and a becoming black beaver bonnet, and roses not so gay as her cheeks, then Jose Antonio, with his

poncho of turquoise blue striped with flowers,
and Frederick de Roos with his grey silk jacket
and sunny British countenance.

I wrote pages of such loveliness, among the
cornfields and olive groves, the willows and the
flower gardens, always against a background of the
Andes in their hoary majesty.

But one evening when, from a further room,
I could hear the soulful sound of a man's voice
accompanying his guitar, I put aside my journal and
pulled a sheet of paper towards me:

Your Lordship,
After ten days in this noble city, after being
received by His Excellency General O'Higgins
on more than one occasion, with marked signs
of favour which I take as compliment to you,
my gallant countryman, after walking or riding
parties to every charming hillside, historic house
or sacred shrine, I have decided to make plans
for a journey south. His excellency has vowed to
help me with acquaintances but, naturally, I wish
you, as my nearest friend in this country, to be
aware of my arrival in two or maybe three weeks,
dependent on the travelling. I trust that your
affairs advanced speedily and that we may meet
in the not too distant future.
    Your affectionate friend
    Maria Graham

No young lover could have chewed her pen more
thoroughly over this brief letter, which I knew to
be a pitiable *cri de coeur*. But I also knew that His
Lordship would read nothing more into it than that

I planned to travel southwards in the near future. I never underestimated a gentleman's deafness to the sensitivities of the lady. A poet, perhaps, a Byron, Shelley or Keats, would have fully understood the meaning of my missive and yet this ability is not altogether masculine; the moment a man listens fully to a woman he is lost. Indeed both my dear husbands paid me too much attention. So, I was content to imagine Lord Cochrane taking up the sheet of paper in his big hands—or perhaps getting Mr Bennett to read it aloud—and thinking, with none of his freedoms impaired, that the female he respected would be coming his way.

Meanwhile, I must survive many more trips to beautiful estates where sketching gave me some peace and satisfaction, more visits to his excellency and his 'orphans', and tours of the mint, the printing press and the Consulado, or seat of government.

'Don't you think it odd,' whispered Freddie, as we sat, somewhat bewildered, on benches near the president, 'that an Englishwoman and an English midshipman may assist at the deliberations of a national representative in Chile?'

'I am glad you know where we are,' I whispered back, with a smile. 'Sometimes I think everything but the riding and eating passes over your head.' But as we crossed the square and made our way home under the arches, I saw an opportunity for education: 'What would once have been romance, is now everyday, matter-of-fact. I was in the Mahratta citadel while it was defended by an English force; I have attended a Protestant church in the Piazza de Foro Trajano in Rome; I sat as a spectator in an English court of justice in Malta.'

'So we can be proud to be English for we are welcomed everywhere.' He looked thoughtful.

'Of course you may!'

'Yet Admiral Lord Cochrane has taken Chilean citizenship.'

This was too clever by half. I felt myself flushing. 'Lord Cochrane has not renounced his Englishness: he has merely added to it a further honour, thereby complimenting an emerging country.'

'I see.' De Roos bent with youthful elasticity and dropped a coin into a beggar's bag.

'Better keep your money for yourself,' I reprimanded him. But he was a fine boy.

The next morning he helped me as I purchased a new horse to give my dear Charles a rest. 'This is the way to spend money,' I told him, as I handed over twenty dollars for a tall roan. He had white feet, two blue eyes and answered to the name of Fritz.

'They say he's never carried a woman in his life.' Freddie helped me into the saddle with what I chose to see as protective admiration.

'Now we can ride twenty leagues without pausing,' I cried gaily, as I made Fritz prance and caper. Although a widow and dressed in black, I was still in my thirties and not above showing off now and again—if not on the Kitty Cochrane scale.

We had, in fact, planned one long trip to the city of Melipilla before going southwards. What shall I say about this? That we visited the beautiful villa of the Marqués de Larrain who owned nine thousand cattle? That we slept one night at an inn where there was only one room for gentlemen and ladies? Poor Freddie was greatly discomposed.

'Dearest boy,' I told him, 'what is the use of

the heavy skirt of a riding habit if not to place it between me and all comers?'

'I am not a boy, Maman, I am a man,' he replied rather petulantly, and in truth he was in that uncomfortable state, like a centaur, of being half man, half child—his body man, his mind child. He slept soundly enough, however, and it was I who rose early and crept into a little closet, mostly filled with wool and potatoes, which I used as my dressing room.

In Melipilla Freddie and I caused universal curiosity among the common populace: I because my black cap and dress decided them that I was a nun of a foreign order, Freddie because his golden locks and bright complexion caused deep admiration. *'Que rubio!'* they exclaimed, as the poor child tried to brush off their attentions. It made me think, of course, of that other *'rubio'*. How I hoped a letter would await me in Santiago!

Each day we rode at least fifty miles until, on our final day, disaster struck. I burst a blood vessel, not large, but enough to make it impossible to me to ride the good Fritz at our usual pace.

Encouragingly, we were only ten leagues from Santiago. Freddie was overcome—not wishing, I may assume, to return his charge in a winding sheet; my Chilean companions brought water flavoured with orange peel, then offered to ride ahead to order a carriage.

As I half lay on a rug, surrounded by all the beauties of nature, and flocks of birds above my head, I pronounced (untruthfully, since I had no wish to die), 'If this is to be my last ride out among the works of God, it will only soothe and comfort me, for I can think more easily than most of my

165

end, detached as I am now from all kindred.'

This grand philosophy agitated Freddie further. Both he and the kind Chileans declared themselves my kindred.

So we rode slowly to Santiago. One attack followed another. I coughed blood. I gasped for breath. A few miles from the city Dr Craig, who happened to be visiting, rode out to meet me. I grasped his hand as at a lifeline. We arrived at Santiago, I was carried to my bedroom in the Cotapos house, and there, in a bundle of letters, was one from His Lordship.

CHAPTER SIXTEEN

The first letter I opened, however, was from my cousin Glennie.

'Oh, no! Please not!' I must have cried out, or something similar, because the youngest Cotapos burst into the room and wiped the tears from my cheeks with their soft little hands, then sat on either side of me with pity in their round dark eyes.

For a moment I imagined what it would have been to have such daughters myself. A moment later, I told them the truth: my young cousin had fallen sick, been brought off the *Doris*, which had recently arrived in Valparaíso, and carried to my home in the Almendral where every day the worst was feared.

Naturally, prayers to the good Dios and His Holy Mother followed, but in this case I could not regret even the most extravagant language and watched calmly as they concluded solemnly, '*En el nombre*

166

del Padre y del Hijo y del Espíritu Santo.' Glennie and I, suffering from the same sickness, needed every bit of help the heavens could provide. Most of all I bewailed the bad luck that meant I could not go to him immediately.

After my guardian angels had left me to rest in the dim quietness of my room, I turned to my other letters.

I had not noticed the envelope from Lord Cochrane because it had been placed, as if with a reverent purpose, in a separate place. The message, written in his own hand, was short:

My very dear friend,
I am happy that your journeying has been fruitful and the supreme director, General O'Higgins—a man with heavy responsibilities—as kind to you as you deserve.

If you are still inclined to visit Chile's south I suggest that, instead of making the very long journey by land—many hundreds of miles—on horseback—you allow me to take you in the schooner *Montezuma* when I sail back there myself.

Oh, how I railed against Fate! Not only was Lord Cochrane already in Valparaíso but proposing, in the goodness of his heart, that I should make a voyage with him. Even when I did return, I could not accept His Lordship's invitation because I must tend poor Glennie.

I began to heal quite quickly. I was not strong, but strong enough to be conveyed by carriage to my house where I might look after my cousin. The most particular aspect of our shared disease

167

is the way it plays with the body, waving forward Death, then dismissing him again, all executed in an arbitrary, unknowable manner. The cough, the bloody regurgitations, the knife-like pain in the chest are the greatest reminder of mortality. Yet one must live with it, crooning over the fragile skin and bones.

The carriage was a ridiculous piece of New World imitating old pomposity. Yet I loved it for that. *The calesa* was mounted on two clumsy wheels painted crimson, while the body was sprigged and flowered like furniture chintz, with old yellow and red Chinese silk inside and striped gingham curtains. In my journal, I wrote with novelettish pathos, 'My spring is past, and my summer has been blighted, yet hope, blessed hope!, remains that the autumn of my days may at least be tranquil.' The truth was different: weak and sick I might be but my heart burnt with fierce passion.

The day before we left, dear Freddie announced his leave had expired and bade me farewell. '*Ma chère maman* . . .' He paused, a little shame-faced for he had not been around my sick bed for a day or two, '. . . how I shall miss you! Your strictures, your conversation, your information. How will I make my way without you?'

'Very badly, if the past days are the pattern,' said I, drily, although I could not resist a smile. He had grown from a boy into a young man during the time we had been away and I knew that his most recent hours had been filled with the kind of dalliance that few young naval officers could resist when on foreign shores.

Poor Freddie blushed even more at my words but it was the rosy cheek of manly pride rather than of guilt or shame. So we parted, and in his place, prancing around my *calesa*, came my very dear friends Mr Dance and Mr Chandler of the *Doris*, ridden especially from Valparaíso for the pleasure of escorting me to my home.

Much to my delight, those scions of youth had assumed poncho, spurs and feathered hat so that we were more like a troupe of medieval mummers than the party of a sickly middle-aged lady on her way to her possibly dying relative.

'Dance!' I called from the window, after an hour or two of rumbling progress. 'Will you come and sit with me for a moment or two?'

My poor Bella was relegated to a mule (Dance's horse being far too fiery for her fearful nature), and I had the opportunity to gossip with my friend.

At first he looked wistfully out of the window where we could see the peasants already trimming the vines in their spring-time freshness. Then, seeing no help for it and being a good-natured young man, he settled down towards me: 'Do you remember our days in Brazil,' he asked, his eyes lighting up at the memory, 'when a civil war was being fought and yet you were determined to land at Pernambuco? I can remember your words, "If it's safe for the officer, then it's safe for me! I have never seen a town in a state of siege before." Captain Graham being unwell, you announced that I must accompany you as your cavalier.'

'Indeed,' I agreed, although I truly wanted to talk about our present times; this past adventure had been on our way from England to Valparaíso.

'We served some use, I remember, by persuading the patriots to release our kidnapped linen, held for washing in the countryside, to be returned to the *Doris*.' He laughed heartily because the contrast between the heavily armed insurgents and our mission to recover our dirty washing had been ridiculous even at the time.

'They sent us off with military honours, a band playing in twenty different keys,' I added.

'Then there was our expedition to Cocoa-nut Island to exercise the party of midshipmen,' continued Dance. 'Even your dauntless spirit quailed when we sailed through Mother Carey's Passage—so-called because few but birds think of swimming there.'

I let his reminiscences go on, thinking that his memories were all of gallantry and dash while I had enjoyed such events against a background of sickness and nursing, of fetid cabins and anxious nights.

Eventually, before he found the tumbrel pace of our conveyance insupportable, I asked him, 'What news of Valparaíso? Are there any rivals for O'Higgins? Where is San Martín? Does General Freire in the South threaten Chile's stability or pacify her enemies?'

He looked taken aback by the urgency of my demands. 'You have been in Santiago at the seat of government,' he answered reasonably. 'You have met the director more than once. I suspect you know more than me, a mere ship's lieutenant, putting in at harbour.'

But I pressed him, knowing that naval gossip is better than any other.

'I can tell you the wages of the Chilean fleet are still unpaid, and by some, in particular San Martín, the Admiral is blamed for every wrong, so much so that Captain Grenfell has written a letter in defence of Lord Cochrane.' He smiled. 'I can even give you a copy for he has been passing it to every man who would take it, quite like a pamphleteer.' At which he took a piece of paper from his pocket.

Grenfell was captain of the *Mercedes* and Cochrane's second in command, a brave man whose words rang with indignation:

May it please Your Excellency, we the undersigned officers of the Chilean squadron have heard with surprise and indignation the vile and scandalous reports tending to bring Your Excellency's high character into question . . .

Prodded by me, the good Dance then revealed what I had had no idea of, that O'Higgins had appointed General Cruz to supersede General Freire as chief of the army of the south but Freire's soldiers had refused to let him leave. 'At the moment,' commented Mr Dance, sagely, 'I am mightily glad to be employed by His Majesty the King of England.'

To which I made no agreement but a smile: I needed still to believe in the settled future of the country in which I found myself.

'There are those who believe Chile and the rest of South America will be great democracies,' said I, alluding, of course, to my hero, a reference not picked up by Dance, whose conversational interest was once more running low.

Outside, the sun picked out almond and apple trees in full blossom and a bee, as if to taunt him, flew in to us. 'Go,' I bade Dance.

He went with all expedition but not without a backwards word: 'Next thing, Mrs Graham,

171

you'll be telling me that San Martín is the Second Coming.'

Since my aversion to the sinuous, opium-eating general was well known, although I had never met him, it was as well that Dance leapt on his horse as quickly as he did. I allowed the weary Bella to return and prepared myself for a rest.

Our journey lasted three days; the Andes was as awe-inspiring in spring as it had been when rain had dimmed the glitter of its snowy peaks, yet my eyes were turned more inwards than out. The jolting of the carriage was no more disturbing than the jolting in my mind. Time seemed to hold itself back as if to taunt my impatience. At one point as the absurd *calesa* struggled up a steep incline, I'd have been glad enough to push it over the edge and watch it fall, like an overpainted ageing whore, to the rocky chasm below, but I would have been sad for the mule and the horses which did their duty without complaint, as dumb animals usually do. Once or twice I rode, shocking my attendants but pleasing myself in proving my strength was returning.

At last, on a warm bright morning at the end of September, our cavalcade arrived at the last stopping post before Valparaíso and there—to see me home as he'd seen me away—was faithful Captain Spencer. Accompanying him were more shipmates from the *Doris* including, miracle of miracles, Glennie, who took his place beside me for the journey back.

'My dearest, dearest cousin!' I clasped his hands and he clasped mine. We were quite the picture of family devotion. 'Faster!' I called, to our phlegmatic coachman. 'We invalids are impatient people,' I told Spencer, laughing through the curtains, and I

172

felt my spirits rising ever higher. Never have I been more aware of the fraternity that binds together those who make their lives on the high seas. It is as if the dangers they face—the wild, tempestuous seas, cruel icebergs and deadly calms—make each always responsible for the other.

Felipe rode ahead, so when we arrived at my home in the Almendral, I found my own and Glennie's bed set up, his in the outer room, and food on the veranda table. There I settled, unwilling to face the darkness of my bedroom when all was bright and cheerful outside. Captain Spencer sat beside me and Don, who had run all the way from Santiago, slept at my feet. Glennie, however, I directed inside, despite his protests.

'You are still unwell,' commented Spencer, attentively, as I stifled a cough.

I glanced at him. Something in his tone and face had given me warning. Although so far advanced in his career, he was only in his mid-twenties, an inexperienced man, as far as women were concerned, and far from home. My glance had caused him to blush and my suspicions were confirmed.

'And how have you been occupying yourself since I am gone? Surely you should have sailed by now.'

He pulled himself together and the tenderness in his hazel eyes was swapped for a more suitable swagger. 'I am expecting orders any day. The *Alacrity* is prepared for whatever may be asked.' Then the tenderness returned. So that was it: he was near departure and regretting our parting, though probably thinking himself a fool for it. I was, after all, thirteen years older than him and, in our society of the day, middle-aged. Yet I had never found it easy to play the part; perhaps my childlessness made me seem younger—it certainly made me more independent.

'Oh, Mrs Graham!' He leant towards me and I saw the danger was not past.

In truth, I would miss him too. I had favoured him more than other officers; I was guilty of encouragement. 'You will make a grand admiral.' I narrowed my lips to imitate elderly patronage. (My prediction was fulfilled and he duly became a rear-admiral, besides succeeding his brother as the 4th Earl Spencer.)

'I do admire your intrepid spirit, so unlike other ladies. I . . .' he began again, and stopped. He pushed his thick brown hair back from his hot brow.

His visits to my house had most often been in the company of Lord Cochrane. Romance is catching, I conjectured, remembering those afternoons of glory. With hindsight, I am forced to admit that those young men circling the Admiral must have been aware of my feelings for their admired hero, and his, in some measure, for me. It would have made me seem less virtuous, less widowed and more accessible. At the time, I didn't permit such thoughts. I have always been good at deceiving myself when necessary.

'I will miss you when you go. The *Doris*, too, is expecting to sail anytime. What will I do without my boys?' I tried a rueful but matronly laugh.

'You will have the Chilean fleet still.' His face had darkened but I refused to understand his mood or his meaning.

'If they are not disbanded without pay. Or civil war destroy the whole country.'

174

'Then what will you do?' He was as intense as I was lackadaisical.

'I have not imagined it.' I imagined nothing further than a face with bright blue eyes, flaming hair and a great nose.

'I suppose you will return to England.'

'I suppose I will.'

He paused, looked down, pulled Don's ears with fingers as slender as a girl's. 'You will always be welcome at Althorp. I shall tell Mamma so. You will be such an addition to her circle.'

I was allied with his mamma now, in a circle, attached to one of England's great houses. He had remembered his place: the danger was past. No *tête à tête* in a rose bower could have the romantic excitement of the solitary lady in the Almendral.

'I thank you very kindly. I have some acquaintance with your mamma.'

I bade him go soon after on the excuse of a rest, but sighed as he cantered away. I crept past Glennie, who slept soundly, and lay down in my own dark hole. My thoughts were disordered. I felt as if only my will gave me a life at all, yet I could not see what that life would be in the future. My chest hurt, and I coughed once, then forced myself to stop before another blood vessel broke and turned me back into an invalid. I closed my eyes but my ears remained sensitively tuned to the sounds beyond the walls. I heard, or imagined I did, the voices of Felipe and Bella with other servants; I heard the crack of the bonfire they were making. I heard the horses, Fritz and Charles among them, eating hay in the stable; I heard Don stretch and yawn, bark once then lie down again. I heard Glennie turn over in his bed, then back. I told myself that I could hear the flowers in the garden opening and thought how noisy they were about it, particularly the great red poppies, unfurling petal by petal. I slept.

'Mrs Graham. Cousin! There are visitors. The Admiral is come!'

Glennie's tousled young head pressed close to mine. I rose immediately, called Bella and made as quick a toilette as any woman who has been separated too long from her beloved.

CHAPTER SEVENTEEN

He was shy. The great man stood on my lawn, a stooping bear of a figure, his face expressing vivid emotion—and surprise at this feeling. The afternoon sun made his face and hair glow.

'I had not thought to see you out of your room.' His voice was soft.

'My cousin Glennie is the invalid. He has sunk back as I have rallied. I am the nurse.'

At the Admiral's side stood Mr Hogan, my whiskery friend, the American consul. Maybe he had cast himself in the role of chaperone. Yet great men are never alone. You would call them 'celebrities' now. Even two centuries ago their personal affairs were seldom conducted successfully in secret.

Behind me, Glennie coughed twice and stifled another. He gave a little gasp.

'Go inside, Glennie.' I knew he wanted to see the Admiral for himself.

We sat down and, in my still weakened state, I

felt as if I had not fully woken from my sleep and that this was a dream. Mr Hogan asked me about my travels and I told him how I had liked General O'Higgins, his mother and sister but had not been totally sure of his intentions towards His Lordship. (Naturally, I made no mention of his mistress or bastard daughter.) But my voice was not yet strong and soon I became hoarse. Then they talked to each other about the almost unbelievable news that San Martín had abandoned high office in Lima and was on his way to Valparaíso.

I asked passionately, 'Does he seek still further acclaim?'

His Lordship frowned. 'Leaving Peru seems hardly the way to securing that.'

'He will not be welcome here!' I said fiercely.

Mr Hogan, as usual more placating, answered me: 'General O'Higgins will not act hastily, I am sure. General San Martín put together and led the forces that won independence for Chile. It was at his invitation that His Lordship came here.'

I wanted to say, 'That is in the past. Now he's a snake in the grass, which opium-eaters generally are. Besides, he hates His Lordship.' Which was, of course, my real point. But, perhaps luckily, my throat was too feeble for such strong reaction.

Nor did Lord Cochrane respond, beyond saying in moderate tones, 'We will see.' Then adding, 'If the Navy and the Army are paid, much of our present instability would be removed.'

A diversion was needed. His Lordship stood and walked on to the lawn. He hesitated, then strolled further until he reached the little stream at the bottom where he had once cast for fish. He stooped, cupped his hand and drank. Slowly he

177

came back to us. 'This is a pretty place.'

'Spring in Chile is of heavenly beauty,' agreed Mr Hogan. 'Nowhere are there more flowering plants, shrubs and trees.'

I murmured,

'By bushy brake and wild flowers blossoming,
And freshness breathing from each silver
*   spring . . .'*

'I am glad your poetic tendency is not subdued by illness.' His Lordship smiled gently at me and my heart beat fast. There was a silence, undeniably an awkwardness. They had expected, perhaps, that I would be in bed and their visit short.

'I should see how Glennie does.' Now I stood, hands to my chest. They must go if they wished. But the usual noise of someone's arrival, dogs, voices—although, I realised, no mules or horses, made me pause.

A strange procession was coming down from the path on the hill. At its head I recognised the tall and dignified figure of La Chavelita; at her side a small boy, loaded with many baskets; behind him a bevy of girls, the younger skipping and dancing, the older cultivating a more sober mien in imitation of their grandmother. All, including the matriarch herself, were decorated with flowers: jasmine, jonquils, carnations, daisies.

I sat again and addressed Mr Hogan: 'Will you greet them for me, if you please?'

He rose politely. The approach of the celestial vision, for the old lady was like a god accompanied by her vestal virgins, came near and an explanation proffered. La Chavelita, hearing of Glennie's illness, had come to cure him by traditional means. She pointed to the boy with a word of command and he opened the basket to show centaury, wild carrot and yellow wood sorrel.

In her beautiful Spanish, the *c* letters slippery, like a young woodpecker's call, she asked to be taken to the patient and for a bowl of heated brandy to be prepared.

All the time this was proceeding, I expected the Admiral to announce his departure but, on the contrary, he seemed deeply interested, following us into the room where Glennie lay suffering. Close after us, the daughters and granddaughters, who might have stayed behind, crowded in so that their youthful brightness and the sweet perfume of their flowers filled the dim room.

His Lordship and I stood side by side at the end of the bed. Just as I had been on our excursion to the Rinconada pottery, I was struck by his curiosity in the things that most great men would consider below their notice. I thought of his growing up in the wilder parts of Scotland, the eldest of five boys, never sent to school, no mother to help him on his way. He was self-made, self-taught and still continued that process, although he had reached the heights of his profession, had been thrown down and had risen once again. When I considered him thus, my love for him became maternal and I longed to guide and protect him.

'What has this magnificent witch got in her hand?' he whispered.

'A piece of cocoa grease, I think.'

The witch gently massaged Glennie's naked shoulders with the grease, which she had previously dipped in the brandy, explaining, as a professor

179

might, the close link between shoulders and lungs. After fifteen minutes, she stopped and gave over some of the herbs to be infused in hot water and spirits. The rest would be used to whip his shoulders.

'Whip?' muttered His Lordship, under his breath, but none of us could question the majestic being in our midst.

She turned to me. 'I assure you, Señora, the pulse will go down and the haemorrhage cease by degrees. If you are still anxious, add a tisane of wild carrot, well sweetened.'

I thanked her gravely and we all proceeded back to the garden where Mr Hogan was still seated, although somewhat impatiently checking his timepiece.

The procession re-formed and La Chavelita, now wearing a tall black hat, which indeed made her look distinctly witch-like, took her leave amid, on my side, many protestations of gratitude. In an age of cupping and leaches, massage and tisanes were the sweetest of cures.

'I hope your time has not been wasted,' said Mr Hogan, disapprovingly, as soon as the last chirruping child had disappeared behind fronds of flowering broom.

'Assuredly, the lady believed in her powers,' said Lord Cochrane, smiling at me. But I could see the sight of his companion had brought back the cares of high office. I myself knew I was risking a relapse in my recovery if I remained active any longer so I wished them God speed with equanimity. There was no doubt in my mind that the Admiral would pay another visit as soon as he was able.

I was not wrong. As spring brought greater

warmth and longer days, he returned to his habit of regular visits, as if my humble cottage and garden could offer him respite he could find nowhere else. Although it was never discussed, neither of us cared about the gossip, he, I believe, because he was angry at the position in which he found himself, caught in the politics of the untrustworthy, and I because my love was far more important to me than my reputation. I have no doubt that our friendship was, however, the subject of comment, and probably the reason for a very surprising visit on the afternoon of 15th October.

Up till my visitor's arrival—and I shall, like a novelist, keep you in suspense as to his identity— the day had been sad. All the hours had been filled with farewells to my friends on the *Doris*, which was to sail the following morning. Their mission to watch over British mercantile interests along the Pacific and the Atlantic coasts, as part of the Royal Navy's South American Squadron, never allowed them to stay in one port for long. The consumption of bread and excellent local honey had been so tremendous that I chaffed the midshipmen they would sink the ship if they ate another slice.

I was consoling myself after their departure with the Honourable Frederick de Roos—dear Freddie, in other words—whose ship, captained by my (love-afflicted) Captain Spencer had still not set sail for Buenos Aires—when we were startled by the sounds of a great company approaching. Assuming it to be the Admiral, I went inside to check on the yet ailing Glennie, who was resting in my bedroom.

When I came out, the whole area seemed filled with people, well dressed and animated, whose horses were being led away by a multitude of *peons*.

181

In their midst stood a striking, tall, handsome figure, dressed all in black, a Hamlet among his court.

'It is General San Martín, Maman,' whispered Freddie, in my ear. He took a step away and glanced at me sidelong, 'He has come to see the Admiral's lady.' Freddie was always more brazen in his teasing than my older and more mature friends because he didn't yet understand the ambiguous nature of truth. At any rate, there was no time to chastise him. San Martín, who had arrived in Valparaíso only a day or so earlier, was advancing towards me with a pompous, purposeful air.

'Señora Graham.'

'Your Excellency, General San Martín.' I performed the sort of sweeping curtsy that flatters men who have risen to their position rather than inherited it. My legs, however, shook beneath me, not because of any bodily frailty—I was well that day—but because in front of me was my dearest lord's enemy, the man I had cast as the devil, expecting my hospitality.

I might have been angry but, in all honesty, I was consumed with curiosity and excitement that I could now judge for myself what sort of man he was.

I saw at once that he would not care to picnic outside so I ushered him into my living room although, since it was only sixteen feet by twenty-six, it could hardly accommodate his retinue. The chief among these was the unlikeable Don Jose Zenteno, the governor of Valparaíso, with his wife and her stepdaughter, once my cabin-mate, Señora Doña Dolores. Freddie seated them in reasonable comfort on the absent Glennie's bed. I did not catch all the names but they included Colonel d'Albe, his wife and sister, General Prieto, Major O'Carol and the captain of the port, Captain Torres.

If anyone thought to cut me from English society, I could turn for comfort to the highest ranks of Chilean. I gave up my own high-backed chair to San Martín and he sat for a moment, took a drink, then put it down before standing again in the recognisable stance of an orator.

My polite enquiries about his health—I had been informed that morning he was in Valparaíso for treatment to an arthritic arm—were brushed aside, 'I shall have recourse to the baths at Cauquenes.' He spoke in only reasonable French, so I assured him I could understand Spanish.

'I am pleased,' he began, in courteous but patronising tones, 'that a lady of such education and with connections to the highest in her own land should find enough in South America to detain her for so many months.'

'The politics of freedom have always been a source of inspiration whether in antique Greece or at the birth of a new society,' I replied, with equal formality.

'You are right. Fair government is at the heart of every man. Whether benevolent dictatorship or full democracy, we must judge each case with the attention of an eagle. Nothing can be presumed. Nothing can be ruled out or in. What is good in one set of circumstances is wrong in another.'

He carried on in this strain for a good half-hour while I was caught, as a rabbit, in the glare of a torch. His companions, meanwhile, occupied themselves by eating as many of the cakes and

183

meats as my servants had scraped up after the ravages of my *Doris* visitors. On the question of government, San Martín had the floor to himself.

When he moved on to philosophy and religion, which seemed interchangeable to him, Zenteno joined him in discounting the superstitions of the people. This might have been to impress my Protestant sensibilities, for San Martín's eyes flashed darkly in my direction. I ventured mildly, 'The Church of Rome is convinced that only she understands how the world should go.'

'Ah, then, Señora Graham . . .' A veritable waterfall of words followed, accompanied by hand gesticulations of the most Latin sort. In his way of bullying with words, however apparently gracious, he was the exact opposite of Lord Cochrane, who was so quietly diffident that, if one did not know his reputation as a dauntless leader of men, one might have considered him a retired admiral from Portsmouth.

By the third hour, San Martín had covered physic, language and disease, in which he spoke most indelicately of the human body. I looked towards the young ladies, but they were concentrating on some fresh-baked cakes procured from my neighbour.

I had more or less despaired of any information of a personal sort when suddenly he fixed his restless gaze on me and took two steps in my direction. I was sitting, quite exhausted, on a stool.

'Do you know how I understood that I must step aside from government and leave Peru?' I muttered a disclaimer, since he seemed to expect a response to what was clearly a rhetorical question. 'At night I put on common dress and, like the caliph Haroun

184

al-Rashid, mingled in the coffee-houses and the gossiping parties at shop doors. I discovered that my people were happy.' Here he paused for an eagle look. 'They no longer needed my presence. After the toils of war, of political unrest, all I yearned for was rest, so I decided to withdraw from public life.'

As he drew himself up proudly, I murmured approbation. But he still had not finished. With eyes flashing to all sides, he declared, 'I have brought with me the flag of Pizarro, under which the Inca Empire was conquered. Its possession has always been considered the mark of power and authority. *I have it now.*'

A woman in love is always going to be cruel to her lover's enemy. Now I must be honest and report that San Martín kept his word and never looked for power again (Pizarro's flag or not) and, secondly, despite everything, I found him an attractive man. Oh, how vulnerable is the unmarried lady, her antennae forever set for a mate! Derision and dislike do not preclude attraction.

When at last San Martín left, I fell on Glennie's bed and closed my eyes as if dead. Don licked my fingers, which dangled over the side. Freddie sat at my side, even he too weary for words. Bella and Felipe stumped exhausted outside, as did, I'm sure, all the servants and animals, even the birds in the trees.

Glennie emerged. I heard his footsteps and waved my hand without opening my eyes. 'They're gone,' he announced unnecessarily. 'Leaving only the smell of cigars hanging in the air.'

'And words,' I waved my hand. 'Words hanging in the air.'

'We could beat a drum to get rid of them,' suggested Freddie, reviving at the thought.

Glennie laughed, then coughed.

'Go back to bed,' I said. 'Or at least sit down.'

We were companionable. I felt the warmth of their loving presence. My dear, dear boys. Gradually I began to think about San Martín again and composed in my head what I would write in my journal. The flattery of his visiting me so soon after his arrival in Chile induced my spirits to rise. Whether he wanted to see 'the Admiral's lady', as Freddie put it, or to impress an educated recorder from Europe with the true nature of his attitudes, he had given me a fine display. What diarist does not revel in good material?

'Dear Mr de Roos, bring me my paper and pen, if you would be so kind.'

Freddie rose obediently and we settled down together, the only sounds the scratching of my pen, Glennie's uncomfortable breathing, Freddie turning the pages of a book he'd picked up and Don's snoring.

I suspended my pen above the ink pot and sighed. 'If the King of England came by for a visit, I would not let him in.'

'No one at all,' agreed Glennie, who was half asleep again.

'No one?' mocked Freddie, putting aside his book and standing up.

I did not answer. The next morning he would be gone, too, and probably should be on board ship now. He would take his knowingness with him and probably I would miss it.

CHAPTER EIGHTEEN

What political creativity there is in a new country!
One morning Mr Bennett rode up. Whereas a
Chilean rider became part of his horse, Mr B. was
like a strapped-on box. Behind him came his *peon*
with a leather bag.

'I am commanded by His Lordship to bring you
these,' he said, indicating the bag. 'He believes you
are the only person in Chile who will read them
from cover to cover.' We smiled at each other. We
had come to an unspoken understanding that he
should not notice the closeness of my friendship
with his distinguished master and I should not do
anything to bring his master into disrepute. My own
reputation he left to my own devices.

'It is hot,' I said. 'The very grass is steaming. You
must sit with me while I arrange for drinks. My
curiosity as to the contents of the bag can wait.'

'How fares the invalid?' he asked, swaying his
way to a chair.

'Improving, whether due to his youth, La
Chavelita's potions or the sunny weather.'

'Milk,' said Mr B., now seated and ready to
converse. 'Beautiful Chilean milk will cure the most
grievous ailment.'

'I have more milk in me than a cow in calf.'
Glennie appeared at the door, pouting like a child.
'If you shook me, I'd turn to cheese.'

'But you enjoy the new warmth at least,' I
suggested.

'Warmth!' Mr B. interrupted. 'You call this
warmth? You must visit the north, the Atacama

187

Desert where the gold mines are, to talk of warmth. There are whole areas where no rain has *ever* fallen. At midday the rocks glow like a red-hot oven and at night they give off an eerie light, like an iceberg.'

Glennie and I exchanged a look. Once Mr B. got on to one of his travellers' tales there was no stopping him. We called him, then, 'Don Benito'.

'What is in that important-looking bag?' asked Glennie.

'We will open it and see.' Mr B. pulled at the clasp.

It turned out that he had brought to me a copy of the newly published *Reglamento* or *Commercial Regulation* and the *Constitución Politica del Estado de Chile.*

'Even a glass of milk would be a better present,' complained Glennie.

'Under normal circumstances, I would hardly find such reading delightful,' I flicked through a few closely printed pages, 'but I have had nothing new for weeks and maybe I shall learn something of interest.'

'Ah, but you are the South American Machiavelli. One week, the supreme director of Chile invites you to his presence, the next, so the Admiral tells me, you are solicited by the supreme director of Peru.'

I shook my head, smiling. 'San Martín is a common man now, if we are to believe his story, while Machiavelli had power and I have as little of that slippery commodity as the bee I can see settling on a flower behind your head.'

'You have given yourself away entirely, my dear Mrs Graham.' Mr B.'s ready enthusiasm was rising again. 'What does a bee do but pollinate the garden

188

as it flies from bloom to bloom? Of all the creatures in the garden the bee is the most powerful.'

When Mr B. had left, being hoisted on to his horse by his patient *peon* (it was extraordinary to think he had travelled all over Chile in this way), I turned my attention to the papers. Three points stood out: the minimum age for electors was twelve years, the government was determined to stop all or most imports from foreign countries, and O'Higgins proposed to give himself twelve more years of rule. Taking the second point, I addressed Glennie: 'A young country can never afford to do without civilising articles from the old.' He turned tail at my lecturing tone.

The want of intelligent company was already wearing away my patience. I could not hide from myself that, by pinning my colours to the Admiral's mast, I had severely limited the number of engagements at which I would be welcome. They were, in ordinary times, not the sort of engagements I would miss, but with the majority of my naval friends sailed to sea, my circle was diminished almost to nothing.

Since His Lordship did not visit that day, I was able to feel thoroughly sorry for myself and also to get to know the *Reglamento* and the *Constitución* in as much detail as the director himself, information, interspersed with my own views, that I shared with the unlucky readers of my journal.

The rest of the evening I spent reading aloud *Paradise Lost* to Glennie, whose speedy improvement might have yet another reason in his need to avoid my poetic ministrations.

How can I live without thee? how forgo

189

Thy sweet converse and love so dearly joined,
To live again in these wild woods forlorn.

The next morning, the sun rose so strong that I put Glennie outside in the shade and went for a walk before the atmosphere became uncomfortable. Felipe came with me, carrying a chair and my painting equipment in case I should find a suitable view. I soon decided to draw a vista down towards Valparaíso Bay and had just sketched in some fresh green vines climbing over a support of stakes when His Lordship and Captain Crosbie came riding up the path. Since I was above them, I watched as they turned into the yard behind the house.

'Direct the gentlemen as to where I am,' I told Felipe, who set off right away. I continued to sketch, thus composing myself into a happy humour.

The truth was that San Martín's visit to me had exceedingly provoked His Lordship. After all, he himself had sworn never to be in the same room with him lest their combative feelings towards each other could not be contained. To make matters worse, the Admiral had not openly rebuked me but shown his disapproval only too clearly in his coldness and the brevity of his visit. It was no mere chance that he had not arrived yesterday but sent up a bagful of documents.

He came towards me walking slowly, his face clouded. There was no sign of Crosbie. I determined to have all in the open as soon as he was near enough.

'Good morning, sir. I fear I have only one chair.'

He did not answer this but stared gloomily at the beginnings of my picture. (It ended up very

190

charming.) 'You should put a ship in the bay.'

'Your ship, my lord?'

'What ship is that?' He turned away and began to beat an inoffensive clump of daisies with his crop.

'You are angry with me because I received General San Martín.'

He increased the vigour of his beating. 'Women are all the same. They wish to dance attendance on anyone who is famous, however tawdry and unworthy the person may be.' He still kept his back to me. 'They are like butterflies drawn to the brightest lights, without the will to resist.'

No sensible man, least of all His Lordship, could liken me to a butterfly, so I began to suspect his mood owed less to politics and more to his marital situation. Kitty Cochrane could certainly be likened to a butterfly.

'Women must often live their lives through men,' I ventured, as humbly as I could, 'but that does not mean they cannot discern the difference between good and bad, between a noble man and a charlatan.'

He looked at me then. 'You are referring to General San Martín?'

'I am.' I laid down my pencil, which I'd been holding poised all the while. 'I am a writer. I must think of my readers and, for their benefit, meet those who, in other circumstances, I might avoid.'

At these words, I saw the look of surprise that attended any mention I made of being a writer. It was not in his nature or background to take seriously such a description of the widow of a naval captain, but he took me seriously so it caused him some confusion, mostly resolved by his forgetting the fact as soon as possible. There was no point in pursuing the issue, so I smiled as loving women have to their men down the ages, and asked the age old question: 'Do you forgive me?'

He did forgive me because suddenly there was nothing to forgive. Regardless of who might come upon us, he took me in his arms and pressed me to his strongly beating heart. Above our heads, little scarlet birds twittered and danced. I do not hesitate to state that love filled both our hearts.

Later I asked, with as calm a voice as I could command, 'Are your plans for the future any further advanced?'

He answered, in a mechanical way, 'I go to Quintero, then to Santiago. I believe arrangements to pay the squadron are at last moving forward.'

I took His Lordship's arm and we wandered slowly back to the house, Felipe following with my equipment. We found Glennie and Crosbie playing chess on a table brought out to the lawn. Although they squabbled like children, over 'piece touched, piece played' or the time taken for thought, it was a pretty scene and I took up my sketchpad again.

His Lordship found his chair on the veranda and watched us through half-closed eyes. Don, a very sentimental dog, laid his enormous head on his master's lap and drooled contentedly. I could willingly have done the same.

'Come, Crosbie, tell us all the gossip of the port.' Glennie pushed aside the chessboard.

'Aha! The gossip that matters most. Miss H. has been jilted by Captain R. although some doubt he ever intended to marry her. Mr Hoseason's butcher has complained of unpaid bills and the quality of his dinners has decreased so much that his guests scarcely make double figures. Don Jose

Zenteno's daughter is to be confined shortly but her husband has been at sea for nearly a year. One of Mr Hogan's whalers went down in the Magellan Strait, and a new fashion for posies, made not from flowers but from stems of the strawberry plant, has taken Valparaíso by storm.' He sat back complacently.

'Now we are quite up to date.' I smiled. 'But I'm sorry for Mr Hogan's ship. Were many lost?'

'Don't be sorry, dear madam, for I made that bit up.'

Glennie began to laugh.

'Then how much of your gossip is the truth?' I asked severely.

'That sounds like a philosophical question. I felt you needed a hint of death and destruction to sharpen the palate.'

'Do all Irishmen tell tales as you do?' asked Glennie admiringly.

'We like to entertain.'

'And have the wit to do so,' I added.

After this silly conversation, during which I finished my sketch, I went to sit by His Lordship. He asked my opinion of the documents he'd sent with Mr Bennett. 'I would that they serve the cause of freedom,' he said. 'Because I am ignobly treated, it does not follow that good may not arise from this newly created democracy. But I do not think General Freire will accept O'Higgins's extended period as director.'

'I thought the same.' I knew that 'ignobly' had arisen because, although he was more certain of payment for the fleet, his own claim for prize money seemed ever less likely to be answered. It was best to say nothing.

'I have a letter from Tunbridge Wells,' he began again. 'From Lady Cochrane. She is proposing to take ship and come here, bringing Eliza, our young daughter.'

I felt the colour draining from my cheeks. It was some consolation that he looked less than overjoyed at the prospect.

'She will need time to make all the arrangements necessary,' he added.

I believe Lord Cochrane gave me that information as an instinctively honourable man. I gazed at him and saw the man I loved and respected struggling to avoid confrontation with a reality that must hurt his conscience.

'It is brave of her with so young a child.' I held his gaze.

'I do not advise it.'

'But Lady Cochrane is a courageous woman.'

'She is.'

There was nothing more to be said. Maybe she would come. Maybe she would not. The sea voyage would take several months. I pictured, with shameful satisfaction, the icebergs circling Cape Horn like knife-edged sentinels, the stormy winds that hurled against the rigging like the giant exhalations of hell, the waves that rose up in mountain peaks and crushed as they fell.

'I wonder,' said His Lordship, with the tentative expression on his face that particularly touched my heart, 'whether you and your invalid might enjoy the greater space and comforts of Quintero. The house is further advanced than it was on your short visit with Mr and Mrs Miers. A woman's eye must advance it in new directions.'

Thus was Lady Cochrane, in modern parlance,

put on the back burner and I rejoiced in future happiness.

This was not to happen immediately, however. His Lordship was to pay a short visit to Quintero and from thence spend a few more days in Santiago with the general. It was nearly a week before I heard he was once more in Valparaíso.

*   *   *

Captain Crosbie came up especially to tell me the story of his return. It was another hot day, and Glennie and I were again on the lawn but Crosbie was too much enjoying himself to sit.

'Imagine! He comes back at last triumphant— the money for the squadron is found. Zenteno and all those in power look forward to a satisfied admiral. But where is he to stay? The governor's house is occupied by O'Higgins because San Martín has taken his in Santiago so another must be found. What could be easier? In the usual way of this country, someone else's house will be volunteered—in other words, the owner and his family removed. Who would best be chosen for this disagreeable experience? Of course. An Englishman! So Mr Campbell finds he must move wife, children, servants—'

'Mr Campbell is a Scotsman,' I objected.

'Don't spoil the story.'

'But it's so unfair.' I remembered the crates marked *DYNAMITE* and *GUNPOWDER* I had seen in my bedroom at the Campbells.

'That is exactly what the Admiral thought,' continued Crosbie, taking a leap sideways so that Don, thinking it the cue for a game, bounded up and nearly bowled him to the ground. After man and dog were separated, the story continued: 'So he refuses the house or any already owned and announces he can make his own arrangements.'

'Where is he?' Glennie and I ask together.

'Camped on the beach, beyond the second fort,' announced Crosbie, laughing heartily.

'He is always his own man,' I responded more thoughtfully, although the idea of a row of tents below the pompous Zenteno's house was a pleasant one. 'How many men has he with him?'

'Well, Mr Bennett, of course. Wilkinson, the colonel, Vicente, half a dozen or more officers of the Chilean Fleet, each of whom has several servants. Then there are the horses, the mules for baggage, the dogs, the carts, all with the rolling waves on one side and the city walls on the other. "The beach is the second best place in the world to be," declaimed His Lordship—I heard him myself. "The best is the deck of a ship."'

*   *   *

Two days then passed, and since I had no visitor, save those who always came and caused no quickening heartbeat, I resolved to ride down to this naval encampment and see it for myself. Glennie was so much improved that I gave in to his animated pleas to accompany me.

Unfortunately, on the morning we chose for our outing the sun was shrouded in a *neblina*, the grey muffling mist that held the day to account. It was so thick that droplets formed on the vegetation and ourselves, causing a sharp drop in the temperature. My spirits correspondingly lowered.

'I should not have brought you out, Glennie.'

'Indeed you should. I am wound about like a mummy so that no damp or coolness may reach me.'

We rode slowly, Fritz, my blue-eyed horse, picking his way carefully as if he had realised that my nerves were fragile. What if Lord Cochrane should reject me? I had never been to him before: he had always come to me. Would he look askance? Plead business? Gallop away along the beach?

The *neblina* had still not cleared when we reached Valparaíso, although it was stretched more thickly and in places torn open to display a sunny day.

We passed along the harbour road, under the wall of the fort, and towards the further beach where the *neblina* clung more closely.

'There they are!' Glennie, who was ahead of me, called out, then coughed. I saw his hand go to his chest and felt the pain.

We had collected an escort of children, who had elected to show us the way, mainly by annoying Don and the horses. But they were beautiful, with their lustrous black hair and eyes, their golden athletic bodies. I recalled the poverty I had seen in India and praised God that even the poorest in Chile were well fed and healthy. They were the future of this new country. My declining spirits rose a little at this move from personal to public awareness.

The tents were arranged in an orderly line, as is always the way with anything under control of the Navy. I truly believe that no one who has spent time on board ship can stomach a hair's breadth of irregularity.

I fell back further, allowing my thoughts to be

197

distracted by the long break of waves on my right. Fritz, too, watched them, dancing sideways if a particular large one came near.

'Señora is well?' Bella became concerned that her mistress, who was always impatient to be at the forefront of any adventure, should be lagging so far.

'Yes. Yes.' I stopped altogether and looked out to sea. Half a dozen ships were moored, their rigging silhouetted against the horizon. I could not see clearly but imagined that at least some of the squadron that had defeated the Spanish were there. The flagship the *O'Higgins*, the *Valdivia* whose renaming from *Esmeralda* (when captured from the Spanish) had caused so much trouble, the *Galvarino*, the *Montezuma*. Like any naval wife, I always knew the name of the ships relevant to a captain's career and could tell you each engagement fought with a particular vessel. One of the reasons for the Admiral's disgust with San Martín was that he thought him a coward since instead of attacking Lima he had sought conquest by negotiation, an idea alien to the Admiral's nature. Meanwhile, as long as the general had talked, his admiral was forced into commanding a nearly endless blockade of Callao. No British sailor worth his salt relishes blockade duty—for one thing it excludes taking prizes.

It struck me, as I continued to look out to sea, that the *neblina* had completely cleared and, as if my mind had become more sharply focused, I realised I must not make His Lordship feel I had come to him as a lover, claiming his attention above all others. He still thought about me, I felt sure, as a sympathetic, educated friend (in short supply around Valparaíso), who happened to have the additional advantage of being an attractive woman. The intimacies that passed between us he disguised from himself—just as a man will beat his wife and honestly deny it in the morning.

I must not pull aside the veils of disguise he had woven around us or I might lose him for ever. I immediately resolved to state as the main reason for my arrival my determination to pay a call on the director, O'Higgins.

Clipping Fritz with my heels so that he set off at a sudden canter, rousing a claque of seagulls that had been floating idly at the edge of the sea, I headed for the tents. A woman in my position is always wise to confront fears and form a plan of action to counteract them. Yet nothing could have been more open and friendly than His Lordship's welcome. Glennie, too pale in the face for comfort, was already resting on a day-bed when I entered the Admiral's tent. Servants and young officers scurried about, taking our horses, bringing drinks. Don, thoroughly overexcited by the many men and animals, tried to lap at his master's face with his great tongue so that he had to be led away by Captain Crosbie.

'Even the dumb beasts wish to express their love to you,' I said, smiling, to the Admiral.

'If only the talking variety were as partisan. I fear O'Higgins believes I wish to sign up with General Freire, who may yet threaten the new government and constitution by a rising from the south. He calls the constitution "a monstrous foetus". I have fought alongside the general. He is an able soldier and a good man. But when have I ever been disloyal to those under whose flag I have taken command?' His voice rose, and he began to stride up and down

199

the small tent so that I worried his huge frame might burst through the canvas. 'San Martín once tried to turn me to Peru and discovered that I am, and will always remain, true to the democratic government of Chile. Disloyalty is not in the heart of a Dundonald!'

Captain Crosbie, having delivered Don into captivity, appeared at the opening of the tent and, then, seeing the way the wind was blowing, beat an ignoble retreat.

I, to the contrary, felt privileged to see His Lordship in his true colours for I had always been aware that when he came to visit me he had determined to put himself off duty. However, like a whirlwind that blew hard and then passed, he recollected himself suddenly and stopped both pacing and speech. The canvas seemed to deflate and hang more calmly.

'You do not need to hear this, dear madam.'

'But I do.' I stood facing him and noticed, with love and concern, his bloodshot eyes and red complexion. 'A friend must always hear what troubles a friend. Otherwise what use is she?'

He did not argue with this but turned and called sharply, 'Crosbie!' When no Crosbie appeared, he addressed a young officer who had been hovering nervously, like a midshipman at his first cannonade. 'Tea. Cakes. Tell the cook we have company.' He turned to me. 'Will you have anything stronger?'

Thus was social intercourse resumed. I set myself in the chair indicated and His Lordship, still fighting a certain impatience, subsided on to a bench, which creaked in justifiable protest.

'This is your chair,' I suggested.

'No. No. I will stand in a moment. There is much

to do. But I'm glad to see you. Very glad.' He paused. 'At least I must be pleased that my efforts to have my squadron paid will be rewarded shortly. *They* are rewarded. Hah.'

As tea was served, laced with 'something stronger', I considered whether my proposal to visit the director was likely to provoke another explosion. But I have never been one to duck under the guns.

'I'm hoping to pay a call on the director.'

'You are? Visiting O'Higgins.' As promised, he stood up, appeared to look for something—perhaps his hat: his hair was uncovered and only loosely tied back.

'With your permission, I might mention my view of your utter loyalty to the Chilean government. General O'Higgins appears to listen to what I have to say. He was educated in Richmond, you know, where I also was educated, and he became acquainted with my uncle, the King's surgeon, Sir David Dundas.'

His Lordship appeared flummoxed at this and perched himself again, frowning.

From the day-bed, Glennie cleared his throat, coughed, sipped tea and coughed again. Everyone looked in his direction. I went over and crouched beside him.

His Lordship wore the kindly look of a good commander. 'Your cousin may rest here while you are engaged with the director.'

So my mission, as it had now become, was given the Admiral's approval. It was true that my second and third visits to O'Higgins, while in Santiago, had been warmer than the first. I had spent the day at his country estate and talked of European politics, which interested him enormously. It was, however, strange to me that the reason he was in Valparaíso was, apparently, because San Martín was installed at Government House in Santiago. It was supposed to be only a brief stay before his retirement but it was often difficult to know what to believe in Chilean politics.

'When do you plan to take your cousin to Quintero?' His Lordship patted Glennie's shoulder.

'As soon as can be arranged.'

'Don't look to my companionship.' The darkness clouded the Admiral's face again. 'How I long to leave this damned bear-garden to join you and other civilised people!' As he finished speaking, in a waspish, carping tone, three men came through the flap in the tent: Mr Bennett, Dr Craig and Colonel Don Fausto.

'There are never such good men!' The Admiral welcomed them as if the sight of his friends restored his faith in a benign world.

'Mrs Graham.' They came to me and Glennie with kind greetings, and I felt the atmosphere in the tent change. Crosbie entered behind them, with my young painting student, Vicente. It seemed that His Lordship, a man of supreme determination on the deck of a ship, needed close support when away from it.

'How about it, Craig, Bennett, Colonel? What do you say to escorting Mrs Graham and her cousin to Quintero? By the look of this young fellow, they need a doctor.'

'But they cannot leave you alone!' I cried.

'Am I a child who needs nursemaids?' His Lordship was laughing at me. I blushed and could hardly meet his eyes for what he had said was so

202

near to my idea of him. He relented, and turned back to his friends. 'It is true I cannot spare quite yet Mr Bennett or Mr Crosbie but the rest of you shall go with my blessing. God willing, it will not be long before I follow you.'

With this venture so happily under discussion, I began to wish I had not proposed my visit to the director but I could not make myself a liar. Leaving Glennie surrounded by the friends I would have stayed with myself, I set off, accompanied by the excellent Dr Craig. He had helped to look after me when I had been in Santiago and now was there to help me again.

A lively, sinewy man, he set off at a canter along the beach while I followed more slowly. However, I caught up quickly enough because Fritz shook his big head and would not be contained.

'You have recovered well,' said Dr Craig, approvingly.

'The weather is so lovely now. Only I pray for no *neblinas*. I believe it is the cold mist that made Glennie cough. The air and peace of Quintero will be restorative.'

He gave me a shrewd look, his eyes, in his sallow face, penetrating. 'His Lordship will be pleased to have company.'

'When he comes. Yes. It is hard for him without wife and children. He tells me they are on their way.'

Both of us looked seawards, as if picturing the long journey between here and England. We advanced off the beach to the main road of the port.

'I'm beginning to hope,' I said, 'that the director is away from home.'

'I am sure his mother or sister will receive you.'

'If they have come to Valparaíso with him, I suppose they will.' I saw there was little chance of escape and pushed Fritz faster. Yet I had been so long away from Valparaíso that I enjoyed the shop fronts, with brightly coloured rugs and garments hanging or patterned china and gleaming brass kettles. Even the simple earthenware pots looked bright in the afternoon sun.

'The city is growing.'

'Every day sees new houses up the *cerros*. There is new business, new trade. It is only money and politics that hold things back.'

'Only?' I smiled.

We turned up Cerro Alegre where some substantial houses were already built with red roofs and ochre- or white-painted walls. The Governor's residence where O'Higgins stayed was distinguished by the new flag of Chile flying overhead, a wide esplanade and the overflowing blooms of a walled garden behind. Several servants appeared to take our horses and told us the director was at home.

'My dear Mrs Graham!' He welcomed me with a crimson rose from which all thorns had been carefully removed. If only the thorns of life could be banished so easily! 'I had hoped and expected you would call on me.'

It was hard not to be won over by his courtesy, which he extended to Dr Craig. 'I am honoured, sir.' They bowed to each other as low as Chinamen, and with as little trust.

The moment we sat—in the room I already knew with its international furnishing—O'Higgins began on politics, with an openness that quite amazed me. 'You know what they are saying on the streets?

204

That there will be revolution, the discontents and exiles uniting to topple the government.' He pulled his stout frame up to its not very impressive height. 'But I am a soldier and a soldier never gives up a fight.'

'Who is to lead this revolt, Your Excellency?' I asked, matching his openness.

'Some say one, some say another.' He fixed me with a dogged glare. 'General Freire is talked of. General San Martín is mentioned.'

'But he is in your own palace in Santiago!'

The director gave me a knowing look. 'If you suspect a man wishes to become a traitor, it is best to keep him in sight. But San Martín is no threat.'

'There is one man I know is loyal to you,' said I, following my mission.

'You speak of my admiral, I have no doubt.'

'I do.' I drew myself up in my chair.

'There are some who say I should imprison him. There are others who say General San Martín plans to have him murdered. Or that the Admiral plans to have the General murdered. Foolish gossip, of course.'

'They are not good friends,' I admitted, 'but the Admiral is always loyal to you and a free Chile.'

'Indeed.' The director circled closer to me, as if to assess the effect of his next pronouncement. 'Loyal to Chile unless, as it is rumoured, Dom Pedro of Brazil offers him greater payment.' He smiled, and even gave a little chuckle.

I closed my lips over a gasp since I knew nothing of this extremely disquieting rumour. 'Your Excellency is rightly amused by such absurdity.'

'All rumours are absurd till they prove true.'

I was saved from answering this philosophical

nonsense by the entrance of the O'Higgins ladies, followed by servants carrying all kinds of sweetmeats and drinks. My heart sank at this extension to our visit and I exchanged a glance with Dr Craig, who had kept silent during our interview. He stood immediately.

'I fear we must decline your generous hospitality. Mrs Graham is not strong and must make several more calls.'

'But you will miss the dancing!' exclaimed the general's sister, who was a most warm-hearted creature, although not as elegant as her mother. 'We plan minuets and the *samba* and the *cuanda*.' Behind her, the mistress and the bastard clapped their hands encouragingly.

'I fear your Chilean dances are too high-spirited for my weary bones.'

Seeing I was obdurate, they did not press me further but allowed us to leave, with many avowals of the tenderest goodwill in which even the director joined.

'You have a magnetic gift,' commented the doctor, as we rode away into the slanting sun.

'I am a poor widow, washed up on a foreign shore. A nobody can be no threat and may benefit from intimacies that others would not hear.' I reined in Fritz, although a cool wind was whipping off the sea. 'Is it true His Lordship may take service with Brazil?'

'Only he knows what is in his heart.'

We rode on again. When we reached the beach, Don came galloping along to meet us. His long body and flying ears made me cheerful again. 'You have escaped from detention, young fellow.' On his hind legs, he could reach as far as my knee. I

206

looked up from petting him to see the tall figure of the Admiral striding towards us. For once, he was on his own.

'It's a fine evening,' he bellowed, as he came nearer, for the waves had begun to crash noisily. 'The wind has moved from north-west to south-east. Most unusual. I believe I will take advantage with a sail round the bay. I've got a little skiff rigged up. Just for an hour, you know.'

It was the most charming invitation I could have imagined and I made haste to agree that an hour spent on the sea would be a joy indeed.

So it was. Anyone who has loved and has the Navy in their blood will know that a lowering sun as a sailing ship runs in a stiff breeze, with the deepening blue of the water below and the brightening colour of the sky above, cannot be equalled. We scarcely spoke. The sailors made it impossible for us to do more than hold hands and that under the pretence of the Admiral securing me against a tipping deck. I certainly asked him nothing about Brazil. A different word passed between us: Quintero.

When we parted, he took my hand again, and said, in his rumbling way, *'Buenas noches.'* It sounded like a promise.

CHAPTER NINETEEN

I am not patient and have seldom been idle but have often found myself waiting. In childhood, I waited for my father's return to me from his long periods at sea. As a young woman, seriously ill at too frequent intervals, I waited for Death to claim me or, if God willed, life to begin again. When I married, although no Penelope, I waited for my husband—until, that is, I joined him on his fatal expedition to Chile.

I understood waiting. It had made an intellectual of me because I turned to books for company. I became stoic, resourceful and, perhaps, opinionated. Never subservient.

At Quintero, I was waiting again. But 'waiting' is too dull a word to describe my state of being. I was *expectant*, full of hope. My lord was on his way. I was waiting for my lord. My mood was feverish; anticipation stoked my heart to a red-hot furnace. I felt myself more alive than I had ever been. Apart from poetry, books had no interest for me. I was active and full of energy, my illness as if it had never been. Each morning I awoke, watched Bella tug back the shutters on my bedroom windows and thought, today he will come!

Luckily, for my combustible heart, the days were full. My primary care was to look after Glennie, who was still an invalid. The warm summer weather helped, and every morning I sat him in front of the house and made sure he had companionship. This was easy because our household comprised Dr Craig, whose undoubted learning did not exclude a pleasure in rousing disputation, Colonel Don Fausto de la Hoya, who had a simple mind but all the polish and sporting enthusiasms of the Spanish aristocracy (although I didn't altogether approve of his new practice of referring to Lord Cochrane as *el tio*, meaning 'uncle'). There was also Vicente, my erstwhile student, who amused us with his youthful high spirits (he had left his paintbrush behind for ever, I suspect) and Mr and Mrs Miers, who had come to visit and stayed to botanise.

We were collecting vigorously; those magic words 'new to science' hovered in the air. We walked for hours over the hillside, through the meadows of Lord Cochrane's farms and into the dense woods where the cattle took shelter at night. When the sole was ripped off one of my boots, a *peon* found a cured hide, cut it to shape and nailed it on.

On the second morning, when the air scintillated like the best champagne, I dug up a bulbous root, called in Chile *mancaya*. I kept it for the beauty of its flower and, with the encouragement of the Mierses, decided to take it to England, whenever my return should be. Indeed, I had the joy of seeing it flourish in a garden at Hammersmith, now called *Cyrtanthia cochranea*.

Whatever I did, wherever I went, it was for him.

'Look at these fruit and vegetables!' Mrs Miers exclaimed, when we had ridden down to the garden. Felipe took hold of the horses, who would gladly have nipped off the carrot tops. We walked among them with the pride of the creator for, although His Lordship must claim ownership, we had planted them on our last visit. It was still early in the season, but we could see the scarlet of ripe strawberries nestling among their frilly-edged leaves.

'Nothing in the world has more flavour than the first strawberry of the year!' Bending, I picked the largest and reddest and, after admiring its beauty at close hand—its satin sheen pulled down into little symmetrical puffs by little yellow studs—I placed it tenderly into my mouth.

Mrs Miers watched me, smiling. 'One would

think you a sensualist.'

I sucked the sweet fruit. 'Merely one who appreciates nature and enjoys a little break from politics!'

Mrs Miers, who gave politics one hundredth of the attention she lavished on her family or her plants, shook her head sadly but firmly. 'Politics can never be shut out in this country.'

She was right. Until the country was settled, politics must determine everything, but I argued the case a little. 'Here on the *herraduras*, it is the politics of the countryside that govern the world. Healthy cattle, plentiful grass, sun and rain.'

In order to prove my point, I pulled out a carrot and waved it in the air. 'Look at the shape of this long strong triangle. Look at the uniform brilliance of its orange colour, study the delicate intricacy of its leafy top. What politician could create such perfection in a lifetime of service? What politician would dare compare his achievement to the glory of the humble carrot?'

Being the least argumentative woman in the universe, Mrs Miers made no answer but joined me among the carrots, although more with the intention of providing a tasty dinner than a philosophical example.

Yet after a few minutes, during which we filled our baskets with carrots, peas and beans, she turned to me and said, with utter seriousness, 'You would make this place a Garden of Eden?'

We were both hot. The morning sun had risen in a perfect globe and we had moved out of the shade of the trees. 'You would not call it Paradise?'

'God made Paradise and man unmade it.'

'But occasionally we catch glimpses. You will

210

allow that?' How childish I had become in my yearning for love. It was what I had been speaking about all along. If Quintero became a Garden of Eden, then Cochrane and I could become Adam and Eve, leaving behind corruption, civil war and an inconvenient wife. I bowed my head over my basket of strawberries. The perfume suddenly seemed sickly. 'We must always be aware of the suffering that fills all corners of the world, must we? Is there no place for simple happiness?' I did not expect an answer because I was talking to myself.

Mrs Miers came over to me and put her arm round my shoulders. I was aware of her soft plumpness as it cradled my thin frame. 'You have had much sadness in your life,' she said gently. 'We all admire your spirit, your indomitable spirit. Mr Miers says that, like Queen Elizabeth, you have the heart of a man.'

I listened to her, sensing there was another message here. I did not like knowing that I had been talked about, even if compared to a triumphant (though virgin) queen. She was talking, I felt certain, about my friendship with the Admiral and her words contained a warning.

I extricated myself from her clasp and walked towards the horses, which were being held in the shade. The darkness there was deep in contrast to the brilliant sunshine; I allowed a single tear to fall. No ordinary woman like Mrs Miers could understand my emotions.

Then we both mounted and rode quietly back to the house. The exercise, the natural beauty all around and the sight of Lord Cochrane's house, so lovingly and quaintly put together, revived my spirits. I sketched it often, concentrating

211

particularly on the whole tree trunks used to support the veranda and the conical tower that joined the main house. As a print it has come down the generations: the famous Admiral Cochrane's Chilean home.

Another day drew tranquilly to its close. A piano had arrived, brought by sea to the beach and then carried up to the house on the back of two mules strapped together. Surprisingly, it had preserved its tune and Mrs Miers played, often to the singing of the colonel—harsh songs of his homeland of lost love and death under a scorching sky. Vicente entertained us more youthfully with Chilean peasant songs about bursting grapes and rosy cheeks. Yet Mr Miers touched me most as he sang the ballads of Old England with melodious nostalgia. We were all nostalgic for one place or another.

Mr Bennett and I made up the audience. 'Don Benito', as he quickly became, had been sent by His Lordship to see how we fared. He had brought news of further discontent throughout the country, of a ship, on the renegade General Freire's orders, approaching Valparaíso before withdrawing again. There was gossip, counter-gossip. He was excitable and his hands flew about.

Once he had settled in, his clothes became eccentric in the extreme; on this musical evening he wore a black fur cap, despite a temperature of nearly eighty degrees, a loose white shirt, looser trousers, nankeen slippers and a scarlet sash. At other times he wore Cossack trousers and a blue jacket with gold buttons and epaulettes. At all times he made a dramatic contrast to my widow's weeds, even though almost eight months after Graham's decease, I had allowed black to lighten towards dark blue and purple. The other alternative, grey, had never been a colour I admired.

Incidentally, in the light of renewed interest in my life, there has been speculation that my favouring of turbans was caused by my wish to cover a childhood injury when I had fallen into the fire. It is a dramatic fiction. The mundane truth is that I preferred to cut short my thick curly hair and found that a turban was not only becoming but saved the many hours of hairdressing to which ladies of my period submitted. There was always something of the hoyden in me.

When I remarked to Don Benito during a lull in the music that I admired his costume, he gave me a full look (as far as he was able for the cast in his right eye) and said, in his odd accent, 'In the early years of the revolution when I was, for a fortunately brief period, acting governor of Esmeraldas, my body was painted, my head adorned with feathers and my clothing as light as that of any wild Indian.'

I did not altogether believe these stories but they were enjoyed by all of us so much that music was forgotten. 'Have you ever been in an earthquake?' I asked. Of course he had, at Barauca.

'Ah, the screams, the *misericordias* as the whole town was swallowed up! All the inhabitants who had legs ran for the hills, and those that had wings flew. The very centipedes crawled for their life.'

We listened, little suspecting that we would soon be in a position to know far more than we could ever have wanted to.

Don Benito moved on to volcanoes: 'When I descended into the lowest crater of Pinchincha, what should I find but that the great Humboldt had left his mark therein!' And on he went.

The next morning Mrs Miers, who had worn a rather *sighing* aspect the night before and retired early, set off immediately after breakfast for her home. One *peon* attended her since Mr Miers was still expectant of His Lordship with whom he had business.

'I could not bear a longer absence from my children,' Mrs Miers told me, as I said farewell. Her eyes rolled languorously as if she spoke of a lover and I, who had always taken great pleasure in the young, felt irritated. In all charity, I try to believe that the boasting of the mother to the childless woman is unconscious. But when there is an undertone of disapproval, charity can seem an unattainable virtue.

So the day progressed. I rode out with the colonel. He carried a gun but held it under his arm in deference to me and my blue-eyed Fritz, who jumped at every pale stone and leapt with all legs straight so I could scarcely hold him.

'He's not usually so girlish,' I apologised to the colonel.

'He has an intrepid rider,' he replied gallantly in Spanish, the language in which I preferred to converse.

We rode along companionably, springy turf beneath our horses' feet, sand dunes and sea to our left, woodland and the endless vision of the noble Andes to our right and, above it all, the sky garlanded with trails of white puffy clouds, like rosettes on blue silk.

'Do you miss your homeland?' I asked him, after we had covered a mile or two.

'I have no choice,' he answered seriously. 'You

are the one with choice.'

'So when old Spain admits defeat and the war is ended not only *de facto* but in the edicts of politicians, you will return to your country?'

'Naturally. I have estates, a family, although not yet a wife. I shall return a proud Spaniard, marry a beautiful well-brought-up young woman and have children. Many children and more than half will be boys.' He smiled.

In the months since Lord Cochrane had rescued a grey ghost, he had become a handsome young man with thick black hair and golden eyes.

I smiled and held Fritz. We stood at the top of a small hill and looked down across the sparkling ocean. A few fishing boats were stationary a mile or so out; otherwise the blue-green expanse was empty as far as the horizon. Yet I did not doubt that, at any time, I would see the sails of a ship bringing His Lordship.

'Were it not for the curve of the globe,' I said musingly, 'we could see as far as the Australian colonies.'

'It is a peaceful scene.'

'To a soldier, yes. To a seaman, or a captain's wife, it is beset with currents and winds, living things that lurk under its depths and great or small land masses upon which a ship may founder.'

'A soldier will always prefer firm land under his feet.'

Was it then I felt a little shudder under the ground? Or was it merely the impatient play of Don and the other dogs, yapping at our immobility and lack of sport?

'Have you never wanted to escape?' I spoke impulsively and foolishly.

215

The colonel answered me coldly: 'It is a matter of honour.' He touched his horse's flanks with the long spurs they wear in Chile and cantered away, followed enthusiastically by the pack of dogs.

I followed more soberly. Women, of course, were not thought important enough to need honour, except for the prescription to 'love, honour and obey' a husband. Yet my thoughts soon turned elsewhere. Any new acquaintance assumed I must be marooned unwillingly in this strange country between the Andes and the Pacific, as if a woman cannot choose independence. I did miss England, seeing, with nostalgia, the Gloucestershire hills in the greener hills and pastures, but that was scarcely enough reason to return. There, I would be circumscribed by the narrow choices of long tradition; here I made my own choices and cared as little if I became a scandal as I did for my detractors.

In Chile, I lived every day with expectations of the highest joy or the cruellest blow. As I allowed Fritz to break into a canter, I heard a gun fired ahead. Obviously, the colonel was still displeased. It made me smile and I slowed Fritz to a walk. I patted his warm shoulder. He had behaved with commendable bravery under fire.

As I leant forward, the tufty grass passing slowly in front of my eyes, I had the curious sensation, once again, that the ground itself was shifting under Fritz's hoofs. I clapped my unspurred heels to his sides and cantered forwards.

*   *   *

That evening the colonel and I were friends again

and, despite the disappointment shared by all of us that the Admiral was still absent, we spent another convivial evening. After dinner Glennie fell into a sound sleep in his armchair by the fireside. We liked the fire for its cheer rather than the heat because the weather was warm and clear. Attracted by the finesse of the evening, Don Benito, who today affected a Turkish style of dress, led us to seats on the veranda overlooking the bay.

I must have shut my eyes to dream the better when I heard Don Benito's exclamation, 'Just look at that show, Mrs Graham!'

I opened my eyes to see the whole bay lit by a violent criss-crossing of lightning. It came from the Andes, illuminating the sea as if it were a vast mirror. Weirdly, it was entirely silent, no thunder, no storm of rain.

I went inside, where I found Glennie still sleeping, and brought out Mr Miers, the colonel and Vicente, who whispered, 'The gods are setting off fireworks.'

'But what are they celebrating?' I asked.

'*Qui sabe?*'

We watched for as long as it lasted, a little bemused, hardly talking, until gradually the deepest of black night brought calm to the skies, followed slowly by a moon sailing majestically upwards.

Filled with awe at, and admiration for, the wonders of nature, but not wishing to leave the invalid longer, we returned reluctantly to the house. The calm continued, except that Don and the other dogs were curiously unsettled, giving sharp twitches and rolling their eyes, occasionally jumping up and biting their flanks, even though they still slept. Once Don let out a high-pitched whine.

'Sssh, Don.' I glanced towards the still sleeping Glennie.

Five minutes later, at a quarter past ten, the house received an enormous shock, like the explosion of a bomb.

Don Benito immediately sprang up and, looking rather comical in his baggy costume, shouted, 'An earthquake! An earthquake! For God's sake, follow me!'

CHAPTER TWENTY

An earthquake! All comedy was banished as Don Benito ran out of the house, followed by Mr Miers, Dr Craig, Vicente, the servants and the dogs.

The colonel hesitated as he looked at me, and I looked at Glennie, who was of course wide awake, both hands pressed to his chest.

'The night air,' I muttered, still bound by normal rules of behaviour. 'He cannot stand it.'

'Señora!' commanded the colonel. *El frío no importa. La Muerte viene.*'

All around us vibrated as if shaken by a giant hand and in a moment I heard the chimneys fall, combining with the moving ground to tear the house apart. I ran to Glennie. Everywhere china and glass fell, clashed like cymbals, and the piano twanged in discordant accompaniment.

Together, the colonel and I half carried Glennie towards the doorway but there we stopped for the veranda had disappeared. In its place a jagged crack scorched across the ground as if the silent lightning we'd admired earlier had fired earthwards.

218

'Gently. Gently.' Slowly we lifted him down for already he had suffered a haemorrhage. But we could not go too slowly for the crash of a wall behind us made it all too clear that the house, the beautiful, solid Admiral's house, was falling in like a game of spillikins.

As we reached the ground, the quick vibrations that had shaken the house apart now turned to rolling, like a ship at sea. Don Benito came to help us and Bella, shuddering and crossing herself, hovered anxiously. Behind us, a trapped dog shrieked in pain. A shot sounded. Putting away his pistol, the colonel picked up Glennie as if he were a child and carried him across to the most open part of the lawn.

There, we were joined by everyone from the house, save two, a builder and his wife who had been crushed together by a falling lintel without even time to shout.

The greatest part of the shock lasted no more than three minutes yet it was only the beginning of our ordeal. My journal for 19th–20th November reads:

Never shall I forget the horrible sensation of that night. In all other convulsions of nature we feel or fancy that some exertion may be made to avert or mitigate danger; but from an earthquake there is neither shelter nor escape; the 'mad disquietude' that agitates every heart, and looks out in every eye, seems to me as awful as the last judgement can be.

Amid the noise of the destruction before and around us, I heard the lowings of the cattle all the night through; and I heard too the screaming of the sea-fowl, which ceased not till morning. There was not a breath of air; yet the trees were so agitated that their topmost branches seemed on the point of touching the ground.

We were like a shipwrecked crew out in that unsafe darkness.

'There will be more shocks,' Don Benito pronounced, 'and some may rival the first.' He'd hardly finished speaking before an explosion, like those accompanying the jets of fire from a volcano, made the ground roll and totter under our feet. A crack, previously only a few inches wide, opened enough for me to imagine that the devils from hell might crawl out of it.

I stood up and shook out my skirts. 'I must fetch medicine for Glennie.' I followed Don Benito, visible enough in his flowing white garments. We clambered one after the other into the ruins, he for drink, myself for medicine, the colonel for a tent and bedding and Mr Miers, only, I believe, for occupation.

Among us, he was the most to be pitied: separated from his wife and children, from his house and the mill on which his whole livelihood depended, he could do nothing but pray to a merciful God that everything he loved should be spared. Even he, in his great longing and distress, knew that he could not make the journey to Concón till first light and perhaps, if the water was up, not even then.

'Oh, why did I not go with Fanny?' he repeated endlessly. 'There was no pressing need to stay. I might have gone. Oh, why did I not go?'

No one could answer this. When an earthquake

220

strikes, everybody caught up in it is only too aware of where they find themselves and who is with them. As with the death of a great man, such a monumental event pinpoints time and place.

I knew why I was at Quintero but, in my heart, I asked why His Lordship was not at my side. And where, indeed, *was* he? If aboard ship, probably the flagship *O'Higgins*, the chances were that he was safe. But if he was still camped on the beach, then the likelihood was that the great waves that followed every earthquake would overwhelm.

Almost as dangerous would be his presence, perhaps for dinner, in one of the houses of Valparaíso. How easily a roof over your head may transform itself from protector to murderer!

As I scrambled over the Admiral's house, now reduced to fallen stones and wood, which seemed to move under my feet, I offered a hungry God General O'Higgins's life in place of Lord Cochrane's and then threw in, for good measure, Miss H.'s. Who in the world would miss her?

I found my room roofless, most of the furniture smashed and tumbled as if a large hand bent on destruction had reached into a doll's house. Yet, miraculously, the bottle of laudanum stood intact.

As more shocks swung what furniture remained into a macabre dance, I fled in triumph. My friends had been no less successful: mattresses and covers, even a surviving chair for Glennie, were being carried out, as if the roarings and rumblings were no greater threat than someone else's tumbrel crossing cobblestones.

We collected together and found ourselves camped under a clear moonlit sky. Poor Miers, alone, stood, waiting impatiently for the first light to show behind the mountains.

I was tending Glennie when a new wave of subterranean fury woke anyone who was dozing and caused the domestic animals to break loose. The dogs, who were already with us, shivering and fearful, were joined by the horses, including my Charles and dear blue-eyed Fritz. He found me out at once and stood shaking all over with his head lowered towards me.

'Even the beasts come to us for comfort,' I whispered to Don Benito.

'They imagine we are masters of the universe.'

I could not resist the question closest to my heart. 'Do you expect your master, the Admiral, to be safe?'

His long, pale face expressed surprise. 'He is a seaman,' he said, 'a warrior.' He paused. 'He will be on board ship. A ship can ride the waves.'

His certainty was reassuring but I tested him further. 'All will be darkness and turmoil—'

He cut me off, 'When is life not darkness and turmoil?'

Along with the roaring sounds of the wild earth, I was becoming aware of a different disturbance nearby: a snorting and snuffling, a squeaking and squealing, a heavy body rolling. In the moonlit darkness, I peered nervously. What new danger threatened? As the eerie noises continued, I approached cautiously and found myself within a foot of the sow, which had come to us for company. Now she had more than enough of that: around her prone body were six or seven piglets and she was still giving birth!

Don Benito joined me and we stood together looking down.

'Mother Nature at her most efficient,' he said.

'I can hardly count, she has so many.'

'And the pigs shall inherit the earth.' Don Benito seemed truly admiring.

'But what an earth to inherit!'

Another loud crack, as if the dark forces under our feet cracked a whip at the more creative side of Nature, made us jump. I felt Don's wet nose pressing at my hand.

'Thirteen,' pronounced Don Benito. 'An unlucky number for any family.'

I turned away. Now I, too, like Mr Miers, waited urgently for the dawn.

* * *

But what a sight met our eyes as a ghostly light illuminated twisted trees, their roots exposed, like a lifted skirt, the ground scored across by deep and jagged cracks, buildings broken into ungainly pieces. Yet the sky and the sea were beautiful as ever and the dew sparkled on the grass.

'Farewell, Mrs Graham.' Mr Miers, already on horseback, came to me. His mare sidled skittishly, rolling her eyes. 'I shall send a messenger with news.' His voice faltered.

'Please.'

During that long, strange day, messengers came, at first from the nearer habitations. Old Quintero was completely flattened, and, a cause for great rejoicing, although the Mierses' mill at Concón was destroyed, the water running mad, no one there had been injured. Rumour, as ever, flew faster than messengers: Valparaíso was smashed to pieces and engulfed by the sea. The English community had been wiped out, although that was quickly amended: a dozen or so killed but most survived. Santiago was hit less badly but a beam had fallen on San Martín's head. (This turned out to be wishful thinking.) General O'Higgins was safe and had watched the destruction of Valparaíso from a shepherd's hut at the top of the mountain, having been forewarned and wafted there by a friendly angel.

Messages about the Admiral seemed more likely: he had been dining on board ship when the earthquake struck but he and his officers had immediately thrown themselves into a boat to go to the aid of those in Valparaíso and found themselves carried on a great wave to the middle of the city. There, they busied themselves in rescue missions of every sort. In fact, Lord Cochrane had been O'Higgins's guardian angel: he it was who had rescued him and installed the general, with his family, in a tent on the mountain.

The seamen feared an even more desperate surge of water but strangely this never happened. Instead the sea receded, leaving rocks on its bed exposed by four feet or more.

As news came in, the earthquake continued to plague us with sudden sharp explosions, followed by lengthy undulations and vibrations. Only the piglets played happily, their gravest danger being the crevices in the ground. Indeed, noticing their number had decreased somewhat, I assumed several had rolled to an early death—or perhaps only the unlucky thirteenth.

We, the survivors, subdued any natural sense of achievement as reports came in of those not so fortunate. One concerned me particularly—a messenger had come from the Almendral. This man, who had bravely ridden through swollen fords, new rivers and land that had risen or fallen in unexpected places, was pale and shaking, his poncho ripped to shreds. I gave him brandy and water over which he coughed and spluttered.

'My home? My neighbours?' I pressed him gently, while Felipe and Bella, as interested as myself, stood at my side.

'Your house, Señora, alone among all the houses, stands. They are calling it a *milagro*. Ah! Ah!' This reference to a miracle caused him to cry out and hold his head in his hands, as doubtless he thought of all the miracles that hadn't happened.

'Proceed!' I said, a little imperiously, to encourage him to recover himself.

'Dios has not been so kind. So much gone! Smashed! Even the Merced!' This was the fine church I could see from my garden.

'The people?'

'*Misericordia*!' He crossed himself fervently, both Felipe and Bella following suit, performing the ritual movement so often that I became impatient but managed, nevertheless, to hold my tongue.

'La Chavelita,' he gasped, 'She herself, five of her daughters, grandchildren, crushed by the great beam of her house. Those who escaped running as wild as bees without their queen.'

An icy shiver crawled up my back. That magnificent household destroyed. I thought of her welcome when I had first arrived in the Almendral, the flowers, the playing children, her long white plait and statuesque air. I thought of her visit to Glennie, her charms and potions. They had not saved her.

The litany of death continued, the surprise escapes—one had left his home to recapture a goat and found, on his return, his wife and children lost under the walls of his house but his baby chortling under a table.

While Bella wailed, the messenger told me more. My house, he said, was no longer mine, for since it was one of the very few left standing my landlord planned to rent it to someone more needy.

'My possessions are there,' I responded, without panic, for I saw this was how the world was. My poor messenger needed food, but even as I sent Bella into the shattered house for provisions, a new series of explosions, followed by a horrid underground sensation as if the layers of the earth fought against each other, made us clutch whatever was nearest, in my case dear Don Benito, who had just appeared to talk about His Lordship's papers. I almost laughed at his screwed-up face as his willowy body attempted to support mine.

The long day turned to another breathless night with periodic seizures as if an animal writhed under our feet. The next morning the head gardener, Don Rafael, arrived with his two grown sons and his wife, whose arm had been crushed. I dressed it as best I could. The men stayed to help us construct a shelter as news was brought of ever more desperate events: the towns of Casablanca, Melipilla, which I had so admired, and Illapel in ruins.

'As soon as the shocks diminish,' I told Don Benito, as we stood together watching the men carrying loads of sappy branches, 'I shall ride to my house and find my things.'

'Ah,' he said wisely. 'Your books.'

Neither of us referred to the fact that, if I

226

reached as far as the Almendral, I should certainly carry on to Valparaíso where Don Benito's employer, and my lord, was employed on heroic deeds. These heroic deeds, I had conceded to myself over the last many hours, would prevent his arrival at Quintero until he felt himself no longer needed.

'I expect rain to follow,' Don Benito added warningly. In fact, he was not so badly off because the little conical study where he worked was built independently of the house and still stood.

'You have your work,' I said, 'and I have my Byron with me. This morning, I found it and read to Glennie.' I took the volume from my pocket. He looked at once more cheerful for, like me, he lived by stories and the imagination.

'Come, read a passage.'

We settled on either end of a bench liberated from the house and I began at once:

'*Nature's law,*
In them suspended, reck'd not of the awe
Which reigns when mountains tremble, and the
*   birds*
Plunge in the clouds for refuge, and withdraw
From their down-toppling nests; and bellowing
*   herds*
Stumble o'er heaving plains, and man's dread
*   hath no words.*'

'*Childe Harold,*' pronounced a languorous voice to our right. It was Glennie, muffled in cloaks, and lying on a day-bed. 'Sometimes I dislike that man Byron exceedingly,' he added, sounding even more bored.

227

'Ah, Glennie, you are recovering.'

'You would prefer sweet ditties, I suppose.' Don Benito smiled kindly.

'Security is for fools,' replied my cousin, 'not for those who, like me, face death every day.'

I wagged a finger at him. 'So wise and yet so young.'

He looked at me reproachfully. 'You, of all people, understand my philosophy.'

'I understand you will soon be well enough to do without me for a few days.'

CHAPTER TWENTY-ONE

Two days later, I rode from Quintero at seven a.m. Those who have lived through more modern earthquakes—in 2010 my dearest Chile was devastated by an earthquake, measuring 8.8 on your so-called Movement Magnitude scale—may be surprised by the amount of travelling that took place as soon as the first quake was over. But there were no tarmac roads to be cracked apart and thrown into the air. We had no cars that we were unable to drive. No aeroplanes to be grounded. Although the death toll was great—only the *ranchos*, built with branches on an interlacing principle, survived— the people were hardy and their horses and mules hardier.

I took Felipe with me, on horseback, and a *peon* riding one mule and leading another that carried my baggage. I left Don behind, not trusting him to the dangers of the journey. The air was heavy and unsettled. Dark clouds massed in thick stripes, then withdrew like battle-lines to take up a new position.

'It will rain,' Felipe told me. 'Always after an earthquake rains come.'

'I know,' I said. Not yet, I prayed. The ravaged landscape, with its raw look of new contours, needed time to settle; I needed time to find some sort of roof over my head.

I was cast back to my arrival in Chile, alone and a widow. I gazed up at the great Andes: their outline had not changed, as if they were immutable gods looking down on us puny earthlings. I felt the exhilaration of wanderlust creep back into my shocked senses. I had needed to leave our little encampment and find myself again.

We rode slowly down an incline towards the beach. The horses were nervous, their ears twitching, their nostrils flaring, yet they picked their way delicately as stones and even boulders rolled from under their feet. I had brought my old Charles who was steadier than the blue-eyed Fritz.

We rounded the headland and followed a slight incline until we were at the usual place of the ford. The water rushed by as if maddened by the turbulence of the earth. I drew up my legs on to the saddle—the great wooden Chilean saddle, which is more like a chair.

Halfway across, the *peon* gave a warning cry; the water had suddenly deepened. Safe on Charles, I watched as the baggage mule broke free and was swept downriver. The clothes I did not regret but, oh, my books, my Byron! But Chilean mules could give lessons in the will to survive. Swimming lustily, he landed himself further down, even managing to reach the further bank.

Soon we were back on the trail, or what

remained of it, reaching first the shattered rubble of the Old Quintero church and house, then Concón and my good friends.

'My dear! My dear!' Mrs Miers seemed overwhelmed that I had made the journey to see them. She sat with her two girls in a newly made *rancho*.

'You have survived!' We embraced and I felt her plump frame shake as if under great stress. Yet they *had* survived, and the two little girls played with a kitten. They dragged a twig, then laughed delightedly as the tiny creature made a tigerish pounce. 'Your daughters are quite unharmed, I see.'

'Oh, yes!' Tears filled Mrs Miers's eyes as if the opposite was true. 'But so nearly, so nearly—' She broke off, too agitated to continue. Eventually, after tea was brought—water boiled on a brazier— she told me her story: she had woken as the house cracked about her, snatched up the youngest daughter and taken her out to safety. But the elder was in another room so she must return.

'It was like the end of the world, the howlings, the ragings, the groanings, the creaking, crashes—I expected the souls of the damned . . .'

'And your daughter?'

Mrs Miers opened her eyes wide. 'She slept. She slept amid it all. I picked her up to carry her out and, until the cool night air woke her, she only murmured, "Mamma," and snuggled closer into my neck.'

All this she told with horror, not triumph, so I could only understand by her repeating 'so nearly' several times that the shock of what might have been still held her in its thrall. Bred up by seamen

230

and on seamen's tales, I could not but wonder at such weakness of spirit, although willing to concede little personal knowledge of the maternal heart. 'And Mr Miers?' I asked. 'His anxiety on your behalf was extreme.'

She shrugged; her tone became more normal. 'His machinery is uninjured. He considers this as much a miracle as the Chileans the survival of their plaster effigy of Maria de los Angeles.'

I could not point out to such a sad, nervous woman that the livelihood of the family depended on the machinery. Already I was preparing to move on again, for Viña del Mar and the Almendral.

It was not yet midday when we reached the outskirts of Viña. We came on the low road between mountain and beach where I was surprised to see little cones from one to four feet high, which I was told had been thrown up on the night of the nineteenth. I tried to ride towards one but poor Charles began to sink into a quicksand.

Viña itself was hit worse than anything I'd yet seen. From the direction of a shattered church, I heard dirge-like singing. I rode on quickly. I knew I would get my first sight of Valparaíso if I took the higher path.

'Hold here,' I told Felipe, as I saw him poised to hasten downwards.

I stood and stared

> *. . . like stout Cortez when with eagle eyes*
> *He stared at the Pacific—and all his men*
> *Look'd at each other with a wild surmise—. . .*

At first the heavy greyness of the afternoon acted like a disguise. The sky was quiet and colourless,

231

the sea quiet too, with the bigger ships at anchor halfway into the bay and the smaller ones closer into port. I turned my eyes towards the land and I could still see the plan of the city as it crawled up the steep hillside towards the dark red glow of the Andes. At first nothing seemed changed. Then I realised that the city was only a plan and no longer three-dimensional for every building was flattened. From church tower to church tower, from substantial house to barn, from customs house to humble dwelling, all was flat. Perhaps my bird's-eye view exaggerated the situation—after all, I believed my own dwelling stood—but, nevertheless, the sight made my body feel light and pale, as if the blood had stopped circulating. This was where I might have been on the night of the earthquake. This was where the Admiral had been. Now I felt more sympathy for poor Mrs Miers.

But the Admiral had been on board ship. Kicking Charles's sides, I set off briskly down the path, accompanied by a waterfall of stones.

*   *   *

My house stood. The report had been true. Fourteen tiles only had fallen from one corner of the roof and the whitewash loosened enough to show the severity of the shock.

As I rode up, travel weary and a little concerned for my health—I must not fall ill—I met a procession coming out from my house. It was led by the fat old priest, who carried an effigy of the Virgin Mary; he was followed by two dozen or more, some with candles, all chanting Ave Marias.

'Why are they here?' I asked Felipe. I could see a

232

dozen more stayed inside my house.

Felipe conferred. He returned, crossing himself. 'A *milagro*!' he announced. 'They are giving thanks and praise. Your home was saved by the intervention of Nuestra Señora del Pilar. She was found in a satin gown, standing close to your stove.'

'And now it is my stove, or indeed my home, no longer,' I said, a little wryly. Yet I admired the faith of these people, which allowed them to find hope where most would see only tragedy.

All around my house and down the rough streets of the Almendral was devastation: children and animals lost under fallen walls or rafters, vines smashed, cows and goats refusing to give milk, fences destroyed so that living stock could escape, often to their deaths—one cow or goat lost meant a whole family's poverty.

'It's best we go to the port,' I told Felipe, after an hour or two of sad stories. 'We will pack tomorrow.'

'Ah, Señora, will you not say farewell to La Chavelita?'

So there I had to go. Still dignified in death, the old lady was laid out in a *rancho*, whose branches yet bore almond flowers and smelt as sweet as any perfumery. Beside her lay the corpses of five young children, dressed as if for a party (although the faces of two were covered, perhaps disfigured). Women draped in black prayed amid guttering yellow candles. God is more present among such people, I do believe. I knelt and prayed; young lives snuffed out without warning must always be affecting.

I stayed much longer than I had intended; eventually Felipe tugged my sleeve and whispered that the light outside my circle of candles and worship was fading. I said my farewells, knowing it was also a farewell to the life I had lived in this blessed and welcoming place. The tears I dashed away were not only for the passing of a great lady and the beautiful innocent children but also for the end of lazy afternoons, coloured by the glow of love.

The Chilean evening is a time of great beauty. How often had I watched apricot and purple clouds reflect over the sea and up to the great mountains behind! But as we approached Valparaíso, the grey day turned seamlessly into a dark night and I was glad of it. What would a gaudy sunset have lit but shabby destruction? Nothing of the grandeur of classical ruins, only the end of ordinary human dreams.

The horses and mules found their way down, as surefooted as ever even after our long journey. Inevitably, my tired eyes were drawn to the sea. There were lights out there, each ship carrying its own lamps. My imagination took me inside the noble vessels and to the staterooms where the captains or the Admiral would perhaps be seated, a glass of wine or brandy in hand, candles of fine white wax glowing golden on the table.

Although I was exhausted, my back aching, my legs sore, I became hopeful and impatient; I was also aware that I presented a scarecrow-like appearance, with my clothes awry and my face and everything else caked with red dust.

We began to see tents and makeshift tents, small fires and bigger ones, men in ponchos, men in long coats, women in Chilean traditional dress, women in European dress. The calamity seemed to have mixed all together as one, a sign of disorder and disintegration.

We reached the harbour. Even in the darkness, I could tell the sea was far further out than before. The beach was littered with smashed boats, many of them now used for shelter. Firelight flickered here and there. A group of drunken English seamen passed by, an oddly cheerful sight in this sad place.

'I wish to go to the Admiral's ship,' I told Felipe, as if he hadn't guessed my intention. As we'd ridden down, he'd conferred with several ghostly passers-by so I knew he would organise what was possible.

Peering along the harbour road, I began to discern old landmarks, now missing. It was a shock to see a pile of jagged walls where the Campbells' house had once stood. It seemed as if something more than an earthquake had destroyed it. I had heard no news of the family.

'Most of the English are living on the ships,' Felipe told me.

'I will wait here.' I dismounted, legs as stiff as a dragoon's, and walked towards a low wall on which I spread my shawl before sitting down. It was a warm night and my riding habit was thick. The fires were more for cooking and illumination than warmth.

A calmness descended on me, such as often occurs when I find myself completely alone and reliant on my own resources. I believe men who live out in the world know this feeling so well as to be unconscious of the sensation, but for a woman of my generation it was unusual, even subversive— which, of course, gave me additional pleasure.

Yet, like the most ordinary of women, I waited to see my man. It was, I believe, the eternal contradiction for the daughter of Eve.

Our *peon*, who had gathered friends, took off the horses and mules, leaving only my two boxes. Felipe strode purposefully to the beach. The moon, the same we had seen before and after the earthquake, rose in all its impassive elegance.

I quoted Shakespeare to myself and, despite everything, was content.

The moon shines bright in such a night as this,
When the sweet wind did gently kiss the trees . . .

What I did not expect to see was a bundled European lady, on a gentleman's arm, who stopped and stared into my face. 'Mrs Graham! You are alive! And here!'

The gentleman gave a choked snort, as well he might.

'Miss H.,' I sighed and thought of quoting 'ill met by moonlight'. I suppose I should have been glad of her acknowledgement since at our last meeting she had cut me dead. The earthquake seemed to have taught her better manners.

'We are on our way to the *Medway*, only a merchant ship but commodious. Captain White has been most generous in sheltering us poor homeless creatures. The Hogans are there and many others of the English community.'

I was, of course, fond of the American consul and his family, although I had no intention of joining them, so I replied, 'I am glad they are safe. May I be introduced to your friend?'

'Oh. Oh. How remiss! This is Lieutenant Tenby, currently of the *Medway*.'

We shook hands and I perceived that the

gentleman was much younger than the lady. 'And your husband?' I enquired.

Miss H. gave a silvery laugh. 'You joke. My husband, God bless him, was lost in the ocean.'

'But your second husband?' I persisted. 'I understood . . .' I allowed my voice to trail away suggestively.

This time her trill was nearer tin than silver. Then, looking out to sea, she cried, 'Is that not our tender come to collect us, Tenby?'

He turned to look and I realized, from the expansiveness of his gestures, that he had drunk more than wise. I also realised that Miss H. had played me for a fool because here was exactly the conveyance I needed to land me on the *O'Higgins*.

'It is such a pleasure to see you so well cared-for!' I exclaimed warmly. But humble pie has never been my favourite food and I saw her give me a crooked glance.

'Yoicks! Tally-ho!' exclaimed the Lieutenant, suddenly, and swayed dangerously towards the sea wall.

'Oh dear.' I cast a meaningful look at him, 'Is your friend unwell?'

'Lieutenant Tenby is in the pink,' said Miss H., with plump dignity.

At which the Lieutenant spewed up the pink with all the energy of the young—luckily over the other side of the wall on to which he collapsed. I saw my chance. 'Perhaps I can help you to the beach.'

As I suggested this, Felipe appeared at my side, like the faithful servant he was, so she could hardly resist our attentions.

We tottered down the slipway to the beach. As he felt the shingle under his feet the Lieutenant, like a wilting flower given water, stood straight, breathed deeply of the sea air and took command.

'You are coming with us, I presume,' were almost his first words and I saw he was quite a well-made individual.

'Felipe will fetch the boxes in a minute,' I replied, ignoring a gulp from Miss H.

Oh, the joy of being in the secure hands of English seamen! They came off the tender, strong, salty men, thrusting among the poor souls camped on the beach. In a trice the largest seaman, seeing I was struggling over the uneven ground in my heavy habit, had picked me up in a firm embrace. I couldn't resist a smile at Felipe's shock to see his haughty mistress treated so, but I was only too glad to submit to naval gallantry—even if it was only the Merchant Navy.

It also meant I was first aboard and able to instruct the man at the helm that my destination was not the *Medway* but the *O'Higgins*.

'The Admiral's ship.' He gave me a closer look. 'They say it's as full as ours and that the Lord Cochrane is camped on his own deck.'

'The Admiral is a hero and a gentleman,' said I, in the kind of severe tone calculated to stop gossip.

But this was an old salt, from Lowestoft or one of those rough ports, not used to holding his tongue. 'I've see him standing there. A fine-looking man, twice the height of the usual. They say the night of the earthquake he saved more than a hundred from under their own roofs. No help from his "Chilean Navy".' He mocked the words in his mouth. 'They'd picked up their pay that very night, hadn't they? Drunk as stoats, all of them.'

So that was the story: pay day had finally

come on the night of the earth's uproar. What an unfortunate conjunction!

I had not been on the sea for many weeks and, despite the uncertainty of my situation, felt a surge of confidence.

'We must watch for new rocks,' the man at the helm told me, as we sped over the water, 'since the quaking.' I stood beside him and let the wind blow on my cheeks.

The men rowed sturdily and almost too soon we had reached the *Medway*, which was moored closer in than the *O'Higgins*.

Miss H. was hoisted aboard, Lieutenant Tenby, quite revived, bounded up the ladder, and I sat down demurely. No words were needed beyond 'Thank you' and 'Farewell'. The gap closed between the two ships and who should I see, standing by the rail of the *O'Higgins* but Captain Crosbie?

Noticing the approach of a lady, he had already signalled for a chair, but as I waved he recognised me with an un-naval yelp. The chair was countermanded, a ladder drapped over the side and the exuberant captain halfway down it to welcome me.

'Of course, we knew you of all people would survive but, nevertheless, His Lordship and I pictured the great trees with which he'd built Quintero and knew they might flatten even your unregenerate spirit.'

Breathless with the rocking of the boat, the climb from boat to ship, I only gasped, 'But messengers were sent. You knew we were safe.'

'Yes. Yes. His Lordship was all for sailing round to see for himself but duty is a hard taskmaster.' Crosbie laughed, as if such things were not for him.

By now we had reached the deck and I understood fully the effects of the disaster. Instead of a scrubbed-clean expanse, there was an orderly but overwhelming mass of boxes, cages, jars, bottles, furniture, even including a large wardrobe.

'Yes. It is odd, is it not?' Crosbie saw my surprise. 'And the Admiral is such a stickler for order. But how could he say no? He himself has pitched his tent above, the staterooms given over to families.'

'And is he on board now?'

'He is, and with that creature, the governor, trying to make some sense out of the chaos. He will be glad to see you. I believe he is coming near to leaving the country he has made his own. But he will tell you all. Sometimes I believe he would prefer to be a simple sailor. But General O'Higgins does not wish to let him go. He is even more afraid of General Freire attacking from the south. He talks of civil war.'

Crosbie stopped talking and stared across the bay to the flickering lights of the city. They were as slight and unsteady as the future of the country seemed at that moment.

'Old Spain had seemed the worst enemy,' I murmured.

'Things will resolve.' Crosbie's future was, I reflected, bound up with the fate of the Chilean fleet which seemed unlikely to survive the present circumstances.

'Come, let me find you a corner to refresh yourself. You're redder than a blushing bride.'

'I think half the dirt of the Andes is upon me.'

I followed Crosbie, and Felipe followed us with the boxes. In any circumstances, coming aboard ship felt like coming home.

CHAPTER TWENTY-TWO

Earthquake under me, civil war around me,
poor sick relative apparently dying; and my kind
friend, my only friend here indeed, certainly
going to leave the country, at least for a time.

There was truth here but also melodrama in this
entry in my journal; nor did it reflect my mood. The
O'Higgins was too crowded for any intimacy with
His Lordship but, as we walked about the deck on
the first night of my arrival, his obvious pleasure in
my company was enough to keep my spirits high.

We strolled up and down, up and down, while he
answered a continual stream of questions, many of
them petty, such as whether more cordage should
be brought in from the town, but during it all he
was calm and even merry.

'They'd give us enough rope to hang ourselves
for sure,' he told me, when the young officer had
gone. 'Yet I am not afraid for the future of this
country. I have worked enough with Chilean people
of the best sort, from highest to low, to know that
whatever storm rocks them now, whether political
or natural, they will overcome it and go forward.'

It was typical of his high-minded character that
he should think of the country before his own
interests. If he did decide to leave he would go
unpaid. His greatest concern seemed to be the
estate at Quintero on which so many of his hopes
had been fixed.

'You must return there,' he told me, his great fingers gripping mine. 'I will come to you as soon as I am able. We will find you a launch,' he told me fondly—I may use that word for his blue eyes, squeezed as they were from many sleepless nights, looked down on me with sweet kindness. 'Your cousin? Is he affected by these dangerous times?'

'The daily shocks make any improvement doubtful.'

By now we were leaning against the taffrail at the stern and thus facing away from poor battered Valparaíso. We were lit brightly by the moon and the stars: they shone through gauzy clouds, which seemed to magnify rather than diminish their influence.

'You have heard I may not stay in Chile.' He spoke with deliberation, his expression sad but not stern, like someone planning to part from a beloved.

'Crosbie suggested it.'

'O'Higgins still ties me here. Yet how can I help him? Officers without men have no role to play. And the squadron is diminished. Perhaps it will be dismissed.'

'You were a politician in London. Could you not be one here too?' It was a daring comment but, although he frowned, he took it calmly.

'A politician elected by the people. All my work was to further democracy. The House of Commons heard me pronounce that "Taxation without representation is a state of slavery." '

'In truth, you have stood up for the people.'

'I became unpopular and unsuccessful.'

This was true too. 'You remained their hero. If Chile is not to be your future, will you return to

England?'

'Heroes are soon forgotten.' Now he became bitter and impatient. 'The Order of the Bath was taken from me. At midnight my banner as Knight Commander, along with my coat of arms, helmet and sword were snatched from my stall in Henry the Seventh's chapel at Westminster Abbey and kicked down the steps. My knight's spurs were severed from my boots with a meat cleaver, while some pathetic fool stood in them as my proxy.' His face, silvered by the moon, glittered with icy fury.

'They were wrong,' I murmured, 'so cruel and wrong.'

He did not hear me. 'I was disgraced!' he hissed. 'I am still disgraced. I shall not return to a country where I am unwanted, unhonoured . . . ,' he paused, then added grimly '. . . forgotten.' He began to beat his hand on the ornamental rail, like a conductor about to raise his baton. 'I shall never go back to England! I was reduced there to a prisoner in a two-room cell. I wept! A hero of the wars wept! I wept for my lost honour, for my people who had voted for me, for my family who faced financial ruin. I wept for the future of England. I turned my back on her for ever as she had turned her back on me!'

'Times change. Governments change,' I ventured.

Quieting a little, he swung round to face me. The lunar pallor became a more human colour. 'I have been approached by an emissary of Dom Pedro de Braganza, the ruler of the newly independent Brazil.'

He seemed to be questioning me, so I responded, 'You had talked of Greek independence as a stirring cause.'

He nodded. 'One may not preclude the other. Rio de Janeiro is on the route to Europe.'

As he spoke I saw that he had truly made up his mind to leave Chile and, unconsciously, I bowed my head. Rumour was one thing, reality another.

A heavy arm rested on my shoulders. I looked up to see a gently smiling face, as beneficent as it had been bitter before. 'You cannot think that I would leave you behind? The widow of a naval officer, alone and unprotected? That would be a scandal no man of honour could countenance.'

I was speechless.

'When I leave, you will leave. Your cousin too.'

'You are exceedingly kind.' Tears in my eyes, I managed to stutter my gratitude.

Slowly, he bent from his great height and kissed my hand.

It may seem odd that I was surprised and grateful for the kindness of a man in whose affection I honestly believed. But I respected him as Lord Cochrane, naval hero, champion of the oppressed, innovator and admiral of the Chilean Navy. In his world, the public world, I was insignificant. Moreover, and I put this at the bottom of my list, he had a wife. A wife, who was at that very time crossing two oceans to be with him.

I slept that night in a chamber, previously the Admiral's, with two other English families. One I knew slightly. Neither were of interest. They were distressed by their experiences. One had lost a young child, and the other included a boy with an injured arm. They slept fitfully, turning on their cots, mouthing disjointed phrases, snoring, heaving, gulping, weeping, crying out, and apologising unhappily if they woke themselves up. Yet, no friends to each other, we were all stuffed in there together until the darkness lifted. Well might we have quoted, 'Misery acquaints a man with strange bedfellows.'

But the creaking of the ship, heard beneath these human frailties and alien to them, was soothing music to my ears and I soon slept.

When I woke, with a sharp light penetrating the uncovered windows, I smiled. Despite the unhappy creatures sprawled about me, I gloated. In such a ship as this, or another like it, I would set sail in the not too far distant future, with his Lordship as captain. I dressed quickly, without waking my companions for I had scarcely undressed, and went to find breakfast. Naval men are always up early and I was not surprised to find that the Admiral had already enjoyed his jug of coffee and dish of kidneys, and was off the ship.

Mounting to the deck and sniffing the fresh air, which seemed prelude to a perfect early-summer's day, it was hard to believe that on land there were still four or five shocks a day, some of them frightening in the extreme. I turned my eyes to the town and saw what I had not seen in the dark evening. The earthquake, like a choosy master, had not flattened all equally but picked out some to stand almost intact while their neighbours lay crumbled to dust. Later, I was told it was the houses that stood on granite that had survived and those on sand that crumbled, yet it felt so jumbled, as soldiers fallen on a battlefield.

Among all my personal concerns and joys, I had not lost sight of my role as a professional travel writer. Although John Murray had been a poor correspondent, I knew he was expecting to publish my journals as soon as they came to him. The earthquake was a modern 'scoop', for no other European traveller had borne witness to what I had on the far side of the Atlantic. Every day I wrote assiduously, reporting exactly what I saw and heard.

It was as well I did for in the 1830s some scientific nincompoop named Mr Greenough made a great song and dance in the Royal Geographical Society, where he was secretary, about my description of the ground rising and the sea retreating as an effect of the earthquake. Even though I had seen and measured it for myself, particularly later at Quintero, this Greenough thought he knew better. Of course I understood that the root cause was an academic man's unwillingness to accept a woman's view—and a woman with no letters after her name or honorary title before. (Yet how could she get them?) Cannon fire was the only answer and that I turned on the poor fellow. He was already missing a limb or two, and half of his already meagre brain, when Professor Charles Darwin, who had witnessed an earthquake a decade or so after me in the same area, added his masculine propriety and professional reputation. My attacker was flattened, squashed like the fly he was, and heard of no more.

I retell this with enjoyable indignation to remind you, my readers—without boasting, I hope—that, although insignificant beside Lord Cochrane in the strange world where we met, in another sphere, that of English letters, travel, the arts and science, I held a not inconsiderable place.

Unfortunately His Lordship, frequenting the adjoining spheres in England of naval affairs, politics and innovative science (for example, the gas lamp he was working on when he left and his passion for steamships), was cast out.

That morning I stared at the wrecked city of Valparaíso and resolved to record it as one might the ruins of Carthage. But as I scrabbled around for my paintbox and paper, Captain Crosbie appeared, bending his bushy head through the door of my dim cabin. The sick child stared curiously. 'Do you wish for a companion to your Almendral house? If so, I am at your service.' He paused. 'I might even bring my gun and see if the earthquake has banished all the game.'

'Yes, indeed. If we can find Felipe and the horses, we can be off at once.'

Felipe found—on the lower deck, wrapped in his poncho and still fast asleep—only needed the sign of the cross to get him going.

We were soon on the ship's boat being rowed to the shore. 'I am sorry to leave the sea,' I told Captain Crosbie, who stood above me.

'You have the Navy in your blood.' He looked at the sky, an unthreatening pale grey. 'But you will be aboard again soon enough.'

'Yes. The Admiral has promised me a launch to make the journey to Quintero as soon as I have arranged my affairs.' I did not presume he referred to the departure from Chile, which was still some time in the future.

Crosbie laughed, obviously amused by my reticence. 'There is that journey and there is a longer journey.'

I glanced up at him. 'You will come too?'

'The job is done here, unless we wish to police warring factions. Like every man, I shall need

247

employment.' I had never heard him speak so sensibly. 'Indeed, we shall be a full ship.' Turning to Felipe, he added. 'What is that heavy darkness over the mountains?'

We were still suspicious of natural phenomena and I, too, stared at the gathering blackness.

'*Lluvia, Capitan.*'

The rain, unseasonable, if the word had meaning any more, hit us just as we arrived at my house. Grasses, trees, vines, blossoms: if they had not been flattened before, were flattened now. It was a sad sight, the whole world disheartened and bedraggled. Yet those Chileans sheltering in my house, for the English who had rented it over my head had not yet appeared, were celebrating.

'Why are you so happy?' I asked the foremost, one of those excellent Chilean matriarchs.

'Ah, Señora, the rain is our friend because it will put out the great fires under the ground.'

Scarcely five minutes later there was the loudest and most continuous shock we had endured for some time. The immediate explosion was terrifying, sending some chickens, who had found their way into my bedroom, flying to the top of my wardrobe and causing my friendly neighbours to give opposing advice.

'Into the house!' It being, of course, miraculous.

'Out into the open!' That being normal practice.

Ominous rumbles continued for more than half an hour but I found myself curiously unmoved. Ever since my conversation with Lord Cochrane, I had felt protected by his invisible cloak and, besides, I was now very keen to get back to Glennie. I imagined what such a shock as we had just suffered would do to his fragile health. Another

248

haemorrhage without my nursing might carry him away. I became impatient to pack and leave with all speed.

But the rain, the turmoil, the suffering meant that my arrangements proceeded with the opposite of speed. Mules were in short supply to bear my boxes to the port. Men were in short supply to carry them—and they had good reason: very often they were burying their dead.

On that first afternoon when the rain had lessened and I needed to get out of the house, I walked through mud and debris to the ruins of the Merced church. It had been reduced to a pile of rubble with the delicate tower entirely gone. I picked my way over it.

Around me the peasants were collecting coloured pieces of plaster, which were all that remained of the effigies of the Virgin Mary they venerated. I felt that, if faith could do it, those pieces would reassemble themselves and bring comfort once more.

I was standing aside, surveying the mournful picture, when a horse, bigger than usual, came down the track towards me. Soon the Admiral stood beside me.

'They told me you were here.'

'I am making my farewell. But there is little enough to salute.'

'They will rebuild. The church and everything else.' He spoke confidently but I sensed his sadness. Like me, he had begun the long process of saying farewell.

We were interrupted when one of the men, also watching, for it was mostly women who were picking up the Virgin's pieces, recognised His

Lordship. 'Señor.' The man bowed and tried to kiss his hand, which the Admiral pulled away. Upright, and with great dignity, the simple peasant delivered the thanks owed to the 'saviour' of Chile.

Both the Admiral and I listened with tears in our eyes. It was extraordinary that he should make such a speech when Chile was, at that moment, suffering under such a disaster. After the Admiral had taken his admirer's hand and spoken warmly about this great new country's ability to defy earthquake and civil war, we parted from this strange scene and proceeded on foot up to my house, the *peon* leading the horse behind us.

'The spirit of freedom will always outweigh material disadvantage,' I said eventually.

The Admiral, who had seemed lost in thought, replied, almost impatiently, 'Yes. Yes. We must leave everything in order. Proclamation. An answer for San Martín. I am sending a printing press to Quintero.'

I was a little amazed by this energetic ordering, but pleased to be included. 'I shall go there as soon as I am able.'

He looked at me kindly, then. 'And I, madam, shall come as soon as *I* am able.'

*   *   *

Yet again, Nature proved more powerful than any human plan. My boxes were finally piled on the quayside, guarded by several sturdy seamen for, although the Chileans were honourable and trustworthy (I found only a smelling bottle and a silver pocket compass missing from my house, even though the whole world had tramped through it),

250

I could not say the same for other nationalities, including my fellow countrymen.

Nature struck with a new weapon in her armament: wind—a harsh and unaccustomed wind from the north, which made it impossible to sail round to Quintero Bay. I found myself forced to spend more time among the shattered remnants of Valparaíso, both material and human. The governor, Zenteno and those who were rich enough to remove themselves and their families, left for Santiago, which was less perfectly destroyed. The merchants stayed to guard their wares. Among them I found Mr Campbell, that sturdy Scotsman. He had built himself a wooden dwelling in the square that had once boasted the elegant Iglesia Matriz but now resembled the waste department of a builders' yard.

'Your house was taken?' I said nervously, for he had the dangerous look of an Old Testament prophet, his one eye wide and bloodshot, hair and beard untrimmed.

'More than my house was taken!'

He seemed about to turn away but, hardly daring, I laid my hand on his arm. 'Mrs Campbell? The children?' I had still heard nothing.

'My son taken. My wife taken. Gone from me. Blasted into eternity. My daughter to be for ever motherless.'

Such was the extremity of his passion that I could not find words. Nor did he want them for he turned away again, saying only, 'I must guard my goods.'

It was a terrible tragedy for he was an old man now, with no time to make another family. With tears in my eyes, I remembered the simple beauty of Mrs Campbell, my first friend in this country.

Her little son too, with his lustrous eyes and curly hair, whose name, Archibald, she had found so impossible to pronounce. It also struck me that his use of the word 'blasted' and the strange demolition of the house might have been due to the boxes of dynamite in my erstwhile bedroom as much as the earthquake. No wonder the sorrowing widower had the air of madness.

As an effort was made to clear the town, more and more corpses were found and the atmosphere—shocks continuing, so that at night many took to the hills—became even more frightful. How to bury the dead or the parts of the dead when the ground might spew them out again?

Amid all this, the rumours of civil war came closer, the principal reason being not politics but the non-payment of the troops under General Freire in the south, although he himself was considered the worst danger.

Even at sea there was disaffection and disquiet. Standing on deck with Captain Crosbie and, as usual, scanning the skies to see which way the wind blew, I spotted a large vessel entering the bay. 'What is that?' I asked, alarmed, because everything seemed alarming at that time. Besides, who would enter an area that was, in biblical terms, a place of plague?

Crosbie hardly needed to look. 'It's Captain Casey's ship. He is captain of the port of Talcahuano, held by Freire's supporters. No doubt he has come to petition the Admiral to join him against O'Higgins.'

'No doubt he will fail.'

We motley collection of guests on board the *O'Higgins* had just finished our afternoon repast

252

when we heard a commotion and the sound of a boat arriving. A conference duly took place between Captain Casey and the Admiral in his tent on deck. As I'd predicted, the captain left without moving the Admiral an inch.

But how I yearned to leave! Nights were worse, stewing in that panelled chamber where the child with the injured arm was feverish and fading, despite all our attentions—I, too, took my turn at nursing.

In the daytime there were other ways to help: I sought out the Campbells' little Rosita but found her, happy enough, with another merchant's family, perhaps not yet aware she would never see her sweet mamma again.

His Lordship sent me on various missions, including to procure ink and paper for various proclamations he planned to print. He told me, 'I trust no one but you.'

I saw him seldom. He was busy. He rode to Santiago to talk with O'Higgins. He came back and conferred with Zenteno. Meanwhile, his steamship rusted to nothing, his fleet was gradually sent away, his crews disbanded and his officers, still, remarkably, on full pay, idle and drunk. Who could blame them? Even His Lordship, usually an abstemious man, would finish a bottle of wine as if it was water. He had started so much and would leave so much unfinished.

We sat in his tent one evening. I was half listening to the noises around us, the creaking of the ship, the slip-slap of the sea, the call of a night-bird. We were lost in our own thoughts, although I held a book. The tent flap was open and the moon, now waning, gave as much light as our candles; it was becoming difficult to procure candles of European quality.

Gradually I became aware of a difference in the atmosphere. I waited a little, to be sure, then jumped up excitedly. 'The wind has dropped! Or changed! I care not which if only that vexatious blow from the north takes itself off.'

His Lordship smiled. An experienced seaman is seldom excited by the vagaries of the wind; he joined me at the entrance. 'I believe you are right.' A midshipman was passing, and he called out, quite affrighting the young fellow, 'Mr Summons! From what quarter blows the wind?'

The poor boy recovered but, untrustful of his own wits, darted off for an answer.

'South-west,' said the Admiral, not waiting for his return. 'Tomorrow I shall procure you the *Lautaro*'s launch.'

'And you?'

'It is my intention to transfer from the *O'Higgins* to the *Montezuma*.'

'So I shall look for the *Montezuma*.' I pictured myself standing on the headland above Quintero Bay, watching for his sails.

The Admiral was not sentimental. Perhaps the only sentimental act in his life had been running to Gretna Green with his pretty, unsuitable child-bride. He was a romantic, of course—as heroes always must be.

A flurry of rain blowing suddenly in our faces, we were turning towards the tent when the young officer reappeared at a run. 'Well, Mr Summons?' bellowed the Admiral.

'South-west, sir,' the boy panted out, receiving for his pains a congratulatory clap on his shoulder.

254

I looked at them together and suffered the sharp heartache of the woman who will never see her beloved with their child.

CHAPTER TWENTY-THREE

Four days after I returned to Quintero from Valparaíso, Lord Cochrane sailed into the bay.

We scrambled down to the shore—scrambled and cantered and tumbled and raced, men, women, servants, horses and dogs—all eager to welcome the master to his home, broken and depleted as it was.

He came with a captain's command. He had brought with him Captains Crosbie, Winter and Grenfell, and a charming little man named Mr Jackson. The seamen who had rowed them ashore were sent in all directions fetching and carrying. Surrounded by the pack of dogs, eager, like all of us, to do his bidding (although they were more of a hindrance as they tried to place their great paws on his chest or tangled among his feet), he strode upwards, noting as he did so the altered scenery, the rocks thrown up, the trees and buildings thrown down.

I did not try to get near him. I allowed Don Benito, wearing that day an exaggerated tailcoat of an earlier century, and the colonel, Don Fausto, graceful in his bowings, Dr Craig, soberly pleased, Vicente, gambolling like the dogs, and the other men to compete for his attention.

I watched as a woman watches, observant to all details. (Is it any wonder we make good writers?) I saw that he trod the ground with great interest but as if it was alien to him. He did not look for loved places: the farmyard where his special implements lay or the garden and his new plantings. He did not even rush to mourn the house he'd had designed with so much love and attention. He was teaching himself not to care.

When he reached the headland, he stood, breathing heavily, and stared out to sea. Eventually he turned to Crosbie who'd come up with him. 'The *Montezuma* isn't a bad little schooner.'

'She did well at Valdivia,' agreed Crosbie, 'although she always tended to a crab-like motion.'

'If I may enquire, why did you leave the *O'Higgins*?' asked Don Benito, swishing his coat-tails.

It was an innocent question, but probing. His Lordship frowned deeply at the horizon as if he wasn't going to answer. Mr Bennett's long, sallow face became longer and his right eye headed out to sea.

We all stared out to sea. It was a beautiful bright day, the bay as lovely as possible with the white waves dashing over the dark blue surface.

'If you were in Valparaíso you would know.' His Lordship turned back to us, 'The director has placed his namesake ship, the *O'Higgins*, and the *Valdivia* under the charge of the commandment of the marine in order, as it is said, to be repaired. He plans to make a storeship of the *Lautaro*. So I must hoist my flag on the *Montezuma*.'

None of us ventured a response to this, although it was clear to me that the change meant Lord Cochrane was deprived of even the slightest authority.

'Now, dear Mr Bennett, my papers. Let us see the wreckage of my papers!' His mood had altered. 'There is much to be done and no one can do it but us.'

Like a whirlwind, he stormed us up to the house, not seeming to notice when a quite considerable shock rumbled the earth under our feet.

At the house he hurried on, kicking or pushing aside any once-loved object or piece of furniture that got in his way. He led us to Mr Bennett's conical study where he had gathered together as many of the Admiral's papers as he could.

Their owner stared with disbelief. 'They are disordered! Dirty! Damp! Defaced!' Poor Mr Bennett was near tears and we all trembled for him. It seemed that an earthquake was no excuse. 'It's a fine day. We'll get them outside and see what we can make of them. Crosbie, find Grenfell and Winter. Fausto, Vicente. Dr Craig. If I may presume.'

We helped remove them to the grass outside what had once been the veranda. But he had not seen the worst: still inside the destroyed walls and fallen roofs of the house were many more papers relating to his early years as a naval hero, his battles with the Admiralty and wrongful disgrace. These Mr Bennett had not managed to remove (or not dared) before the heavy rains came and turned them to a sodden mass. With bitter consciousness of failure, he now led his master to them. Sensible of the probable reaction, we dropped back, yet heard the cries.

'History! My history! The means with which I may confound my critics. My life! My world! My past! My defence! My everything!' he raged. He wept. He was King Lear in his grief. This was the worst homecoming imaginable, revealing to all of us the misery that lay at the heart of his every day. He had believed that these now sodden papers were the means to his restitution when he finally returned to England.

I took a breath and stepped forward, climbing to him over lumps of stone and jagged rafters. I laid my hand on his arm. He looked at me wildly. 'If you can remove them,' I said gently, but with an air of challenge, 'without the walls falling on them or on your own head, then, like the others, we can carry them out into the sun and soon they will be dry as new. Look how warmly the sun shines.'

He listened, became calmer, and soon we were carrying out the bundles.

Sometimes, as I laid a pile carefully on the grass, they would come apart and words would leer out at me: 'Action on Aix Roads 11th, 12th, 13th April 1809. Court martial on Lord Gambier'—beside which was scrawled in His Lordship's hand 'Prosecution of myself'. I knew this was true, though not legally so. He had been exonerated of any blame. But Lord Cochrane's outspoken criticism of the ways of the Admiralty had won him many enemies. Why else was he in this far-off place?

Despite a dozen or more helping, it was several hours before all the papers could be rescued after which, in a grand finale, a wall fell down, happily upon an empty space. We cheered, Crosbie loudest as usual, before repairing to the *rancho* where a meal had been set out for us.

Meat, cheese, the unvanquished vegetables and fruit from the garden were laid on an admirable dinner table composed of the great door from the house. Looking at my cheerful friends around me, I felt that I could love this picnicking, in which informality made everything simple and good-natured. I had strengthened the walls and made shapely windows from the shrubs and branches of the *quintral* so that we might look upon the sea and hills. No dining room could have been finer.

His Lordship, second bottle of wine at his elbow, pronounced that there were two rooms of the house, aside from Mr Bennett's little vestibule, that were habitable. 'Where the frame is wood,' he pronounced, patting an outlying branch of the *rancho* round us, 'it will withstand anything.'

'With the exception of cannon-balls,' suggested Captain Crosbie, hopefully remembering his times at sea rather than predicting any present danger.

'Yet even then,' said I, the captain's widow, 'wood can be replaced and put back together quicker than any other material.'

This led to a lively description by the Admiral of bringing in his ship after one of the battles against the French with only one mast left standing and hardly a beam or a plank that didn't need replacing. 'Yet a good shipyard—like Malta or Chatham— would have a ship fit again to take on Napoleon himself within a few days.'

Captain Winter, a prematurely balding young man whose pigtail started halfway down his head, then described an eccentric ship's carpenter who filled his mouth with nails as the place where they would be readiest for use. I smiled, and I thought, once again, that the naval officer with his courage, practicality and modesty outdoes any other

259

professional.

Time passed, coffee was brought, cigars and pipes were lit. The sun was moving to the west so it painted our faces with a rosy glow. Contentedly, I imagined the magnificent Andes, blushing red at our backs. Sea-birds, with their curiously human cries, were making their way back to their night resting places in the cliffs.

We would soon move, for we needed to bring the papers under cover before darkness fell. Indeed, we were about to move when Nature, as if angry at our composure, tore apart the tranquillity. A violent wind, as terrible as it was unexpected, shrieked inland from the sea, bringing with it huge plumes of sand and grit that doused us as liberally as if we'd been in an African desert.

'My papers!' shouted the Admiral. Jumping to his feet, he knocked over our makeshift table so that everything on it slid helplessly to the earthen floor.

I will not detail the efforts to save them that followed, all undertaken in a hurricane of sand. Only Glennie was exempt and I heard him murmur, 'Never shall I commit anything to pen and paper if it leads to such anguish.' No one but I heard him and I did not reprimand him because the sick, as I know from my own experience, speak with the voice of the outcast.

We collected many of the papers but not all. Some had been lifted high out of our reach and carried, perhaps, as far as the Andes themselves. I imagine eagles' nests lined with fragments of paper on which a few sentences remained: 'Lord Keith's forces being fifteen sail-of-the-line' or 'the lower bomb-proof of Fort Trinidad' or 'my services altogether unrecognized!!!'

In 1860 the Admiral, by then the 10th Earl of Dundonald, published his defence, in two volumes, under the unassuming title of *Autobiography of a Seaman*. If I had been alive, I would have advised him to tone down some of the more strident language because by then his reputation had been restored to him and he could write after his name 'GCB', as well as 'Admiral of the Red' and 'Rear-admiral of the Fleet', etc., etc. Let us not overlook the 'etc., etc.', which indicated that his honours were endless and that he had no more need of rage. My other particular interest in this publication lies in a note written by His Lordship:

In the great earthquake at Valparaíso in 1822 my house shared the common destruction and from the torrents of rain which accompanied the unusual atmospheric disturbance, my papers were saturated with water, to such an extent it became necessary to lay them to dry in the sun. Whilst undergoing this process one of the whirlwinds common on the Chilean coast suddenly came on and scattered them in all directions. Many were lost, but more torn, and rendered almost indecipherable; whilst all that remained have been ever since in confusion. The labour of accurate compilation from such materials may be imagined.

At first nostalgic as I pictured our distress and our labours, I became saddened instead. Whoever should receive warm thanks for making sense out of chaos but a Mr Earp. Earp! I could not invent such an unattractive name, redolent of an uncontrolled exhalation of odorous fumes from the stomach. 'I must express my thanks to Mr Earp, who has exhumed from documents, almost in my own estimation, beyond comprehension or arrangement.' I was hurt, I admit it, hurt on behalf of all of us who'd striven to save His Lordship's history. It is true that the dead can be hurt, and if I did not turn in my grave, it was only because my second husband left me little room.

On that Chilean evening, we were still seeking the white sheets, illuminated by the stars and the waning moon. The wind fell and His Lordship, instead of relaxing, arranged that the two rooms he'd designated safe should be prepared for habitation. The long day ended for me in comparative comfort. Glennie and I shared one room with a hanging between us and the Admiral took the other.

Before we retired, he came to me. Glennie, dosed with laudanum, slept soundly. 'Tomorrow I shall rise early,' he said, taking my hand, 'then walk for two or three hours. Perhaps you will accompany me.'

I had just assured him that it would be my pleasure when Bella appeared to undress me. It was annoying, and I noted, too, that she had the distracted, excited air of a young woman who has been too much in the company of young men. For her own sake, I decided, it would be wise to send her away; Mrs Miers would be pleased for her help.

That night I woke now and again to the twin rumblings of small earthquakes and Lord Cochrane's snores. Neither disturbed me more than the other. My kind of romantic love could always encompass reality.

CHAPTER TWENTY-FOUR

The next morning we awoke in Paradise. We took coffee in the *rancho* where the sun, rising from behind us, turned the sea into molten quicksilver with, here and there, a tinge of apricot. We walked towards it, chiefly for the purpose of tracing the effects of the earthquake along the rocks. The air was still and so fresh that after a few inward breaths we were as intoxicated as if we'd drunk strong liquor. I felt that I was *living* poetry but, perhaps luckily for His Lordship, had no urge to quote it.

The walk was about a mile from house to beach and on the way we studied the huge cracks in the granite, filled, many of them, by shining white quartz forced up from below.

'We're being admitted to the secrets of Nature's laboratory,' I suggested, a little fancifully.

But the Admiral was gentle that morning and agreed. 'At Valparaíso,' he said, 'the beach is raised about three feet and some rocks are exposed, which allows the fishermen to collect the clam or scallop shellfish, which were not supposed to exist there before.'

I was surprised he had had time to remark such things, but when we reached the beach and he bent this way and that, noting in detail all the changes, I recalled the scientific interest that was such a strong part of his character. It was a sad sight to see the dead fish where the sea's withdrawal had left them high and dry. We returned by way of a little fishermen's cove to which the men had just returned from the sea. They had many stories to tell of narrow escapes and horrible deaths during the first great earthquake, and I was surprised that they dared venture to sea at all, such was their terror of what the waters might hold, until I thought that a poor man has no choice but to be brave. For a gold coin, they cooked us a breakfast of freshly caught fish.

'In England, ten gold coins could not buy such a breakfast!' I exclaimed. It was an ill-chosen remark, reminding the Admiral of the insecurities of his position. Seeing he was about to leave the rock that we had each chosen for a chair, I added, 'As a child in Scotland, you must often have breakfasted on fish just caught.' He only nodded gloomily. But our surroundings were still exhilarating, the air warmer now, and by the time we reached the house, he was happy enough to welcome, with a bellow, the pack of dogs released from their pen, and a troupe of men wishing to serve him.

From that day on, we walked together, left to go alone without comment, every morning or evening. 'Returning at sunset, the snowy Andes was decked in hues of rose and vermilion and the nearer hills in dazzling purple, streaming to the ocean, where the sun set in unclouded radiance,' as I wrote in my journal.

In the daytime, I worked hard with Mr Bennett (harder than Mr B'Earp, in his well-appointed study, I'm certain) because I was put in charge of editing (writing in part) Lord Cochrane's answer to the defamations proclaimed by San Martín since, even now, Lord Cochrane felt the sting of his gibes. More important, to my mind, I helped write the farewell letter His Lordship planned to distribute.

264

My labours would have been lighter if I had not also been in charge of the lithograph press. In fact, it was in my room. Our main difficulty was with the ink: it was so very bad that we were obliged to renew the writing on the stone very frequently, so that we might have multiplied the copies almost as quickly with a pen.

The original earthquake having taken place on 19th November, time seemed to gallop by so that soon we were halfway through December.

Meanwhile, the various news of approaching civil war grew: Coquimbo in the north had gone to Freire's side and raised twenty thousand dollars to support him. Freire himself was marching towards Santiago and O'Higgins had ordered Major Hynes, head of the Navy's marines, to march them to the capital so that they could join other defensive troops.

Whenever Lord Cochrane rode or sailed to Valparaíso, which he did frequently to arrange his affairs, I feared for his safety. Despite his intention to leave Chile, he was still nominally admiral of the Chilean Navy and thus in a very exposed position for any ill-wisher to the government. Sometimes I went with him, or rode with Felipe. I could never stay long from his orbit. Often he brought back new strays to swell our numbers.

Happily, I had made a friend in Mr Jackson, an adventurous character who had helped set up the first Chilean newspaper, *La Aurora de Chile*. Although he was without Benito's thrilling experiences or eccentricities, he shared his love of words. We were, indeed, a motley crew, headless until His Lordship was present when we fell into line like the best ship's crew.

On one of the Admiral's and my evening walks we had strayed far enough left of the bay to see the newly exposed wreck of the *Aquila*, a prize ship. As we stood in contemplation, the sun set slowly behind it, shooting scarlet flares on to its jagged spurs. I wondered whether it was strange to be faced by the sad remains of a triumphant day, but His Lordship said only, 'I took her at Guayaquil,' before turning away.

As we walked back together, a longer way than usual, I said, with perhaps too much emotion, 'I like this wild life we are living here, half in the open air; everything is an incident, and as we never know who is to come, or what is to happen next, we have the constant stimulus of curiosity to bear us to the end of every day. Only these walks of ours are constant.'

At first I thought, by his silence, that he was not listening but it turned out my words had touched him in a way I wouldn't have guessed. He stopped and faced me, his big open face filled with the glow of the lowering sun. 'You do not miss the drawing-rooms of London? The sophisticated talk? The learning? The persons of power and influence? The bright chandeliers? The crystal glasses and painted plates? The rich silks and satins? The diamond earrings, emerald necklaces, the comfort and dignity bestowed on the household by Turkey carpets, well-trained servants and the acquaintanceship of the rich? You do not miss such things?'

I answered calmly, although he had been heated, 'I have sophisticated talk and learning here, and the comfort of those around me.'

'Yet there are some, I would dare to suggest

most often women, who consider the delights of the drawing-room indispensable.'

'Indispensable.' I rolled the word consideringly. I had guessed almost at once he was referring to his wife, the beautiful and vivacious Kitty, Lady Cochrane, who had begun her life as the bastard daughter of a Spanish dancer. (Why should I not repeat this heredity?) What could I say? There was no point in blackguarding her because I was always aware that he was a man who would be loyal to death, if not always faithful. In much the same way he was loyal to the present Chilean government, despite his own criticisms and their ill-treatment of him. In the same way, he was a patriotic Englishman, despite his flirtation with Napoleon Bonaparte and even though he was cast down from the highest office to spurned fugitive. Yet I could not help mourning what might have been. If only we'd met in Edinburgh when I was a charming young blue-stocking and he an heroic naval captain!

Saying nothing, I reached my hand up to his cheek, which was warm and faintly moist. He closed his hand upon it and we stood together for several seconds before breaking apart.

'I persist in my view,' I said, laughing gaily, always aware no man likes emotion to linger, 'that our *rancho* is the best-appointed and best-attended dining room in the world.'

Unfortunately this became less true in the following days. On a visit to Valparaíso Lord Cochrane, in his mercy, brought back one of the English families who had camped aboard the *O'Higgins* and since its decommissioning had found no home. The Davenants consisted of a quiet, biddable father, whose merchant business had been

267

destroyed by the earthquake, an hysterical mother and three wild boys. Not witless, perhaps, although they had no interest in displaying it, but certainly wild. As soon as they arrived off the *Montezuma* the middle boy, William, a short-nosed, low-browed lad, tried to drown the youngest, George, egged on by the eldest, Harry. Harry was the boy with the crushed arm whom I'd helped to nurse on board the *O'Higgins* and not expected to survive. As a result of the attention lavished on him, he was thoroughly spoilt and believed the whole world revolved round him. If anyone took him to task, however mildly, he whimpered and cradled his arm as if suffering. This was always enough to bring his mother running to his defence.

It was this unattractive family who joined our previously happy group, and poor Glennie had to listen to many of my complaints. It was he who reminded me of the answer. 'How often, dear cousin, have you told me that education is the key to successful living? You have enough clever people here to make a whole school of Quintero.'

So, there arose another tent: the schoolroom, in which Harry, William and George were taught in turn by myself, Don Benito and Mr Jackson. Even their foolish parents understood, if not the merits of education, the joy of being released from the company of their frightful progeny for a few hours. In the usual way, the boys' co-operation was procured by a mixture of coercion and bribery, both delivered by a strong seaman: a thrashing if they failed to attend lessons, a trip to sea if they behaved themselves.

I do believe the desire for learning is planted in any halfway senseate being. At the end of the

268

week, every one of those reprobates could sit still and listen and even, on occasion, take in what they heard. I gave myself the task of educating them about the world, present and past. In fact, I grew quite fond of the Davenants and was glad to receive a letter from Mrs D., on the death of her husband, informing me that William had become a notably erudite vicar, who fathered thirteen children, ten of whom were boys, Henry a sea captain, and George a luckier merchant than his father. She concluded, 'I cannot thank you enough, Lady Callcott [as I had become], for instilling in them the gift of discipline during our time together on that far-off Chilean coast.'

With order comes peace, and with peace happiness. One evening, as we sat contentedly in our *rancho*, our attention turned to how we might celebrate Christmas, fast approaching. There being no religious among us, prayers would be a mere formality. Imagination fixed instead on the Christmas pudding.

'What is Christmas without a pudding?' enthused little Mr Jackson, who was rather the shape of a Christmas pudding himself. He explained to the first bewildered and finally unconvinced Colonel Fausto the ingredients necessary for the perfect result: 'Shredded suet, flour, eggs, breadcrumbs, mixed spice, nutmeg, cinnamon, brown sugar, sultanas, raisins, currants, lemon and orange peel, almonds, rum, barley wine and stout.'

As the list lengthened, the handsome Spaniard's face grew more and more disgusted till I burst out laughing. 'Say no more, Mr Jackson, or the poor colonel will see Christmas as a threat.'

This led Don Benito, tonight shrouded in some

long striped garment, to embark on one of his stories. 'We were in the Atacama Desert,' he began, in a hushed voice, 'the temperature never below a hundred degrees, our breakfast the proverbial fried egg on a stone. Christmas approaching, we decided to devise a pudding out of what ingredients were available. The principal of these turned out to be raisins, if not as old as the ancient mummified heads found in the caves then curiously similar in appearance: hard, black and wizened.

'Crouching together, like a posse of witch-men, we poured what we had, including brandy enough to make up the lack of suet or nuts, into a black cauldron set over a fire. The desert night fell, the mixture bubbled in the darkness. We peered hopefully. Suddenly, without warning, there was a mighty explosion. Raisins, boiled to a great heat and even harder than before, fired out of the pot like round shot from a gun. We went down, as surely hit as a clutch of sitting pheasant. Ping! Ping! Ping! We clasped our arms, our faces, our necks, our chests.' He spread out his arms, Christ-like. 'I have the marks still!'

'No! No!' we cried, as he seemed about to lift the hem of his robe.

'No,' he agreed. 'Ladies.' He bowed to myself and Mrs D. 'That is the true story of the Exploding Christmas Pudding.'

As Mr Jackson and I expressed our appreciation, the colonel suggested that we might strive to find a more appropriate way to celebrate the peace and joy of Christmas.

'The haggis,' intoned a deep voice from the corner, 'is a far deadlier instrument of kitchen destruction.' It was the Admiral. When he was not poring over indecipherable papers he sat with us, brandy in one hand, cigar in the other, staring meditatively up at the stars, a habit ingrained in all naval officers.

'Haggis?' enquired the colonel, politely, although the aspirate *h* made the word even odder than it is.

'A feast for Burns Night,' said I (the only other Scots person present), which, of course, explained nothing.

'Of what is it composed?' asked the unwitting Spaniard.

'Ha! Ha!' His Lordship boomed, and beamed towards us. 'One sheep's stomach or ox secum, the heart and lungs of one lamb, beef or lamb trimmings, onions, oatmeal, salt, pepper. All these must be spooned into the sheep's stomach and, here comes the trick, sewn up with exceptionally strong thread and pricked a couple of times. If this is not achieved, the cook or anyone else will find themselves plastered with slimy ordure as the whole explodes like a cannon, with a crack.'

As he spoke with all the relish due from a true Scot to an ignorant Sassenach, Don Benito translated into Spanish so that the elegant Spaniard might shudder at the frightfulness of the foreign savages.

It was Don Benito who took the conversation a step further. Since he spoke in Spanish, Mrs Davenant was at first spared his suggestion, 'Surely, my dear and honoured Colonel Don Fausto, the Spaniards take special pride in a dish made of bull's testicles, coated with a sauce composed equally of tomato and chocolate.'

Even I, with the digestion of one who had eaten the python in India and the tiger in Africa, couldn't hide a face of disgust. The Admiral was made of sterner stuff. 'Bulls balls!' he roared, more than once, so that even Mrs D. could not shut her ears.

Not all our evenings were so ribald. Often we sat quietly, as if in a Sidmouth drawing room. However, the notion of a Christmas pudding had taken hold, and the next time I accompanied His Lordship to Valparaíso, I gathered as many of the ingredients as I could find.

His Lordship's mood varied intensely. On the verge of being released from the Chilean Navy because O'Higgins needed all his attention for the oncoming civil war, and could not pretend a fleet was the answer, His Lordship found himself straddling two lives: the past and the future, with the future by no means certain.

As we rode back to Quintero, on a sultry day when even the birds were quiet, I asked him about this new emperor of Brazil, Dom Pedro de Braganza, once a Portuguese prince.

'I am confident in the Emperor's good faith,' he told me, scanning as he did the low hills ahead. (A seaman's eyes are always drawn to the horizon.) 'But I am not so certain of the Brazilian fleet or whether there may be one at all.'

'I have no doubt you will create a navy, as you did in Chile,' I said.

He reined in his horse and looked not at me but at the wide river ahead. His horse was small for him and his huge torso above the saddle and dangling legs below might have looked slightly ridiculous, were it not for the nobility of his bearing.

'You know already that I have grown to admire the Chilean man's spirit, his courage, discipline and capacity for hard work. I have not heard such good

272

reports of the Brazilians.'

He might have said more but at that moment, a man appeared on the other side of the bank, waving. It was Mr Miers come to show us the new place of the ford.

'I had thought you would travel by ship,' he commented, once we had safely crossed.

'Exercise,' was His Lordship's brief answer. Behind us our mule train loaded with packages, including sultanas, suet and spices, scrambled nimbly across the water.

We proceeded for a while together. Mr Miers told us that Mrs Miers's state of mind had improved but she still suffered with her nerves so he would not leave her long.

'You are remaining in Chile, I assume?' His Lordship asked sympathetically.

'What choice have I? All my money is in the equipment I brought here. We are remote enough to be perfectly safe, if not from nature, from the attentions of opposing armies.'

'I have no doubt.'

We parted soon after, never to meet again.

We arrived back to find that Mr Jackson, in anticipation of my successful ingredients foray, had produced an ode, nay, a rhapsody in the pudding's honour. Very pleased with his powers, he recited its one hundred lines to us twice all the way through and we were all much amused. But since he was neither a Lord Byron nor even an Alexander Pope, I can only now recall his opening words: 'A gleeful globe of glory . . .'

It was the last day of the old year, not Christmas, that left a lasting impression on my memory. After dinner His Lordship and I walked to the seaside to enjoy the prospect and the music of the sea, which comes 'like the memory of joys that are past, pleasant and mournful to the soul'. (Pedants may like to know that I have corrected this from the version in my published journal in which an editor pointed out my errors.)

We sat long on the promontory of the *herradura* and watched the last of the sun of 1822 go down into the Pacific. Then we saw how his rays gilded the snowy tops of the Andes even after he himself was hid in the ocean. The sea was beating nearly round us. As far as the eye could reach, there were only the ruins of one human habitation, and the deep shadows of evening concealed the narrow traces of cultivation that, here and there, encroached on the wild thickets below the mountains. The cattle had retired to the woods and only the night-birds flitted around us.

'Do we still belong to the human race?' I murmured, hardly expecting Lord Cochrane to pick up my words.

'Man is always alone, even in the midst of society. We only trick ourselves when we think otherwise.'

'Misery and death may make a man or a woman *more* alone.' I was referring to my situation after poor Graham's departure from this world, but it was hardly honest since the only companion who meant anything to me was seated at my side. Yet, in my weak woman's way, it hurt me that my presence did not alleviate his aloneness.

'I have seen too many deaths to place my trust in any man's continuance. Life is given to us as a great battle between good and evil and each must struggle on his own path.'

It is natural at the end of a year to review past failures and glories—if glories there have been. In my published journal, I comment, 'So ended, perhaps, the most disastrous year of my life.' Never believe the whole truth of a journal for its author chooses the entries for a particular effect in just the same way as an author of fiction!

Even the snowy peaks were dark when we eventually walked back to the house. Sweet earthy odours arose around us but not a star came out to light our way so that we lost our track and stumbled out of our path. There was no chance of falling over a cliff but my ankles were at risk from the broken ground.

'Take my arm, if you please.' Cochrane had come out of his dream and chosen to help me.

I did so, feeling its warmth and strength through his coat. After a while, he moved and placed his arm round me so that I was contained within his huge body. I stood straight and proud. When he kissed me, such intense joy flooded me that I was not surprised, on opening my eyes, to see a brilliant star blink over our heads.

CHAPTER TWENTY-FIVE

Lord Cochrane to the inhabitants of Chile:

CHILENOS – MY COUNTRYMEN!

The common enemy of America has fallen in Chile. Your tri-coloured flag waves on the Pacific, secured by your sacrifices . . .

Chilenos! You have expelled from your country the enemies of your independence: do not sully the glorious act by encouraging discord, and promoting anarchy, that greatest of evils . . .

It is now four years since the sacred cause of independence called me to Chile: I assisted you to gain it; I have seen it accomplished; it only remains to preserve it.

I leave you for a time, in order not to involve myself in matters foreign to my duties, and for reasons concerning which I now remain silent, that I may not encourage party spirit.

Chilenos! You know that independence is purchased at the point of the bayonet. Know also, that liberty is founded on good faith, and on the laws of honour; and that those who infringe upon them are your only enemies,— among whom you will never find

COCHRANE
Quintero, 4th January, 1823

Sterling, well-judged words. I was proud of them, not only because they perfectly expressed Lord Cochrane's lofty sentiments but because I had a hand in them. Genius is seldom moderate and His Lordship's passions sometimes led him to intemperance in his public utterances.

The 'silence' in which he 'remained' concerning his reasons for departing was of my making. Mr Bennett and Mr Jackson concurred but could not have made it so. His Lordship trusted me and I loved him and knew what was best for him. We printed it all day, and another addressed to the merchants of Chile.

276

The schoolroom being closed while we worked, the three boys reverted to their brutish behaviour and happened to cross His Lordship when he wished for peace. 'We are too close here!' he announced, striding out of the sad remains of his house. In a second the plan for our living quarters was entirely changed. 'The infernal Davenants must have the run of the house. I shall remove myself to the sea-beach. In a tent.'

Our new settlement was arrayed in naval order, like ships-of-the-line prepared for battle. First came the dining *rancho* nearest to the hill, where a fisherman's hut served as a kitchen, and where there was a well of sweet water. Next was erected a very large tent, across which a screen was placed, thus forming two apartments for the still unwell Glennie and myself.

'Ah, cousin,' he said, on seeing the arrangements, 'will you never be free of me?'

'Who would be free of a person she loves?' I replied. Surely Glennie was the most tried and patient of us all. In my last years when I found myself bedridden and incapable, I often pictured his drawn young face, so used to suffering. Yet he recovered, I reminded myself, to continue his career in the Navy, and I could compliment myself that my nursing, added to his natural strength, made that possible.

Lord Cochrane inhabited the next tent. The very converse of an invalid, he was up every day at dawn, sometimes riding to Valparaíso and back before dinner. The third tent was appropriated for packages, the fourth was Mr Jackson's, the fifth Don Fausto's, and in the sixth Vicente was as irrepressibly useless, yet charming as ever.

Don Benito, expressing his individualism, pitched his tent out of line and behind the rest. 'I am a world traveller,' he explained, 'and must pick my own resting place.'

'World' was a somewhat exaggerated term since he had not gone beyond South America, while I had visited continents including Africa, India, Europe and South America. But I did not mock his pretensions because, only too aware of our precarious circumstances, we were kind to each other.

General Freire had reached Maule, only six days' march from Santiago. His Lordship's efforts intensified to remove us to safety.

At last, on one of our evening walks, he told me, with satisfaction, 'I have secured the brig *Colonel Allen* for our departure. It is a dark, closed ship but it will take us round the Cape.'

Instead of rejoicing at these words, I had a shuddering premonition of a different sort of departure, when we would arrive at Rio and he would leave me. It was impossible to pretend otherwise. Moreover, Kitty must make her arrival on the scene sooner rather than later.

'What is it? You've become so pale.' He bent to me with concern. 'Are you ill?'

'No. No. Thank you.' I clapped my hands together. 'A chill caught my heart. It has gone.' Never, in our time together, did I show weakness. My experience of life had taught me that my two greatest attributes were intelligence and a proud strength. He must not pity me, and I believe he never did.

Despite our circumstances, I still caught myself feeling sometimes, particularly when we all came

278

together for dinner, that we were enjoying an extended camping holiday. The fishermen had shown us that the wreck of the *Aquila* had been possessed by shellfish; this gave us one of our prized dainties, the large edible barnacle, peculiar in Chile to the bay of Quintero and known as *picoroco*.

At first I found it strange without Bella to wait on me, bring water, look after, hook and unhook my dresses, but I managed, and the freedom her absence gave me was delightful. A royal or aristocratic person had no hesitation in carrying on the most intimate details of his life in front of a servant because that servant was, to their way of thinking, nobody. But I could never think like that. I found it easier to visit His Lordship's tent in the fond conviction that nobody knew or, at least, cared enough to gossip. We were a band of survivors, waiting to set off for a new life.

Nevertheless, people did come to find us, most often to bid His Lordship farewell, usually in praise of what he had done and meant to them, sometimes in a less friendly spirit. One afternoon I was passing his tent when I heard voices raised angrily. I entered freely, as I was accustomed to do, and found His Lordship being harangued. He was dejected, chin in his hand, elbows on his splayed knees. I recognised the three men facing him as officers from his Chilean fleet, two young, upstanding, one older; two Chilean, one English.

His Lordship stood up when I came in and made a kind of wave towards the men, part disclaimer, part introduction, although he said no names, perhaps assuming I knew them. Sometimes I thought he assumed I knew everything he knew.

279

'Gentlemen.' I bowed coldly. They were fine men and they bowed politely back. But there was no need for them to distress His Lordship with their complaints. He had already done what he could to have the financial or other promises honoured. He could do no more and it was this inability that brought him so low. His heroic spirit was not formed for failure, whether in himself or on behalf of others.

So they terrorised him, but, interrupted, they became milder.

'You have heard of the famous Quintero *picoroco*?' I asked them. 'It is a delicacy you will find nowhere else and, taken with a glass or two of white Chilean wine, it is quite sublime.'

'Sublime' was overdoing the joys of the ugly mollusc but my feminine presence had already reminded them of civilised behaviour, and we went off to the *rancho* with a reasonable appearance of accord. Indeed after half a dozen bottles of wine and several stories from Don Benito, they seemed quite resigned to their fate, and even began to praise Lord Cochrane for his brilliant tactics as an admiral—two had served with him at Valdivia.

They loved him, I could see, but they could not properly understand his genius outside the deck of the ship. *'Ce n'est pas tout d'être aimé, il faut être apprécié'*: I scarcely knew anyone in Chile who was capable of appreciating him justly, so that even the very homage he received was unworthy of him.

Oh, why is he not at home? I thought, before recalling that I would not then be at his side. I looked up and calmed myself by watching the waves, rolling smoothly in to a few yards of us. Every day like this was precious, I told myself.

When I look in my journal I am reminded of the preparations necessary for a sea voyage that was likely to last for several months. It would be my first for nearly a year and I was not immune to the excitement.

All hands are now employed; the overseer's people on the hill salting beef, the carpenters nailing up boxes, people cutting up strips of hide for cordage, secretaries writing [a reference to myself and Don Benito] the press at work [me again] sailors fittings bars across the light logs, called *balsas*, to make a raft to ship the goods with when the expected brig *Colonel Allen*, arrived.

This happened without warning and suddenly we were really leaving. Berths needed to be allocated, possessions and provisions, including live animals, pushed and squeezed aboard. The ship was not commodious, as Lord Cochrane had indicated. Two days running, a vile wind blew up from the north-east which had the double effect of rolling the ship till anything unlatched slid and toppled, covering our household goods with sand and sparkling grit—the very same grit that the earthquake had forced up from the intestines of the earth.

Pulling up my shawl, I used it to cover my nose and mouth. Captain Crosbie, who had been away but was back with us, laughed at my appearance. 'We are going to Brazil, not the mystical Orient!'

'More *odalisque* than *nomade*, you think,' I joked back.

At that moment, His Lordship came out of

his tent. His beautiful hair was spread over his shoulders as if his mental exertions had led him to pull it out of its ribbon.

I smiled at him, but he frowned at us both. It struck me that it was not just the disturbance caused by our high spirits that vexed him. 'I need you, Crosbie—that is, if you can make the time.'

It was the only time I saw His Lordship jealous and I treasure the memory still. As always, he was unconscious of the cause of his disturbance.

Giving me a slightly wicked backwards glance, Crosbie followed Lord Cochrane into his tent and I went in to Glennie.

*   *   *

The next morning His Lordship and I took our last walk on Chilean soil. Blasted by natural causes as it was, and threatened by the foolishness of men, we nevertheless shared a great love for the country. Lord Cochrane had been there for four years and, during that time, had added new honour to his name. He had done good to the people by giving them ideas for improvements in their agriculture, their arts and their government that would eventually bear fruit. I had been there less than a year, arriving desolate and only saved by the hospitality of the Chileans and by the presence of one man who was to give my life meaning.

We walked slowly, gathering seeds and roots that we could take or send to England. Many survived and some still exist nearly two centuries later in the Botanical Gardens at Kew. But perhaps I have boasted of that before.

We made no sentimental statements, but our

feelings were in our sober expressions and silent reflection.

Yet we were both by nature impatient, restless, so we were happy enough to be thrown out of our reflection into a last boisterous dinner on the beach. We were to sleep on board ship that night and the servants had finally removed everything to it.

Like children, we competed to make rude forks, carving them from pieces of wood. A seaman is never separated from his knife so there was no shortage of those. The wind had blown itself away and it was a fine, quiet afternoon, with only the sea-birds squawking over old bits of food thrown into the sea. The two ships, the *Montezuma*, still flying the Admiral's flag, and the *Colonel Allen*, rode at anchor. Around them bobbed a flotilla of little boats, fishermen mostly, come to see the sights.

While we spread rugs and tarpaulins on rocks, the servants dressed and roasted a side of beef and two suckling pigs, which, in perfect symmetry, came from the litter born on the night of the earthquake. The meat was accompanied by potatoes cooked in the ashes while bottles of beer, wine and brandy stood open on upturned caskets. Even Glennie, who should have been fearful at the prospect of the voyage ahead in his state of health, was strong and cheerful.

'A health to the Admiral!' he cried.

'To the King!' responded Cochrane.

'To O'Higgins!' shouted Crosbie. 'And, if he doesn't last, to Freire!'

'To the King of Spain!' called Vicente, winking at Colonel Fausto, who, as a captive of Chile,

283

would not be coming with us and whose future was uncertain.

'To poesie!' said I, in order to change the subject.

'To democracy!' answered Cochrane.

'To Lord Byron and democracy!' I replied, which shows just how much I'd enjoyed the Chilean wine.

The toasts grew to a litany and gave way only when Don Benito told us of his last journey round the Cape, which started everybody (except myself whose tale was too sad to tell) competing with 'icebergs as tall as the Andes' and 'waves as high as St Paul's Cathedral set on top of the Andes'.

Then songs took over, Lord Cochrane leading the way with a booming rendition of 'Rule Britannia' in which we all joined, ignoring the irony as he moved from the service of one foreign country to another.

Darkness fell, and the moon had risen amid scintillating stars before we finally flung the last bone, the last wooden fork, into the sea and gathered ourselves to board the *Colonel Allen*. We stumbled, heads down—even His Lordship—but were soon gripped by strong seamen's arms and taken to the boats.

I gasped in wonder for the water sparkled with phosphorescence, as if a sequined mantle was laid across its gentle undulations. It was sublimely beautiful; a poet could have described it, but I found tears falling down my cheeks. Lord Cochrane sat hunched nearby and I caught a tear glistening on his cheek too. Only a man without feelings could have withstood the emotions of such a farewell.

Somewhere on shore a dog barked, and all my sorrow focused on my poor Don, left behind to the less than tender mercies of Don Rafaelo.

284

I mourned, too, my faithful horses, the steady Charles and flighty blue-eyed Fritz. They had been partners in my adventures and now I had abandoned them.

Slowly, slowly, we were rowed across the silver sea.

CHAPTER TWENTY-SIX

Glennie and I had small communicating cabins on board ship and His Lordship's next to mine. Once I'd settled Glennie and undressed, I lay down on my bunk and watched a sliver of moon come in through my window, lighting on my boxes. It was some comfort to have all my worldly possessions so close around me.

At first I thought sadly of the friends left behind to an uncertain fate, of Don Fausto and Vicente, of the Miers family and the Hogans but, lulled as always by the gentle waves, I had fallen into a calm sleep when I was roused by a knock at my door.

'Mrs Graham. Are you awake?'

I was now, so I put on slippers, a better cap, a long Indian jacket and shawl over my nightdress, then went next door.

His Lordship was bent over a map spread across a large oak table. He scarcely looked up as I came in, so certain was he of my attention. I went over and stood at his side. He had three candles lit.

'The coast of northern Brazil,' he said, putting a finger on Bahia, the place on which his concentration was fixed. 'The unvanquished Portuguese fleet is based there. The Brazilian government wishes me to scatter it and join the two halves of the country together again. As in Chile, there are royalists inside and outside the country who have not given up restoring the rule of the old country. The difference is that Brazil's emperor is only twenty-four and was destined to become King of Portugal. What can a Portuguese princeling, turned freedom fighter, know about the nature of civil war?' He looked up, although his eyes saw me only partly.

'Nothing, my lord,' I murmured. 'But what does he need to know, with you at his side?'

'Yes. Yes.' I saw this was not altogether the right answer. 'My crusade for liberty,' he carried on, 'must look for the most oppressed of states.'

'And Brazil is not?' I paused.

This time he did see me. 'Your Lord Byron is gone to Greece. Greece is a country cruelly yoked. Why should I not go to Greece?'

'You pointed out to me once that Rio is on the route to Greece. Fighting for one may not preclude the other.' I understood that at this dark hour of the night, when he was finally leaving behind glory, disappointment and turbulence, he was suffering from doubt and needed me for reassurance. 'You understand the Americas,' I continued, laying my hand on his so that a good section of the Brazilian coastline was obliterated. 'There can be no country in the world where, at this time, you can do more good.'

Almost instantly relief unclouded his face. Without more words, he clasped me to his bosom.

My love and admiration made me content that I had restored his confidence. But, looking back, I can't help wondering how much happier I might have been if I had persuaded him to skip over Rio and head back across the Atlantic. The *Doris* under Captain Graham, with myself on board, had stopped at that city on the way to Chile and I had been fascinated and appalled by the slave markets where naked girls were forced to parade their charms under the lascivious and estimating ogling of immoral traders. It was a disgusting place, where slavery was only the most obvious symptom of corruption. I should have suspected that such a hot, musky city, home to a sniggering fledgling court with an emperor and empress who were hardly more than children, could only bring me bitter suffering.

* * *

The next morning opened with what might have been an affecting scene: His Lordship's flag was hauled down by Captain Crosbie from the mast on the *Montezuma* and brought to him where he stood on the deck of the *Colonel Allen*. A single cannon fired in salute, not very loud.

'The deed is done,' whispered the irrepressible Crosbie, as he passed me on his way to the Admiral, although perhaps I should no longer style him 'admiral' as he was admiral of the Chilean Navy and none other.

' "If it were done when 'tis done then 'twere well it were done quickly," ' I riposted, as I had once before when circumstances were adverse.

Lord Cochrane, however, scarcely glanced at the furled flag. I suppose that if your insignia of the Noble Order of the Bath has been thrown down the steps of Westminster Abbey lesser pennants hardly

287

register.

Besides, he was eager to get the final stores aboard and weigh anchor while the wind was favourable. For a seaman, a favourable wind trumps everything. Later I found the flag poking half out of a chest in his cabin where his servant had unsuccessfully carried out his master's orders to stow it.

The wind *was* favourable and so was the day; white clouds scudded across a blue sky and the sun beat warmly. I had stepped on deck with Don Benito, Mr Jackson and a group of others who had come to watch the show; we stood, like eager animals, sniffing the fresh air.

'I understand we must put in at the island of Juan Fernández,' I said to Don Benito. 'I am told the water is plentiful and pure, which is why we use it as our watering source. Perhaps you have been there.'

'A desolate place,' responded Don Benito, unwilling to admit he hadn't.

'I had surmised that,' I continued, glancing with a smile at Mr Jackson, 'since it was the lonely shore on which the famous Robinson Crusoe found himself shipwrecked.'

'Ha! Ha!' Mr Jackson began, prelude to some entertaining information, I felt sure, but at that moment the bellow of repeated commands instigated a veritable relay of fleet, barefooted seamen dedicated to carrying them out.

'Perhaps we should go below,' I suggested, suiting action to words, as the profusion of sails going up and ropes coming down made our presence on deck both dangerous and unpopular.

We found Glennie in the dining saloon, furious

with me for forbidding him to go on deck and himself for obeying. 'I don't know why you think this stinking, airless hole will do me good,' he said sulkily, and took a gulp of coffee from a mug in front of him.

'Buffeting wind will do your lungs even less good,' I replied severely, but sat down to keep him company. Dr Craig and Mr Jackson sat, too, and after we'd poured ourselves mugs of cold coffee, Mr Jackson reverted to the subject of Juan Fernández.

'Reading *The Tempest* gave me a longing to set foot on a desert island.'

'It won't be very deserted with all of us,' objected Glennie.

'Three and sixty miles west of us here,' I said mildly, 'in the middle of the great Pacific Ocean. Only twelve miles long and four across. Would you not call that a desolate island?'

'Do you know everything, Mrs Graham?' joked Mr Jackson.

'I have been reading about it,' I admitted, 'and looking at Lord Cochrane's maps.'

'You are drawn to remote places, perhaps,' surmised Mr Jackson, before Glennie interrupted with a frown.

'Such an island is no more desolate than a ship in the middle of the Atlantic or your precious Pacific.'

This was too rude, and Dr Craig intervened, 'My dear young man, may I suggest that in future you drink less coffee? I would also suggest you lie down for a rest since your bright-coloured cheeks indicate a raised pulse.'

Poor Glennie! I felt sorry for him as the doctor led him away, yet glad that Mr Jackson and I could now have our literary talk.

'I must confide in you,' Mr Jackson began, 'that on my first reading of *Robinson Crusoe*, some fifteen years ago in Bognor where I was writing an article on the new esplanade, I determined to visit his island. Indeed, I have carried the novel with me on my travels. I love, in particular, the opening: "I was born in the year 1632, in the city of York . . ." ' he quoted lovingly.

'But, my dear sir,' I leant my elbows on the table and addressed him eagerly, 'how can you so commend the opening of a book that tries to purvey a lie? The author, Mr Daniel Defoe, pretended even through publication that Mr Crusoe had in truth been born in York and shipwrecked on an island, whereas the whole invention was based on the adventures of a seaman, Alexander Selkirk.'

'I had not thought of you as placing such an emphasis on the facts, dear lady, even though you yourself are the master—or should I say the mistress?' he gave me a sly look from his remarkably small eyes '—of them all. I thought that, like myself, you had a more *poetic soul*.' He emphasised the words, his raisin eyes rolling heavenwards. 'Although, of course, unlike myself, you are a *reader* of poetry not a *writer*.'

'An ode to a Christmas pudding hardly makes you a poet, Mr Jackson,' I responded tartly, because we were good friends.

'It does not make me Lord Byron, perhaps, although the great man did write odes to the dinner bell, which he referred to as "the toxin of the soul", to a Newfoundland dog and to his own thirty-sixth year.'

'We seem to have strayed from the island or

group of islands, to be precise, of Juan Fernández. Earlier you mentioned *The Tempest*.'

'You are so keen, then, to leave an argument of artistic reality?'

'So that is what we were discussing.'

'What else is there to discuss between two artistic souls? You may not write poetry, but you are a writer. You create, just as Daniel Defoe did.'

'I do not write fiction.'

'Then as Robinson Crusoe did.'

'He *is* fiction.'

We were pleased with our discussion, Mr Jackson and I. We did not expect to find the boundary between reality and fiction—or even if there was one—but we complimented each other with our mutual understanding. I wrote travel journals that employed the material of my life and yet I considered it art. He wrote about plum puddings and considered that art too. His real *métier* was as a journalist.

We talked more. We wore ourselves out with abstract theories that never could be decided.

Eventually we were silent, and I became aware of the immense swell of the ocean beneath us. We were moving fast; I could tell instinctively by the sounds all around us, even though the three small portholes showed only a blue sky that seemed unmoving. Ships are living things, like a powerful animal when it runs: the muscles expand, the tendons stretch, the skin ripples.

'We're moving fast,' I said.

My companion, unused to ships, caught the tone of my voice. 'You are excited.' He smiled a little patronisingly.

The ship made me think of her captain. What

291

I would have given to be by his side at the wheel! But Crosbie was there and other young lieutenants eager to be on the move after all the uncertainties of the last month. It was not clear still what their future was although, if given the choice, I have no doubt they would follow Lord Cochrane into any navy in the world.

'To return to Juan Fernández,' said Mr Jackson, as if he was jealous of my lost attention. 'I promised myself a particular course of action if I ever landed there with which I hope, perhaps, you'll help me.'

'Anything that is within my power and does not include murder,' I replied, failing to match his seriousness.

His plump face screwed up. 'It will be a secret until the time comes.'

'But how can I help you then?'

'You will know at the time.'

'What if I am otherwise engaged?' Now he understood I was being playful and his face deflated in sorrow. I thought that we all have dreams and how they may appear ridiculous to any but the dreamer. 'I will not be otherwise engaged!' I amended hastily. But he had risen already and was making a dignified retreat, until a sudden greater roll of the ship threw him unceremoniously into the door jamb.

'Mr Jackson!' Guiltily, I flew to his side.

He was a dear, kind man and he allowed me to pick him up and set him on his way. 'I shall look forward to your "particular course of action",' I said, and looked hard at him so that he had to believe me.

When he had gone, I told myself that in a ship full of men a lady must behave herself with the gentle sympathy expected of her sex. But I did not convince myself. Restlessly, I walked round the room, adjusting my steps to the flowing movements of the ship. Like the birds that follow all vessels, I spread my arms and flew a little.

Over the next four days, the weather did everything in its power to curtail my spirits. Low fog surrounded us in the morning, coating every surface both on deck and below with a clammy wetness and making the action of breathing an unpleasant necessity. In the afternoon, a bad-tempered wind blew the fog away but it would not make up its mind to persevere in any one direction, causing a tedious shifting in sails and heavy work for the seamen.

None of this affected Lord Cochrane, who was used to far worse. When I said to him one evening, 'I am thinking of setting up an entertainment for our passengers,' he looked quite astonished.

'Can they not entertain themselves?'

A man whose mind is ever active can never imagine the lassitude into which a lesser mortal may sink. 'They are not used to being confined in a ship.'

'Confined?' he repeated, in wonderment. In his bright eyes (any hint of red cured by a few days at sea) I saw reflected the great Pacific, tumbling away to a horizon of endless sky.

'There was the fog,' I faltered. 'The fog depressed.' I stopped as His Lordship gave a derisory snort. No entertainment, I thought.

He came closer to me. It was late, darkness outside for thousands of miles, only a couple of guttering candles inside. He had been drinking with Crosbie and some of the other officers earlier and his breath smelt of brandy.

He said gently, '*You* are not depressed.'

I smiled. I wanted to say, 'I wish this voyage would never end,' but instead I asked, 'How long before we sight Juan Fernández?'

The naval man has his sights always on the next landfall. Yet I believe his heart is in the open sea. I've known many a retired captain who walks each day from his house at Plymouth or Portsmouth or Hove, and stands leaning on his stick, staring at the grey or green or black waves, and if a ship comes into view, he lifts his telescope (saved from his seafaring days) and fixes it on the deck. 'Captain Shillingbeer's son,' he may say, but it is himself he imagines on the deck, not coming into harbour with the swirl of birds above but setting out on the vast tide of water.

Six bells rang, making me start, quickly followed by a relay of commands and the scurry of bare feet on wood.

His Lordship reached for his coat and hat. 'I shall go for a breath of air. Tomorrow I expect to see Juan Fernández, although an adverse wind may well hold us offshore.' I listened to his heavy tread pass confidently along the corridor and disappear up the steps. Then I sat down and turned to my journal.

CHAPTER TWENTY-SEVEN

24th January, 1823
Yesterday and today in sight of Juan Fernández, and working for it, but could not reach it till

near sunset. It is the most picturesque place I ever saw, being composed of high perpendicular rocks wooded nearly to the top, with beautiful valleys; and the ruins of the little town in the largest of these heighten the effect. It was too late to go ashore when we anchored; but it was a bright moonlight, and we staid long on deck, admiring the extraordinary beauty of the scene.

When we eventually went below, Mr Jackson read long passages from his precious copy of *Robinson Crusoe* and I competed with stanzas from *The Deserted Village* by Oliver Goldsmith:

Where once the garden smiled
And still where many a garden flower grows wild.

His Lordship left us at this point but it was another hour before we managed to quell our excitement for the morrow and retire to our separate berths.

The sun arose, a golden-faced bride swathed in white gauze. As the veils lifted, the calm sea glowed in coral hues. Wrapped in shawls, I stood on deck and watched Lord Cochrane rowed slowly across it. At his side sat the upright figure of Mr Shepherd, a young officer, and Mr Tizer, a Valparaíso builder, whose business lay literally in ruins.

I yearned to be in the little boat too but, led by the *Colonel Allen*'s boatswain who had spent time on the island a few years earlier, they planned to climb the highest peak, and a lady in skirts, however agile, would not have been welcome. Besides, I had promised Glennie to take him ashore and he would need a close eye to prevent him scaling a height of his own.

The light was thinning and brightening: Cochrane's back, with its thick golden pigtail—no grey visible from where I stood—was the size of a small doll. Sighing, I turned to go down and almost bumped into Captain Crosbie coming up. His face was so fresh it hurt.

'Ah, Mrs Graham! Ho! Ho! Left behind, eh?'

I couldn't help smiling. 'Don't "Ah, ho ho, eh" me, young fellow, or I'll think you've turned into a Chinaman. I am heralding the new day. What time will the boats go to the islands?'

'At your command, madam. What time does Madam desire?' He beat his hands together, then stamped his feet on the wooden planks. 'I'm just a simple seaman,' he said, in an accent half Irish, half West Country.

I laughed and passed by him. It struck me suddenly how differently the affairs between His Lordship and I might stand if we were younger, if our energy was untainted by long experience, by earlier joys, defeats and violent happenings. We could not recapture the single-mindedness of youth. Yet even as I thought this I denied it. I, at least, was single-minded in my devotion.

It was eleven before we landed on the island. I was carried across the deeper water, my skirts bunched up around me. The men went in splashing, water drops glittering in the bright sunlight. Even the plump and fastidious Mr Jackson was too exhilarated by our arrival to complain of wet legs and feet, while Don Benito held up his skirts and danced about like a Dervish.

In front of us the reddish ground stretched upwards into a green valley bounded by black pinnacles of rock, up one of which Lord Cochrane and his companions had climbed—and not yet appeared. We proceeded more sedately to view the remains of the small town, at first enclosed by the most luxurious vegetation that nature can provide: large entwining fig trees, wild mint, giant fuchsia, andromeda, myrtles and, above all, a lovely monopetalous shrub with shiny, thick-set leaves, flowers and berries of the richest purple.

Inside the abandoned town we found the tangled roses, sweet herbs and fruit trees that human hands had planted and, on departing, left to careless Nature. A few houses and cottages were still in tolerable condition, though most of the doors, windows and roofs had been taken away or used as fuel by whalers and other ships touching here. Standing on its own, its portico and walls still intact, was a church.

'I don't remember a church on Robinson Crusoe's island,' commented Mr Jackson, disapprovingly.

'We've already established,' I replied, 'that you favour imagination over reality.'

'My gout does not much enjoy reality either,' muttered Dr Craig.

I glanced at my companions. Glennie was pale, the others pulling various faces of discontent. There is nothing more annoying than when in the heights of historical romance to find oneself among unwilling explorers. At any moment His Lordship might appear, God-like, on a mountaintop.

'The sun is high. I will stay but you should return to a shadier place.'

So it was that I read alone the inscription over the church door: *La Casa de Dios es la puerta del cielo*—The house of God is the door to Heaven. I stood for a long time staring in, cool in the shade cast by the heavy stone. I thought of the faith behind the simple words, carved by simple men, brought here to establish a small colony on the island. I hoped that their faith had lasted longer than the door: another line of the inscription informed me that the church had been built in 1811, only seven years or so before the Spanish, who had inhabited the island and used it mainly as a prison for Chilean revolutionaries, had been defeated. Here I stood, companion to the very man who had caused their defeat.

The moral, I supposed, is that one should not put one's faith in a doorway, even a doorway of God, if it stands in the path of history. Giving up the question marks of theology, I set off up a steep incline to a battered fort. The dry grass that coated the ground was slippery and made the climb far harder than I'd expected so when I arrived at the top I sank down beside a fine brass gun. Thus I did not see Lord Cochrane's arrival.

'Spanish, 1614,' he announced, in his grand, booming voice, although he panted afterwards, as if out of breath.

I raised myself. 'Your Lordship!'

He sat astride the gun and I saw that his face was scarlet and streaming with sweat. Indeed, his whole large body seemed to steam, like a horse after he has run a race. He was still wearing his heavy coat, which couldn't have helped.

'Damned fool, that boatswain! Takes us up a pinnacle as sharp as a needle so our hands are raw with clinging on—and I've been climbing up ropes since I was a babe. He told us we'd see the whole back of the island, said it was the highest point, and when we get there, what did we see? A whole forest of higher pinnacles. Damned fool! Probably dreamt he was on the island before. I've had men flogged for less.' He wiped his forehead with a large handkerchief and focused on me. 'You here alone?'

'Mr Jackson is looking for Robinson Crusoe, Dr Craig is tending his gout, Mr Bennett has not yet disembarked, and Glennie is still weak.'

'Shepherd and Tizer swore they must plunge into the sea before their brains fried. So we are both abandoned.'

I nodded and shifted my position as the commander of an army of well-disciplined ants assessed the toe of my boot. 'I suppose this was the barracks.' I waved my hand at a row of fallen buildings.

His Lordship looked around him without too much interest. 'Yes. Some sort of insurrection occurred not long ago, perhaps among the political exiles.'

'And was this under Chilean rule?'

'I believe so. They did not want the island to become the centre of the disaffection as they themselves had tried to use it when under the Spanish yoke. More often it has been a prison. Do you not find it a melancholy place?'

'I have always found romance in ruins.'

'We have seen too much of that lately.'

I was reproved. I pictured the flattened houses of Valparaíso where men, women and children were crushed of life. I remembered Mr Campbell, Old Testament prophet in his destitution. His Lordship gazed out to sea where the stubby *Colonel Allen* rocked gently on the swell. The sight seemed to restore his spirits, or perhaps it was the boat being rowed backwards and forwards from ship to shore, filling barrels with the famously pure Juan Fernández water. He removed his gaze to the sun, shrouded now, having reached its peak and slowly descending.

'Dinnertime,' he announced, jumped off the gun, took my hand and pulled me upright. We stood side by side for a moment or two. A little cooling breeze sprang up. Behind us were the great black turrets of stone; before us the green valley flowing down into the sea.

I reached for a Byronic line but could think only of Cochrane's large warm hand holding mine. Perhaps Milton's *paradise*, before the 'Arch-fiend' arrived, might have served but sometimes even a blue-stocking must put away her books.

When we rejoined the rest of our group, we found a tablecloth of broad fig leaves had been laid under interlocking trees that bent together to make a domed roof. On one side a rivulet sparkled downwards over the stones, playing host to a clutch of claret bottles from the ship. Our ordinary supplies of meat and biscuits were supplemented with fruit from the island, cherries, apple, pear and quince, although some were still hard to the teeth.

His Lordship and I took our places, as hungry as anyone who has enjoyed early rising and long exercise. But we had hardly lifted our glasses before Mr Jackson, with an eye to me, scrambled to his feet. Beckoning me to follow, he skipped over to a particularly large rock. 'My secret!' he exclaimed, when I reluctantly joined him. He fumbled in a box and produced, with a reverential flourish—a violin. '*Voil*à! Violin! The sweet music of the island. *The Tempest*. Act one, scene two, verse 387.'

'You play the instrument?' I was taken aback.

'A little. I have been practising in the hold. The men were kind enough to say that I made a more agreeable sound than the cats chasing the rats.'

'That seems a poor compliment,' I said doubtfully, but he was already tuning the instrument with a concentrated air. 'What role do you wish me to play?' I asked, as he paused for a moment in his squeaking.

'You,' he announced, producing a small book from his pocket, 'will read the relevant passage by way of introduction. After which, I shall strike up behind this rock, off-stage, as it were, by magic.'

I took the book, it seeming to me that the sooner we began the sooner the affair would be over and I could regain my place at our leafy table.

How strange it is that so often the most unlikely and ridiculous of events succeed by the very outrageousness of their fantasy! I read, the rivulet tinkled accompaniment, the audience clinked their glasses and Mr Jackson struck up with remarkable dexterity and musicality.

When he had finished and appeared once more among us, His Lordship rose and clapped him on the shoulder. 'You are a man of surprises, Mr Jackson,' and added to me, out of the side of his mouth, 'Now you have your entertainment, Mrs Graham.'

After our meal, His Lordship and I took a walk together, as if we were back at beloved Quintero. We gathered plants, and he began to talk once more about his childhood in Scotland and the responsibility he felt for his three younger brothers. 'From an early age,' he said, 'I knew that I must rely on myself and that no one in the world would pause their own tasks to lend me a hand.'

'Surely your father,' I queried.

'My father least of all.' He frowned heavily. I did not know it then but, at this point in 1823, the Earl of Dundonald, who was nearly eighty, had run through several fortunes, three wives, and was living with his mistress in Paris.

'My father is a madman,' His Lordship continued gloomily. 'A spark of genius and a gutful of drink. He never did anything for me but tried to make me a soldier when my whole being was turned towards the sea.' He became agitated. 'At the time I was thrown into gaol, he gave an interview with the *Sun* newspaper,' (believe this, you modern readers,) 'accusing me of allowing him to sink into penury when, in truth, I gave eight thousand pounds over ten years to keep him in women and drink. He was never a father to me!'

He fell silent while I regretted wholeheartedly ever mentioning the unloving earl.

'Your life has been a triumph over adversity,' I said eventually, and I thought that we were not unlike in this.

'Yes. Yes.' He was impatient. Bending, he plucked a long slim grass that had forced its way out of a crack in a boulder that blocked our way. 'If a single grass can break open the hardness of stone, then how much more should man be able to achieve?'

'So you are set upon freeing the Brazilian nation from her oppressors?'

'I am.' He straightened to his full impressive height, gazed for a moment out to sea, then, just as I was feeling myself forgotten, turned back to me with a sweet smile. 'At least you will be at my side for another four or five weeks. Rounding the Cape is ever unpredictable, particularly in an old boot like that.' He stabbed his finger at the poor *Colonel Allen*.

'I am happy . . .' I began, but he was already making his way back to the landing stage.

CHAPTER TWENTY-EIGHT

Oh, Rio! Rio! Would that I could rewrite history as the cleverest historians take pride in doing. But this is my own story, with its joys and sufferings creating the ink with which I write—if a ghostly reporter is allowed to use such a concrete metaphor.

Rio ended the gentle dreaming into which I'd been lulled. I spent the final day of our mooring off Juan Fernández sitting on the deck of the *Colonel Allen* and painting the island. There were seamen to serve me, officers for a chat, Mr Jackson for a laugh and His Lordship for love.

Then followed the long, difficult sea voyage; yet when I picture the great cliffs of ice in the southernmost tip of Chile, where others see danger, I see tranquillity. I soared like a sea-bird when the skies were blue and raced with furled wings on the black clouds of storms. Even the nightly performance on the violin by Mr Jackson, whose early praise had given him overwhelming confidence, was part of it. 'Bliss was it in that dawn to be alive . . .'

Until Rio.

As we approached, there were natural intimations of disaster:

1st March

We came in sight of the land about Cape Santa Marta. At night there was the most beautiful lightning possible; and while we were looking at it, we heard something fall into the sea like a heavy body from a height, at some distance from us, and about half an hour afterwards, Mr J. saw, and some of the others heard, a second body fall into the water. Could these be meteoric stones? The thermometer for some days not under 80°.

4th

We are going slowly along the land, thermometer 82° morning and evening; 89° at noon.

9th

Sailing along the land and among the islands of the Bay of Santos, not one half of which appear in the charts. They are mostly high; many of them rocky, and many covered with palm trees. We have had the thermometer at 94° but last night a wild thunderstorm and heavy squalls of wind and rain have cooled the air.

13th

We anchored in the harbour of Rio de Janeiro.

The heavens falling to earth, a thunderstorm and an unlucky date: I should have been warned. Thick rain fell from boiling skies, hitting the cool seas with a hiss of steam. It was so drenching that we couldn't get off the ship, and six extra hours were bought aboard. Mr Jackson became aggravated by Mr Tizer, who mounted to the deck three or four times in his impatience to be off, each time reappearing as wet as a drowned rat (and there were plenty of those too).

'Tomorrow, my dear Mr Tizer, will be time enough to start making money.'

This infuriated Tizer so much for the implication he was not quite a gentleman that he shouted, 'If you were not such a poet, I would throw you a challenge,' meaning, I suppose, pistols at dawn, which I thought very old-fashioned of him, besides being unconvincing from a working man. Angry men always incline me to laughter.

The Admiral (as I began to think of him again) was shut in the stateroom with various officers discussing the situation *vis-à-vis* a Brazilian fleet. The one messenger who pierced the monsoon gave a gloomy report of the state of the ships and even worse of the available seamen.

Passing by at one point, perhaps hovering just a little, I heard the Admiral's voice raised in wrath: 'If I am forced to fight the Portuguese with the dregs of their own seamen, I cannot vouch for success!'

It was possible through certain windows and the shrouding rain to perceive the ghostly shadows of ships nearby, but when Crosbie emerged briefly and I queried if they were the Brazilian fleet, he gave his most snorting laugh and answered, 'There is no Brazilian fleet.'

We endured an uncomfortable dinner together. The water fell on the ship with so much noise that it was difficult to hear one another speak, besides the moroseness of Lord Cochrane.

At one point, I shouted, 'How sad to think of those poor slaves, naked in this deluge!'

By chance, the rain diminished for a moment so that my exclamation, at shrill volume, surprised everybody, though pleased none.

'What rain?' His Lordship raised his head.

'It will give those blackamoors a much-needed clean-up,' commented Crosbie, merely to annoy me.

'Water is nothing when you're used to whips,' said Mr Tizer. He gave me an irritable look. 'If I could run a business here without slaves, I would, but I am assured that in Brazil they are all the workers one can find.'

'Every family has its slaves,' said Mr Jackson, 'but they are treated no worse than servants in England.'

'Slavery is an abomination,' bellowed His Lordship, returning to the fray, 'but while the vast majority of English people are disenfranchised, we are in no position to pronounce on another country's regulations.'

This silenced us all so that we listened to the rain, once again raised in volume, for the rest of the meal.

The next morning dawned dry and bright, although a damp haze hung over Rio de Janeiro. I could see that, since my visit nearly two years ago, the city had grown remarkably in size and even elegance, to judge by the crescent habitations, towers, spires and even what looked like parkland.

'It has become beautiful,' said Glennie, at my side, receiving only a baleful glance. He stared around him at the many ships in the harbour, flying flags of every nation except Brazil. 'We will find friends here, I believe.'

The first visitor, however, was a Brazilian, an officer from the port who, since Crosbie, Cochrane and everybody else was busy, I was asked to entertain. We sat in the cabin, drinking tea.

'Did you come from Chile?' he asked me,

although I thought he should have known.

'Indeed. We leave earthquake and civil war.'

'Have you ever had the honour of meeting Admiral Cochrane?' He uttered the name solemnly, his swarthy skin flushing darker with emotion.

'Indeed. He is a friend.'

'A friend!' His eyes widened. 'All our hopes are on his arrival. Oh, that it may be soon!'

'It is now,' said I, lifting my teacup. 'He is arrived in this very ship.'

'Now? In this very ship?' Leaping to his feet and crying, 'Where? Where? Oh, that I may kiss his hands!' he tried to drag me from the cabin.

'Allow me to replace my teacup,' I said, smiling. 'I'm sure you may salute His Lordship, but as for kissing his hand, I'm equally sure he will not allow it.'

Yet his enthusiasm was affecting and he collected an audience for his moment of homage. That achieved with all speed, he gave instructions that we might anchor where we liked, then disappeared over the side of the ship, calling, 'I must make haste so I may be the first to tell of our admiral's arrival!'

This excitable gentleman was followed by a procession of interested parties: Perez, the port captain, who welcomed us in flowery but sadly, incomprehensible Portuguese; Captain Garção of the frigate *Liberal*, a handsome man who, as he paid his respects, reminded me of the abandoned Colonel Fausto. Then Captain Taylor, once of the *Doris*, now of the Brazilian *Nitherohy*, taught us about the state of His Imperial Majesty's fleet which did, after all, exist.

I sat quietly in the corner of the stateroom taking notes for my own purpose. A great sun had risen and soon this fierce heat, combined with the seamen's exhalations, made the atmosphere feel combustible.

'The *Pedro Primeiro* is out of the dock yesterday,' began Captain Taylor, a cunning but truly clever man. 'She had been in a sad state but the Emperor has repaired her and I'm told she sails well.'

'Huzzah!' responded Crosbie, somewhat ironically.

'The *Caroline* is a fine frigate,' continued Taylor, impervious to high spirits, 'but not commissioned for want of men. The *Unao* is a very fine ship, although in want of copper, and commanded by young Captain Jewitt. Captain Beaurepair commands a fine corvette, the *Maria da Gloria*, and I myself labour on the *Nitherohy*, a corvette, well found and in good repair but a heavy sailer. There we have it: ships enough, perhaps, but where are the sailors?'

Spirits, which had been rising, subsided. His Lordship, who had never changed his attitude of calm, called for more coffee and then, although it was scarcely eleven, brandy, which, when it came, they mixed with water and drank like water. Faces became redder and more cheerful.

'I hear the Emperor is fond of the Navy,' said His Lordship.

'He wishes to rule the whole of his country,' said a young officer come along with Taylor. 'If he is to take the north, he must have a navy and an admiral to go with it.' We all knew this but it was pleasing to hear it said.

'So. So.' His Lordship pushed away his glass

308

and called for his servant. He ordered his dress uniform to be brought and his feathered hat. He stood, rolling his great shoulders. 'We will pay our respects to the Emperor.'

So it had to be. The Admiral was about his business and I must be about mine. Glennie had suffered yet another relapse and I needed a quiet place to nurse him. While Lord Cochrane met His Imperial Majesty and his empress in all the state of a court, I took a boat with a single servant at my side in order to make enquiries about where Glennie and I might stay.

The rain had started again in a dull drizzle but, even so, I was able to admire the aggrandisements of the city: two massive arches, under which the Emperor had passed on the day of coronation, designed in extremely good taste and well executed, new fountains opened, aqueducts repaired, all the forts and other public works visibly improved, and the streets new paved.

However, when I arrived at the opera house, a famous centre for gossip and even information, I found it closed and realised we were in Lent. Not only were public places closed but the English and many others of importance, who might have been able to help me, had gone to their country houses.

Bedraggled and despondent (my attendant bedraggled and complaining), I returned to the brig. There, at least, good news awaited me. I might have Admiral Sir Thomas Masterman's house for a few days. I tried to cheer Glennie with the news, 'He was a fine sailor who fought with Nelson at Trafalgar so I have no doubt he has a fine house.'

'A fine house to die in,' responded Glennie.

'You will not be there long enough to die,' I told

him bracingly.

Mr Jackson had already left to negotiate a passage to England; Mr Tizer had been away since first light. Mr Bennett and the other officers had accompanied the Admiral so only Dr Craig was left for company. Like Mr Jackson, all his thoughts were on the next ship that would take him home to England.

We did not see Admiral Lord Cochrane that evening, the only indication he had come aboard the bustle and piping of his arrival late at night.

More rain, as warm as a bath, fell the following morning, but I was determined we should leave. All travellers know when they must rely on themselves or lose heart entirely. I had fallen asleep just at dawn so missed the Admiral's departure for another meeting soon after.

I wrapped Glennie in a rug and put another over his head.

'It is not cold, Maman.' The word brought a little tear to my eye. 'In truth it is blisteringly hot.'

'Come! Come!' I called to the seamen, who were manhandling our boxes into a boat. 'Those boxes have not travelled across two oceans and more continents to end up at the bottom of Rio harbour.'

Admiral Masterman's house was fine indeed, but on the day we arrived, I would have given up the pillars for a loaf of bread since it was completely unprovisioned. Nor were the Negroes, hanging around in a surly way, at all helpful. Eventually I persuaded one called Antonio, brighter than the others with a handsome physique, to lead me to a huckster's shop in the area. The damp heat, making the air heavy and the pavements slippery, almost undid me.

310

'Oh, madam!' exclaimed the slave, catching me against him as I fell. It was a measure of how low I had come that, despite his strong odour, I was comforted by the warmth of his body.

'You look quite cut up,' murmured Glennie, from his bed, on my return.

In answer, I poured for us both significant doses of laudanum. The next few days passed in a blur of loneliness, sickness and self-pity.

This was broken by a visit from a certain Mrs May, who insisted on being shown into the large day room where I lay on the sofa half dressed. She was just the sort of woman I disregard: practical to her core, she had never read a book, thought an original thought or aspired to anything beyond serving her husband and anyone else whom she perceived in need.

'My dear Mrs Graham, I am so sorry to burst in on you so early.' This was her excuse for my *déshabille* because it was not in fact early. 'But I heard you were unwell and in want of a house and I have found just the one.'

It is remarkable that one can despise and love the same person and I soon doted on dear fat Mrs May—how she kept the fat on her in that heat I cannot imagine.

'The house is small, but clean and light and almost surrounded by sea, which makes it especially airy. Perfect to restore the lungs. It is on Gloria Hill. Such a charming name.'

'Gloria,' I repeated. My mood hardly accorded with 'Gloria'.

Mrs May, assuming everything agreed, settled in for a good chat, having first organised the servants (I will no longer call them slaves and, in fact, they

311

were freed slaves) to bring delicious fruit drinks
and cakes that I had not known were in the house.
'So,' she said, bright eyes beaming at me, 'Lord
Cochrane still here and events not much further
forward. They say he was asked to serve under two
Portuguese admirals and for Portuguese pay. That
is, Brazilian.'

'Can that be true?' I sat straight for the first time
in days.

'He's certainly still living on board the ship he
arrived in.'

'Still in that mean little brig?'

'You arrived with him, of course?' She was
too good a woman to look more than ordinarily
curious.

'But I have heard nothing of the latest news.'

'He has been given a house on the same Gloria
Hill but perhaps he may not stay.'

'He is a man dedicated to the principles of
freedom,' I avowed, somewhat stiffly. Suddenly
'Gloria' seemed more apposite.

'Oh, yes. I have no doubt everything will be
worked out to everyone's satisfaction.' Her voice
carried the optimistic tones of a kind nurse and
teacher.

Yet she was proved right. The next day I had
a note from His Lordship. He announced that
he would be hoisting his flag at four o'clock that
afternoon on board the *Pedro Primeiro*. Later, he
planned to visit his temporary residence on Gloria
Hill and also to call in on myself, as he understood I
stayed in that area.

'Oh! Oh!' I shrieked, so that all the servants, for
once, came running.

Even Glennie tottered to my side. 'What is it?

Cousin, are you ill?'

'We must be in our new home by evening. His Lordship, now admiral and commodore of the Brazilian Navy is to visit us.'

The problem was how to remove ourselves in time. How often have I had occasion to remark that the Royal Navy will rescue any situation? A kind Captain Bourchier of His Majesty's Ship *Beaver*, happening to call an hour after I had received His Lordship's news, at once offered me the use of the ship's boats to convey ourselves and our goods to Gloria Hill.

'I shall oversee it myself,' he said, bowing heroically. 'A captain's widow must always deserve our care.'

It is a fact that intense activity with a purpose almost always improves my health. The heat was intense as we moved at midday, the sea unusually choppy, but I tied a gauze scarf over my face and my sea legs did not desert me.

'You should be carved in wood like that,' commented Captain Bourchier, as I stared forwards, 'and set on the prow of a ship-of-the-line.'

Glennie snorted derisively at the extravagant compliment, but I was pleased. My spirits were high enough to greet the Admiral.

*   *   *

He did not arrive until after ten that night and came in a cohort of young officers and even a couple of midshipmen. They, however, went in to visit Glennie, who had already retired.

The house, hardly more than a cottage, was filled with loud male voices and my heart beat louder and faster in response.

'You have been ill,' His Lordship said gravely, taking my hand.

He sat on a chair too small for him and I couldn't take my eyes off him.

'I am well now. And you are very well, I know. When will you leave for Bahia?'

'Tomorrow, if we could. Probably in a week. The *Pedro Primeiro* is a most elegant ship, a two-decker without a poop. I will take you aboard her as soon as she moves into harbour.' Here was a changed man from the dismal bear holed up in the *Colonel Allen*. I rejoiced in it, even though I was aware it would take him from me. After the miseries of the previous week, I could feel nothing but joy. How lucky is the human animal who lives in the present!

'I shall see you every day,' promised His Lordship, as reckless as a schoolboy. He took both my hands and leant forward so that his strong knees touched mine. Underneath his cotton flannel and my peplum our hot skin melted together.

In honesty, I knew that the fire in his eyes was aroused as much by the prospect of adventures on the high seas as any feeling he had for me, but I made the touch of his body and the declaration of a daily visit enough. 'It will be like your visits to my house in the Almendral,' I said softly.

But he was never a man to look back. 'You have everything you want here?' His glance swept round for a moment, the naval eye that looks for cleanliness, comfort and order.

'Perfectly.'

'Then I must go.'

I watched from the window as they set out into the blackness, heading downwards to the sea wall.

314

Clearly, their evening was not yet over.

I put out the candles and sat on for a while. As my eyes grew accustomed to the dark, I saw the line of sea and sky and the lights from the great ships anchored there. A naval man will always be sailing for the horizon, leaving his wife sorrowing. I was not even his wife.

On the fifth of His Lordship's daily visits, he arrived by sea at four o'clock, accompanied only by Crosbie on whom I had not set eyes since I had left the *Colonel Allen*. It was a brilliant day and Crosbie shone. 'I am come to pay my respects before leaving at once.'

I smiled. 'You captains are all the same. Get yourself a ship and you forget old friends.'

'You have heard!' He blushed charmingly.

'That you are captain under His Lordship's command of the *Pedro Primeiro*. The whole world knows.'

'I have responsibilities.'

'Go. Only yesterday I said farewell to Mr Jackson and Dr Craig. No one can be held in one place. Go, my dear Crosbie. The Admiral and I have serious matters to discuss.' In fact, I could tell from His Lordship's preoccupied face that he did have some news but I little guessed what it was.

Captain Crosbie bowed and left. We took up our accustomed places, the low sun streaming through the windows; Antonio brought us coffee and wine.

'This morning early,' began the Admiral, the moment we were on our own, 'His Majesty's Ship *Tartar* came into Rio. It has sailed from England and brought distressing news: Lady Cochrane, not knowing of my removal to Rio, is on her way to Chile. She has little Eliza with her, a sickly infant.

Think of it! They must perform the rough passage round Cape Horn twice before they find me and then, indeed, I will be gone for Bahia.' His beautiful wide mouth drooped and his blue eyes looked to me for comfort.

Despite my thudding heart, I hastened to provide it. 'Lady Cochrane's ship must touch this port before heading for Chile.'

'They will be making all speed. The winds may help them forward. Why should they put into Brazil when their destination is Chile?'

I could have answered, 'Because almost every ship does,' but I saw he was determined to be anxious.

So I offered him wine and listened as he told me of the dangers of rounding Cape Horn, as if we had not just performed the feat together and I myself had not lost my own dear husband on the same stretch of water.

As my heartbeat settled, he turned happily to his own future. 'Captain Brown of the *Beaver* gives the most formidable account of a Portuguese fleet bound for Bahia.' Leaping to his feet, he showed me, with demonstrations on a nearby table, exactly how he would suffocate the Brazilian fleet and starve the citizens of Bahia into submission. 'The Imperial Army,' he conceded, 'will play their part but, as always, it is the actions at sea, that will determine the outcome.'

So Lady Cochrane was forgotten. I could almost have been sorry for her and her child, were it not that I would be myself forgotten, both of us in a far-off country without our lord.

*   *   *

Two days later, I had a message from His Lordship to prepare myself and descend to the seafront when a boat would take me out to the *Pedro Primeiro*, now dropped down the harbour as far as Boa Viage. Only a short walk from my cottage, I could see its masts and flags, a cheerful sight, as warlike shows usually are.

An English officer, Lieutenant Gulliver, a hearty youth with long chestnut hair, and a midshipman accompanied me over the water. Their uniforms were so fresh that I imagined this would be their first engagement and wondered whether blockading the enemy would satisfy their lust for glory. The officer was determined to tell me about the morning's excitement.

I put my face up to a warm breeze and listened.

'The Emperor and Empress came on board this morning, pleased with everything they saw until some Portuguese officers began to complain that the English sailors had been drunk the night before.'

'Ha! Ha!' intervened the little midshipman, as if to suggest that drunkenness in sailors was hardly a surprise.

'The Empress,' continued Gulliver, 'as impressive a lady as ever looked down her Hapsburg nose' showing here a surprising grasp of history, for the Empress had been the Archduchess Maria Leopoldina, 'turned to the officer nearest to her and announced, "Oh, 'tis the custom of the north, where brave men come from. The sailors are under my protection. I spread my mantle over them." '

'Was that not a great put-down?' chortled the midshipman, so infectiously that Gulliver and I joined in.

We came aboard the grandeur of the *Pedro Primeiro* with fittingly sober faces. His Lordship met me at once, wanting to take me over every corner of the ship so that I was reminded of our trip on the ill-fated steamship the *Rising Star*. Every minute with him now was clouded by my sense of his imminent departure. When I reclined on the green morocco cushions in his cabin, I thought only that soon he would lean against them but not I. His mind was on cordage, gunpowder and, most of all, the training of an untried crew. I was too afraid of breaking down to carry much conversation.

But as Gulliver swung himself along to collect me for the return journey, the Admiral said, nonchalantly enough, 'I shall see you for breakfast tomorrow. We shall not sail till noon.' So it was not yet farewell.

The next morning was dull and grey. I had been up since dawn, expectant. I had made Antonio pick a huge vase of lilies and set it by my chair so the Admiral's last view of me should be beautiful. Imagine my horror when I saw the entire Brazilian fleet, the *Pedro Primeiro*, the *Maria de la Gloria*, the *Unao* and the *Liberal* get underway and sail.

I could only watch, trying to hide my tears from Glennie, as the squadron came abreast of Santa Cruz and the fort began to salute. Just then the sun broke from behind a cloud and a bright yellow flood of light descended behind the ships to the water, where they seemed to swim in a sea of glory.

My eyes dried in wonder. At length, in a kind of inward prayer, I said my farewells. Much later, I discovered that the Emperor and Empress were on board the *Pedro Primeiro*, and stayed there till they

318

reached the lighthouse. Consequently the Admiral could not leave them to visit me.

Such is the fate of illicit lovers.

CHAPTER TWENTY-NINE

I should have left Rio the day that Kitty Cochrane arrived. Beautiful, young, high-spirited, titled, the wife of a hero, the whole city was at her feet.

What was I in comparison? My world was confined to the little house on Gloria Hill for I had neither station nor friends in Rio, aside from the naval men who came off the British ships. I had not been presented to the Emperor and Empress so had no visibility at Court or, therefore, to the grander families. More painful still, my arrival with the Admiral had given rise to gossip in this sweltering, indulgent place, which relied for its very existence on the infamy of slavery. Vulgar splendour and despicable hopes had bred a lowly race, and many who should have known better thought themselves too good to visit me.

While His Lordship remained, this was merely an insult to be borne bravely enough. But once he had sailed, I fell back in solitude and desolation and soon became ill. The news that General O'Higgins had agreed to abdicate in favour of General Freire on 28th January, only a few days after we'd left Chile, should, perhaps, have made me more sanguine: it proved we'd left in the nick of time. Instead I felt as if my months in Chile were already being negated and relegated to history. My correspondent wrote that the new Supreme

Director's 'countenance bespeaks great mildness and benevolence'. Yet Chile was to have four constituent congresses in five years.

Oh, what a saga of misfortune! Glennie endlessly ill, and then myself. No kindly Bella or Felipe but only a sluttish freed slave called Elizabetta, whose brutal treatment by her owners had turned her into a brute. Dealing with her slipshod work and sly answers, I regretted Bella and Felipe, and rehearsed daily their loyalty and tact where before I had seen only foolishness and dull minds. I was unhappy before Kitty Cochrane sailed into harbour in the merchant ship *Seostris*, but how much worse thereafter!

Her Ladyship called on me almost as soon as she arrived. It was early morning but the temperature was already in the nineties, the air sultry, and I had just put my swollen feet into a bucket of cool water—at least, what remained after Elizabetta had slopped most of it on the floor, causing an invasion of thirsty flying centipedes to drop from the ceiling.

'Maman!' Glennie came to me in a rush. His health had improved as mine had declined. His long illness having broken his connection to the Royal Navy, he was planning to join the Admiral in Bahia as soon as possible.

'Be careful!' As I feared, he slipped on the puddle but righted himself with the agility of youth.

'We have visitors. Coming up the hill.' This was unusual enough to cause not only Glennie to come running but Elizabetta and the three Negro servants who at this hour (and most other hours) took their leisure in a small garden at the back of the house. 'It is Lady Cochrane, who arrived yesterday . . .'

'I know she arrived yesterday.' Slowly, I took one foot out of the pail and held it up, white and dripping. If Bella had been with me, a towel would already have been wrapped round it.

'. . . and come to see you today!' continued Glennie, with unflattering wonder.

I lifted out the other foot. 'How many are there?'

'A dozen, perhaps.' Glennie peered out of the window. 'They have come by sea.'

'I did not expect them to come by air.'

My slightly bad-tempered calm, which dear Glennie, being male, didn't question, disguised violent emotions: dread, excitement, jealousy, curiosity and even admiration that she wished to confront me so soon. I had no doubt it was rumours of my close friendship with her husband that had brought her halfway across the world. I even felt a kind of ignoble pride that I could be so important.

'Bring me my stockings and shoes,' I told Elizabetta, and to Glennie: 'See what drinks we can provide and that the glasses are clean.'

I looked around the room as I spoke. It had a few charms: the pretty French furniture was not entirely eaten by worms, while some of my paintings and a few prints I had picked up on my travels adorned the walls. There were books in every corner—but I did not expect Kitty to admire those.

'Half close the shutters,' I instructed Antonio, the youngest Negro, whom I had begun to train. Coming out of the sultry heat, a cool dim room would be welcome to my visitors.

I need not have worried. 'Vivacious' was the word most often applied to Kitty, when 'beautiful' had passed along. She came in with her escort of English and Portuguese gentlemen, her maids, her Negroes, her sad little daughter, and lit up the room with her gaiety. She wasn't even as stupid as I'd hoped.

'I trust you are recovering?' she asked, leaning forward tenderly so that her shiny black ringlets fell round her rosy cheeks. 'This climate is so cruel. I would not have come back to South America if I had known we were to be in Rio. Poor Eliza is not strong and I fear for her health.' She glanced at the little girl, bundled up in bonnet and plum jacket peering out from behind her nursemaid. 'I have not brought the boys since they are at school, as boys should be, but from Lord Cochrane's letters I knew that he needed his family around him. He has the strongest ties to his family, and if we are separated too long, his spirits become depressed and his health suffers.'

After this charming speech, redolent of uxorious understanding, she looked up at me again with a kind of coy questioning.

'Lord Cochrane is a most outstanding commander,' I said politely, diverted for a moment by her companions' actions. They were examining every object in the room like ill-disciplined children. 'It is a pity he is not here for you,' I added. 'Would you like tea or juice?'

The pretty bow mouth curved into a drawing-room smile. 'Coffee, if you please, and juice for Eliza.'

'She has the same name as my servant,' I said.

After coffee was duly served, Her Ladyship resumed her conversation. 'I understand Lord Cochrane is starving out the Bahians. Our ship did not pass that way to gain any news.'

Glennie, who had not yet spoken, now

intervened enthusiastically: 'Bahia is on the point of capitulation. We expect to hear from His Lordship very soon. Already prize ships are coming this way.'

At that I thought Kitty's bright eyes sparkled more—I knew her demands for luxury and expensive entertaining had vexed Lord Cochrane over the years. Certainly, as Glennie elaborated on the condition of the ships in the Brazilian fleet, her attention waned and she soon signalled to her grand Portuguese escorts and her attendants that she must be off.

We bade each other farewell with as much goodwill as would satisfy our audience and I immediately called for the return of my bucket, although I would as easily have poured it over my head as used it to cool my feet. Jealousy is a fiery emotion, which even the strongest will might not subdue.

By coincidence, not many days after this meeting, I was offered a berth in His Majesty's Ship *Creole*, which had come from Bahia and would shortly be returning to England. I was once more in bed; Glennie was leaving me that afternoon, and every breath I took was like a knife in my body. The journey would have been hard in my condition yet everybody urged me to it. I hesitated, put off the decision for a day, a week, and then a note arrived from His Lordship.

My dear Madam,
I have been grieved to learn of your
indisposition, but you must recover now that I
tell you we have starved the enemy out of Bahia.
The forts were abandoned this morning, and the
men-of-war, 13 in number, with about 32 sail of

323

transports and merchant vessels, are under sail.
We shall follow to the world's end. I say again,
expect good news.

Ever believe me your sincere and respectful
friend,

Cochrane

2nd July 1823
Eight miles north of Bahia

After such glorious news, sent to me but not to
sweet Kitty (admittedly, he might not have known
of her arrival), how could I cede my position in
Brazil? Instead of making the decision to depart,
I decided to get well and find my way into Rio
society. I had heard much of the Empress, and all of
it portrayed a clever, lonely young woman, snatched
unhappily from the cultured court of the Habsburgs
to the intrigues of what so recently had been a
colonial outpost. Like myself, she read books,
spoke several languages and was not interested in
frivolity. She would make a perfect subject for my
Brazilian journal. It also seemed to me she was in
need of just the kind of friendship I could provide.
I, therefore, set about arranging it.

My introduction, oddly, was through the modest
Mrs May who, in her artless way, had made a
friend of Doña Ana, the wife of Señor Luis Jose de
Carvalho e Melo, both of them aristocratic, rich,
well connected and, more of a surprise, very well
educated.

I had already entered their house, brought by a
French naval captain of my acquaintance, La Susse,
who had taken me there to watch the procession of
the Emperor and Empress to the state opening of

the Constituent and Legislative Assembly. Inside the state coach, which was pulled by eight mules, sat the young and handsome Dom Pedro, dressed in a cape of yellow feathers over green robes. Beside him sat his wife and on the seat in front perched his jewel-encrusted crown.

Of all this I had been merely a spectator, mocking to myself the absurd gala carriages and *calèches*: many looked as if they'd been built in the age of Louis XIV and were decorated with all kinds of savage hangings, absurd liveries, gaudy silver harnesses—pea-green being a favourite colour. Even the houses around were hung with damask and satin, and the balconies were stacked three deep with ladies decked out in gala finery, including diamonds to rival any I've seen in the world. They waved their handkerchiefs and scattered flowers on the royal coach.

Now, many painful weeks later, I entered the Rua do Ouvidor with greater humility. Nevertheless my interest was solely focused on the Empress, who must be superior, from her European background, to the rest of the Court. I was formally presented to her at the palace of São Cristóvão, where the imperial family presided, just outside the city.

It was a morning of suffering, following a night of the same, so I took a good quantity of opium to dull the pain and was glad that several other English visitors were to be presented since I did not expect to shine. Indeed, as my carriage turned towards the elegant neo-classical palace, set in its own ample grounds, I feared that I might faint or otherwise disgrace myself. (Later I painted the palace but since the Empress begged the picture from me, I cannot recommend where it may be viewed.)

Lady Amherst and her daughter were presented first, by the stout Mrs Chamberlain, unfortunately attired in blue and yellow stripes, which would have more suited an armchair. She was the English consul's wife and very aware of her station. It was correct for the Amhersts to take precedence since her husband was not only an earl (originally William Pitt) but also a governor-general of India. Yet my insignificance as I waited, dressed once more in the darkest widow's black—that was the convention in this country—lay heavy on me.

The Empress instantly dispelled such doubt. 'I have heard so much of you, Mrs Graham,' she said, speaking in perfect French.

As I was trying to curtsy and kiss her hand, I failed in any sensible response so she continued to set me at ease. 'You have published journals of your travels, I know. Perhaps you will write of our newly independent country here.'

I straightened and was face to face with the sweetest expression I had ever seen on a royal countenance. Not beautiful, admittedly, but alive with intelligence. Her figure was more rounded than slender, which was hardly surprising since she had given birth to a daughter for every year of her marriage to Dom Pedro, but she carried off her purple satin morning dress with grace. We talked about Europe, which I could tell she missed greatly, and her children. The name of the Imperial Princess, Doña Maria da Glória, brought a particular light to her eyes, as eldest children so often do.

This first meeting with the Empress was soon to be followed by many more; of course, I did not know then that her daughter's fate was to be connected to mine—not, I'm afraid, for the good. But that goes for almost everything in benighted Rio. Even poor Captain Graham's fever, which eventually proved fatal, had been contracted during the *Doris*'s time there. Owing to his illness, my visits ashore had then been in the company of Mr Dance from the *Doris*, or the midshipmen, my own dearest 'boys'. It was a strange coincidence, therefore, that the *Doris* should sail into Rio, with the same Dance, about to become acting captain of HMS *Beaver*, and many of the midshipmen I had known.

So now I had companionship, an entry into the court, which also gave me access to the highest society, and soon a preoccupation: slavery! It was enough to hold me in Rio.

*　　*　　*

'You are so very grand, Acting Captain Dance, that I don't expect you will be escort to a humble widow.'

I stood outside my house on the walkway and hailed Mr Dance as he approached with a springy, youthful step. It was a fresher morning than usual and my lungs felt correspondingly more energetic. Behind him straggled a group of naval young men, suffering from the lassitude that attacks those hybrid of child and man, and behind them the great harbour, alive with a constant movement of ships and small boats. Two years earlier I had written that neither Naples, the Firth of Forth, Bombay harbour nor Trincomalee could surpass the beauty of the bay.

I could still admire it as a tourist, for the ships were graceful, the sea brilliant and the sky clear, but I could not love it as I had Valparaíso. After

327

all, the Admiral's ship was not anchored there, nor could be expected, and—a nobler preoccupation—too many vessels were coming from Africa, bringing their shameful human cargo.

Mr Dance began a retreat: 'If you were not such an intrepid explorer, Mrs Graham, I would have more confidence in my ability to be your escort. As it is, my duties on the *Beaver*—'

'Young men!' I interrupted him and turned my attention to the boys. 'Mr Chandler, Mr Witty, Mr Tunis, you shall be my guard.'

I led this little band to the Val Longo, the slave market of Rio. The day had already heated up and my escorts and I would rather have been sucking oranges in the shade. Tunis, a lanky youth (who later became an earl and a very respectable admiral of the Blue), was clanking marbles in his pocket.

'Mr Tunis, my dear,' I resumed the school-ma'am's voice that I had used on them to good effect over many months on the *Doris*, 'I wonder how your Greek is progressing. Perhaps you would like to try me with a touch of Homer.'

He laughed uncomfortably and the others sniggered, moving away surreptitiously in case they became my next target.

Dear little Mr Witty, braver (although he died of the fever too young to become even a lieutenant), addressed me: 'We are not in the schoolroom now, Mrs Graham. Besides, we've seen such things since we last met.' He began telling me about their journeying round the globe, about the glaciers, polar bears, the storms with waves erupting like volcanoes, about true volcanoes sending up flames as high as the sun . . . They were good boys. I loved them and they knew it.

328

The slave market was a curious place, disturbing for so many different reasons. The Val Longo, as its name suggests, was a very long street in which almost every house was a depot for slaves. The doors were cut in two, as with stables, so that the slaves, like animals, might look over at the world, should they have the will. Most sat on benches or lay inside, their bodies emaciated, their heads shaved and the marks of recent itch upon their skin. The contrast with the bright cheerfulness of the day and the health of my companions, of the same kind of ages, made me set my lips with shame that God's creatures should be treated so callously.

'Let us go.' Witty plucked at my sleeve.

'*They* exist whether we go or stay.' I knew the poor boy's wish to deny the very existence of such unhappy fellow human beings. But the Val Longo was as much a part of his education as Homer. I noticed that three or four captives, with their heads over the doors, were staring at us.

'Let us go now,' said Chandler, which determined me to go closer.

'They are Africans,' I said, over my shoulder, for none of my boys had followed me, 'far from home, wondering at things here as you wondered at icebergs and polar bears.' As I neared the door, the captives began to chatter in their own language and point at me with smiles and even laughter. Though more inclined to weep, I smiled back at them, looked cheerfully and kissed my hand to them, with all of which they seemed delighted, jumped about and danced, as if returning my civilities.

'Oh, you poor things! You poor, poor things!' I could not restrain myself from exclaiming out loud, at which they danced the more. To my eyes it was a dance of death, their childish glee certain to be cut short by miserable suffering. They were already lucky to have survived since one in five died on the passage from Africa.

I returned to my boys, my sight blurred by tears. They, heartless little brutes whose fathers might well have profited from slavery (even though the trade had been abolished throughout the British Empire in 1807), were gathered in a huddle outside one of the few houses without slaves. I said nothing and wiped my face firmly. The sight of that vale of tears was enough of a lesson and, although we walked back soberly to my house, cakes and a jug of beer soon restored their good humour.

My own spirits remained low but I found some consolation in writing my experiences in my journal with the knowledge that superior persons in England would be forced to face up to the reality of the situation in which the British were certainly complicit. I have a naturally interfering cast of mind, not so different from His Lordship's—it made us both unpopular. During my stay in Rio, I questioned any officials I met for the true figures on the slave trade. Eventually, I obtained a statement of customs house entries: 21,199 slaves imported in 1821, 24,934 in 1822. These were shocking facts.

The immediate result was that I became far more tolerant of my own freed slaves, Antonio, Elizabetta and the others, and soon placed so much reliance on Antonio that I took him as a companion when I felt well enough to make a little exploration of the countryside behind the city.

I do not intend, however, to give a full account of my stay in Brazil. Any vitality in my story comes from my feelings for its hero and he was far, far away. In his absence, my emotional satisfaction came from my growing association with the Empress. I was soon quite in the habit of going to court functions. At first it was hard going there on my own but I always took the trouble to make friends. One of them, a French gentleman, remarked to me, 'There are but four English ladies present, yet you hardly ever converse together.' He was a fine, humorous man with jet-black hair.

'You are quite right,' I answered firmly. 'I like, when I am in foreign society, to talk to foreigners, and think it neither wise nor civil to form coteries with those of one's own nation.'

He smiled, or rather leered, under his great black moustaches but added nothing to his observation. Of course, one of the ladies to whom he referred was Lady Cochrane. I had to get used to seeing her everywhere. Her companions on this occasion were Mrs Chamberlain, the English consul's self-important wife, and the wife of the commissioner for the slave business. Neither of them appealed. A more charitable lady might have felt sorry for Kitty, who never looked particularly happy, despite her famed 'vivacity'. But I had never had any time for women whose sole interest lay in the effect of their beauty and their social position.

We bowed to each other and said, 'Good evening', without quite looking into each other's faces.

With the Empress it was another matter. I was flattered by her picking me for conversation in her private apartments. Sometimes we talked about the places we both knew in Europe for which, although she doted on her husband far more than he deserved, she was thoroughly homesick. She liked to try out her English on me which was not as good as her other four or five languages.

'Meesees Graham,' she began one day, pursing her full Habsburg lips in what she hoped was an English mode, 'do you read a book today? I would like to know the book.'

'I am sure Your Imperial Majesty would not,' I began, then saw her surprised frown and realised one does not contradict an empress, however gentle and affectionate. Even the black maids stiffened as if they understood English, which they certainly didn't. In fact none of the court spoke anything but Portuguese and most had never read a book, being only educated enough for gossip and intrigue. 'What I meant to say,' I continued carefully, 'was that I am reading a novel, a *roman*, and perhaps such stories are not suitable for an empress.'

'*Un roman*,' she repeated, and then, catching my meaning, went off into a gale of laughter. At which all the maids—one I came to know well, called Black Anna—also began to laugh and even clap their hands.

'But I love the novels. Your Maria Edgeworth was everything in Paris. Tell me the one you read.'

'It is not by an English writer, madam, but by a Scottish man called Sir Walter Scott. It is a history, *Peveril of the Peak*. The principal figure is the Duke of Buckingham, at the court of the English King Charles the Second.'

'*P-e-ve-reel de la Pic* . . .' tested my august companion.

'*Exactement*, Your Imperial Majesty.'

'*Parfait*. I will like to read. And your *mal-élevé* Lord Byron, you read him too?'

'Poetry is my greatest weakness, particularly that of Lord Byron.'

'You have many books with you?'

'Too many.'

'You will bring here? And my English will soon be good like my German.'

She was a clever lady, excited by the adventure of a new democracy and the charms of her handsome husband, but at heart a lover of privacy and study.

He, Dom Pedro, with his swaggering airs, soon lost any charms he had had for me. It was impossible to avoid knowing what he didn't attempt to hide: that he had many lovers. Neither did he deny his bastards. Like other self-indulgent monarchs, he had *une maîtresse en titre*—the only *titre* in which he was likely to show any interest. Madame de Castro, who favoured spectacular pea-green wigs, disliked me from the start, although I did not know why.

As the weeks passed and my friendship with Her Imperial Majesty drew closer, my popularity, such as it was, declined. The Brazilians, who talked of their empress as 'the stranger', began to talk about me as the 'second stranger'. The so-called 'Portuguese' diehards, who still had not given up hope of Portuguese association, if not rule, hated my championship of the new order. The English— leaving aside a few good friends, my doctor, the Mays, Mrs May's brother, Mr Dampier, who was happy to escort me wherever I wanted—continued to shun me, led, I believe, by the ladies. For example, Mrs Chamberlain, a close companion of darling Kitty, poisoned her husband, the consul, against me so that I was never invited to their house.

One sultry evening, when Mrs May and I were trying to catch a breath of air in my little garden, I

333

broke down and wept. 'What is it that I have done to these people? Am I not clever enough? Am I not well bred enough? How is it I am not deserving?'

Mrs May picked up a dead palm leaf that had fallen to the ground and began to fan herself. 'My dear Mrs Graham . . .' she hesitated, looking sympathetically at my still falling tears '. . . I understand you did not follow normal practice and visit the consul's wife on your arrival.'

'But I thought hers was that duty!' Indignation dried my eyes. 'Besides, I was ill. You took pity, why not she?'

Mrs May fanned faster without answering. We both knew the truth was that the gossips had spoken ill of me, and after the injured wife had arrived, with sick child in tow, I had had no chance at all.

'Never mind, my dear Mrs May, I have lived through worse and at least I have the consolation of being received in intimate circumstances by our august empress.'

I must have sounded smug because even the kind-hearted Mrs May frowned. I saw her deciding to speak. 'It is said that you would like to become governess to the little Princess Maria da Glória.'

I was quite taken aback and laughed falsely. It was true I'd been foolish enough to confess some such idea to Sir Thomas Hardy, a most charming gentleman who had flattered me with his attentions at a *soirée*. 'Oh, no, no! How could I consider such an idea?'

My denial cut no ice with the practical Mrs May. She put aside her fan and spoke clearly, with the intonation of someone brought up in the north of England. 'Then what reason have you to remain here?'

CHAPTER THIRTY

They all wanted me to leave—save Her Imperial Majesty. I could well have exclaimed, with Shakespeare's Rosalind, 'Oh how full of briers is this working-day world!' Yet I was still in Rio on 1st October when the news arrived of another great victory for the Admiral: he had taken Maranham, the final and most intransigent northern state in the hands of the Portuguese royalists.

Lieutenant Gulliver, who had escorted me across the bay to the *Pedro Primeiro*, brought a personal letter to my cramped quarters in town where I had been forced to move for reasons of economy. His visit was like a reviving burst of fresh air.

'Tell me, dear Mr Gulliver,' I grasped his large, calloused hands, thinking that not so long ago they would have held his Admiral's, 'was it a difficult engagement?'

'His Lordship fooled them entirely,' he replied, laughing heartily at the memory. 'We were in there flying an English flag, with Mr Shepherd playing a desperate part with utter ease, and then the *Pedro Primeiro* followed and anchored under Fort San Francisco. From there the Admiral sent a message to the authorities, assuring them of perfect good treatment if they surrendered, but all the horrors endured by Bahia if they held out. The junta, headed by an excellent bishop, soon saw their way to becoming part of free Brazil.' The lieutenant laughed again. ' "Impossible" is how they described the taking of Maranham to the Admiral, which is why he went at it.'

I agreed that the word 'impossible' was a red rag to a noble bull and reminded him of the same having been said before the taking of Valdivia. I added, 'I'm happy that Mr Shepherd, who I travelled with from Chile, performed well.'

'Then you sailed with the Admiral?'

I contented myself with an 'Oh, yes', a little surprised that my reputation was blank with this young man. But simple confirmation was enough to set him questioning me about his hero. Calling for meats, wine and brandy, I settled down for a few hours of what I enjoyed most: extolling the merits of His Lordship.

'You saw him in London too?'

Here I was a little more sketchy, emphasising our shared Scottish background and his role as a Whig Member of Parliament before his enemies had engineered his downfall.

At this hint of politics, the good lieutenant noticed it had got dark and leapt to his feet, crying, 'I've been expected on board two hours since.'

'Go! Go!' I told him tolerantly, and imagined with envy his boat trip across the bay to his tall, creaking home.

But I had my letter. I carried it to my room and read it gloatingly by candlelight. It was not a love letter by any normal standards but His Lordship's desire to tell me, in person, of his triumph, assured me that I was first in some part of his heart. Indeed, tender words could hardly have meant more to me than his celebration of the facts:

Maranham, 12th August, 1823
My dear Madam,
You would receive a few lines from me, dated

*from off Bahia, and also from the latitude
of Pernambuco, saying briefly what we were
about then. And now I have to add, that we
followed the Portuguese squadron to the fifth
degree of north latitude, and until only thirteen
sail remained together out of the seventy of
their convoy; and then judging it better for the
interests of His Imperial Majesty, I hauled the
wind for Maranham; and I have the pleasure to
tell you, that my plan of adding it to the Empire
has had complete success. I ran in with this ship
abreast of their forts; and having sent a notice
of blockade and intimated that the squadron
of Bahia and Imperial forces were off the bar,
the Portuguese flag was hauled down, and
everything went on without bloodshed, just as
you could wish . . .*

*. . . Thus my dear Madam, on my return I
shall have the pleasure to acquaint His Imperial
Majesty, that between the extremities of his
empire there exists no enemy either on shore or
afloat . . .*

Oh, how wonderful such a declaration! Not only
was it victory for the principles of liberty but also
a promise of his return. Indeed, the letter ended
with his intention to sail for Rio as soon as possible
where he had every expectation of having the
pleasure of my company once again.

I should have rejoiced. I did rejoice. Yet how
could I expect to see him in any sort of intimacy
when his dearest Kitty was waiting with jealous
arms? Despite the increasing illness of her little
daughter, she stayed on, determined, I believe, to
sit me out. I could not guess that the very next day

337

there was to be a further twist to my story.

I was at court in a gathering attended by Their Imperial Majesties. We had first to go through the ceremony of kissing the royal hands, which I had come to detest—at least, when Dom Pedro's hand was the one held out to me. We were all given the opportunity, and when the room was full, as it was on this occasion, it could take a very long time. Both majesties were splendidly attired, the Emperor in a vaguely military uniform, with many silver buttons, sashes, medals, and a ridiculously long sword that was in danger of tripping anyone who came near. The Empress was dignified in white satin embroidered with gold, a headdress of feathers tipped with green, and opals liberally sprinkled over her person, including around the portrait of the Emperor she wore always on her bosom.

At the front was Lady Cochrane and beside her the proud consul's wife. I was with my friend Madame de Rio Seco, a powerful lady at Court. I whispered, 'How charming it is to see those clumsy Negro hands take up with such care the little white hand of the Empress and hold it to their pouting African lips.'

(To a modern reader, this must seem an insufferable racist comment for which I might even be clapped in gaol, but two hundred years ago we were still uneducated in racial equality, although I can boast of holding dear the abolitionists' maxim, 'Am I not a man and a brother?')

'Indeed the Negro soldiers are an important part of the Imperial Army,' agreed Madame de Rio Seco.

It was because of this little interchange that I

338

found myself unprepared and at the front of the kissing queue. As I came forward, the Emperor hesitated, turned towards Lady Cochrane, who was still in his circle, and announced to her, in the hearing of us all, 'Today, madam, I have conferred on Lord Cochrane, the admiral of our naval fleet, the title of Marques of Maranham so that I now address you as the Marquesa of Maranham.'

A little clapping broke out but, since he had spoke in French, the new Marchioness looked quite bewildered until Mrs Chamberlain whispered in her ear. Then she blushed prettily, gave the lowest curtsy possible, without reaching the floor, so that everybody clapped again. The Emperor turned back to the kissing queue.

Taken by surprise, I put forward my hand to take his before realising I was still wearing my glove. What a catastrophe! There were sniggers from behind while the Emperor, Zeus thunderbolts flashing from his black eyes, abandoned us for the assembly room. There, he gave a long speech celebrating the Brazilian victory and its perpetrator, the new *marques*.

Covered in confusion and suddenly friendless, I resolved to find the Empress and make my apologies. But she, too, was retiring towards her private apartments where at that moment I did not quite dare follow her.

My anger with myself and at the whole ridiculous charade was increased by seeing the Empress stop by the proud Marchioness and have several earnest words with her. Although they seemed to glance my way several times, I had no hint of the next act in the drama. Only pausing to collect a few ladies round her, Kitty swept over to me.

I curtsied to her. 'Marchioness, may I be the first to congratulate you.'

She bowed, the diamond stars in her diadem sparkling among her dark curls. 'I have been speaking to the Empress,' she said, her voice childlike and fluting. 'She wishes me to convey to you what is in her mind.'

I smiled politely, wondering why the Empress couldn't convey her thoughts in person. In the last months, we had shared so much of what was in our minds, finding that we had in common not only a love of books and the study of languages but also of botanising and geology. Her Imperial Majesty owned a remarkable collection of shells, which I had helped her collate by providing drawings.

The Marchioness drew herself up. 'Her Imperial Majesty would like you to accept the post of governess to her daughter Princess Maria da Glória.' After this little speech, she took up her fan, made of lace as fine as a spider's web. Her dark eyes, with their long lashes, assessed me over the top.

'I am honoured, my lady,' I began. I *was* honoured. Despite Sir Thomas Hardy, I had never really thought the post could be mine. Yet it was hard to accept gratefully the role of governess when the news had been conveyed by an illiterate bastard who had just been made a Marchioness.

'The Empress suggests you meet the Emperor at five o'clock,' continued the Marchioness, 'when he will confirm the appointment.' I became aware that the odious Mrs Chamberlain and all the ladies around us were staring at me with a curious unwinking gaze. The sense of being an outsider which I have carried with me all my life, became painfully strong.

'It is very gracious of Their Imperial Majesties,' I managed to stumble out.

'Your learning is known throughout Rio,' said the Marchioness, 'perhaps even Brazil.' Around her the faces smirked.

'You are very kind.' It is easy for the uneducated to make fun of the educated. 'I will attend at five,' I replied calmly, and started as if to make my way out of the room.

But the Marchioness stepped close to me, 'The Empress wished me to advise you further that you have her leave to visit England before taking up your duties. She will not expect you for some months so that you can collect the books you may need for your work as governess.'

'I understand a packet will be leaving for England within the next week,' added the consul's wife.

I left quickly, aware, in your succinct modern parlance, that it was 'a stitch-up'. Sweet Kitty had seen a way of removing me before the Admiral's return and turned it into a royal command.

Elizabetta and Antonio noticed my distress as we waited for my carriage outside the palace for, by now, I had learnt they had tender hearts.

'Are you ill?' asked Elizabetta, fanning me with her apron. The sun blazed down since it was one o'clock in the afternoon. But I was not ill, merely angry, cornered, confused and almost despairing.

By chance Mrs May called immediately after my return so we sat in my dark little room trying to pretend it was cooler with the shutters closed, and talked of my future.

'Once gone, you must not think of returning

here!' Mrs May's round face flushed with conviction. 'You belong among your family and your intellectual equals.'

How kind is a sincere friend! How soothing her sentiments! I put my hand over hers. 'I shall, of course, arrange the publication of my journals while I am in England. But otherwise nothing awaits me there.'

'Nothing?' She could not believe me.

'I deeply admire the Empress and wish to educate Princess Maria da Glória up to the highest European standards.'

'And the Emperor?' Mrs May sat straighter and took back her plump little hand. 'Does he wish his Brazilian princess to look back to old Europe?'

For a practical woman, Mrs May was sometimes very astute, but I was not listening to her. I knew only one truth: while His Lordship was west of the Atlantic, I must be there too. I could only bear my banishment from his side, for that was what it seemed, if I had a certain reason to return.

'I shall see the Emperor later today,' I told Mrs May. 'If he formally confirms my appointment as governess to his family, it would be wrong to deny him.'

'Wrong,' repeated the good lady, who had often heard my views on the delinquencies of that royal personage.

'Improper,' I tried—with no more success. So, we sipped our tea quietly until it was time for me to return to the palace.

Yet what would I have been in London? A writer, true, but a widow, first, a displaced lady just as I was here. There was no job open to me, as there would be for a woman of my talents two

342

hundred years later, or, at least, only one job: marriage. But I was not ready for that yet. Even if my love had allowed it, my sense of adventure was still too strong. I would rather be confidante of an empress and governess to a princess.

So, three days after my interview with the Emperor, when I had kissed and curtsied and he, fully bemedalled, was gracious, I and my twenty or more boxes, including botanic samples from Her Imperial Majesty and many I had collected previously, were loaded on to the packet for England.

Mrs May walked down with me to the shore. Behind us, Antonio carried my personal baggage on his broad back. Elizabetta had wept as we parted at the house. 'It's only *au revoir*,' I had told her, which did not console, perhaps did not convince. Hers were the only tears my departure was likely to inspire. It was another humid morning with only a soft wind and I wondered whether or not we would be able to sail. I looked at the boat come to take me out.

'It is kind of Sir Murray Maxwell to lend his boat to me,' I said. I thought how agreeable it would be not to depend on the kindness of strangers.

'So long since I've seen England.' Mrs May sighed. 'I shall miss you.' I smiled. 'My brother will miss you, too,' she added, with a perfect understanding of my smile.

'Mr Dampier and I made some interesting expeditions together.' This was true: we had visited many small towns and large estates where I had seen up to two thousand slaves working, many exploited unmercifully, others as well looked after as any good employer treasures his employees. Our

343

experiences had given me much useful material for my journals. This, of course, was my lasting talent and profession. The idea cheered me. I had already written to John Murray, announcing my arrival.

'Your brother is a great horseman but I beat him at a race once.'

'That won't have pleased him.'

'But it did. He decided on it. He said that to be beaten by a woman like me was a greater honour than to win.'

Mrs May smiled doubtfully. She knew her brother had fallen a little in love with me. My spirits lifted another notch, then fell again. It is the way of an outsider and a traveller always to be meeting new people, then soon saying farewell. I would have had a more rousing send-off, except that none of my naval friends was in Rio. I glanced behind to where Antonio waited patiently.

'I should go before Sir Murray's boatmen drift away. I must thank you before everyone.'

Mrs May dabbed her eyes. 'I do not like to see a woman on her own.' This was irritating. 'And your health is hardly reliable.'

'I was born to the sea.' I chose to take her remarks as referring to the long voyage ahead and started walking towards the trickling waves. The pebbles crunched under my sensible boots and a strong smell of salt, fish and sewage filled my nostrils. I raised my head and imagined the *Pedro Primeiro* appearing on the skyline with the Admiral on deck. I would direct Sir Murray Maxwell's boat towards him and he would hold open his broad arms.

'*Au revoir*, my dear friend.' We embraced, Mrs May so small and comfortable, and myself as stiff as a marble column.

When I arrived on the packet and had properly taken charge of my little cabin, I climbed the steps back up to the deck. No one took much notice, which pleased me. There were no other paying passengers and, still more happily, the captain's wife and daughter were on board. I felt as if I had taken lodgings with a quiet English family, all so decent, orderly and clean.

I stared at the great bay of Rio de Janeiro, the very opposite of those adjectives, and imagined the brilliant colours of wealth and corruption disguised in the steamy haze. My attention was diverted by a line of seamen about to haul up a sail on our ship. One carried a monkey on his shoulder, which chattered at me in the most friendly way.

Thus cheered, I retired below.

CHAPTER THIRTY-ONE

It took us nearly two months to reach Falmouth, our course always eastwards, so any dreams I had of meeting with the *Pedro Primeiro* on the northern coast of Brazil were sunk. On 7th November 1823 my journal notes with admirable restraint:

Lat. 5 ° N, long. 25 ° W. For several days the thermometer at 80 °; the temperature of the sea at noon 82 °. We spoke to the *Pambinha [a ship]* 60 days from Maranham. She says Lord Cochrane had gone himself to Para, whence he meant to proceed directly for Rio; so that he would probably be there by this time, as the

Pedro Primeiro sails well. I had no opportunity of learning more as the vessel passed hastily.

This was the extent of my contact with His Lordship for the next many many months. Yet his presence never left me. After passing the Azores, the captain summoned me on deck to watch one of the miracles of nature: two great winds, meeting in the open sea and driving the water furiously before them, forced up a vast line of spume that broke upwards as high as any ship's mast. Soaked to the skin and wondering how our small vessel survived, I likened this majestic event to the meeting of Lord Cochrane and myself.

*   *   *

I arrived in England near Christmas when, then as now, people took the opportunity to become less efficient than usual. I therefore hastened to London and to Albemarle Street where John Murray held literary court.

Murray met me at the entrance. As we entered I glanced backwards at Piccadilly. 'The streets are noisier than ever,' I commented, 'the carriages driven by savages.'

He offered me his arm and led me up the elegant staircase. 'You are the one who has stayed among savages,' he told me suavely.

I took hold of the banister. After my long sea voyage, my legs rolled weakly and I was glad of all supports. As soon as we were settled and tea poured, he began with what was on his mind. 'It is good to see you home after so long. If only others would or could return!' His handsome brow on which the hair was brushed fashionably forward, wrinkled in a doleful frown.

I knew at once to whom he was referring. 'I understand Lord Byron is in Greece.'

'You are sitting on his chair. He arrived in Kefalonia in August when he insisted on raising four thousand pounds of his own money to refit the Greek Navy, then sailed for Messolonghi where he may arrive at any time. Oh, why does a poetic genius dissipate his energies on the politics of a nation synonymous with deceit?'

We had always talked of Byron so I defended him briefly. 'Like all great men, he is a romantic.' I wanted, reasonably enough, to talk about my own affairs, which, for once, seemed more pressing than the poetic m'lord's. 'I have witnessed the coming of freedom in two countries over the last years. It is politics like none other. Men of honour can never turn aside.'

Murray twiddled his thumbs for a moment before peering at me curiously. 'You became friendly with Lord Cochrane while in Chile, I understand.'

I blushed, but as I have a naturally high colour and Murray's eyes were myopic, I don't expect he noticed. 'He is a principal in the story of Chile's independence and I am honoured to count him a friend.'

'He is a surprising man. Where is he now?'

'After taking northern Brazil from the Portuguese, His Lordship has rejoined Lady Cochrane in Rio.' I spoke a little stiffly.

'And returns to England soon?'

'I am not party to his plans.'

'No. Certainly not. These naval men treat the

world like Ariel, who promised to put a girdle round the earth in forty minutes.'

'"Round *about*".'

'What. Oh, yes.' Murray laughed. 'You always were a devil for accuracy.' Which was not true; it was just that I was irritated by him. 'Now, shall we do some business?' He looked at his watch. 'You will stay for what Sir Walter calls my "four o'clock friends". You have read *Peveril*, I am certain. The great man himself has promised to attend.'

I assured him I had read *Peveril* with great delight and even passed it to the Empress of Brazil. Then we did talk business and his terms were so gentlemanly for my two books that I found enthusiasm to stay for his gathering of authors and journalists.

The beautiful room filled quickly. The smoke from the men's pipes and cigars wreathed the portrait of Byron, the busts of Wellington and Cicero, as if it were laurel crowning the brows of the great. Among the noisy confidence of braying English voices I had enough writerly acquaintances to feel part of the scene and, after half an hour, as if I had never left it. Indeed, I gathered a little circle round me as I expounded on the iniquities of slavery in Rio de Janeiro, which I had seen with my own eyes. Cards and invitations were pressed upon me but best of all was a letter Murray gave to me as I took my leave.

'Spencer would have shot me if I forgot. Mad keen to have you. Fine house, Althorp. Fine people. A great collector. You know the naval son, I understand.'

I didn't answer his question but thought that dear Captain Spencer, my young admirer, had been

348

true to his word. A well-run country house was just the place I needed to pass the winter months and see my journals through publication. Captain Spencer could not be importunate under his parents' eyes and, besides, he had probably found a malleable wife by now.

I wrote that very night accepting the invitation.

*   *   *

A single lady who can make herself agreeable will always find a place in a house, if it is large enough. My bedroom was spacious, the fire lit early and kept in till late, my duties light: I was to be talkative but not too talkative, to attend at meals and at other times when invited, to admire the gardens, shrubberies and hothouses—this a pleasure (I unpacked some of my plants there), to visit by carriage dull neighbours and, another pleasure, to accept the use of a riding horse from Althorp's extensive stables.

None of these activities interrupted the main purpose of my visit: to complete my books, which in practice involved long hours of copying out those parts of my journal that I wished to be published. I had a desk by the fire since the weather was bitter, particularly coming as I had from the torrid airs of Brazil. I had pens, ink, blotters, a stack of notebooks. In short, allowing for the strange hiatus of my situation, I was as happy as possible.

In January Captain Spencer came for a visit.

'My dear Mrs Graham!'

I was standing on the mounting block, having just descended from my mare, when he rode into the stables. He seemed as surprised to see me as I was

349

to see him, his parents having assured me he was at sea.

'Freddie! Freddie!' His younger sister, who had been riding out with me and Lord Spencer, ran towards him and, agile as a monkey, climbed up in front of him. The horse, tired though he was, capered protestingly.

I took the opportunity to gather up the skirt of my habit and, despite the perfectly good steps, jump down. The ground was still hard from a sharp frost the night before and I must have winced aloud because Spencer directed his overloaded horse towards me. 'I'm not sure I can add another lady across my saddle.'

History has painted Frederick Spencer as a dry stick, who, through compliance to duty, became an Admiral, an MP, a Knight of the Garter and, like Lord Cochrane, a recipient of the Order of the Bath. But I met him when he was young, a third, fourth or even fifth son, I can never remember which, who never expected to inherit and never had any money. He needed a profession and I knew him both as a good sailor and a charming man.

Later in the day we walked round the gardens, keeping up a brisk pace.

'Are you enjoying my father's library?' he asked me. 'One hundred thousand books must be enough even for you.'

'I am working on my own little books,' I said, smiling. 'But the intellectual stimulant is dizzying after my time in South America.'

'But I heard you were one of the court in Rio. Surely there you found intellectual entertainment.'

'Only in the company of the Empress.' I looked at his handsome face and remembered in whose company I had always seen him. 'There is no group of men I like better than the Navy,' I said, quite seriously.

'Oh, yes, yes. I know that!'

'I think of my little house in the Almendral with great affection.' I paused, but then continued quickly, 'I am here to see my journals through publication, for which purpose your father has generously welcomed me to Althorp.'

'He does so worship his books,' said Spencer, irreverently.

'Five splendid rooms full, the majority bought by your father. He is a great collector.'

'Let us stand for a moment.'

We had turned in our walk and saw at a distance most of the great house revealed. In my description of a 'large house' I may not have given enough majesty to what was, in fact, a palace. There were forty indoor servants and fifty outdoor. My readers, used to my small cottages and expeditions on horseback with a single attendant, may be surprised by the grandeur in which I was living. Literature was partly the explanation, the 2nd earl's love of it, and my own place, however humble, in its annals. That I came from an aristocratic Scottish naval family and that the 2nd earl had been an excellent first lord of the Admiralty (promoting Nelson, for example) was the other part.

We walked back slowly. I beat my numbed hands together, stamped my feet and waited for Spencer to mention my most noble of friends.

'Lord Cochrane is still in Brazil, I understand?'

'I believe so.' When the name came, I found myself quite unable to speak. We were already crossing the driveway and Spencer paused enquiringly.

'Victorious,' I added.

He nodded, before looking up at me with a frowning face. 'Is it true you are returning to be governess to the Emperor's children?'

Up till then he had shown no emotion but his obvious disapproval was too strong to be objective.

'I am honoured with an invitation from His Imperial Majesty, Dom Pedro himself.'

'Dom Pedro!' Disapproval turned to disgust. 'A corrupt court when you could have this!' He spread his arms to indicate the house, the estate, with its new planted trees like clumps of black-lace fans, and the wintry Northamptonshire countryside beyond.

I looked. Then, not sure of his meaning, I pronounced, 'England is always very lovely but I must make my way as you must make yours.'

He bowed, moved forward with a young man's elastic stride, and our conversation came to an end. He had come only for a few days' hunting; I continued my work and we met at mealtimes where there were never less than thirty places set. Yet he was my friend and, in the years to come, brought his wife, a second cousin, and two charming children to visit me.

*　　　*　　　*

Since John Murray had been generous with his terms of publication, I had money enough to buy the books and equipment I needed for a royal schoolroom. However, more and more friends and acquaintances tried to dissuade me from returning to Brazil. Around this time I made a short visit to

Paris, where I made a friend of the famous novelist, Maria Edgeworth. When I told her of my future plans, she was aghast and, on her return to her home in Ireland, wrote to me warningly:

Dame d'honneur sounds well—and Gouvernante des enfants de Brazil, very grand! But be clear before you take the weight of labour and responsibility that is to hang upon this title, that there is a solid well-secured remuneration balancing the weight on the other side. Be pleased to remember a truth and a truism which enthusiastic geniuses are apt to forget while they are in the heat of racing after some favourite flying colour of Hope's rain-bow. Be pleased to remember that not only life is not to be bought with heaps of gold but the poor possession of a day's health is not to be had for the wealth of the Orchominian town or the mines of Peru ... Look once,—look twice,—look three times,—before you leap.

It was paper, ink and epistolary invention wasted. Neither my always doubtful health, nor pecuniary concerns, nor normal good sense could sway my fixed intention.

As winter turned to spring and my journals were turned over to the printer, I went up to Scotland to visit my family. I have revealed little about them in this book. If I was a modern writer, I would make much of my younger brother, deaf and dumb, who lived his life in an institution, and my sister, who managed so much better than me the conventions of the age. (She had no particular talent, however.) But my separation from them at a young age—as I described in my short memoir at the opening of this narrative—had always encouraged me to believe that I was, essentially, alone.

Let them think I was crazy! I looked at the cold black mountains of Scotland and told them how I yearned for the warmth of the southern hemisphere. 'So much gentler to my lungs,' I said, and never told them how ill I'd been in languorous Rio. Instead I described my expeditions with Mr Dampier.

'Mr Dampier?' My aunt's eyes sharpened.

'The brother of my friend, Mrs May. A much younger man,' I continued quickly. 'He rode a tall bay horse and wore a huge straw hat, a short jacket, and a brace of pistols. I was astride a little grey mare, my boat-cloak over my saddle, otherwise dressed as usual, with a straw riding hat and a dark grey habit. Antonio, the merriest of Negroes, followed us on his mule, with Mr Dampier's portmanteau behind and my bag in front of him . . .'

'And what did you see?' they asked me. I described picturesque villages interspersed with vast slaver estates.

With such circumscribed story-telling they soon began to believe my time in Brazil one long picnic, although sighing dutifully over the fate of the slaves.

Yet when I returned to London, a guest with yet another generous host in the newly developed area of Highbury (referred to as 'airy' in Jane Austen's *Emma*), my spirits began to fail a little. I had become too comfortable; Murray's 'four o'clock friends' filled the whole day.

Then, in late April, appalling news struck London with the force of an earthquake. Lord

Byron was dead. He had died in Messolonghi, Greece—free Greece, because with his leadership and money the city was free. He died in a thunderstorm, followed not long by an earthquake in reality. His body was to be brought back to England, the country that had effectively exiled him. He was thirty-seven years old, the age that a fortune-teller had warned him to beware.

Albemarle Street was in mourning, although that seems too respectable a word for the convulsions of grief and desolation. Why do I write about it here? Because his spirit and his poetry (indissoluble) flew like a meteor through my life. Because he was the only genius I had known, apart from one other. Because his poetry and his passionate sense of justice inspired the same emotions that I felt for that other. Because death teaches us how we must live.

One early afternoon I found John Murray alone in his drawing room.

'Hobhouse is determined to burn all Byron's private papers. Friends and family will do it here. In this grate!' He pointed dramatically.

I could find nothing to say, but tears of horror at such desecration rolled down my cheeks.

'And they will not bury him in the Abbey. The Dean is adamant. He quotes "questionable morality". We have a Poets' Corner and the greatest poet of the century may not be buried there.' Murray, the most sanguine of men, slumped in defeat.

I still could not speak but I thought that genius always causes disturbance in the people around them. I told John Murray, 'The moment my journals are published, I return to Brazil,' but he did not attend.

Lord Byron, spurned by authority, lay in state in Great George Street, Westminster. Whig and Radical peers mixed with the common people to visit him. I went once on a perfect May morning when the heart should celebrate the bright leaves and the clear sky. I went again when it rained and looked on the beautiful face with its wide brow and great eyes, like a marble sculpture—and thought of another.

In July the funeral cortège drove through the city, the black plumes gathering dust, the horses straining up Highgate Hill.

Though the night was made for loving,
And the day returns too soon,
Yet we'll go no more a-roving
By the light of the moon.

I had planned to watch the procession but letters came from Brazil that took my attention away. Once more there was insurrection in Pernambuco; revolutionaries had set themselves up as a republic under the leadership of Dom Manuel de Carvalho Pais de Andrade. The Admiral was expected to sail there in the next few weeks. In passing, my correspondent referred to Lady Cochrane: 'Lady C.'s daughter has never been well since she arrived and now her anxious mother has packed her bags and gone in company of a doctor, two servants and her maid.' So Lady Cochrane was no longer in Rio. But neither was her husband.

My journals had been published successfully, 750 copies of each, and were selling well (although some objected I was too kind to Lord

Cochrane); my friends and family had stopped trying to persuade me to stay. I had my boxes of schoolbooks, my good English pens, my preferred notebooks. In short, there was nothing to hinder my departure and everything to urge me forward.

It seemed likely that if I passed by Pernambuco in August, the Admiral would be there.

CHAPTER THIRTY-TWO

18th August, 1824
On making the land near Pernambuco saw a Man of War—Soon made her out to be the *Pedro Primeiro*—a midshipman (young Da Costa) came on board—I sent a message to Lord Cochrane. Soon after Captain Grenfell boarded us, and then I went with him towards the *Pedro Primeiro*—Saw the Admiral leave the ship as it proved for the purpose of calling on me. I returned and dined—and had pleasant and satisfactory conversation with Lord Cochrane— See papers—The Empress has another child whether male or female I don't know—mail landed.

'Pleasant and satisfactory'. Oh, how must we star-crossed lovers express ourselves with such sublime understatement! It was midday, the tropical sun made operatic the azure water, the long reef and, far away, because we stood three miles out to sea, the beautiful white city of Recife.

We stood on deck together for a few minutes, the billowing swell reflecting our swelling hearts.

There were officers all around, of course—dear Glennie, ebullient Crosbie, Shepherd, Grenfell, Dance, Gulliver; they were mostly old friends.

I looked at His Lordship and saw he had aged, the folds of his great face dropping, his shoulders further stooped, his brilliant hair as thick as ever but now more grey than gold. I loved him all the more.

'Your journey has been good, I trust? Not too many thunderstorms.' He stared around the ship, a humble packet, as if he thought it not fine enough for me.

'I never see a thunderstorm at sea but it reminds me of the vision of Ezekiel: "The Sapphire blaze, Where angels tremble while they gaze."' I was nervous so I quoted and blamed myself for it. But he only smiled, either because he had not listened or because it reminded him sentimentally of my poetic propensities. Either way, it was a gentle, tolerant smile. Soon after, we were called down to dine.

Picture the scene: a low panelled room with many small windows through which the sun pierces in bright balls of light; a room full of naval gentlemen, handsomely dressed as always, with their hair tied back in neat pigtails; a long table laden with all our captain could provide, augmented by fruit and bottles from our guests; we are seated and each chair has a sailor behind it, acting servant with the mixture of efficiency and independence that only sailors can achieve. There were fourteen of us sat down and once the captain, a religious man, had prevailed on the Admiral to say a prayer, we all set to with a will, tongues only leaving aside eating for talking and talking for

358

eating.

Naturally, the Admiral led the subject, speaking with the open frankness that I particularly admired in him. 'The self-styled republican president, Manuel Carvalho has convinced me he is an honest man. He believes that the Emperor is not to be trusted and, if he acknowledges his rule, Pernambuco will, sooner or later, find itself once more under Portuguese government. I would rather persuade him he is wrong than starve him out or blow his men to pieces.' Since he had a whole guinea fowl in front of him, admirably boiled with onions and capers, he paused here.

We all gave our views then, and I saw the Admiral listen attentively when I talked of the importance of dialogue in any form of government. 'You are acquainted with Carvalho, I believe?' he asked me.

'I have met him,' I answered. 'You know I was in Pernambuco three years ago. In the *Doris*.' I didn't mention Captain Graham's name. 'Tomorrow I plan to visit an old friend, Lord Stewart.'

'But you will be free at breakfast?'

I nodded in agreement. Over and over again I had to remind myself he did not admit to himself that he loved me, which in no way decreased his feelings for me.

That afternoon he left the packet with his officers, although allowing me my cousin Glennie for an hour or two. After commenting on his sunburnt health I asked him how it was with the Brazilian fleet.

'Politics,' he answered moodily, 'and the men fall sick, with little to do and a fetid climate. The Admiral is unhappy too—he has received hardly a

359

fraction of the prize-ship money owing to him.' He stopped and smiled, a sweet, boyish smile. 'We are all cheered to see you.'

'And I you.' We sat on together, drinking coffee in that strange world where your ship is in harbour but you are not on land, and I answered all the questions I could about England, although in my heart I had left it far behind.

'I am surprised, in truth,' said Glennie, innocently, 'that you have left England for such a hell-hole as Rio. Lady Cochrane and her daughter left with Dr Williams in February. They were both too ill to endure another day.'

'I heard they had returned to England,' I replied, with as much nonchalance as I could. 'Some women cannot stand the heat. For my own self, I find Rio a fine city and my health improved by living there.'

Glennie laughed. 'Would I dare contradict you, even if we once inhabited the same sick bay?'

'I fall ill wherever I am,' I said crossly, 'but less so in the warmth.'

To which Glennie contented himself with a mocking 'Amen.'

*　　*　　*

True to his word, His Lordship was escorted to our ship early. The air was still fresh, the swell not so pronounced. Mr Bennett accompanied him so I had to tell him all the London gossip and describe Byron's funeral until the Admiral became impatient and demanded a private room. He had papers, he said, which he wished to discuss with me alone. He snatched a bundle from Bennett, followed me into a cabin, quickly cleared, and shut the door.

Storm shutters were already up against the sun so the light was dim and cool. Laying the papers on the table, he took me in his arms. I felt very small against his large body. I sighed and pulled his face towards me. I knew he didn't want to take all the trouble of undressing me or himself. The minimum would do for us. The floor must be our bed.

But how joyously we came together, with far more abandon than our circumstances suggested. Mostly we were middle-aged, or even old, but for those few minutes we were as young and ardent as first loves.

Afterwards, we tottered upright, our cheeks flaming, our eyes brilliant.

'You look well,' he said. 'You always look well on board ship. Even a packet like this,' he added, after a pause.

In another moment he had turned to the bundle on the table. I was not so quick to recover and dreamt a little as he talked. I had picked up by the end, however. He truly did have private matters to discuss. 'I understand that you would like me to go as your emissary to the self-styled president and see if I can persuade him to step down.' I stared up at him, wanting to touch his face but he had gone from me. 'Men do not like to abandon power,' I added.

'He is a man of principle.' He took a chair and I took another beside him.

'Even men of principle do not like to abandon power.'

'He will listen to you, an Englishwoman on her way to take up a position in the Brazilian court. He will trust you in the way he will not trust an admiral who stands behind two tiers of twenty-five guns each.' He leant closer. 'In Chile we both met men who abandoned power. Perhaps you heard that eventually General O'Higgins was taken by a British warship to Peru, where he remains.'

'I think we can agree that in O'Higgins's case the departure from office was not voluntary.' I did not argue more but studied with him the papers in which he strove to argue that the inhabitants of Pernambuco would be better served by agreeing to his terms, which included letting Carvalho go free. I had seen too much of the fiery Brazilian temperament to believe in the success of my mission but I could never deny His Lordship anything he asked.

*   *   *

Pernambuco, created of the two cities Recife and Olinda, was a pretty place with as many churches, convents and monasteries as is customary with those lands colonised by papists. But constant unrest since my last visit had reduced many of the grander parts, although churches and long shopping arcades survived in a tattered state. Uncertainty had caused many of the richest to leave or at least not invest. In the convent there were only thirty-seven nuns and no pupils.

Nevertheless, a bright sun and all the glories of tropical flowers, the scarlet, yellow and purple where birds, butterflies and insects feasted in unceasing celebration of life, echoed my mood. Lord Stewart, my friend who had come in from his country estate to secure his property in the harbour, led me to the self-declared republican president's house.

'It appears that since I was here three years ago there has been scarcely a day's peace.' Grim words but I found myself smiling as I said them. A woman who has had her heart's desire after being deprived for more than a year is hardly likely to suffer from someone else's political turmoil.

'And not finished yet.' Lord Stewart was a sensible man but it was his sister who was my true friend and, being of nervous disposition, she had stayed in the country.

Carvalho received me most politely. His men and a crowd of freed slaves led me into a large room, heavily shuttered against the sun. Just as well, perhaps, as I could still see that it was remarkably filthy, although I suppose there is little incentive to sweep the floor if you expect a volley of enemy shells at any minute.

'Mrs Graham. This is an honour!' The president spoke excellent English with a very charming accent. He kissed my hand with a flourish. Or perhaps the flourish was for his daughters, who entered the room carrying large bowls of fruit, which they set on a round table in the corner.

'I come as an emissary from the Admiral,' I said, enjoying the sound of the words on my lips.

'Ah, your admiral! How much I admire his honourable character!' He indicated two chairs in the middle of the room.

'He has sent me with proclamations.' I waved to my servant to bring over the papers.

'Papers. Yes. I have some papers, plans, maps. All is open to you to view.' His servants produced a great many maps with detailed placing of troops and other information that might be thought secret. 'I have men who will die for freedom, men and even

363

boys, like these who stand here.' He made another flourish, which directed my eye to a silver-headed Negro and a boy of not more than ten years old.

'But you are responsible for their safety,' I suggested, as he began to look at the Admiral's terms.

'My party will never yield on less terms than these: that the constituent assembly, consisting of the very *same* members, should be reassembled as it is now, that they should meet at any place but Rio, and must be out of reach of the imperial troops.' Working himself up into a patriotic frenzy, he jumped up and cried out, 'I am resolved for freedom or to die on the field of glory!'

At which all his men closed round and yelled their support, which made quite a stink around us of garlic breath and overheated bodies.

Alas, I thought, that men will be careless of blood! When the brave followers had retreated, I turned the talk to more abstract politics for I feared that I might otherwise be in for a San Martín-length harangue. But he was less arrogant than that, only aware of the sad treatment of Pernambuco by the Portuguese and now what he called the 'Portuguese imperialists'. He was determined to keep faith with the cause.

I left aware that putting my toe into history was likely to change nothing. Lord Stewart and I were rowed to the *Pedro Primeiro* and there I reported to the Admiral my warm reception and lengthy conversation with Carvalho. 'You will never be able to agree terms,' I advised, 'however much you respect each other.'

'We cannot choose our adversaries.' The Admiral was glum. We were all silent and I heard, above the eternal creaking of the ship, the long, splashing roll of waves breaking against the reef. That would be here whichever political party triumphed.

I would be gone as soon as the packet had dealt with its correspondence, received more supplies and a few more passengers. It would be no more than days and I felt that every time I went ashore, where, of course, the Admiral as Carvalho's enemy could not follow, I was cutting myself off from him. Yet I was excited to be once more in an exotic land. I took my saddle (which this trip I had brought with me) to an equable horse and rode out to meet Miss Stewart, who greeted me with only less warmth than her pet blue macaw, Jack, who put his claw on my arm and cawed, 'Hallo, shipmate!'

I could also have visited Mrs Parkinson, the English consul's wife, or Mrs Bennett (no relation to my Mr Bennett), the American consul's wife, but I preferred to gather plants. I would have enough of consuls' wives in Rio. It is a fact that little status is needed to turn the head of a person when that head has little content.

On the last day of my stay, the Admiral came to me in restless mood. I had been sketching on deck with an awning over my head. When I saw his boat approaching with the usual ceremonial noises, I began to pack up.

He strode up and down around me, stopping to peer down at me every now and again, although making no comment on my picture.

'You are always occupied.' He frowned, as if in disapproval.

'I have learnt through illness not to waste a moment. I shall be free immediately.'

'Free, yes, you are free enough. Free to come and go as you please. While I . . . I must stay in this damned place, like a child in a nursery.'

His analogy, although not well chosen, was a clue to his emotions, which always had a childish petulance when he was upset. 'I wish you could sail with me,' I said, 'or I could sail with you. I wish we could never be parted.' It was hard for me to make this declaration but I knew he never would and I needed it said. My tone was matter-of-fact, without a trace of sentiment, which, I hoped, would make the words more acceptable to him.

'Yes. Yes.' He took off his hat and beat it against his thigh. Then he came closer. 'We must part and I am sorry for it.'

It was the nearest he had come to a declaration, and even though we were on the open deck, I could not resist putting out my forefinger and placing it against his full red lips. 'We will meet again,' I whispered.

He clapped his hat on his head, so hard that an approaching band of sea-birds took off with a great deal of screeching. 'Now tell me you have a piece of poetry to put that in fine language.'

But I hadn't.

'Then, *buenos días*.'

Wednesday, 25th August 1824
Anchored about ½ a mile from the shore of the arsenal of St Salvadors commonly called Bahia. The French frigate *Magisienne* being in the *Doris*'s old berth and decked in honour of St Louis' day . . . I find the people here expecting impossible things from Cochrane, that he was to land the troops at Grande and in one night end

366

the business at Recife.

For the record, the Admiral did achieve those 'impossible things'. He landed his twelve hundred troops, and Carvalho, valiant or not, escaped on a raft, from which he was picked up by HMS *Tweed*.

None of this concerned me any longer for on 27th August our ship left Bahia and made a speedy voyage of ten days to Rio de Janeiro, where my new independent life was to begin. 'Thus have the gods spun the thread for wretched mortals: that they live in grief while they themselves are without cares.'

CHAPTER THIRTY-THREE

Everything was as disagreeable as possible in Rio. The weather was either steaming or raining. My supporters in court had either died or lost favour. My apartment was not ready in the palace and the Empress, recently delivered of yet another baby daughter, informed me that she had tried to delay my departure from England. Her message had been sent too late. Yet I would not have heeded it.

I set myself up with the ever-solicitious Mrs May while I waited for an invitation to the palace of São Cristóvão. My room smelled of English lavender and Brazilian drains.

'Mr May and I could hardly believe you would return.' She surveyed my sea of boxes, chest and crates. 'By the look of it, you mean to stay.'

Of course I meant to stay. Lady Cochrane, the Marchioness of Maranham, or whatever she liked to call herself, was in England. Sooner or later His Lordship must return to Rio.

'Among other necessities, I have a pair of Carey's two-foot globes, handsomely mounted, and several instruments for making observations on the weather and climate, such as Leslie's hydrometer and gynometer.'

Mrs May expressed herself amazed at all this for one five-year-old girl.

'I wish her to be as well educated as any princess in Europe,' I replied, with what might have seemed foolish pride, although as Doña Maria da Gloria eventually became Queen of Portugal, I was not so far off the mark.

Eventually my waiting ended and I was summoned to the palace, where the Emperor met me personally in an outer courtyard. I would have appreciated the honour more if he very obviously had not come straight from his siesta: he wore slippers but no stockings, a light gingham jacket and trousers, and a straw hat bound and tied with a green ribbon. He was leaning with one hand on the iron rail leading to the principal door and the other he stretched out to me.

Flustered, I presumed he expected the kissing homage, but as I bent, he smiled and took my hand. '*A mode Ingreza,*' he said.

So, we shook hands and I complimented him on his health. He told me to go to the veranda where the Empress's equerry of the day would escort me to her private apartments. Just as I left he called, in a voice just short of insolent (even an emperor can be insolent), 'I hear you saw my admiral in Pernambuco.'

'The packet I travelled on stopped for several days in Pernambuco,' I said cautiously.

'Yes. Yes.' He seemed suddenly to lose interest

and went swiftly into the palace by a side door.

At least the Empress was as gracious as ever, although her figure and face were puffed up, clearly the pregnancy had taken its toll. She showed me my apartment, seven rooms, just above her own, with a view of the beautiful palace gardens and the mountains of Tijuoa. With royal kindness, she joked that when it was finished, every other wall would be a bookcase. Then she introduced me formally to my pupil, Doña Maria da Glória, a high-spirited girl, in looks like her Habsburg mother, in temperament like her father.

She spoke in French: 'When may we start? Please. Please. Tomorrow? The day after? Soon? Now! Perhaps now!'

How sweet is a little enthusiasm to a lonely heart! Yet I was not so happy when she had gone to another room and I saw through an open door how she treated her playmates. They were two or three little black slaves and one little white girl whom she tyrannised and even beat without mercy. I managed to say nothing to her mamma, the Empress, but I thought that if my job was to educate the princess both in *physical* and *mental* matters, as my contract stated, then behaviour like this must surely be included.

No one, I told myself, with English certainty, is born a despot, and what is learnt as a baby may be unlearnt as a child. Remembering all the spoilt, lazy, dirty midshipmen I had turned into bright, articulate young men, I looked forward to the challenge.

More than a week passed while, yet again, I waited at the Mays. I wrote a letter, full of politics, to the Admiral and received one he had sent soon after I'd left, full of complaints. It turned out that Carvalho, far from being the honourable man I had understood, had offered him eighty thousand pounds, if he would change sides—a huge sum that only provoked the Admiral to anger. He wrote, 'It did not follow that, because the Brazilian ministers were unjust and hostile to me, I should accept a bribe from a traitor to follow his example. I did not for San Martín, a far more considerable force, and I shall not for Carvalho.' Such was South American politics of the time.

I had some of my prints framed ready for my new home, took care to avoid the consuls' wives, and became used once again to living among Negroes. This last was useful because when eventually I was summoned to take up my post, I found that my principal servant was 'Black Anna', the mighty Negress already mentioned who could as easily have dandled me on her knee as a newborn baby.

I liked her, however, for she was full of enthusiasm. Together we unpacked my chest and, like two children, displayed the contents about the rooms. Soon her excited cries brought other slaves and ladies running and even the magnificent person known as the Barber, who ran the royal household.

My dresses were pronounced disappointing—they were black, as was decreed for widows in Rio, and most of plain cambric muslin—but my turbans were much admired and within a few days copies were all over town. I soon realised that Black Anna's endless curiosity about my life was fuelling her subsidiary role as a spy for the Barber. I did not blame her, for that was the system at the court so she had no choice, but I made certain to lock away my most private and treasured possession: the letters from His Lordship.

It was a sad fact that he had many enemies in the Brazilian government. Indeed, in June of that year, when I was still in England, he had been warned of a threat against his person so imminent that he had had to jump out of the window of his house. Intrigue against foreigners is to be expected, particularly among the unsophisticated, and I was fully aware of my own unpopularity in certain quarters: unscrupulous courtiers coupled me with their foreign empress and fuelled their suspicions with salacious gossip.

None of it concerned me. My focus was on my pupil from whom I gained pleasure and pain: pleasure to find how quickly she learnt—languages especially for, since she already spoke Portuguese and French, English was no problem for her; pain to watch how the slaves and ladies treated her.

For example, on our first morning together I went to the princess's apartments to find the women washing her naked, not in the bathroom but in the open apartment, where the slaves, male and female, were passing, and through which the Empress's gawping guard always paraded. When I approached the dressers, they flatly refused to alter this unseemly practice until I had obtained a written order from the Emperor. Her breakfast was equally inappropriate: thigh of a fowl stewed in oil with garlic, accompanied by a glass of strong wine and water, followed by coffee, toast and sweetmeats. No wonder that in later years she had continuous problems with her weight.

My disgust at her early-morning routine was so great that I even told Mrs May, who'd been given special permission to visit my apartments.

'How can she learn Christian propriety when she is brought up in such a careless, uncivilised way?' I cried.

Of course Mrs May expressed herself as shocked as I, although she added, in a warning note, to which I should have listened, 'We must always remember this is not England and we are here as guests of Their Imperial Majesties. Their customs may sometimes differ from ours.'

Our conversation ended as I spotted Anna lingering in the doorway where she had doubtless stood for some time.

'I am bringing you water, madams,' she said, entering in her splendid way and setting a jug on the floor. Even Mrs May smiled at her, for she was indeed a powerfully attractive woman. I was told that she was mother to some of the princess's abused little playmates, and it was as much for her as the children that I eventually spoke out.

I had already tried approaching the mother of the little white girl, hoping that she would co-operate in correcting the princess's improper behaviour. The lady answered with an expression of supreme moral rectitude, 'I would put a child of mine to death who did not think it an honour to receive a blow from the princess.'

So, I must tackle the culprit herself. I chose a moment in the schoolroom when everything was as quiet as it could be in a Brazilian court and we had just finished reading *Little Charles* by Mrs Barbauld, which has a good moral tone. The princess sat at her table and I beside her.

'Tell me, Doña Maria, do you not admire your mother's gentle manners better than those of any lady and wish to resemble her?'

She gave the question a little thought. 'Oh, but everybody says I am like Papa—very lively.'

'Yes, but ladies do not show their feelings as men are allowed to do,' I persevered. 'Your mamma was taught to be gentle when she was a little princess like yourself. In our country, none of the great people are permitted to beat common folk.' She seemed to be listening, so I carried on; 'I must not have you beat your companions any more—it is not like a lady or a princess.'

This was quite a daring lecture and halfway through I remembered my own childhood nickname, Tiger, and had to stop a smile. Yet who is the more suited to preach than the reformed sinner?

Surprisingly, perhaps, my words bore fruit because only a few hours later, I once again saw the princess grow exceedingly red and high-passioned with her hand outstretched towards her playmates. However, instead of bringing it down on innocent shoulders, she ran quickly to me.

She stood in front of me, her thick hair tumbled, and cried joyously, 'Now was that not behaving like a lady and a princess?'

It is only feeble boasting to tell this story— indeed I dictated it to my good friend the Honourable Caroline Fox many years later— because, in truth, it was the peak of my success as a governess. In less than two months it was all over and I had left the court. In my journals and letters I left few clues as to the cause. The little history that has been written about me recognised a mystery and made the reasonable assumption that my departure was due to my over-closeness to the Empress and my staunch defence of the Admiral at every opportunity. Indeed, I myself hinted at the problems of 'court politics'.

My cousin and biographer Rosemary Gotch, more honest, left the blank blank, admitting she had no real understanding of what had gone so wrong.

How often is the least obvious answer the most true! In my case the least obvious event in the world had occurred: I was with child. Remember, I was forty years old and had never once been pregnant, even during my twenties when I was a married woman, with a doting husband who longed for a family; he had whispered it in my ear as he asked me to marry him. I had assumed I was barren, another cross in my life but one I felt equal to bearing. I had my midshipmen, my 'boys', who called me 'Maman'.

My ignorance made me slow to recognise the signs of maternity. Not so Black Anna who gave sudden tweaks to my bosom when she was dressing me and brought me nanny-goat's milk with some folklore promise of goatish strength. I was old. I was a blue-stocking; blue-stockings did not became pregnant. (Apart from Mary Wollstonecraft and she died in childbirth.)

But it was nearly three months since I'd left Pernambuco and even I began to notice changes in my body. I, who had never felt seasickness, now was queasy half the day; I ate pineapples and pomegranates and chillies by the handful. My skin was sensitive; I was tired one minute, then filled with energy. I suppose that only my age and black widow's weeds saved it from being clear to everyone.

I was still ignorant of my condition when one

374

early morning I took the carriage into town to oversee the making of ink, about which I was most particular. As I waited for my orders to be carried out, I called on Mrs May.

Her parlour was gay and bright, the shutters not yet closed. A brilliant parrot blinked on a rail.

'Coffee, my dear?'

'No. No.' I shuddered. Recently, the very thought of coffee made me ill. I sat down and took off my gloves with which I fanned myself. 'Today the heat is even more humid than usual, I do believe.'

She looked at me oddly. 'My brother will be sorry to miss you. He was here scarcely five minutes since.' She paused. 'Are you quite well?'

'Quite well. I . . .' I, too, paused. In that moment, with her kind grey eyes on me, so unlike Anna's black gaze but wearing the same questioning expression, I knew the truth.

It was, of course, a catastrophe. But I have never allowed catastrophe to overwhelm me. When poor Graham lay dying in the *Doris*, I had noted for my journal the ludicrous aspects of the storm raging above, as the breakfast table lurched and unloaded itself into the lee scuppers. I was a governess at the court of Brazil. I was pregnant. The serious and the ridiculous always border on each other.

That day I said nothing to Mrs May but, forgetting to collect my ink, went straight back to my apartment where I gave out I was sick. I sat upright and thought about my situation. Only then, in semi-darkness and solitude (noises below and around but not with me), I took in the reality and a hot, heavy warmth spread through my body. I was carrying the child of the man I loved. Knowing I could tell no one, I longed to boast, to shout, to

375

glorify. I sat up all afternoon and all night, and even managed to ignore Anna's heavy tiptoes.

The next morning when I still gave out that I was sick, she stopped her attentions and it struck me that this was the moment when she would go to the Barber and tell him my secret. I realised I should act, perhaps appeal to her, but I was reluctant to leave my private sphere of rejoicing. I gave myself till the afternoon.

At two p.m., the hottest hour of the day, Anna reappeared, a substantial shadow at the side of my bed. Behind her was a creature in no recognisable human shape that I gradually made out to be a woman wearing a turban as high as herself.

'Madam,' said Anna, in her strange variance of Portuguese, 'this Lilia. She will help you. A good clean lady. Without her I have not ten children but twenty, thirty, forty.' She spread her huge arms.

'But, Anna,' I smiled at her, accepting at once the situation, 'I have only the chance of one baby and I do not want to lose him.'

'No other little ones over the sea?' she asked, amazed.

'This inside me now is the only one.'

Anna stared, then turned to whisper to Lilia, who also stared, before crossing herself and retreating quietly with her turban nodding like a drunken person sitting on her shoulders.

My afternoon of decision had come and now I was ready for it. 'Anna, my dear, have you told anyone of my condition?'

She shrugged. 'What interest is one more baby? Now, if you were the Empress, and the Virgin and her angels had brought you a baby boy . . .' She giggled.

'It *is* a boy.'

'You know that? Who has told you? You have a baby today but will you have it tomorrow? You are a grandmother. Your body is thin and old. You cough blood.'

Strangely, I was not angry with her for presenting the truth. 'I shall leave the court.'

'Ah. Ah.'

'I shall find a nice cottage in the country.'

'Ah. Ah.'

'And my son will be born.'

'With the help of Maria, the Mother of God.' Now she crossed herself.

On impulse I put out my hand. 'Will you come with me to my cottage?'

She stepped back, her large bare feet making no sound on the stone floor. 'I am the thing of the Emperor and the Empress.'

'You are. Yes, you are.' I asked her to bring me water and let some sunlight in, and when the Empress woke from her siesta I let it be known that I was well again.

*   *   *

Now followed some very strange weeks in which I tried to perform my duties while harbouring my secret, my miraculous secret, as I thought it, not without reason. My task was made harder by the length and constriction of my days: they started at seven a.m. with my royal pupil and ended as darkness fell and our wing of the palace, the wing of the Empress, myself and the ladies of the wardrobe, was locked up.

I felt like a prisoner, a prisoner whose time might

well end with public sentence and humiliation. Yet I was also filled with joy and in the early morning, with my head at the window where the sweet smell of the orange blossom in the gardens below filled the air, I dreamed, smiled foolishly, and felt I had never been so happy.

The most difficult part of the day was my *tête-a tête* with the Empress, which usually took place in my room while the Emperor had his siesta. We were so intimate in conversation that I could scarcely believe that she, who knew so much of childbirth, had not noticed my condition. It was true that my natural slimness had changed in only small ways, but I suspect her ignorance reflected more the way she thought of me: a woman of letters, tutor to her daughter, almost sexless. It pained me not to be able to tell her the truth.

Yet it was these daily meetings, so important to the Empress's lonely soul and so unpopular with the court and, I'm sure, the Emperor, which provided the answer to my dilemma.

Gradually, the court gentlemen and ladies, the servants, the very slaves who should have obeyed my orders as their princess's governess, became openly contemptuous. When I ordered tea to be brought into the garden, it was taken to the veranda or the nursery. When I demanded the carriage to be brought up so we might make an educational expedition, I was told no horses or even mules were available. When I was supposed to accompany my charge to the opera where, bejewelled and crowned, she played the little queen, the ladies so crowded around her that there was no room for me in the carriage.

I now had respectable, if humiliating, cause to

leave the court. Everybody, except the Empress, would be happy. On the afternoon that the Barber pushed me against the wall of the corridor, I resolved to talk to Maria Leopoldina the following day.

That night I lay awake from darkness until dawn. Now that my life was changing again, I must confront my choices. Most important of all: should I tell Lord Cochrane of my situation? His name was often on the lips of the Empress: her anxieties about the plots that seemed to multiply against him, her gratitude that he was still fighting the cause of a united independent Brazil. I blushed and shook in the black night when I considered if she should find out.

I was scarcely less afraid of His Lordship's reaction. He had a wife, he had three children already and, though it hurt me to think it, might well have more. His feelings for me, which I did not doubt, were bound up with his life as an admiral in foreign service. When we came together, he was fully himself, and we met as equals. A child was not part of it.

Yet in my dreams I saw his noble face bent over a cot wherein lay our baby son. How hopeful! How ridiculous! As the light trickled under the shutters and the slaves' feet slapped along the corridor, I admitted to myself that if I told His Lordship, he was more likely to be astounded, shocked, perhaps even horrified. I turned and tossed miserably.

Anna stood over my bed. She pushed the hair back into my cap and put a cool palm on my hot forehead. 'It will rain today,' she said. 'Storms of thunder to cool the air.'

Yes, today I would tell the Empress that my

position had become intolerable.

Great waves of rain pounded the windows of my room, reminding me of a ship in a storm. The heat was still intense. The Empress and I sat together and drank mango juice as we talked. When the sweat trickled down our cheeks, we mopped it up with squares of cambric.

'Oh, oh,' murmured Maria Leopoldina, fanning herself, 'do we not sometimes wish for the cool snows of the Alps?'

The 'we' caught my heart but I knew I must not hang back. Quite distinctly, I felt a flutter in my belly, the first time, as if my baby was encouraging me forward. I stood up.

The small plump princess stared unsuspectingly up at me. 'I laughed so much when this morning Doña Maria came running in to tell me that, on your globe, Brazil is very much larger than Portugal.'

I longed to join in with her happiness but instead I told her, almost brutally, that I could not continue as governess. 'My health is on the point of breaking down. It is impossible for me to be of the use I had expected to be and it has made me ill. Were it not for my friendship with Your Imperial Majesty and my affection for your daughter, I would have left sooner. Excepting the pleasant hours you have allowed me to pass in your company, my life has been that of a state prisoner, and one, moreover, subjected to all manner of impertinence and incidents from persons of the lowest description, in which I include the Barber Placido and the female attendants in the palace.'

By the end of this horrible little speech the Empress was in tears so that, with rain outside,

380

sweat and tears inside, we were in a very watery place. But what could she do? She knew what I said was true, and as I wept, too, her kindly nature felt only pity.

'I had hoped for so much,' she said, 'but now I see it was selfish of me to bring you here. To have made you absolutely ill is a sad responsibility. The support I have relied on has not come and now, indeed, you would be best leaving the palace.'

She was so decided that, for a moment, I doubted her love, although I knew she had only my interests at heart. 'You must write to the Emperor and ask that you may withdraw. We must make sure it is given after a siesta where there have been no interruptions.'

This was a reference to Dom Pedro's extreme bad temper, in fact, fury, if woken untimely. Now the suddenness began to make me heartily sorry for myself and it took another flutter in my belly to pull me back from what might have become hysterics. Anna, coming in just then and seeing the situation, gave me a glass of water stiffened with wine.

'May I beg Your Majesty to delay my letter for a week so that I may make some plans? Although I shall eventually leave your country, I do not feel strong enough for the voyage just now and will withdraw to a quiet place until my health is restored and a ship can be found.'

This was agreed, sadly.

Two days later, I managed to escape my captors and ride, on horseback, into town. It gave me the impression I was in charge of my life. I went directly to Mrs May.

Our interview was full of the unspoken.

'I overestimated my strength,' from me.

381

'We must find you a cottage,' from her.

'Not in Botafogo or Gloria Hill.' From me— these were where the fashionable villas were situated.

'Perhaps in one of the small valleys at the foot of the Corcovado,' from her.

'"Hill and Valley, fountain and fresh shade",' quoted I, which meant little to dear Mrs May as it was written by a Scottish phrenologist called George Combe who described landscape as 'the banquet of the mind'.

She contented herself with a wise nod. It may seem strange that we could not openly acknowledge the subject of conversation but our silence saved the good lady from either moral condemnation or complicity.

'I will get Mr Dampier to ride out and see what is available. You must have room for servants, a shady garden and running water nearby.'

We did not talk much longer but three days later I received a message that the perfect cottage had been found, among orange groves, recently vacated after the death of its owner. Not perhaps the perfect omen but I was as eager to leave the palace as a child to go on holiday.

With the help of the Empress, a firm and dignified letter was composed for the Emperor. He accepted it although, in an ungentlemanly way, ordering me to return my letters of contract. For this reason, I left the service of Brazil with substantial sums of money owing me, since I had not yet been repaid for the educational equipment bought out of my own purse.

I left very early one morning. Before most of my enemies had risen from their sluttish beds, I was in a carriage with my most immediate necessities. Behind me four mules carried the rest of my boxes while on either side of my carriage, lest my departure might seem too ignominious rode Mr Dampier and an American naval-officer friend of his.

Beside me, sat Black Anna—a shock to many, I expect, who thought she should run behind. The Empress, showing her sensitive nature, had noticed her attachment to me and thought her most suited to care for me in my 'illness'. A cheerful note was added by Anna's youngest children, who decided not to be left behind and at the last minute jumped into the carriage. They stuck their excited faces through the windows.

'Let them stay,' I ordered, knowing that the loss of three small black children would count for less in that court than the loss of three pins.

CHAPTER THIRTY-FOUR

My cottage, amid the orange groves below the mountains, had four rooms with a shed outside for the kitchen. It seemed luxurious compared to my home at the Almendral but then Anna and her children were joined by Antonio, the cheerful Negro from my previous stay on Gloria Hill, and Antonio was joined by Elizabetta, her young brother, Carlos, and two large dogs. The establishment was ruled by Anna who, coming from the court, although a slave whilst they were freed, decided she should be empress. I might have been reclusive, but I was never, therefore, without entertainment or without a companion for my rides after Mr Dampier had procured me a horse.

Mr Dampier was my only outside visitor—apart from the local priest, Padre Francisco Xavier, who invited himself every other day for a glass of wine at sunset. This practice gave such pleasure to my servants, my companions, that I could not deny him. Mr Dampier, eventually, I was forced to deny.

I have not described Mr Dampier, I believe, which is easy enough because he was a drawn-out version of his sister with the same kindly grey eyes but the addition of a beard, a not very substantial beard. Mrs May, to my sorrow but understanding, did not visit me, forbidden, perhaps, by Mr May or even on her own account.

As a man, Mr Dampier was allowed to be bolder—too bold, as it turned out. One early morning when the still pale oranges were swathed in a hazy mist and the sun rose slowly like a golden lantern, I saw him appear on his horse. I was standing at the door, as it happened, drinking coffee, which I had begun to enjoy again, and admiring the view but, with some premonition, I retreated to my private room immediately.

He found me there and, still overheated from the ride, fell to his knees immediately. His hollow eyes and trembling hands gave away his intentions. Since he could not find words for a moment, I did my best to avert the crisis,

'Mr Dampier. Please. Take a seat. Tea, perhaps? Water?' It was no good.

'I have come to ask you to join your life to mine. The first time I set eyes on you, I knew there could never be any other woman for me.'

As he took a breath, I intervened severely, 'You

384

must not presume, sir, on a lady who is old enough to be your mother. I know you cannot be serious so, please, rise up, and we will forget your unfortunate words.'

He did rise but only to speak more passionately. 'You must not make fun of me when I will be thirty next birthday. You are my most beloved, my inspiration, my goddess. I know I am a merchant, a poor, uneducated fellow compared to you, but—'

'Mr Dampier! Remember your sister! Remember your excellent brother-in-law, Mr May—'

'I know your circumstances but I do not care a fig for what the world will say. Neither will all the Mays stretched from here to Plymouth curtail my sentiments for one second—'

'You have not told Mrs May of your intentions in coming here?'

'No. But I will do so proudly.'

'Then it must be forgotten. I may be an immoral woman in the world's view but I am not a cruel one. I cannot blight your future. Now, we shall have coffee, and it will be forgotten.'

Taking my chances while he reeled back under my determination, I darted to the door and threw it open, calling, 'Coffee!' at which, in the time-honoured way, three bodies fell backwards while staring upwards with more reproach than guilt. They would have me married, it being long established in their society that a father is seldom the best husband.

I was sad to say farewell to Mr Dampier, but not too sad. He was the kind of ineffectual man who likes to hitch his star to someone else's drama and, if that is to happen, I prefer to do the choosing myself.

However, although I could not regret my handling of the situation, which always verged on farce, it did unsettle me. By chance, the next day Antonio collected a letter from Lord Cochrane. He was full of discontent, still not free to return to Rio and, in the weeks before Christmas (it was early December) remembered our days together in Quintero where all around us was desolation, but we were happy and together. He even made reference to Mr Jackson's Christmas-pudding rhapsody, which I had thought beneath his notice.

I was now five months pregnant, healthy, still small, and a mad fever gripped me that I should go to him in Bahia. There, he would see my condition for himself. Cut off as I was, I might have pursued the idea no further if a letter had not arrived from the Empress—we wrote to each other frequently since she believed I was recuperating out of the city. She happened to make reference to a British ship, the frigate *Blanche*, which would be leaving for Bahia shortly. The captain was called Mends and I wrote immediately asking for a passage, sending the letter by Antonio.

A different captain, and how different my fate might have been! To my misery and fury, I received a letter back from a shipping agent by the pantomime name of Jack London informing me that Captain Mends would be unable to offer me a passage on the ship because 'it lacks the proper facilities to accommodate a lady and her luggage'. He deeply regretted being unable to comply with my wishes. He continued, causing me to strike my head in humiliation and Anna to come running, 'Since it seems that your intentions were to see

Lord Cochrane, I can imagine your disappointment at your arrival in Bahia or Pernambuco, when you found out that he had already sailed back to Rio, since rumour has it that he has been recalled.'

'Wrong! False! How dare the lackey?' I cried aloud. 'To insult me so!' For I had discovered that this very same frigate had brought a Mr and Mrs Hayes and their luggage to Rio. It was not that Captain Mends *couldn't* take me but that he *wouldn't*. Nor was the Admiral returning—or, at least, not imminently.

After days of impotent fury, despair followed. My head ached, my belly, suddenly swelling, seemed to mock me. I threw away any letters that arrived (although Anna astutely retrieved them) and for many weeks I ate little and refused to leave my room. Selfishly, I felt if I lost the baby I could not suffer more. At my lowest point I even desired its loss. I wept more than I had at any time in my life.

But the cycle of life is strong and my good companions determined that neither I nor my baby should slip from them.

The youngest child, Mo, who was considered the most likely to charm, with his beaming smile and innocent joy, was sent into me with tasty morsels. Anna decided she was too abrasive for my delicate state and delegated Elizabetta to ask at any moment when I seemed more nearly human, 'And how feels the baby, madam?' varied occasionally with pieces of information, such as 'A crib has arrived from Mrs May this afternoon' or 'Alicia [my mare] is missing you every day.'

They won. By January I was resigned, and by February I had even begun once more to feel the excited anticipation I had enjoyed before.

'You must walk now,' ordered Anna, who had become bossy again. 'You can watch the orange pickers at their work or go down to the stream where the washerwomen labour. The children will go with you.'

'No more riding now,' she told me in March. 'But I have a letter for you.' They all knew everything about me, I believe, although I never told them anything. They saw my absorption if the letter came from Bahia, my pleasure if it came from London (from John Murray) and my seriousness if it came from the court. The Empress Maria Leopoldina and I still talked politics, and if she found it strange that I was still in Brazil, she never expressed it. I assumed she thought I was still too unwell for the long journey home because, not infrequently, hampers of exotic fruit and herbs would come via Mrs May from the palace. The fate of Lord Cochrane was still one of our principal subjects for conversation, never, I fear, with much hope of a happy outcome from his point of view.

In April Anna looked at me assessingly. 'The baby will come early.' She called in Elizabetta for confirmation. 'Any time. Any day. We must send a message to Padre Xavier.'

'Why should we do that?' I was surprised. I was reading comfortably on our little veranda while silvery rain fell on the wintry trees, although in this tropical country true winter never came.

Now they looked surprised. 'For baptism. It is safer. So, if God wills, the little one can join him in heaven.'

I smiled. My first child, my only child, baptised a Catholic when my whole life I had inveighed against the Pope and papists as only slightly better than the devil and his crowd. But I was at the mercy of these true believers and could not object. So I smiled. God would work it out and I had grown fond of Padre Francisco Xavier, who was not ill-educated for a parish priest. He was also, apart from the estate owners and managers with whom I did not mix, the only white man in the area. In fact, I had become, by now, quite colour-blind and would have shocked my contemporaries at home by the equality I accorded Anna, Elizabetta, Carlos and Antonio. I think if my son had been born a little black baby, I would hardly have been surprised!

*　　　*　　　*

Arthur Thomas Cochrane Dundas Graham entered the world on 11th April 1825 at three o'clock in the morning in the middle of a thunderstorm. In my delirium, for I had insisted on a good deal of opium, I rode the high seas and heard cannon fire, shouted commands and, at one terrifying moment, the topmast breaking in two and crashing to the deck.

Afterwards Anna told me she had been surprised by how quick and easy the birth had been, considering my age, narrow frame and delicate health.

They swaddled Arthur and brought him to me. 'He is small but strong,' they said. They left me alone as they went to bury the placenta and cord. Outside the dogs barked as if in celebration.

I cannot, even now, describe my emotions as I looked down for the first time on the son of my only great love. It was quite outside my experience before or since, and I knew life could offer me

389

nothing nearer perfect happiness. To my eyes, he was a small replica of the Admiral, from the tufty golden hair to the wide-spaced eyes, the reddish skin, large nose and perfectly shaped hands. They said he was small but I had little idea what size a newborn should be. He was strong and he would grow bigger with milk from the wet-nurse Elizabetta had found.

He was swaddled and I felt cocooned, too, in my overwhelming love.

It is not in the nature of life to stay still, yet for a month or so, an utter calm descended. Everything in my little establishment revolved around Arthur. If I thought of the outside world at all, I pictured the time when the Admiral would return to Rio and I would meet him with Arthur in my arms. That was how he would discover our child.

Sometimes my imagination went even further and I saw Arthur, a sturdy little boy, dressed in a midshipman's uniform, joining the line of all the other midshipmen I had cared for over the years. But this time the cry of 'Maman' would be for his very own mamma.

It is a strange and terrible fact that at the same time I was enjoying the exaltation conferred by motherhood—never had a baby been more handsome, his smile divine, his intelligence supreme—another woman on the other side of the Atlantic was also celebrating a baby son, born about six months earlier and also called Arthur Cochrane.

The Admiral wrote to me—always disgruntled: he had become utterly disgusted with Brazilian politicking, although he still trusted the Emperor (I can't think why); he had sent his admiral's frigate *Pedro Primeiro* back to Rio without him and transferred to the smaller *Piranga*. Since he and his men were sicker every day and since the Emperor would not accept his resignation, he planned to sail northwards forthwith where the cooler climate would restore their health.

This letter arrived in May. That night I placed a kiss on Arthur's silky warm forehead before going out to the veranda where I often liked to sit and hear the nightjars calling to their mates. Now I shuddered with a premonition of what might follow the Admiral's decision to sail north. How easy it would be for Lord Cochrane to reach the Azores and decide not to make the long, difficult voyage back to the country that no longer honoured him!

After an hour or two's sleep around dawn, I woke aching and feverish. In another day or two, I began to cough blood. Sickness is never worth describing. It is ugly and dull. A doctor was brought—against my wishes: he did not know who I was—and the baby was hid. Father Xavier came and rubbed me with holy oils, sadly reminding me of La Chavelita's anointing of Glennie. I also took the precaution of dosing myself with laudanum and teaching Elizabetta to put on blisters.

I heard no more news and began to recover a little strength. Enough time had passed for Arthur to learn to chuckle at Mo's antics and aim his chubby fingers at any bright object dangled in front of him. I allowed myself to hope.

Then a batch of letters came all together. I eyed Antonio suspiciously. 'These are just arrived?'

'Oh, yes, Señora.'

I knew they had kept them from me while I was ill. The Empress wrote: 'Our dear Admiral has taken his destiny back into his own hands, and left us for England. I cannot blame him, although others will.'

Mrs May wrote, with a heartlessness I could not have believed possible: 'I think you would want to know that Lord Cochrane has returned to England. He sailed into Portsmouth on 26th June where he received a 15-gun salute as befits an admiral of another country, then went directly to Tunbridge Wells to join his wife and new son.'

John Murray wrote, in his worldly way:

Your friend Lord Cochrane is making all the news here. He kidnapped his ship and crew and now he gallivants in Scotland with his beautiful wife. I hear they had a standing ovation at the opera the other night when South America happened to be mentioned. Of course the Brazilian government is outraged and pressing him for reparation; to which he counter-attacks, totalling the hundreds of thousands of pounds he is owed.

Much the longest letter came from His Lordship. I could not open it at first, knowing too well what must be contained therein. A week passed and the nights were so long that, fearing I might do damage to myself and there was still Arthur to consider, I invited Anna into my bed, as an animal looks for friendly body heat. One night, I rose quietly before anyone was stirring and, after stroking little Arthur on his rosy cheeks, went onto the veranda with a single candle.

My dear Mrs Graham,
Our long and valued friendship must be

interrupted. The stress of dealing with internal wars, anarchy and revolution had begun to make serious inroads on my health; whilst that of the officers and men, in consequence of the great heat and pestilential exhalations of the climate, and the double duty which they had to perform afloat and ashore, was even less satisfactory.

In my misery, I saw that he was to give me his public defence—to me with whom he need defend nothing. I read on:

I shifted my flag into the frigate Piranga *and sent the* Pedro Primeiro *back to Rio. Perhaps I already informed you of this. I resolved upon a short run into a more bracing northerly atmosphere, both to restore our health and give us a clear offing for returning to the Brazilian capital, always my intention. But when we were northward of the Azores island of São Miguel, strong gales descended and we made the unpleasant discovery that the frigate's main top-mast was sprung, and, on putting her about, that the main and main top-sail yards were unserviceable. Besides that, the rigging was rotten and we were low on provisions. With 9000 miles between us and Rio, it became absolutely necessary to seek some nearer harbour.*

I put the letter aside. Whatever else followed, he was gone and, I felt sure, did not intend to return. I sat for half an hour without moving as if my whole body had turned to ice. I could not even weep. But I had to drain the chalice of suffering.

393

*We could hardly expect a welcome in Portugal
or Spain, nor had France yet recognised the
Brazilian independence.*

As insects attracted by my candle battered and
singed themselves to death; the letters on the page
began to dance in front of my eyes. But I forced
myself to carry on.

*So, with much rejoicing from the men—all my
officers and most of the seamen were English—
we sailed up the English Channel and dropped
anchor at Spithead. There I hesitated. I had no
wish to sneak into Portsmouth like a thief or
renegade so I ordered the largest Brazilian ensign
we possessed to fly at the stern and the flag of a
Brazilian admiral at the main-mast. Then I let
loose a salute of 15 guns to Admiral Sir George
Martin, on the Victory, the flagship of the port,
and raised the Union Jack to our fore top-gallant
masthead. To my great pride and joy the guns
of the Portsmouth forts answered with a 15-gun
salute, which rolled and thundered round the
port and far out to sea—as far as France, I
wouldn't be surprised. Never since the great days
of my battles with Napoleon have I felt more
properly honoured.*

He had then scribbled in the margin—clearly an
afterthought to his sense of a glorious personal
welcome, 'This was the first time the flag of
independent Brazil had been formally saluted by a
European state.'
Even as I suffered the bitterness of cruel

abandonment, I imagined the ranks of warships, the heavy merchant ships, the busy little boats, an audience of many hundreds for a popular hero. He might be anathema to the authorities, in the words of *The Times* correspondent (I read it later), he was 'a brilliant ornament' to the British naval service. He was loved, he was applauded, he was home. To me, his only true confidante, he revealed the depth of his satisfaction.

I was rowed to King's Sally Port and put my feet on English soil for the first time in seven years at around 10 o'clock. Cheers broke out from a crowd ashore. I bowed. Crosbie, Shepherd, Glennie, Dance, Grenfell, Mr Bennett, and other officers were with me as we walked up the High Street to the George Hotel. That night and the following morning a number of naval and military officers visited me there.

Later, I read (again in *The Times*) that His Lordship had been wearing a blue undress military coat and a forage cap with a gold band. While my whole miserable body quailed and shook under the knowledge that I had lost him for ever, I was yet able to rejoice in this theatrical triumph. There were two further paragraphs:

You who have stood at my side through so many difficulties, and understand better than anyone my hopes and ambitions, will understand also that I must begin another life, as long as I have the strength, and be at the service of those who need me, wherever that may be. As you know, Greek independence has long been a cause close

*to my heart. Meanwhile I must fight for my rights
with both the British government who accused
me of breaking the law by taking service in a
foreign country and the Brazilian who accuse
me of kidnapping their ship yet owe me many
thousands of pounds.*

*Thus have our paths parted, dear Mrs
Graham. If I read poetry as you do, I am certain
I could find a line that would make beautiful
words out of what must be a sadness to us
both. But as a mere naval man, I can only say
farewell, sure in the knowledge that we will only
ever wish the happiest future for the other and be
grateful for such an affectionate friendship in the
past.*

May God bless you.
Cochrane

There, in the drab light of a cloudy dawn, the only
romance of my life ended. Or very nearly. It was
even more nearly the end of my entire life, for,
once I had finished reading the letter twice and
once again, I fell unconscious. When Anna and
Elizabetta found me, I had a fever so high that they
despaired of saving me.

They laid me like a corpse in my bed and there
I stayed for many, many weeks, so long that the
blossom was once more on the orange trees when
I finally came to my senses. For the first time since
my illness I saw steadily the great dogs by the door
and the dark kindly face half asleep at my bedside.

'Elizabetta.' I put out my hand. She sat up and
immediately saw the change. She placed a hand
on my forehead. Then, instead of smiling as I
expected—a return to health is always received

happily—she burst into tears and ran from the room. The dogs followed her, although I called them weakly. It was the emotion of relief, I told myself, but I began to shiver again as if the fever had returned.

Where was Arthur's crib? Where was Arthur? They had removed him while I was ill, I answered myself, and lay back, waiting for Anna to come to me. Elizabetta was always a fearful creature.

He had died. I can write it only simply. My son, our son, had died. He, who was expected to live, who should have lived, died and I, who should have died, lived. No wonder Elizabetta fled with her apron over her head and the dogs slunk away in shame.

Over the next few days Anna told me the tragic story. It was about contaminated water, the river where I had admired the women washing their clothes, singing, forever singing. Many of the workers and their families had fallen sick, my little household too. They did not recognise the dangers. The aged and the little ones died; the adults were strong enough to survive.

'They were baptised. They were buried,' whispered Anna.

'They?' I thought that if I had nursed Arthur he would have survived.

The youngest of her children had died, little Mo with the wide smile, and I had not even noticed his absence.

'Oh, Anna.'

'God has taken them because He loved them. He will care for them better than we can.' She had seemed careless of her children and yet now I could see that sorrow had changed the contours of her face. Even her body as she stood beside me, seemed less magnificently immense.

'Father Xavier said the mass and buried them. I will show you where.' She turned to see where I was staring.

I was sitting on the veranda swaddled in as many shawls as a mummy although I did not feel the cold. In truth, I could not feel at all. My eyes had fixed beyond the orange groves on the range of mountains shrouded, like myself, in shawls of grey mist. They told me that my time in Brazil, in South America, was over.

'This is a bad place now.' Anna was close to me, her beautiful black eyes reflecting my own pale face. I understood they had been waiting for me to lose or win the fight for life. Now they would go back to their other lives.

'In a few weeks I will be strong enough to leave.' I spoke mechanically. 'I will find lodgings in Rio. Antonio must enquire what ships are in harbour.'

'Ships for England, madam?'

'Ships for England, Anna.'

The day before I left for Rio, I found the courage to go with Anna and the others—even the dogs accompanied us—to the church where my son was buried. The sun shone gaily, lighting up the marks of damp on our black clothes. Father Xavier met us. He seemed smaller and older than I remembered.

'He has been ill too,' whispered Anna.

He must have seen so many deaths, conducted so many funerals. He led us into the church—no more than a stone room with a roof of branches and palm. It was cool and smelled of damp earth. A few candles lit the darkness; there were no windows.

'He is buried here,' said Father Xavier, walking to a corner. He coughed. The floor was earth. I imagined men digging. 'He will be safe here.'

I wondered whether this was a spiritual reference or more mundane.

'You see, they are near the Virgin,' said Anna, kneeling. Everybody, except the priest, also knelt.

I saw that one of the flickering candles was set in front of a figure, her white dress gleaming. 'They?' I enquired.

'How many holes could they dig?' whispered Elizabetta, in a slightly reproving tone.

I asked no further. It was better that Arthur lay with his little friend. All skeletons are white.

Father Xavier began a prayer in Latin. It went on and on repetitively, broken at intervals by a refrain from my companions. I did not try to understand the words, although I know Latin well enough.

As my eyes grew more accustomed to the darkness, I saw there was a roughly hewn stone over the spot to which they prayed. I still had not knelt but now I crouched down and laid my fingers on it. My tears fell gently.

Around me the incantation continued and I realised that, if I could not join in with them, I could open my heart to my God and beg for His mercy on my son's soul.

Afterwards we went outside and the sun still shone and Antonio produced a bottle of some fiery liquid that we all drank eagerly.

Not far away, in a group of palm trees, a bevy of parrots set up a violent squawking.

Father Xavier took my hand. 'We will not forget your baby,' he said. 'Our blessed Virgin already holds him safe in her bosom.' The words sounded

399

beautiful in Portuguese.

I nodded, thanked him, and gave him some coins.

'For the poor,' he said.

'Yes,' I agreed, although I would have liked them to be his.

On the way back to the house, the dogs gambolled round our slow procession, and Antonio produced a large scarlet handkerchief to mop his brow.

The front room was filled with my packed boxes.

CHAPTER THIRTY-FIVE

I arrived back in England on 14th October, 1825. By then Lord Cochrane who had still not settled his differences with the government, was living in France with his wife and family. From there he tried to negotiate conditions for his expedition to Greece.

My return was a great shock to me—hardly surprising since it was more than four years since I'd sailed from Portsmouth at the side of Captain Graham. Admittedly, during that time I'd returned for some months, but that had been in preparation for the publication of my South American journals and for my post in Rio. I had not had the intention of settling in England and my heart had remained on the other side of the Atlantic with Lord Cochrane. But now I had come to stay. I was still physically weak and suspected that gossip had not been kind to me in my absence. I was quite certain that nobody knew about Arthur, and those who were interested in my past accepted the version, which I encouraged, that I had been pushed from the Brazilian court by a faction jealous of the Empress. That was humiliating enough.

Unless I was to become a charity case, looked after by family or rich friends—a fate I had fought against all my life—I needed work, paid work. So, I abandoned the soft, autumnal delights of Althorp, where I had first found rest, and set off for London and Albemarle Street. My reputation, both personal and professional, had suffered from envy and prejudice against my sex, but I had made good money for the publishing house of John Murray, and Mr Murray was not only a firm friend but also knew I would work harder than any other of his writers. Genius I might lack but never application.

'You are thinner, my dear Mrs Graham,' commented Mr Murray, as we sat together in the famous upstairs drawing room. 'I trust you have not been ill.' He leant forward in sympathy.

He could not know that if my true state was to be shown I would be beating my breast and tearing out my hair. I gave a half-smile and cast my eyes up to the famous Thomas Phillips portrait of Lord Byron, hanging above the mantel. 'At least I am alive.'

In the past, I had fancied a certain similarity in this portrait to the one of myself painted by Sir Thomas Lawrence. Now I felt more like a dismal affair painted at the same time by John Jackson RA, an unromantic soul who liked women to be meek and mild, if not actually downtrodden.

Murray sighed theatrically and gave me an approving look from his protruding eyes. 'No one could be more alive than Mrs Graham.' I knew from this that my sufferings had not diminished the effect of my striking appearance, which, in truth, had never relied on youthful charms.

He, in his turn, gazed up to the noble lord: 'That portrait, painted in 1814, has spawned a series of men in open-necked white shirts across England and Europe, including Chateaubriand and Pushkin among others. Such is the power of a great personality!'

'A great poet,' I said.

'Ah, yes, indeed.' He never liked a reproof.

To soften him I admired further points of the drawing room, the collection of first editions by Jane Austen and Sir Walter Scott among others. 'This is a room where a scholar may feel happy,' I said, 'or even an historian.' I paused. 'I have come to you, my revered publisher, to ask for work. Do you have anything for me?'

Indeed he did: manuscripts to read, articles to write and, when I was more settled, a mass of notes written by the chaplain, Mr Bloxham, on a voyage to the Sandwich Islands, which Mr Murray wanted fashioned into a book. He was my good friend—as were Mrs Murray and their three nice girls (I was godmother to one)—but he could never be my confidant.

My confidence and health restored for public purposes, I set about finding myself lodgings, at first in Park Street, before fixing on Kensington. This area, leafy and residential, although without the fashionable pretensions of Mayfair, had all the charms of my neighbours, artistic, literary and scholarly with the great Whig salon of Holland House at its heart. After the miseries I had suffered during the last year or more and with the object of my affections quite out of my reach—His Lordship still could not return to England for fear of being arrested, even though the steamships he insisted on for his Greek effort were being built here—I settled into an energetic routine of work and social life.

My address was 8 High Row, Kensington Gravel Pits, hardly romantic, yet romance came. Nearby lived Mr Augustus Wall Callcott, forty-seven years old to my forty-two, a painter, a bachelor, handsome, charming, well connected, and with no thought of marriage in his head until he married me.

He went down on one knee exactly a year after I'd moved back to England. I was not surprised by his declaration but by the passion with which he announced it. He was a gentle soul, who had formed the habit of drinking tea in my little drawing room and talking about art most afternoons.

'I have loved you since I first saw you in Rome in 1819!'

'Surely you were not there,' I said, foolishly enough, for he could hardly forget the whereabouts of his falling in love.

'You were married to Captain Graham. You did not notice me.' His sweet brown eyes did not lose their look of devotion.

'Perhaps I am confusing you with Eastlake,' I suggested, hardly kindly, 'for surely he was there. Why have you never reminded me before?'

He smiled. 'Because I knew you hadn't noticed me. You were being painted by Sir Thomas at the time. You would not forget *him*.'

'Forgive me.' I pulled him to his feet. 'We will go to Italy together and then I'll remember you.' Thus I accepted his offer—much to the annoyance, I may already have mentioned, of many of his friends and relations. In my afterlife, I discovered that Lady Holland, anxious that a married Callcott might not be so much at her own beck and call, wrote:

Poor Callcott is to marry the intrepid Mrs Graham. He is a quiet man, hitherto very happy with his own family, who live round him, and many who depend upon him entirely for subsistence. Unfortunately he fell in with this undaunted lady, and there he sank. It vexes all his friends for she will quite sink him, being a most determined lady and as proud as Lucifer of her family and connections. Besides she has not a penny, probably debts, a bad prospect for him, poor man. She is writing a history of Spain, so her pen and his brush are the fond du ménage.

I am glad I did not know this was her view at the time for I soon made good friends among his family and wider circle. Indeed, the Holland House librarian, who recorded her ladyship's unkind comment, also noted the truth: 'Lady Holland's gloomy prognostications, however, were falsified by a most happy marriage . . .'

I did not say I loved Callcott because he knew I did not, not the kind of love that can be formed into declaration. I was very fond of him. A fortnight or so after his proposal, I wrote to the Empress Maria Leopoldina telling her my news. We had remained in contact ever since I'd left her side and I was more honest with her than anyone. It was an unlikely friendship but important to us both.

Weary of being alone in the world, I have decided to marry again and the wedding will

*take place in February next year. The man I
have chosen is a painter, yet already some of my
relatives have cried out against this misalliance.
What fools they are! As if an honest background
combined with superior talent, integrity and
kindness were not much more desirable than
the dubious privilege of being called the cousin,
in whatever degree, of certain lords who don't
care for me enough to give me even the time of
day! His name is Callcott and he is a good forty-
seven-year-old man who loves me very much
and has loved me for a long time.*

Even to my dear empress I did not pretend to
a love I did not feel, but defended myself against
criticism of his too-low birth. I need not have
worried: my husband was soon knighted and
became Sir Augustus Callcott, making me 'Lady'.
Tragically, my dear Maria Leopoldina died giving
birth to her first son a few weeks after receiving
this letter and had not time to answer. It was
an unhappy ending to her difficult life, which I
discovered four months later when my next letter
was returned to me. I like to believe, however, that
she was happy her wandering friend had settled in a
safe home.

Her untimely death made me regret that I had
never confided in her the existence of little Arthur.
I had thought it would end our friendship but
perhaps I had done her an injustice. Lying awake
on his second birthday, I allowed myself to imagine
that Anna, on returning to loyal service, had not
been able to resist passing on such a piece of news.
Alone in the dark night (Callcott and I did not
share a room), I allowed myself to imagine that the

Empress, who so loved babies, had rejoiced at my motherhood and sympathised with my loss.

Despite Mr Callcott's declaration, after our marriage we lived more as brother and sister than husband and wife. Our natures complemented each other: I galvanised him and he soothed me. He did not mention his love again but I was perfectly secure in the knowledge. His only show of independent spirit was to forbid me his studio when he was working.

'You raise my spirits too high,' he told me, 'and then I cannot find the dispassionate calm which is necessary for my art.' His work, landscapes mostly, was very calm, some might say insipid, although always well executed. One contemporary described the delicate silvery colouring that predominated in his pictures as 'ghostly' but I never saw that for his feet were planted steadily on the ground.

Immediately after our wedding in 1827, I chivvied him into a year's travel through Holland, and what is now Germany and Austria. We looked at art galleries and I took notes for a book.

It was humiliating to gather that Callcott did not rate me as much of an art critic. On the other hand I was glad, at least at first, that he felt superior to me in something. Even the meekest of men need to feel superior to a woman. In fact, my so-called 'German Journal' owed so much to Augustus's pontifications that it lost any real interest for me.

You, my reader, will be wondering how this new life I was leading fits in with the story I have promised of an enduring love. Had I finally forgotten Lord Cochrane, soon to inherit and become the Earl of Dundonald? Had my head finally squeezed him out of my heart? Not at all.

406

How much easier would my life have been if it had! But for the early years of my marriage he was in Greece, trying to release that poor brave country from the Turkish yoke. I followed his progress as closely as I dared and was both shocked and saddened when his usual success evaded him. His passionate insistence on steamships made the whole project far more complicated and expensive. I was reminded of our abortive trip on the *Rising Star* and smiled, while I mourned him.

It was not until 1830 that he finally returned to England. King George IV had died in June and his successor, King William IV, who had spent his youth in the Navy, was one of Lord Cochrane's admirers. He was talked of, naturally, although more among London's Whig circles, which I sometimes entered, than the artistic. I learnt that he had prepared a petition for his pardon to the King, which he had also sent to cabinet ministers. Lady Cochrane was active on his behalf, having several meetings with Lord Grey, the prime minister. In 1832 his petition was granted and he was reinstated in the Navy.

During all this time we never met. But as the years passed I began to believe it was my duty to tell him about my—our little Arthur. I owed it to this baby, conceived in love, that his life, however short, should be recognised by his father.

Then in 1831 I suffered a severe illness, breaking a blood vessel. At the height of my suffering, when I was in a hallucinatory state, I pictured my little son in his chuckling baby joyfulness. His death I could only imagine with dreadful horror because I had been ill myself. I imagined his tiny corpse in the humble stone chapel on the other side of the world, without either friend or family to visit him. Scarcely conscious, I heard his baby voice calling for me, as my midshipmen had in the past.

'*Maman! Maman!*'

Feverishly, I called back to him, 'Arthur! My darling! Arthur! Wait! Don't give up hope. Your mamma is coming for you.'

When I recovered consciousness, I remembered none of this and, ironically, it was Sir Augustus who reminded me. Among his gifts, was a willingness to act nurse so he had spent many hours tending my sick bed.

'Who is this Arthur you dream about?' he enquired one evening, as he sat at my side. The bed had been removed to a large day room, filled with all my books and treasures that I liked to look on. A Virginia creeper trailed like a blind over the west-facing window so that the sunlight was gracefully filtered. Since I was to spend the remainder of my life—eleven long years—in that room, it was as well that I liked it.

My body was still so languid that it was not difficult to appear calm, although my heart beat heavily in my breast. 'Arthur,' I repeated, and found, at the name, tears slid out of my eyes and rolled gently down my cheeks. 'Arthur,' I said again after Callcott had wiped my eyes.

'Yes. A child, perhaps. You talk as if he may be a child.' He looked closer at me. 'Maybe an imaginary child. I don't think we have any children visiting of that name, although it is popular enough.'

It is strange how idle words, certainly unknowing, can lead to startling results. As Callcott hazarded 'an imaginary child', I saw a sturdy little boy, about seven or eight years of age with thick reddish hair

408

and bright blue eyes. He seemed to be looking at me questioningly, as a confident child looks at his mother.

'Oh, yes. Now I remember,' I whispered. 'As I lay in the night, hardly awake or asleep, I promised myself that if I recovered, I would write a history book for children. I christened it in my fevered head *Little Arthur's History of England*. Of course, Arthur will stand for all boys and girls who have curious minds and want to know about their own country. Perhaps their mammas and papas can't give them enough answers. Perhaps they live in a foreign country.'

After this inventive little speech, I fell back into my pillows. For the first time in years I had a warm glow at my heart.

Callcott took my hand and held it to his cheek. 'Now you will have to get better.'

He knew I loved children because he had seen how I encouraged to the house his nephews and nieces, great-nieces and -nephews of whom he had an inexhaustible supply. We played games, composed little magazines and, partly to amuse them and partly to remind me of Don left behind in Chile, I imported a very large dog called Lillo, which they rode as though he were a charger.

My little history book, written to assuage a mother's grief, became by far the best known of all my works. Published in 1835, it was reprinted seventy times over the next hundred years, selling more than a million copies around the world. Indeed, it was last reprinted in the 1970s, as far as I can be certain from so far underground. But far more important than the fame or money it brought me was the part it played in bringing the Earl of

Dundonald to my side.

Since God helps those who help themselves, I wrote him a letter and had my maid take it to the House of Lords. Below is the sense of it, although I did not take a copy for reasons of secrecy:

The Mall, Kensington
My Lord,
It is some years since we were together in Chile and Brazil. I do not presume on that friendship. Time, as the Bible teaches, turns everything into dust. However I will shortly be publishing a book which, although a trifling thing, has some bearing on yourself and your family. It is called Little Arthur's History of England, *a history book for children. John Murray, who publishes it, is already pleased by the number of orders, so it is set to be at least a modest success.*

My purpose for writing after such a long interval is that I would like to present you with a first copy since not only have your heroic deeds been an inspiration but you are also the father of a son called Arthur, now just the age to read the book and whose birthday is, I understand, imminent.

Unfortunately I may not come to you, since my failing health has kept me confined to my room for the last years. I would count it a great honour if you would pay me a visit, where I live with my husband, the painter and Royal Academician Sir Augustus Callcott. It would give a woman who may not live much longer in this world great joy and satisfaction to give you, with my own hands, a copy of my latest and certainly last work.

410

To conclude, may I congratulate you on your ennoblement and your highly deserved title of Rear Admiral of the Blue . . .
Yours etc,
Maria Callcott (Graham)

This letter, which I sealed quickly with my usual blob of red wax, said everything I wanted to say, including the announcement of the birth of my Arthur in coded terms. I also mentioned a date when it would be suitable for him to come at five or six o'clock. I selected a particular day when Callcott habitually enjoyed an evening in Piccadilly with his fellow Royal Academicians. If this month, I wrote, could not be managed, the next would have to do or the one after, although by then *Little Arthur's History* would be in the public domain.

I did not expect an answer and did not receive one. But on the evening I'd proposed for his visit, I saw off dear Augustus with a tremulousness that caught his attention.

'Would you like me to stay?' he asked, laying aside his hat.

'No. No. I am merely a little fatigued.'

'No one cares or will even notice if I'm there,' persisted my kind husband. 'It is twenty-five years since I was elected and I think I'm quite part of the furniture now. I'm surprised I don't get sat on.'

'I want you to go,' I said, irritated by his gentle humour. 'When you come back you will tell me how everyone is doing and we will be able to talk about it for days.'

'That is true,' he agreed, cheered that what he wanted to do, for he was an intensely sociable man, could also be of service to me.

'Then, go, my dear.' I turned away, and added petulantly, 'It is quite wearing me out, this hanging around and "Will I go? Won't I go?" '

His hat was on his head quick enough then and off he went, although unable to resist a backwards wave.

I returned slowly, almost luxuriantly, to my bed, the same I rested on whether day or night. The room, I thought with satisfaction, had something of the look of a stage set about it. Lillo, my great white dog, lay by the fire, more heraldic beast than domestic pet. Every wall was hung three or four deep with paintings and prints of scenes from around the world, painted mostly by Augustus and sometimes by my own hand. On the occasional tables and many bookcases were objects I had picked up on travels, including an Indian cup with slender straws from which I had supped *matee* in those far-off Chilean days. I looked at it tenderly, as one might an old friend. An even more intimate memorial was the little fishing fly I had made one afternoon from His Lordhip's and my combined hairs, dark and gold strands interwoven. It lay on a painted dish and I wondered if Cochrane (I could not think of him as Dundonald, although must remember to say it—men, even men above the common run, can be offended by retrograde nomenclature where the peerage is involved) would recognise it. I dismissed the thought at once for his brain was too active for him to use his eyes to the full, unless he was on board ship, and then he had his eye-glass to help him.

I dreamt a little then, before returning to my inventory: Wedgwood vases holding flowers, cherubs' heads on the mantel, letter-cases and baskets, boxes, drawers all crammed. I wrote a piece of doggerel about it once to amuse the children:

> *Beyond, an arch sustains the ceiling;*
> *on either side with tasteful feeling*
> *Hang carved wreaths, a Surzana hat.*
> *A modelled gem and over that . . .*

My straying thoughts, or perhaps 'the inward eye that is the bliss of solitude', were interrupted by a loud bark from Lillo. He barked so seldom, used as he was to the constant comings and goings of assorted family and friends, that I knew at once he was the trumpeter who heralded the advent of the King.

'Sssh, Lillo.'

I sat up higher in my bed and put one hand under the shawl covering it so that I could feel the copy of *Little Arthur*.

'You have come,' I said.

CHAPTER THIRTY-SIX

He stood in the doorway, apparently bewildered by the scene in front of him. Perhaps he did not even see me at first because his gaze went from corner to corner of the elaborately cluttered room.

It gave me a chance to look at him by the evening light that spattered through from my window to exactly where he stood. Used as I was to a gentle, unassuming husband (except in matters of art, and then only to his wife), I stared shamelessly at

413

the flamboyant giant who was entering my room. My loving gaze noted that he stooped now, his hair was nearly white and his figure and face had been dragged downwards by the weight of age. Compared to the victorious admiral I had met in Chile, he was a mountainous ruin but, nevertheless, he remained a hero, with all the charisma of a man who had stood above the general run.

'Is this your dog, Mrs Graham?' he asked, finding at last where I lay. I had forgotten the simple directness of his speech, so typical of a naval man, however elevated. He took a step towards me, his hand automatically fondling the dog's head and ears. I remembered, with a sharp pang that made me gasp, how thirteen years ago in the Almendral, I had watched that same hand stroking a dog and had longed to feel the fingers on my own skin.

'He is my dog. His name is Lillo. But my name is no longer Graham.'

'My apologies. Of course. Lady Callcott.' Embarrassed, he looked round searchingly as if Sir Augustus might be hiding inside a cabinet.

'And you are the Earl of Dundonald.'

'True. True.' He still seemed uneasy.

'Pull up a chair, please. And forgive me for not rising to greet you. Would you like tea? Or perhaps sherry? There are glasses on that side table. Sir Augustus sends you his regards,' I added, then enlarged with a perfect lie. 'He hopes to be back before you leave.'

He poured himself some sherry, offered me a glass, which I declined, and chose an overstuffed wing-chair. He sat down and was silent.

'I am glad you are an admiral in England now.'

'Yes. Yes.' He seemed bored at the idea before a

gleam brightened his eyes almost to their youthful bloom. 'If you read of my reinstatement and promotion in *The Times*, you may also have seen who ranked immediately ahead of me.'

'Who, my lord?'

'None other than your very own relative the Honourable George Heneage Lawrence Dundas. When I saw that, I thought, This will raise a smile from Mrs Graham.' He gave a hearty bellow of laughter before remembering himself and saying, 'Lady Callcott, that is.' He paused and looked at me properly for the first time. 'So we have both changed our names since we last met.'

We were on terms now. His legs were stretched out comfortably, and when my black cat jumped onto his lap he hardly noticed it. I thought, like a love-sick girl, I'm glad my animals love him too.

'I read that you are involved in steam engines more thoroughly.'

'The future. We must always look to the future.' As all inventors, he could never resist an invitation to inform. Soon I was hearing about the London and Greenwich railway trials with his own rotary engine, which, only a month or two ago, had seen very promising results. 'The Rocket was a disappointment, I have to admit, but my latest design is much superior. Besides that, the Admiralty is at last showing interest in my marine condensing engine. Perhaps I can do you a sketch.'

In his enthusiasm, he had stood, not noticing as the poor cat dropped and fled. He was no longer the mountainous ruin who had entered the room, but the man I remembered, fully alive with the power of his great mind. Obsessive, yes, but always to a magnificent purpose. He might be in his sixties but the future beckoned him.

'Please draw for me,' I said. 'There is paper and pen in that scroll desk there.'

So he sat and drew, clenching the pen in his fist like a schoolboy. I can see him now, hunched and determined, filling my room with animation and my heart with love.

'There you are.' He brought the paper to me and, unwilling to summon a candle, although the light was going, I peered at it closely.

'Not up to Sir Augustus's standards, I fear.' He watched me looking but did not attempt to explain the lines and circles. He sat back in his chair. 'Of course, it's an expensive business,' he said, 'but I cannot let that stop me.'

'Certainly not.' I folded the paper away. I knew from London gossip that Lady Dundonald was out of sympathy with her husband exactly over this matter. 'Is your family well?' I asked.

'My eldest sons get themselves into debt and expect me to bail them out. My beautiful daughter picks men who would disgrace a butcher's daughter. My wife complains that I pay her less attention than a rotary wheel. This is normal family life, by all accounts.' His sardonic tone did not seem, I felt, to suggest the very deepest suffering.

'I am told you have a fine house in Regent's Park.'

'Hanover Lodge. A noble pile, with colonnades, pediments and wings. I came back from Brazil to find that Lady Cochrane, as she still was, fancied herself in love with another man. A fine fellow, became Lord Auckland, we're still in touch, although he took himself off to India. Too many children involved, you know. But love was never

416

foundation for a future—at least, not if you want contentment. Or so I've found. I thought the house would keep the countess content—not my sort of thing—but now she needs Chinese vases, crowds of statues and *fêtes champêtres* to which she can invite such living statues as the Prince of Canino or the Duke and Duchess of Padua. I tell her she can have as many princes as she likes but she may not have me.' He spread himself lower in his chair. 'Tonight is one of her brilliant evenings, flares in the garden, dancing till midnight. But where am I? Here, at ease, with you, my dear friend, Mrs Graham, now Lady Callcott.'

'I am glad you are here,' I said softly, but could not speak further. His Lordship's nonchalant remark about Kitty's love for another was spreading ripples in my mind. If she *had* left him when he had returned from Brazil, that would have been the same time that I was awaiting our baby among the orange groves. If I had told him, if the miserable Captain Mends had allowed me aboard his ship, might there have been another outcome? From his tone, it was extremely unlikely, so there was no point in torturing myself with fantasies. Arthur had died. That was fact.

The time was approaching when I must show him my book. My body, although enjoying a stronger day than usual, was always unreliable. If a fever rose, I would lose my strength and my opportunity. But His Lordship's outpourings seemed to have depressed him into a glum silence.

'Perhaps you would pour me a very little sherry.'

He rose with alacrity, refilling his own glass to the brim and bringing a thimbleful to me. He was always precise in his measurements.

He stood over me and said, 'At least I can be proud of my son, Arthur. Soon he will join a ship and I have no doubt will make a better admiral than his father ever did.'

I clasped my book, still secure under my shawls. As I said nothing he returned to his chair, although I noted a certain restlessness.

I withdrew the book slowly and held it out towards him. 'Here is the little history book I wrote about. You have your own story printed there. It is a humble offering to reward you for your kindness in coming here.'

'I like your place.' He turned his head to see the room, which was now so dim that he could scarcely recognise what was there. His eyes returned to me and, dragging the chair forward, he took the book from me. Our fingers touched. I sighed. An old man and a dying woman, yet I still sighed.

'It is a pretty book,' he said, but distractedly. He opened the pages but it was too dark to read so he put it aside and instead took my hand.

'Your fingers are as white as a ghost's.' He stroked them gently. Jealously, Lillo rose from where he'd been lying and tried to come between us. He hardly noticed and the dog lay down again.

'Am I not a ghost from your past?' I spoke so softly that he didn't hear—or pretended not to. I was glad because today I wanted to be more than a ghost.

'Have you lain here long?'

'I broke a blood vessel while travelling in 'thirty-one.' But I did not want to talk about that either.

'You are dying of consumption?'

Death was nothing special to him. 'I am *living*

418

with consumption, as I have all my life. When I die it will be of something else.' I held out my glass to him. 'More wine. Bring me more wine.' I sat higher and he took the glass.

When he came back he took my hand again. I sat up straighter and spoke boldly. 'I, too, have an Arthur in my life.'

'Indeed.' He nodded politely. 'There are many Arthurs. The fame of the Iron Duke added to them, I have no doubt. A fine soldier, although I have no time for his politics.'

'My Arthur was very close to me. He was born in Brazil, you see, when I was there.'

My friend said no more but looked at me with the same attentive concentration I'd seen him give a map of a coastline filled with swirling currents and underwater rocks.

I looked at him although, either due to the darkness or the sherry, his face was blurred, even wavering. 'He was born on the eleventh of April 1825.' I found I was gripping his hand like a lifeline. 'His name was Arthur Thomas Cochrane Dundas Graham.' I saw he might speak then, so I continued quickly, 'He was a handsome, healthy baby, in looks very like his father. But when he was three months old, a fever like a plague swept through the place where we lived, and his short time on this earth ended.'

So far I had sustained my courage but now it failed me. Gasping for breath, I fell silent. I had already said everything.

Words can be no comfort for the deepest sorrows. He held me and allowed my tears to fall upon him. How long we stayed like that I do not know. Perhaps I fainted. I hope I was not so foolish

419

for I would not wish to have missed one second of our closeness.

The first of the outward world that came to me was the sound of the nightingale outside my window. All sorts of birds flew to my sill as I put out scraps from my trays. Many of them were quite tame, but this nightingale sang with a wild independent beauty.

I listened and my grieving was solaced. I thought that the nightingale would remain after my lord had left.

Slowly he eased himself away from me. His great body seemed to creak, like the ageing timbers of a fine ship. He towered over me. 'What will you do when I'm gone?' I understood he was referring to the rest of my life, however long or, more likely, short that might be.

I smoothed my sleeves, straightened my cap, wiped my eyes—although they were already dry. 'I will play with my pen. Then with my little friends, the leeches. Then back again to my pen.' I paused. 'Then I will die.'

He looked neither happy nor convinced by this so I added, 'Sir Augustus has a very large family for whom this room is a favourite playground. I am only alone when I wish to be so.'

He bowed more contentedly. 'Then I leave you in safe hands.' He walked slowly towards the door before turning. 'I have not been a good husband. My poor Kitty! What she has suffered.'

Despite everything, I almost smiled at his lack of tact. Did he truly expect me to feel sorry for *Kitty*? Kitty had been given everything.

He continued, 'But I have been an even worse friend to you. I . . .'

420

I held up the hand that he'd called ghostly and it must have had a spectral sheen in the almost complete darkness for he stopped instantly, relieved, I am sure. I had wanted him to know about our son, nothing more.

As my hand fell back to the bed, it rested on something hard and I realised he was about to leave without *Little Arthur's History of England*. Again, I felt like smiling. Instead I held it up and said, with mock severity, 'My lord, you have forgotten my gift to you.'

'What? What?'

'My book. Arthur's book.'

He paused. He wavered. Like a ship that had lost is bearings.

I had an idea. 'Come back for a moment. Do you know how to light a gas lamp?' Absurd question to an inventor but we had only recently installed two lamps so that I could read and write more easily in the evenings. 'There's a taper on that stand.'

A warm yellow glow spread through the room. He sat down. 'Now I can see you.'

'No longer a ghost?'

'Not a ghost.' He frowned. 'Never a ghost.'

I picked up the book and it fell open at the introduction, dedicated 'To Mothers'. I reflected a moment then read: ' "Though I have not the happiness to be a mother, my love of children has led me to think a good deal about them, their amusements, and their lessons. This little history was written for a real little Arthur, and I have endeavoured to write it nearly as I would tell it to an intelligent child." '

I shut the book and handed it over. 'It makes history fun,' I said, in as lively a tone as I could muster. 'It is cruel about the popes and kind about the kings—English kings.'

He began to look serious, as if he might dispute the efficacy of kings, but then smiled. 'And queens?'

'Oh, yes. But not Queen Mary.' As I spoke, I pictured the tired face of Father Xavier who had christened and then buried our little Arthur. Unable to restrain myself, I said, low enough, but he heard me, 'A papist priest buried our son.'

'There was none other to do the office?'

'No one.'

'I am sure God will understand.' His tone was not ironical but neither was it natural and I knew he was only trying to please me. Why should he worry about the funeral arrangements of a son he had never known?

'I should not have brought us back to this,' I said. 'I want Arthur's short life to be remembered cheerfully by this modest book. Forgive me.'

'You ask me for forgiveness?' He leant forwards in his chair, then, sighing, fell back again. 'As the years pass, there are so many regrets . . .'

'I do not want to be part of your regrets.' I stopped him fiercely. 'I came to you freely. I asked for nothing then and I ask for nothing now.'

'You were always proud.' He smiled.

'If, by that, you mean I did what I wished to do, that is true and I am proud of it.' We smiled at each other. 'So now I command you, go! Leave me!'

He rose, clasping *Little Arthur's History of England* in his strong hand—the sight nearly started my tears again—and walked quickly to the door. I hoped he would not let go of the book too soon.

He turned back. '*Buenas noches.*'

422

'*Buenas*.'

So we parted. He to his life. I to mine.

Nonchalantly, Lillo rose and came to lick my hand.

CHAPTER THIRTY-SEVEN

The Admiral's bewildered appearance at the doorway, his beautiful hands on the decanter, on the gas lamps, on my grief-stricken body, stayed with me for the remainder of my life. It was a comfort that so much had been touched by his presence. The winged chair he'd sat in, the pictures he'd peered at, the table upon which he'd placed his glass became a source of happiness; even my cat and dog bore witness to our meeting, and I saw him again in their glowing eyes. Most important was my sense that on that dusky evening he had become the father of our son.

Outwardly, my days continued as before: I wrote books, but none so successful as *Little Arthur*. I enjoyed Augustus's kindly company and the company of all who came to visit me, particularly small children. Gradually, my health declined and, as we entered the Victorian era, I became less interested in myself and more interested in God. When I no longer had the stamina for professional writing, good works became a poor substitute for good writing.

In 1840 Augustus, who knew that I was happiest with a pen in my hand, persuaded me to attempt one last journal. Its inelegant abbreviated style reflected my abbreviated mental ability due to daily sufferings. It is a sad come-down from my past efforts, with the ink, like many of the people referred to, dying in splutters on the page. Yet it also reflected my continued interest in life outside my room:

Sunday, 22nd November
After a miserable night—a disturbed day! Wrote to Miss Fox to propose a holiday to the schools on account of the birth of the Princess.
Monday, 23rd
Brought a post-mortem drawing of Ld Holland— so calm so peaceful—what a sweet expression: the Rapture of Repose—
Tuesday, 24th
Poor Lady Holland, even after such a loss as hers cannot do without society—has had some to dinner already.
   W. Hawes and Sophia called—talk chiefly about proposed buildings on site of Kensington Palace—Kitchen Garden and public walks generally—very good—liberal and right. Wife a daughter of Brunel—immortal Brunel!
   Dr Chambers called—he says the quickness of my pulse don't signify but he seems sorry it is so weak and flickering—Does that mean I am near my end?
Thursday, 26th
Letter from Miss Fox—children not to have holiday—only pence.
Friday, 27th
Finished Miss Martineau's 'The Hour and the Man'—one of the most fascinating books that I have read these many days—Toussaint has been a hero of mine ever since I began to feel that

there might be other models than Achilles or Alexander for a hero. Thick fog.

Saturday, 28th

Had Watson the gardener's two boys in, to play about the room: charming children: the eldest too delicate—both intelligent: gave them oranges in honour of the Princess Royal.

Sunday, 29th

W. Allen and J. Horsley dine—discourse on decorating the Houses of Parliament with pictures—I joined—was snubbed—I hope for self command NEVER again to join in conversation when artists are here or Art the subject—

Tuesday, 1st Dec

A kind and affectionate letter from Capt Frederick Grey, bewailing himself that loving his country he dare not wish for war—yet having the finest imaginable frigate under his feet, he will have no opportunity of serving his country or distinguishing!

Thursday, 3rd

Miss Rogers reports Ld Monteagle as going to be married to Miss Marshall!—nonsense—marry his daughter's sister!—No! No! Miss R growing large and coarse.

This was the last entry to my last testimony—hardly an uplifting epitaph.

It is affecting to see my concern for the Queen's first child; I still found birth a cause for rejoicing. I continued my friendship with the Hon. Caroline Fox (strangely, Miss Fox in this journal) but I could no longer help in the schools she had founded. My family became more important to me, including my dear cousin Glennie, now healthy and exalted in the Royal Navy—and dear Augustus's family too. I continued to resent his proprietary air where Art was concerned, but he nursed me faithfully.

I could still read. Harriet Martineau was the sort of clever, forceful writer I admired but, after my death, I was shocked to find in her *Autobiography* spiteful comments about my character and, worse still, the accusation that my husband's devotion to me had 'cost him his health and life'. Writers, particularly female, have a tendency to competitive jealousy. I could never be jealous, however, of one who caused Charles Darwin to exclaim, 'I was astonished to find her so ugly!'

My somewhat grand reference to Toussaint l'Ouverture as the heroic inheritor to Alexander and Achilles reflects my enduring admiration for the men who change the world—not thinkers but doers. Toussaint's bravery and political acumen won him status as freedom fighter for the enslaved races of the world; Lady Nugent, the wife of the governor of Jamaica, complained that whenever Haiti was discussed at dinner, 'the blackies in attendance seemed so much interested they hardly change a plate or do anything but listen . . . What must it all lead to?' We now know the joyful answer.

Martineau's book reminded me, unsurprisingly, of my time in Brazil—of Anna and Elizabetta, who oversaw the most painful year of my life. I dreamed sometimes of the little house in the orange grove at the bottom of a mountain. My stay there had never been much more than a dream—a dream that turned to tragedy.

Once a gentleman called Dampier came to our house and, tentatively, I asked after my erstwhile

426

admirer, but this Dampier disclaimed all knowledge of a Brazil-living relative. At one time a fancy took me to make contact with the Empress's eldest daughter, Princess Maria da Glória, who had been my pupil so briefly, and had become Queen of Portugal. But my letters were unanswered.

The reality—at least, the public reality—of my years in South America existed in my published journals. Their imprint remained black, while I faded. Sometimes I looked through them, lingering over the engravings and marvelling that my now feeble fingers had once been capable of such precise paintings. I stayed particularly long over a picture of the landing stage at the island of Juan Fernandez. It shows row-boats pulled up and two small figures walking and talking. Behind them conical mountains rise in vertical challenge and in front a gentle, lapping sea. I remembered our picnic on a fig-leaf table, how I had read from *The Tempest* and dear Mr Jackson played his violin.

I slept over the scene, awoke, and found Augustus had tidied the book away.

Although I lived on another two years, my ill-health made me too incapacitated to write another word. My mind, however, remained intact.

About the time this journal ended, I heard that the Earl of Dundonald had separated from the countess, who was living in France. She never returned to England but set up home in Paris. When you are touched by death, the line between the real and the imaginary becomes blurred. I don't doubt that heavy doses of opium encouraged the process. On misty summer dawns, when I woke to my birds calling at the window, I looked up and saw my door frame filled with a burly figure. The stoop

427

had gone, the pendulous effect of age undone and I could feel, although I could not see, the brilliant blue eyes upon me.

He never spoke, however. But then, words were never his strength, and when he did embark on a speech or proclamation, it needed a good editor to sharpen the ponderous cadences. (His autobiography, even to me, is almost unreadable.) Genius sometimes needs an interpreter.

When a naval man, as Captain Frederick Grey, mentioned in the journal, came into my room, I sighed over his blue coat with brass buttons and instructed him to tell me about his latest voyage. Having spent so much time at sea or in towns that depended on the sea, I could picture everything and, not sharing his yearning for war, was satisfied by his descriptions of wave and sky. If he had been round Cape Horn and up the Chilean coast to Valparaíso, I plagued him with questions and tried to excite him with tales of earthquake and civil war.

Returning from scenes as dazzling as any painted by Turner or John Martin to my own dim room took me further towards the dark realms of death. Exhaustion and pain should have made me ready for it. But I was not.

'Have you heard anything of Dundonald?' I whispered to Captain Grey one murky afternoon—my inward eye saw Crosbie or Dance or Spencer.

He looked up, surprised, from the book he was reading to me—too often, these days, a moral work. 'He makes his inventions, I suppose. He is quite in with the Admiralty now, and they say the Queen admires him nearly as much as the great Nelson. I expect he'll get all his old orders back.'

'The Order of the Bath was thrown down the

steps of Westminster Abbey,' I murmured, and lay back, pleased.

The good captain, thinking I dozed, put aside the book and dozed himself.

While my lord lived, it was hard for me to die. Yet, as my days were spent with blood-lettings, greedy leeches, daggers in my head and chest, swollen legs, falling hair, itching eyes, twitching feet, disgusting odours, insidious sweats and secret pangs, it became harder and harder to live. (The doctors who eventually laid out my corpse expressed themselves amazed that I'd lasted so long.)

It was only when I came to the conclusion that, although my body should lie underground in the fashionably new Kensal Green cemetery, my spirit would roam beyond the grave—in earthly rather than heavenly realms—that I allowed my beating heart to slow, then stop.

My death, on 21st November, 1842, affected some, although my long illness lessened the shock. Doubtless most thought me dead already. Poor Augustus was utterly miserable, yet a little consoled (as who wouldn't be?) by a message of condolence from the Queen and Prince Albert. All the Callcott family mourned my passing and my sweet relative, William Callcott, wrote very prettily: 'There never was a greater example of courage, self-control or of the influence of spirit over matter than was exhibited in her.' His comment appeared in the 'Annual Obituary'. If I'd been a man, it would have been written in *The Times*.

I would like to record that the Earl of Dundonald was struck down by grief or at least took a walk in Hyde Park without noticing the heavy rain. But I

429

would not have expected it and it did not happen. Robert Harvey, one of his biographers, wrote about us, '. . . it is clear that something powerful flared between them in Valparaíso that continued on the long journey to Rio . . .'

Not very much to be recorded in this way but I like the word 'flared', with its fiery glow. I like even better the label on my photograph in the Valparaíso *Museo*: 'Maria Graham. A personal friend of Admiral Cochrane's'. 'A personal friend' has a good ring to it. Some biographers scarcely gave me a footnote and history never made us lovers but I cannot care about that. Who writes the history owns the characters in it and I am writing our own story.

Thomas, 10th Earl of Dundonald, Marquess of Maranham, GCB, Admiral of the Red, Rear-Admiral of the Fleet, etc., etc., died, aged eighty-four, on 30th October 1860. He was accorded all the honours of a memorial stone in Westminster Abbey (an honour then still denied to Lord Byron). Fame and fortune were his, although his estranged wife had described him as 'a very weak headstrong old dotard'. She changed her tune after his death.

There is a saying that we do not choose whom we love. But I *chose* to love Lord Cochrane. That morning in Chile when the child ran along the streets crying out, *'The Admiral has come! Our great and good Admiral!'* I knew that he was to be my fate.

I believe that women are programmed to make heroes of their men, which is, doubtless, not very modern of me, but Lord Cochrane was already a hero when I met him.

In 1812, thirty years before my death, I wrote in my private journal,

> Talent is the power, born more or less with every man acquiring all or any of the arts or sciences as circumstances or early impressions may decide—genius is a rare qualification, which may once in a century illuminate a mind and guide it to ends which would cost years of labour to ordinary mortals.

I was of service to a genius briefly, and briefly his lover. This is the story I have been proud to tell.

*   *   *

Every year on 21st May the Chilean Navy pays tribute to its heroes and its fallen at the grave of Admiral Cochrane in Westminster Abbey. A wreath is laid by His Excellency the Ambassador of Chile. The current Earl of Dundonald reads from Psalm 107:

> . . . *They that go down to the sea in ships,*
>   *that do business in great waters;*
> *these see the works of the Lord,*
>   *and his wonders in the deep.*
> *For he commandeth, and raiseth the stormy wind,*
>   *Which lifteth up the waves thereof.*
> *They mount up to the heaven,*
>   *they go down again to the depths: . . .*
> . . . *Then they cry unto the Lord in their trouble,*
>   *And he bringeth them out of their distresses.*
> *He maketh the storm a calm,*
>   *So that the waves thereof are still.*

Then they are glad because they be quiet;
  So he bringeth them unto their desired haven . . .

Men and women, fashionably dressed for a spring morning, a few wearing extravagant hats, group conspiratorially around the memorial slab. Above them and on either side, the soaring columns, the black vaults, the secret altars are haunted by the dark ghosts of other stories.

As the people crane forward to hear the speakers and admire the wreath, brilliant in the Chilean colours of red, white and blue, I am there too, peering attentively over the shoulders of the living.

It is the place of a lover—and a writer.

AFTERWORD

Much of this novel is based on Maria Graham's Chilean and Brazilian journals first published by Longman and John Murray in 1824. All the direct quotations are accurate.

The exact nature of the friendship between Maria and Lord Cochrane can never be certain.

There is a year in Maria's life from the end of 1824 when she was in Rio de Janeiro during which there are no records of her movements or explanations for her disappearance from view. I have drawn my own conclusions.

BIBLIOGRAPHY

For those who might like to read more about or around the lives of my protagonists:

Akel, Regina, *Maria Graham. A Literary Biography*, Cambria Press, Amherst New York, 2010

Birkenhead, Rt. Honourable, the Earl of, *Famous Trials of History*, Garden City Publishing Co. Inc, New York 1926

Brunel Gotch, Rosamund, *Maria, Lady Callcott: The Creator of 'Little Arthur'*, John Murray, London, 1937

Collier, Simon and Sater, William F., *A History of Chile*, Cambridge University Press, 2004

Cordingley, David, *Cochrane the Dauntless. The Life and Adventures of Thomas Cochrane*, Bloomsbury, 2008

Dundonald, Thomas, Tenth Earl of, *The Autobiography of a Seaman*, 2 vols, Richard Bentley, London, 1860

Dundonald, Thomas, Tenth Earl of, *Narrative of Services in the Liberation of Chili, Peru and Brazil from Spanish and Portuguese Domination*, 2 vols, James Ridgeway, no. 169 Piccadilly, MDCCCLIX

Forrester, C.S., *Captain Hornblower R.N.*, Penguin Books, 1987

Graham, Maria, *Journal of a Residence in Chile during the Year 1822, Voyage from Chile to Brazil in 1823, Journal of a voyage to Brazil and Residence there during part of the years 1821 1822 1823*, Longman and John Murray,

Albemarle St, 1824

Graham, Maria, *Journal of a Residence in Chile during the Year 1822, and a Voyage from Chile to Brazil in 1823*, ed Jennifer Hayward, University of Virginia Press, 2003, Charlottesville and London, 2003.

Maria Graham's Journal of a Voyage to Brazil, ed Jennifer Hayward and M. Soledad Caballero, Parlor Press Anderson, South Carolina 2011

Harvey, Robert, *The Life and Exploits of a Fighting Captain*, Robinson, 2000

Longford, Elizabeth, *Byron*, Weidenfeld & Nicolson and Hutchinson & Co Ltd, 1976

Marryat, Captain Frederick, *Frank Mildmay or the Naval Officer*, McBooks Press Inc., Ithaca, New York 2003

Miers, John, *Travels in Chile and La Plata*, 2 vols, Baldwin, Cradock and Joy, 1826

O'Brian, Patrick, *The Aubrey/Maturin Novels*, HarperCollins Publishers

Souhami, Diana, *Selkirk's Island. The Original Robinson Crusoe*, Phoenix, 2008

Southam, Brian, *Jane Austen and the Navy*, National Maritime Museum, 2005

Thomas, Donald, *Cochrane*, Cassell, 1999

Vale, Brian, *Cochrane in the Pacific*, I.B. Tauris, 2008

ACKNOWLEDGEMENTS

The idea for this novel arose out of a visit I made to Valparaíso, Chile in 2003 where my daughter, Rose, and her husband, Sebastián Gaete were living. Without that Chilean connection and the help of the Gaete-Hurtado extended family, in particular Maria Elena, and her husband, Raúl Hernan Oyanedel my task would have been much harder. Also in Chile, my thanks to historian Piero Castiliorgue, Valparaíso's Honorary Consul, Ian Hardie and, most particularly, to Regina Akel who not only shared with me her own research and dissertation on Maria Graham but also checked over my manuscript.

In the UK my thanks to historian Linda Kelly for reading my manuscript, to Tim Moreton at the National Portrait Gallery for arranging a special viewing of Maria's portrait by Sir Thomas Lawrence and to Virginia and John Murray for their support and suggestions. Also thanks to the librarians at the Bodleian library, the British Library, The John Murray Archives at the National Library of Scotland and the London Library. All helped me to track down manuscripts and early publications. My agent, Andrew Gordon gave me total enthusiasm and support, as did my friend, Belinda Wingfield Digby who typed the manuscript. Jon Wood and Laura Gerrard at Orion expertly steered *Maria and the Admiral* into harbour, with Rebecca Gray waving the flag. My family, Nat, Hannah, Rose, Sebastián, Chloe, Caspar, and my sister, Antonia Fraser Pinter, helped me in various important ways. Especial gratitude, as always, to my husband, Kevin, who returned with me to Chile for further research, as well as doing invaluable work to unravel the tangled skein of South America's history of independence.